HOME TO THE GLEN

Recent Titles by Gwen Kirkwood

FAIRLYDEN
THE MISTRESS OF FAIRLYDEN
THE FAMILY AT FAIRLYDEN
FAIRLYDEN AT WAR

THE LAIRD OF LOCHANDEE *
A TANGLED WEB *
CHILDREN OF THE GLENS *
HOME TO THE GLEN *

Writing as Lynn Granger

THE LAIRD OF LOCHVINNIE
LONELY IS THE VALLEY
THE SILVER LINK
THE WARY HEART

* *available from Severn House*

HOME TO THE GLEN

Gwen Kirkwood

WEST BEND LIBRARY

This first world edition published in Great Britain 2006 by
SEVERN HOUSE PUBLISHERS LTD of
9–15 High Street, Sutton, Surrey SM1 1DF.
This first world edition published in the USA 2006 by
SEVERN HOUSE PUBLISHERS INC of
595 Madison Avenue, New York, N.Y. 10022.

Copyright © 2006 by Gwen Kirkwood.

All rights reserved.
The moral right of the author has been asserted.

British Library Cataloguing in Publication Data

Kirkwood, Gwen
    Home to the glen
    1.   Dairy farmers - Scotland - Fiction
    2.   Scotland - Social conditions - Fiction
    3.   Domestic fiction
    I.   Title
    823.9'14 [F]

    ISBN-10: 0-7278-6326-6

Except where actual historical events and characters are being
described for the storyline of this novel, all situations in this
publication are fictitious and any resemblance to living persons
is purely coincidental.

Typeset by Palimpsest Book Production Ltd.,
Polmont, Stirlingshire, Scotland.
Printed and bound in Great Britain by
MPG Books Ltd., Bodmin, Cornwall.

The Maxwell Family

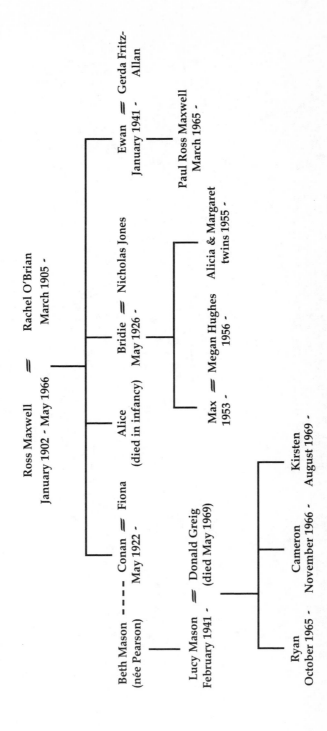

One

Paul and Ryan struggled valiantly to help the heifer bring her calf into the world.

'It's so big for a first calf,' Ryan gasped as he held on to a slippery foreleg and shoved the rope above the first joint as he had seen his uncle do.

'Aye, I expect it'll be a bull,' Paul muttered gloomily as he tried to ease the pressure around the calf's head with a gentle finger.

'I know we're desperate for heifer calves to build up our herd but even a live bull would be better than a dead heifer,' Ryan panted. 'There! I've got the ropes on properly. On both legs this time so they shouldn't slip.'

'Slot this through the other end of the ropes then and we'll both be able to pull,' Paul said, passing him a smooth wooden baton. 'That's what they used to do at Glens of Lochandee before Aunt Bridie bought one of those calving jacks.'

'Aye, I think that ought to be one of our first investments if we ever have any money to spare,' Ryan agreed, releasing the pressure slightly to give the heifer time to regain her strength ready for the next contraction.

'The head's nearly there, and it's still alive,' Paul said, pulling away the skin which had covered the calf's nostrils.

'Right, pu–ull . . .' Ryan ordered. 'If only the bloody thing wasna so big.' They relaxed again briefly, allowing the heifer to pant. 'Our first calf. Imagine what they'll all say if it's born dead.'

'I know, I know. "They're too young. They shouldn't be farming on their own yet" . . .' Paul mimicked. 'Right! Pull again . . .' After a mammoth effort the head of the calf squeezed out but the heifer roared in pain and panic and

1

rolled to her feet with the calf hanging half in and half out.

'Oh bloody hell!' Ryan didn't often swear but he felt like weeping in frustration.

'Maybe she'll lie down again in a minute,' Paul said. Slowly he moved closer to the frightened animal, talking softly, soothingly. But the heifer was afraid of the violent pain racking her body. To make matters worse they were outside in one of the small paddocks and she had too much space to get away from them. She moved away as far as she could get with the calf's head swinging behind her. Then suddenly she stood still and arched her back as another spasm convulsed her. Swiftly Paul and Ryan moved forward but the calf fell to the ground with a slithering thud.

'Aye, aye, just a pair o' stupid college boys! Ye should have had yon heifer tied up in a shed to calve her!' Paul and Ryan swung round at the sound of the jeering voice. It was a still November afternoon with a gossamer mist hanging over fields and hedges. Neither of them had noticed the man leaning over the fence. Paul recognized him as one of several farmers who were renting Wester Rullion's acres for summer grazing.

'Never heed him,' Ryan gasped, rubbing frantically at the calf's side, massaging the glistening black skin, willing the young animal to breathe. Paul knelt beside him, though he was fuming inwardly. What sort of neighbour would stand and watch their struggles and not offer to help?

'It's not breathing!' Ryan muttered.

'Let's hang it over the gate! Hind feet first. Come on. We've nothing to lose.' Panting they struggled to lift the dead weight of the long slippery body and haul it over the gate. Paul held it while Ryan massaged frantically, round and round, again and again. The neighbour, a man named Bardrop, had now been joined by his son. They stood watching incredulously, grinning and jeering.

'I've seen them do this when I was doing my year's practical in Ayrshire,' Paul muttered to Ryan. 'It does work sometimes, even if those grinning idiots don't believe us . . .'

Suddenly the calf coughed and choked, and coughed again.

'It's beginning to breathe!' Ryan exclaimed in excitement.

2

He continued to massage a little longer then between them they lowered the calf carefully to the ground. The young mother came running, mooing angrily. She walked all round nosing her offspring none too gently, then she began to lick it with an urgent, rasping tongue.

'That's a better massage than I can give it!' Ryan crowed triumphantly. Within minutes the calf lifted its black and white head from the ground and its mother nosed at it as though giving instructions to stay still a bit longer.

'It's a heifer calf too!' Paul grinned at Ryan. His smile faded when he realized their unhelpful audience was still watching.

'Thanks for offering to help!' he muttered. He was not given to sarcasm but the leering pair irritated him intensely. He was sure they had hoped the calf would die. No doubt they would have enjoyed telling the rest of the farming neighbours of his and Ryan's inexperience. He frowned, recognizing the son now that he'd had a closer look. He had made several snide remarks about Wester Rullion and the Maxwell family one night at a Young Farmers' Club meeting.

'Oh shut up, Jeremy!' one of the other members had said irritably, giving Paul an apologetic smile. 'He's just jealous because his old man will be losing the Rullion grass lets.'

'Ye're just like your auld grandfather the way ye glower,' Mr Bardrop mocked Paul now, 'but ye'll never make a go of farming this place the way he did, not with a mother like yours. Breeding aye comes to the fore whether it be in man or beast.' Paul's face paled. None of the family ever mentioned his mother. He barely remembered her himself but he had overheard snips of conversation from time to time, and recently there had been some pointed remarks about her from people he hardly knew. He gathered she'd run away with another man and cheated his father of every penny she could lay her hands on, and more beside.

'Never heed him,' Ryan hissed through his teeth. 'That family must be all alike when it comes to nastiness.'

'You know his family?' Paul stopped and stared at Ryan.

'Well he's Nigel Kent's uncle. Didn't you realize?'

3

'Nigel from college? Lord Nog?' Paul asked incredulously. 'But he comes from near Glasgow.'

'Bardrop is a brother of Nigel's mother. At least I think that's what old Nig-Nog said. Thank goodness his father got him away to a job in Australia instead of sending him down here to his relations. One lot will be enough to cope with.'

'And he talks about breeding! Malice and jealousy must run in the family,' Paul reflected. He turned to face Bardrop.

'You'll be removing your cattle from Wester Rullion now?'

'Not for another three weeks. We've paid to the thirtieth and ye canna shift us off before then.'

'Well that's your affair,' Paul shrugged, 'if you want to starve them. There's certainly no grass left on the field now.' He would have liked to add that the Bardrops had put so many cattle on they had churned the grass field into a sea of mud but he turned away to follow Ryan back to the farmyard.

He knew that many of the temporary tenants kept their cattle on the seasonal lets until the very last day, longer if they could get away with it, preserving their own pastures at the expense of the Wester Rullion fields, uncaring if the grass was ruined.

Paul understood now why letting the grass had always worried his grandmother but there had been nothing she could do about it. It would be up to himself and Ryan now to restore the land to productive leys again.

He frowned as he walked, reflecting on the various remarks he had heard about his mother, especially since he returned from college and news leaked out that he and Ryan were taking over Wester Rullion. He felt a shaft of bitter anger towards her. How could any normal mother desert her own child? Obviously she must never have loved him. He would have liked to hear the full story of his parents' marriage but none of his family seemed to want to discuss it. He suspected they held his mother responsible for his father's accident and his subsequent death.

He knew it was because of his mother that the Wester Rullion herd had had to be sold as well as all the farm implements and equipment. His grandmother had struggled to hang on to the Wester Rullion land because it was his inheritance from his grandfather, Ross Maxwell. It was her dearest wish, and his own, that he should farm the land himself, and one day rebuild the herd which his grandfather had founded and which his father had carried on.

Deprived of capital his grandmother had had little option but to auction the fields each year for seasonal grazing to other farmers who needed supplementary grass for their own cattle and sheep. The Bardrops were one of these seasonal tenants, and it occurred to Paul now that he was one of the two farmers who had tried to stir up trouble and claim security of tenure when news spread around the glen that Wester Rullion would not be available for seasonal grazing next year.

In three weeks' time, the end of November 1986, the grazing term would end and the neighbouring farmers would remove all their animals from Wester Rullion's fields for the last time. Most of the farmers accepted the forthcoming changes and had wished them well. The fields had been let for the last fifteen years or more, ever since his father was killed and his mother disappeared. It was a long time.

Fortunately his grandmother had taken advice from their lawyer at the beginning and Peter Forster, her one faithful employee, had made sure all the animals were removed from Wester Rullion during the winter months, so any claims to a permanent tenancy had been foiled. When the ruse to claim a tenant's rights failed Bardrop had tried to claim compensation for disturbance to his established farming policy. That had failed too but the claims and the unpleasantness had caused his grandmother considerable stress. Now Paul had a clearer understanding of the reason for Jeremy Bardrop's hostility at club meetings.

Paul wished the next three weeks would fly away so that he and Ryan could really feel the farm was theirs. Meanwhile they had some serious decisions to make. A meeting had been arranged with Aunt Bridie and Uncle Conan, his father's elder brother and sister. They were the trustees for Wester Rullion, along with his grandmother. He needed their support and help before he could carry out any of his plans to farm

5

Wester Rullion land, even though it was his inheritance from Grandfather Maxwell.

Uncle Conan was also Ryan's grandfather so his support was even more crucial. They were depending on him to put up enough capital to make Ryan an equal partner at Wester Rullion. Without his money they could not even begin to farm. The few cattle they owned already had come from Aunt Bridie and cousin Max at Glens of Lochandee but they needed more cows to produce milk and make an income from the farm. First they needed to repair the buildings to house the animals and that cost money.

Ryan had set his heart on having a pedigree dairy herd. It was his sole ambition but already they had run into a huge problem. Too late they both realized it should have been one of their first considerations. Wester Rullion land had no allocation of milk quota and with the new rules brought about by the EEC this meant they were not allowed to produce milk.

Would Uncle Conan be willing to give them the help they were going to need with this new burden to overcome? Could he afford to do so? He had built up the Rullion Glen Coach Company from nothing. His business appeared to be successful but appearances could be deceptive. Would he trust Ryan and himself with the huge sum of money they would need to get started on their own?

Paul would have been surprised to know his grandmother's apprehension about his future at Wester Rullion had also resurfaced recently. After his father's death and Gerda's treachery, Rachel had lived in fear in case she returned to claim her rights as his mother, taking him away from all that was loved and familiar. Her daughter-in-law's deceit, and the cheating evil man who had enticed her away, were totally beyond Rachel's understanding of decent human behaviour. She was afraid there might be no end to their treachery.

Time had passed without any contact from Gerda and Rachel had almost put her out of her mind. She had concentrated on Paul's happiness, and on preserving Wester Rullion land as his inheritance. But in March Paul had celebrated his twenty-first birthday. Gerda would be sure to remember.

No mother, even one as unnatural as Gerda, would forget the birth of her child. Would she remember Paul's inheritance of the land she had expected to inherit herself on Ewan's death? It was only the wisdom and forethought of her beloved Ross which had protected Wester Rullion from Gerda's unscrupulous clutches then. Several times recently a cold shiver had passed over Rachel when she considered the possibility of Gerda returning to their lives and bringing renewed heartbreak.

In the cold light of day Rachel's sound common sense usually asserted itself. Even if Paul wished to sell Wester Rullion land he couldn't do so without the consent of the trustees until he was twenty-five. Gerda would not know that of course. Would any woman who had been so callous, so larcenous, and worse – would she be brazen enough to return when she believed her son had become a man of property? Rachel wished she could rid herself of the frisson of fear which haunted her in the darkest hours when sleep eluded her.

Two

Rachel was just clearing away the supper dishes when she remembered the phone call from Ryan's mother, Lucy. She turned to Paul and Ryan who were still discussing their ideas prior to their meeting with Conan and Bridie tomorrow. She knew they were nervous about it and she understood.

'I almost forgot,' she said. 'Your mother would like us all to go for lunch on Sunday, Ryan. She says she's barely seen you since you finished at college.'

'Well we've a lot to do before we can start building the new milking parlour,' Ryan excused himself. If he was honest he hadn't been getting on too well with his younger brother lately and it had seemed easier to avoid Cameron altogether rather than get into silly arguments and upset their mother. It worried her that Grandfather Maxwell would be providing the money to enable him to become a farmer, as his father had been, and Cameron resented his grandfather being generous to anyone except himself.

'You'll both be free on Sunday?' Rachel made it more a statement than a question and they both nodded.

'And there's one other thing. Megan called in this afternoon. She has a friend coming to stay at Glens of Lochandee for a couple of weeks but she's supposed to take it easy until her baby is born, as you know. She's not taking any chances this time and Max suggested you two might entertain the girl some of the time. Maybe take her to some of the Young Farmers' Club meetings and social events?'

'Is she interested in farming and Young Farmers' events?' Paul asked doubtfully.

'Her father is on the neighbouring farm to the one Megan's

family had on the Herefordshire–Welsh Border. Though she's going in for teaching as a career I think.'

'Teaching!' Paul snorted.

'Hey, my mother was a teacher,' Ryan reminded him. 'There's nothing wrong with that. So was your mother . . .' Ryan's voice tailed off in embarrassment. Close though they were they had never discussed Paul's mother.

'I believe she is very fond of children,' Rachel said. 'Megan says they are lovely people. They came from Ireland. They had only been there about a year when Megan's father had his heart attack. She says they were wonderful neighbours when she needed help.'

'What's the girl's name?' Ryan asked with interest.

'Augustine but Megan says everyone calls her Tina. Tina Donnelly. You will do what you can to make her stay in Scotland enjoyable, won't you?' Rachel looked them both in the eye. 'I know Megan would be grateful. She wants to repay Tina a bit after all the help they gave her.'

'Doesn't she have a mother then?' Paul asked curiously.

'No. Apparently she had had a long fight against cancer and died before they left Ireland. I understand Tina was only about fourteen at the time.'

'Hasn't she any brothers and sisters?' Ryan asked.

'Not as far as I know. At least Megan didn't mention any other family.'

Rachel left them to their discussion but Paul gave Ryan a hefty poke in the ribs.

'Entertaining girls is more up your street than mine, old boy. I'll leave the Irish damsel to you.'

'Ye canna do that!' Ryan exclaimed in consternation. Paul glanced at him curiously. Ryan was always more than willing to entertain a girl for an evening's dancing. He had inherited his mother's sense of rhythm, although Aunt Lucy had never managed to teach him to play a musical instrument.

'Why ever not? You're usually keen enough . . .' He broke off, observing Ryan's rising colour. 'A-ah, see! There's someone special you're chasing. Is that it?'

'I'm not chasing! We-ell . . . not exactly. It's just that I've fixed up a date with Molly Nairne and I don't want her to think I'm two timing.'

'Molly Nairne? Is she old enough for dates?' Paul's surprise was genuine.

'Of course she's old enough,' Ryan snapped irritably. 'She's seventeen.'

'Mmm . . . younger than your usual selection . . .' Paul teased and ducked quickly to avoid Ryan's bunched fist. 'You don't usually care if you're seen two timing. You even had three on the go at once when you were at college.'

'That was different.'

'I'll bet! Hasn't our Molly got two big brothers? Are you afraid they'll deal with you if you hurt their little sister?'

'I doubt if her brothers know anything about Molly and her friends. They're at least ten years older than she is. They're both married with farms and children of their own to see to,' Ryan said seriously. Paul's eyes widened.

'You're not that serious about her? Are you?'

'Why not?' Ryan demanded defiantly. 'Anyway it's too soon to know, but Molly's not like the rest. She's not confident or a flirt like most of the girls we knew at college. They knew the score and they were no more serious than we were.'

'I see . . . so this is serious, is it?' Paul grinned, his green eyes sparkling. Ryan had never minded being teased about his numerous girlfriends before.

'I don't know, do I! I just don't want Molly to think I'm taking out another girl, even if it is only to please Megan. She'd never believe that.'

'Not with your reputation, she wouldn't!' Paul grinned and just managed to avoid a well-aimed punch in the ribs.

'So *you*'ll have to entertain Megan's friend. You'll be safe enough there, old boy. She's probably the same age as Megan so she'll not be interested in snatching you from your cradle.'

'Well I'm not going to risk it. If we must entertain her we'll make up a foursome. How about that?'

'We-ell . . .' Ryan frowned. All the girls liked Paul with his tall slim figure, his thick blond streaked hair and the slow smile which always made his eyes sparkle like green emeralds. 'I suppose we could go as a four if you insist.'

10

'I most certainly do. You know I never lead any girls up the garden path and I'm not about to start now.'

'Don't go turning on your famous Maxwell charm with Molly then! She's still a bit shy.'

'Is she still at school?'

'Yes, she is. She's studying languages. She's waiting for the results of her Highers. She wants to go to university.'

'A-ah, same as your little sister, Kirsten, then?'

'Yes, they're in the same classes for most things this year.' Ryan blushed. 'As a matter of fact they're quite good friends. That's how we met. But I've had a job persuading her to go on a date with me so don't you be putting her off with your tall tales.'

'By the sound of it, the truth about Ryan Greig the Lothario would be enough, without any tall tales. OK, OK.' Paul held up his hand for peace, grinning widely. 'I do believe you've been smitten, old fellow. I promise to be on my best behaviour and give you an excellent reference if she asks for one.'

There was no banter the following day when Paul sat beside Ryan on one side of Conan Maxwell's desk in his office at the Rullion Glen Coach Company. He had never seen his uncle look so severe. He had always been a benevolent uncle, a man to be relied on when he needed encouragement at school, or an avuncular pat on the back when he had achieved some small success or other. Uncle Conan and Aunt Fiona had been more than generous too, including him on family holidays with his half cousins Ryan, Cameron and Kirsten, and their mother, his beloved Aunt Lucy. How often he had wished she had been his mother as well as Ryan's. They had had great fun together then, but they were adults now. Young men wanting to become farmers. Young men with enthusiasm but without money.

He looked more closely at his uncle's stern face. He didn't look old enough to be Ryan's grandfather. Paul considered this. Conan Maxwell must have been even younger than he and Ryan were now when Aunt Lucy was born. He squared his shoulders. That was one trap he was definitely not going to fall into. No woman was ever going to influence him or deflect him from his ambition to farm Wester Rullion and he would make it as successful as Grandfather Maxwell whatever the neighbours might think – if only he and Ryan had sufficient capital to get started.

He glanced sideways at Ryan and wondered whether he found his grandfather forbidding when they were on opposite sides. Uncle Conan probably frightened his competitors into submission when he was taking over smaller touring companies. Well he and Ryan were not competitors.

'We know it is a big responsibility,' he said in a clear voice, willing himself to speak slowly, not to gabble with nerves. 'But we're both prepared to work hard, aren't we, Ryan?' He glanced at his companion for support, then at Aunt Bridie. She was sitting beside her brother on the opposite side of the desk but she remained silent, neither discouraging nor criticizing, simply surveying them both with the same level look she had when judging cattle in the show ring. She would always be fair, but not always pleasing.

Ryan Greig looked at his grandfather, Conan Maxwell, the founder and managing director of the Rullian Glen Coach Company. He would never have dreamed of asking for a loan if Grandfather hadn't offered to help, but did he realize how much help they were going to need? A nervous shiver ran down Ryan's spine.

Grandfather Maxwell had no interest in farming but he understood how much he had always wanted to follow in his father's footsteps. His only chance of achieving his ambition was as a partner with Paul at Wester Rullion. His own father had died when he and Cameron were very young and his sister Kirsten was not yet born. Grandfather Greig had forced their mother to give up their farm in Ayrshire. She had returned to her childhood home in Lochandee and taken up teaching to support them. They had enjoyed a secure and happy childhood, but he had spent all his free time at Glens of Lochandee or Wester Rullion. He'd had no worries until now. It was difficult having to ask for money from Grandfather Maxwell.

Paul and he had always been more like brothers than half cousins. They had been five years old when Paul's father was killed and his mother absconded with another man. Rumour had it that she had left behind a huge pile of debts as well as taking all the money she could get her hands on. It was one of the few subjects they avoided.

So here they were, Paul with his Wester Rullion acres and no money, and he, sitting like a tongue-tied infant, hoping his grandfather would advance enough capital to get them started in farming.

'Well, Ryan?' Conan prompted, watching the earnest young face intently. 'It's not too late to change your mind just because you've been to agricultural college. You can put that down to experience and join me in this business if you like.'

Paul gasped in dismay and turned to look fully at Ryan, his friend and confidant for most of their twenty-one years. They had planned to be farmers since they could walk and talk. There were just six months between them. Kirsten and Cameron were intending to join their Maxwell grandparents in the Rullion Glen Coach Company. Surely Uncle Conan didn't want Ryan as well? Ryan was so different to his brother, Cameron. Ryan met Paul's alarmed green gaze. A slow smile spread over his craggy features.

'You know fine I'm not going to change my mind, even if I have to be a farm worker for the rest of my life. And so does Grandfather,' he added, giving Conan a steady look. 'I know you're just testing us, Grandfather.'

'Am I? I want you to be absolutely certain your future lies in farming.'

'But it does! You know it's what I've always wanted to do. You'll not regret helping us, I promise. We're not afraid of hard work.'

'We know that well enough,' Bridie said, speaking for the first time. 'You have both proved it ever since you were old enough to help at Glens of Lochandee. But you're both so young. It's not just hard work that's needed. It's making the right decisions, at the right time – when to buy, when to sell, when to plough and sow and harvest, when to turn the cows out to grass in the spring and when to bring them in. You have to get the right balance, both with nature and with the economics – with each changing season and situation. It isn't easy. It needs experience.'

'But we have to start sometime, Aunt Bridie,' Paul insisted.

'Yes, you have.' She sighed. 'I just can't believe you could make so many plans about the way you want to farm Wester Rullion as a dairy and build up a pedigree herd without considering the biggest problem of all . . .'

Both boys flushed.

'The milk quotas,' Paul mumbled.

'I'd forgotten Wester Rullion wouldn't have a quota allocation,' Ryan said unhappily. 'We can't even begin to restore Wester Rullion to being a dairy farm again without quota.

'Apparently not,' Conan said grimly. 'I hadn't realized you'd missed that out of your careful calculations until Bridie pointed out the recent changes in milk marketing. It's the first thing you two should have considered.'

'If only we'd started milking three years ago,' Ryan lamented, 'the government would have allowed us quota . . .'

'If the Wester Rullion herd hadn't been sold the farm would have had its own quota, and a big one at that,' Paul said bitterly. Once more he felt a stab of anger against the unknown woman who was his mother. It was all her fault.

'It's no use saying "if only" in business,' Conan said irritably. 'As far as I can see you've either to farm Wester Rullion with beef and sheep or—'

'Beef! Sheep!' Ryan protested. 'But you know I've always wanted to breed dairy cows like my father . . .'

'As I was saying . . .' Conan raised his dark brows at his grandson. 'Or . . . your only other option is to use some of your capital to buy quota and make do with fewer cows to get started. Am I right, Bridie? That's what the European legislation means, isn't it?'

'I'm afraid it is.'

'It seems a strange sort of business to me. Buying milk quota means you're paying for the dubious privilege of milking cows twice a day, seven days a week,' he said dryly, 'but then I never did understand why so many people think there's nothing in the world like being a farmer.'

'It's a way of life for some of us,' Bridie defended.

14

'However hard it is neither Ewan nor I ever wanted to do anything else. I believe the boys feel the same way?'

'We do!' they chorused.

'Well it's not going to be easy to get started, not now, with all this over-production and intervention boards and butter mountains and the Europeans rationing production.' He shrugged. 'It seems a mug's game to me so I'm asking one more time, Ryan. Are you certain you want to enter into a farming partnership with Paul? Have you considered doing any other kind of work?'

Paul tensed, waiting for Ryan's reply.

'No.' He shook his head slowly. 'Farming's what I want to do more than anything in the world. And I want a dairy farm and pedigree cattle . . .' he added stubbornly.

'It seems no time since you were both going off to college. Where has all the time gone?' Bridie sighed. 'You should be enjoying yourselves instead of tying yourselves down in business. What happens when there's a cow calving and you want to go out to a dance, or escort your favourite girl-friend to a party?'

'There's no fear of that in my case,' Paul assured her swiftly.

Bridie and Conan both raised their eyebrows at the vehemence in their nephew's tone. Ewan, his father, had already been smitten by his attraction for Gerda Fritz-Allan even before he left college.

'I've heard that before, laddie,' Conan smiled wryly.

'In Paul's case it happens to be true,' Ryan asserted. 'The girls at college ran after him but he never took any of them out more than a couple of times. We threatened to get him on that new television programme – you know, the one with Cilla Black. *Blind Date* they call it . . .'

Conan responded with a fleeting smile but his green gaze met Paul's and a frown drew his dark brows together. Paul was a good looking lad, half a head taller than Ryan, long legged, slim hips; with his green eyes and blond streaked hair Conan could well imagine him being attractive to girls. His frown deepened.

'I know what you're thinking,' Paul said almost accusingly.

15

'You think I might be like my father and jump into an unsuitable marriage before I've begun to farm! Or maybe you think I'm like . . . like her! Is that it?' he demanded angrily. 'Oh I know none of you ever talks about what happened, but I've heard enough rumours to guess how it was. My father must have been a fool to trust a woman the way he did. I shall never make that mistake. I shall never get married!'

'Calm down, Paul,' Bridie said hurriedly, disturbed by her nephew's smouldering anger. She turned to Conan. 'I seem to recall you saying something similar yourself. Look what a dark horse you turned out to be. All of a sudden there you were – married to Fiona.' Conan knew she was trying to smooth things over. It was true none of them ever mentioned Paul's mother. She had left too much grief and bitterness behind but perhaps it was time someone put Paul straight on a few things concerning his parents. He would not care for the task himself though. He summoned a smile.

'I was just as much against women and wives as you are, young Paul, but I'll tell you this, I've never regretted taking your Aunt Fiona for my wife. The secret is to choose the right one. Speaking of Fiona,' Conan said, turning to Bridie, 'She thinks they should have a partnership agreement drawn up. A proper legal document.'

'I agree with that,' Bridie nodded. 'It's essential in case either of you decides to dissolve the partnership.'

'But we'll never do that!'

'We'll be partners for life.'

'That's what your Uncle Nick and Conan thought when they were young,' Bridie grimaced wryly. 'I never thought my husband and my brother would ever quarrel. They were the best of friends too, and they'd come through the war together. Hadn't you Conan?'

'We did,' Conan agreed wryly.

'It seemed an ideal arrangement but friendship isn't always the best basis for a business partnership. So if you're going ahead with this venture it needs a properly drawn up agreement. You can't just have a heated quarrel and think you can split up at a moment's notice, not in farming. As one of Paul's trustees I insist on a legal agreement before you go any further.'

16

Her tone was implacable. Both boys knew her well enough to know she would never be swayed once she had made up her mind. She had once been in partnership herself, with Grandfather Maxwell. Granny Maxwell had often told them how hard she had worked to prove she could manage Glens of Lochandee on her own. She had built the Lochandee herd into one of the best in Scotland and now she had handed it over to cousin Max, but she was still invited to judge at the agricultural shows.

Ryan felt a shiver run down his spine again. Aunt Bridie had been right when she insisted they should both go away for a year's experience and then go to college, but he hoped she wasn't always right. It was unthinkable that their partnership should be a failure when they both wanted it so much.

Paul frowned anxiously. The idea of getting the farm going, only to sell everything up again to settle a dispute was unimaginable.

Conan, watching them carefully, read their minds.

'Bridie's right. We'll have everything drawn up legally. I reckon Mr Niven will know what's required. He and his father have been the Maxwell family's solicitors for as long as we've ever needed one.'

Paul and Ryan looked at each other, grimaced, then shrugged.

'Oh yes, I know you think we're old fuddy duddies,' Bridie chuckled, 'making a fuss about nothing, but one day you'll thank us. I hope for your sakes you do remain good friends and partners, but there's no telling what might happen if you do get married, or if one of you gets a wife who begrudges the time spent working. After all it's seven days a week all year round when you keep livestock. You can't blame some women for resenting that.

Paul scowled. Was this another hint about his mother, or was he becoming hypersensitive?

He had a hazy memory of himself as a small boy and hordes of farmers who had come to buy the Wester Rullion herd, and the dreadful emptiness and desolation after the cattle had all been driven away. All that had been his mother's fault. It had— Bridie interrupted his thoughts.

'How are the heifers doing that Max sent over from Lochandee?'

Both boys brightened.

'One of them calved later that day. The travelling must have brought her on a bit early,' Ryan announced happily.

'Oh!' Bridie frowned anxiously. 'Is she all right?'

'Oh yes,' he assured her proudly. 'And it's our first heifer calf. The foundation for our new herd.'

'Well make sure you find out about buying some milk quota before you go any further,' Conan cautioned. He looked at Bridie. 'How much will they need?'

'We-ell, we have a million litres at Lochandee. Wester Rullion has just as many acres so they'll need to aim at building up to that eventually if they're going to concentrate on dairying. Oh not in the beginning!' she amended quickly, seeing Paul's startled gaze. 'At fourteen pence a litre, and the prices jumping up and down, you'll be lucky if you can afford to buy a quarter of that. You could lease some though to get a start, but the bad thing about that is you'd have to pay out again each year and the prices depend on supply and demand. They're fluctuating all over the place.'

Ryan and Paul looked dejected.

'Maybe we're mad to want a dairy,' Paul muttered. Ryan looked at him sharply.

'Since the Chernobyl fallout a lot of farmers round here haven't been able to sell their lambs,' he said. 'I wouldn't like to depend on sheep for a living.'

'They'll lift the ban on most places eventually, when the land tests clear again,' Bridie said. 'But I certainly feel you'll have to compromise for a few years until you get established. You may have to see the bank manager about a loan to cover the purchase of quota. After all it is a capital asset and you can't expect Conan to finance everything . . .'

'Not at this rate, they can't!' Conan said darkly. 'It's a damned shame about the quotas though. You'd have thought the government would have made allowances for young folks starting up.'

'They don't want any more milk,' Bridie said flatly. 'There's plenty in Europe just waiting to come into our

18

supermarkets as it is, and look at the butter mountains. We've just been too efficient and done what the various governments thought they needed us to do. The subsidies were really aimed at the small European farmers but in Britain we've made good use of them and produced more than the politicians anticipated.'

'It doesn't make it easy for young farmers starting up though, does it?' Conan reflected, wondering just how foolish he was being to encourage his eldest grandson in such a precarious business.

'Do you think the bank would give us a loan?' Ryan asked anxiously, homing in on his grandfather's train of thought.

'Probably, but they'd want Wester Rullion land as collateral,' Bridie said. 'Times have changed. The banks are almost too free and easy with loans these days.'

'You mean if we can't make a go of it they'd sell Wester Rullion to get their money back!' Paul exclaimed. 'That would kill Granny . . .'

'Mmm, I'm glad you realize that, as well as the enormity of what you'll be taking on,' Bridie said. 'But you're young and healthy. If you're willing to make sacrifices for what you want I see no reason why you shouldn't make a go of it. After all you've no rent to pay. Though you will have the expense of bringing the buildings up to standard for modern milk production.'

'Whew!' Conan raked his hair back. 'I must be mad to have anything to do with such a venture. Are you certain it's what you want, Ryan . . .?'

'Yes, Grandfather, it's all I've ever wanted. Honestly.'

There had always been a strong bond between Paul and Rachel. There was no one in the world he cared for as deeply as Granny Maxwell. He couldn't bear the thought of letting her down when she had struggled to keep Wester Rullion for him all these years. She never blamed his mother, at least not in his hearing. Recently he had tried to broach the subject but she had twisted her hands together as she did when she was agitated, then she talked of other things. When he was younger he had never thought about his mother much. Now

19

he knew she must never have loved him or she could not have left him.

Then there was Peter Forster who lived in the neat little house on the other side of Wester Rullion farmyard. Paul knew he had come to work for his grandfather as a young prisoner of war and had stayed on ever since. Granny Maxwell often said she didn't know what she would have done without Peter to look after things in the years since his father's death. Even letting the land for seasonal grazing needed someone to look after things. Peter had carried out the rolling, harrowing and fertilizing each spring so that the fields would fetch the best price at the spring auctions. Afterwards he had tended the cattle and sheep during the summer, alerting their owners if any were ill or injured. He had mended the fences and kept them in good repair, but there had been no animals to keep in the buildings and no money to maintain them, nor the little cottage where Paul had lived as a baby with his parents. It had been sold to an elderly couple but they had allowed it to deteriorate over the years.

'I don't know whether we'll be able to afford to employ Peter,' Paul said slowly, speaking his thoughts aloud. His voice faltered as he saw Aunt Bridie's frown. Her lips tightened. 'Afford his wages I mean . . .'

'I don't think you can afford to lose him either,' she said sharply. 'Peter has probably forgotten more about stock and farming than you two know between you. Oh yes, I know what you think. He's about the same age as I am. In your eyes that makes him an old man. He'll be about sixty. That's five years until he retires – if he ever does retire completely. Wester Rullion has been his home and his life. He may not be able to do heavy work any longer, but you'll find he's worth his weight in gold if you're prepared to listen to his advice and his observations.' Then more gently. 'I know it's a worry at the beginning, wondering how you'll pay for everything, but as soon as you can start selling milk you'll have an income, not like beef where you'd have to wait a couple of years. You already have the heifers I've bred for you. They go all the way back to the blood lines your father was using, Paul. They're good. You may be able to sell some of the bull calves for breeding. You will probably get some ewes and lambs when this Chernobyl catastrophe has blown over. I think you'll be glad of Peter.'

'We shall have to build a milking parlour first,' Paul said doubtfully. 'The old one was dismantled when father died I believe?'

'Yes.' Bridie's voice was tight, remembering the circumstances of her younger brother's death and the trauma which had followed. She swallowed hard. 'It would have been out of date by now anyway,' she said briskly. 'This is a good opportunity for you to modernize. I expect the environmental health people will insist you build a new dairy too, and you'll need to budget for a decent sized milk tank, and make sure it's accessible for the collection tanker coming into the farm. Those lorries seem to get bigger every year! Do you still want to farm?'

'Well you've done your best to put us off,' Ryan grinned wryly, 'but for me there's never been anything else.'

'You're so like your father,' Bridie said warmly. 'Don was a born stockman.' She turned her questioning gaze on Paul. She saw the pulse in his square jaw.

'You know I want to restore Wester Rullion to the way it was when my father had it,' he said tightly. 'It's what Granny wants too. She'd like that more than anything else in the world. I'll do it if it kills me.'

'Even Wester Rullion is not worth a life,' Conan said quietly, his thoughts on Ewan. It was uncanny the way Paul resembled him in so many ways. Except for the blond streaks in his mop of brown hair he bore no resemblance at all to Gerda. Thank God for that, he uttered silently.

'It may be what my mother would like to see,' Bridie said cautiously, 'but such improvements take a long time and Mother is an old lady remember. She'll be happy just to know you're both doing your best. But before you build anything for goodness' sake rethink your budget and sort out the milk quota problem.'

Bridie was dismayed at the look of desolation on Paul's face. Suddenly he seemed young and vulnerable, not at all ready to take on the responsibility of running a farm, let

21

alone a farm without stock or machinery and only a collection of old-fashioned buildings. She thought of her own son, Max. He had a real affection for his younger cousin, and for Ryan too, and he had been more than generous with his gift of six pedigree heifer calves from the Lochandee herd. Max appreciated his own good fortune. He'd had a fine start in farming at Glens of Lochandee, and Megan was proving a lovely wife and daughter-in-law. Bridie loved her own two daughters dearly, and their children, but soon she and Nick would have another grandchild. This one would be brought up at Glens of Lochandee as she herself had been, and as Max had been. Surely nothing will go wrong this time, she prayed silently.

She looked again at Paul and sighed. Should she have insisted Ryan and Paul should work on other farms until they were older? She frowned. No, she couldn't do that. Her mother had borne the responsibility of Wester Rullion and its problems far too long already. It was fortunate Rachel Maxwell had lived to see him grow to manhood, but no one could live for ever and Paul would miss her dreadfully. He had lost so much when he was young.

'There's just one more thing. You do know you will have to keep on employing Joanne Williams? Your grandmother was eighty last year, even if she doesn't look it. She couldn't manage without Joanne now.'

'Oh I know that, Aunt Bridie,' Paul exclaimed reproachfully. 'Anyway Granny told me she has enough money from the summer grazing to pay Joanne and keep the house until March.'

'Good, I'm pleased you've thought about that. It will mean extra work with two healthy young men with good appetites and lots of dirty clothes to wash . . .'

'I'm quite domesticated.' Ryan grinned. 'Mum saw to that. She used to say if any of us grew up as inconsiderate as Grandfather Greig she would put us out of the house.'

'Good for her!' Conan cheered. 'All the miserable old sod thought about was making other folks work to earn more and more money, but he hung on to it all himself. He'd have cut a currant in two to get the juice.'

22

'Conan!' Bridie remonstrated. 'That's Ryan's family you're . . .'

'Oh that's all right, Aunt Bridie. Aunt Chris says the same and she was his own daughter. She says her and my dad were like Grandma Greig, and my two uncles take after Grandfather. She never sees them unless they want something,' he grinned, 'and they always want it for nothing.'

'No, well . . . we can't be responsible for our relations,' Bridie conceded.

'Mum says we've to treat other people as we like to be treated. She was annoyed with Cameron the other day and she told him he's growing just like Grandfather Greig.'

'Well I hope she's wrong about that if he's coming to work for me!' Conan exclaimed. 'Anyway if you treat Joanne all right she'll look after you. She's a good sort and she hasn't had the easiest of lives.'

'Joanne has come to Wester Rullion as long as I can remember,' Paul smiled. He knew Joanne had a soft spot for him. She had never married but she always said she liked young people around. 'She often says she wouldn't know what to do if she didn't help at Wester Rullion.'

'I suppose it's become part of her routine,' Bridie agreed, 'especially since her mother died and with her sister, Wendy, and her husband in Australia. She came to Wester Rullion as a farm secretary, though, not a house help. She stayed on to help Mother when your father was killed, Paul. Gradually she has taken over the running of the house as well as any book work but she must be at least sixty-two, I think. So don't be making too much extra work.'

Conan pushed back his chair and rose to his feet. 'Well boys, once a legal partnership agreement has been drawn up and signed, I'll put my money into your account. The rest is up to the two of you, but for the next five years Bridie and I need to be kept informed of any major decisions, including a bank loan if you go for one.'

Bridie nodded agreement and was rewarded by a smile of relief from both young men.

Three

A couple of weeks later Ryan and Paul were discussing how many animals they would have to eat the grass in the spring, and whether they might need to continue letting some of the grazing to other farmers after all.

Neither of them heard Rachel enter the kitchen.

'A lot of the pasture is getting unproductive after all the years of tenants tramping it in wet weather, or overstocking,' she said regretfully. 'Your grandfather used to plough some fields each year in rotation. He grew corn for two or three seasons, then sowed them back to grass.'

The two young men looked at each other.

'We should have thought of that,' Paul grimaced. Ryan nodded shamefacedly.

'Aye, we should. Maybe we should ask Peter which fields are most in need of improvement. He should know . . .'

'I'm sure he'd be pleased to be consulted.' Rachel smiled at them both. 'And while you're at it perhaps you could re-assure him about his job?'

'Oh but we've agreed we must keep him on.'

'Maybe the two of you have agreed, but have you told Peter?'

They looked at each other and slowly shook their heads, giving Rachel a rueful smile.

'I thought not. You will need to consider your workers if you want to get the best out of them. Take Peter into your confidence. Tell him your plans, and listen carefully if he does make any comments or suggestions. He has a wealth of experience, even if you two do think some of his methods are a bit old fashioned.'

*   *   *

Ryan and Paul were both surprised when they met Megan's friend, Augustine Donnelly, for the first time. They knew Megan had recently celebrated her thirtieth birthday but this girl looked considerably younger.

'We thought you'd be the same age as Megan,' Ryan blurted. 'I mean she said you were good friends . . .' He broke off, confused for once.

'Age doesn't matter between friends.' Tina chuckled at their surprise. 'I liked Megan from the first time we met. She was so friendly and hospitable to Daddy and me when we first arrived in England and we didn't know anybody in the area.' Her expression sobered. 'Besides, we had one big thing in common. We had both lost our mothers.'

'Megan said you were wonderful neighbours when her father had his heart attack,' Ryan said. 'And later when he died and she needed help with the farm sale and everything.'

'Ach, we only did what any decent neighbours would have done.' Tina smiled, brushing the air with a wave of her hand.

'Well we know Megan appreciated your kindness,' Paul assured her. 'So might I ask what age you are then?'

'Well it's not usually a question a gentleman asks a lady,' she teased, 'but then I never pretended to be a lady, as my daddy would be telling you if you knew him.'

'And Paul's no gentleman either!' Ryan grinned, but his grin quickly turned to a wry grimace when he saw the mischievous threat in Paul's dancing green eyes as they darted from him to his young companion and back. Paul could be an incorrigible tease at times and Ryan didn't want Molly to hear of his past exploits at college. None of them had been serious or anything he was ashamed of but Molly might not believe that. 'I'm no gentleman either,' he added swiftly. 'So how old are you then, Tina?'

'It's no secret. I was twenty on the sixteenth of March this year.'

'Gosh, that makes you exactly a year and a day younger than I am,' Paul exclaimed.

'A year and a day? Then I shall remember you were born on the fifteenth of March, 1965. Is that right?'

'Yes, it is.'

'And what about you Molly?' Tina asked the younger girl, gently drawing her into the conversation and earning Ryan's undying loyalty for her kindness.

Soon the two girls were engaged in animated conversation and Paul realized that what Tina had said about ages probably didn't matter one jot in her case. She seemed to be a naturally warm hearted and friendly person who probably chatted to everyone from nine to ninety. There was nothing pretty about her with her elfin face and wide mouth, but she had a neat figure. He studied her surreptitiously and decided it was her thick auburn hair and dark brown eyes, coupled with her warm chuckle, which gave her such a vibrant personality, rather than physical beauty. She seemed to radiate happiness. She only came up to Paul's shoulder but he guessed she must be stronger than she looked if she worked as hard as Megan said she did, helping her father on the farm as well as keeping house.

'How will your father manage without you when you are at teacher training college?' Paul asked suddenly. He saw her reddish brown eyebrows arch in surprise at his question. 'Er . . . it's just that Megan told us how much you help him, and how he depends on you.'

'We depend on each other, Daddy and I,' she said softly. 'He's the best father in the world to me, but you see we only have a small farm, and we are tenants, not land owners like Max and Megan. Daddy can't afford to pay for a regular full-time worker. We have contractors in for silage and harvest. The rest we manage between us. That's one of the reasons I have chosen to attend a college within travelling distance of home, so that I can still live with him and help a little. Or at least I can still do the cooking and keep the house. I would have liked to stay at home all the time, but Daddy insists I must have a career. He says the farm would be too small for me to carry on alone and make a decent living on my own.' She sighed. 'It isn't the best of reasons for being a teacher, I know, but we both thought it would fit in so well if I have the long holiday in the summer to help him. That is so long as I can get a job near home. But you're right, it will not be easy for him while I am at college. I just hope

I'm doing the right thing in going along with his suggestions.'

'You make me realize how lucky I am with my family,' Molly said. 'I have both my parents, and two married brothers, and they each have two adorable children.'

'You're fortunate indeed then,' Tina said sincerely. 'And are your parents farmers?'

'Oh yes.'

'Three farms between them and all owned by them.' Paul filled in the picture, appreciating Molly's reluctance to boast of her family's wealth. She smiled up at him and blushed.

He didn't know her father but he knew the family had been in the same farm for several generations and Granny Maxwell had told him her grandfather had bought the farm as a sitting tenant about the same time as his own grand-father, Ross Maxwell, had bought Wester Rullion. Since then the Nairnes had progressed sufficiently to buy an additional farm for each of Molly's brothers.

My father might have done the same, he thought morosely, and felt a shaft of fierce anger against his mother. She had ruined Wester Rullion with her greed and selfishness, and if the gossip was true she had been the reason for his father's accident and death. Several times recently he had wondered where she was now, what she was doing, would they ever meet. He didn't think he could be civil to her if . . .

'Don't look so grim!' Ryan hissed. 'We're supposed to be entertaining the girls, remember.'

Paul shook off his melancholy mood and set out to enter-tain both the girls with a charm which Ryan frequently envied. It seemed no effort to Paul. He had no idea how many girls had sighed for him and been sadly disappointed when they realized they were no more special than the next dancing partner.

In fact Paul found he was enjoying himself immensely. Both girls were intelligent and neither wasted their time batting false eyelashes or uttering inane remarks calculated to keep his attention and boring him rigid instead. Moreover he had had little time for pleasurable pursuits since he and Ryan left college.

*   *   *

27

Paul and Ryan never did hear whether Tina had enjoyed her evening with them. They had arranged to take both girls to a Young Farmers' dance at the weekend but on Thursday Megan was rushed into the Cresswell Maternity Hospital in Dumfries. Her baby was not due for at least another month. She had previously suffered two miscarriages. Now it seemed this baby would be premature. She was in great distress, and so was Max, both for his unborn child and, more importantly, for Megan.

Later Max told them all how calmly and competently Tina had taken charge, soothing Megan, urging him to accompany her in the ambulance and stay for as long as he was needed.

'I'll tell your parents what has happened and between us we'll see that everything is taken care of here.' Max admitted he had needed no urging to comply with her suggestion.

'It was such a relief to know I could rely on Tina to see to everything.'

Bridie and Nick were equally upset. They knew how much Megan wanted a baby, even more than Max, whose first concern was his wife's health. Bridie was astonished and grateful for Tina's calm efficiency.

After two long weary days of waiting for news she was jubilant when she heard Megan had given birth to a baby boy and both mother and child were going to be all right. She went over to Wester Rullion to share her relief and joy with Rachel.

After she had passed on the good news and rejoiced she went on, 'And Tina fed all the calves instead of Max. Megan still keeps nearly as many hens as you used to keep, Mother, but Tina fed and watered, collected the eggs and cleaned them ready for the packing station. She seemed to know exactly what to do without the slightest fuss. She even insisted Nick and I sat down and ate a proper dinner. We didn't feel like eating but she was right, we did feel the benefit. She had made it so appetizing, and we have needed all our energy with Max away.'

'I expect the lassie has got used to coping with crises if she has no mother,' Rachel reflected, recalling her own painful teenage years – so much to learn and so much work to be done. Cruel years they were for her. 'I just hope she can take time to enjoy herself while she is still young.'

'She would certainly make some lucky man a good wife but I doubt if she'll ever leave her father. They seem to be very close and she telephones most nights to make sure he's managing, and looking after himself.'

'Megan has been truly grateful for her help. Both she and Max are wishing she could stay longer but she returns to college next week and I expect she has things to do at home and probably some course work to prepare. If there could be a degree for caring and common sense I reckon Tina would get a first class honours.'

Ryan and Paul were pleased to hear Max and Megan's news and genuinely sorry not to be seeing Tina again. She had proved cheerful company without any of the coquettish, or clinging ways of so many of the girls they knew. Even Paul had felt easy and happy in her company. More important to Ryan, she had put Molly at ease. The younger girl had forgotten her shyness and Ryan felt their friendship was making steady progress since their outing as a foursome. She had been reassured that she could mix with his friends and her confidence was growing.

Megan called at Wester Rullion to show her baby son to his great grandmother. Rachel stroked his silky head with a gentle finger. She was proud of all her offspring but she always felt each new baby in her family circle was like another miracle, and this one was a particularly welcome one. Maybe one day this little fellow would take over Glens of Lochandee.

Paul and Ryan duly admired the small scrap of humanity but their minds quickly moved to other things.

'When you write to Tina, Megan, tell her we'll look forward to taking her to another dance next time she comes up,' Ryan said, 'won't we, Paul?'

'Mmm . . .' Paul murmured absently, his attention on a sale catalogue he was studying.

'I doubt if she'll come back for quite a while,' Megan said, cradling her baby son closer. 'Tina and her father rarely take a break from their farm and she'll have so much work to do between home and college. I don't know how she manages to keep so cheerful. I was just so fortunate she was at Lochandee at the crucial time.' None of them guessed the events which would affect their lives before they saw Augustine Donnelly again.

'Some people thrive on working all the time,' Ryan said with a pointed nod in Paul's direction. Megan followed his gaze to the oblivious Paul and sighed.

'Well I've learned there are some kinds of work more important than others.' She turned to Rachel. 'I've decided to sell most of my poultry. It's impossible to compete with the specialist poultry farms where the hens never see the light of day and the feeding and egg collecting are all done mechanically. There are so many eggs imported by the big supermarkets too. The shoppers don't seem to mind that they're not natural eggs so long as they are cheap enough.'

'I expect they consider they are "natural" eggs,' Rachel smiled. 'After all many of them will never have tasted an egg from hens which run around the fields and in and out of their huts as they please.'

'Well they certainly don't want to pay any more money to let hens like ours have that privilege,' Megan said dryly, 'so from now on I shall keep just enough to supply the family and I'll spend my time looking after this wee chap and his daddy.' She smiled down at her sleeping baby and Rachel felt Max really had a lovely wife in Megan. She hoped they would all be as happy as she and Ross and their own children had been at Glens of Lochandee.

Paul and Ryan felt anxious and frustrated as they tried to make plans and get estimates to build the new milking parlour and an adjoining dairy. The milking equipment and the milk tank cost a small fortune, even without the buildings. Everything seemed to take such a long time and meanwhile they had no income.

'Peter has asked me to buy wood to make new doors for the cubicle shed,' Paul announced over breakfast one morning. 'It would save a bit of money if he could make a decent job. Do you think we should risk it, Ryan?'

'Risk it?' Rachel demanded, before Ryan could reply. 'Whatever do you mean, Paul?'

'Well if we buy the wood and then the doors don't fit or—'

'Of course the doors will fit if Peter makes them. Have you forgotten how good he is with his hands? Look at that picture on the wall in the hall!'

'The one with all the pieces of wood made into a picture of Wester Rullion?' asked Ryan. 'I've always thought it was a real beauty. I wonder who made it.'

'Peter did,' Rachel said flatly. 'He made it as a wed—, as a gift for your father, Paul. Ewan really treasured it,' she said softly, almost to herself. 'He knew it must have taken Peter months to get each piece in the correct shape and colour and then to fit them all together so perfectly.' She didn't tell them that Paul's mother had despised the gift. She was incapable of appreciating the love and care which had gone into making it, not to mention Peter's consummate skill. Rachel felt the old burning twist in the pit of her stomach at the thought of her daughter-in-law. It had plagued her more often since Paul had celebrated his twenty-first birthday. She didn't doubt that Gerda must remember the date, although she had never once sent him even a greetings card. Would she also realize he had now inherited Wester Rullion Farm?

Paul purchased the wood and Peter made the new doors as well as repairing roof lights and several windows in the old stone buildings which had made up the original farm steading many years ago.

'They're still useful sheds for storing fencing materials and tools, or housing a few calves,' Peter said wisely. 'The biggest shed will make a good calving pen if I make a door to fit it.'

'That's a good idea, Peter. Aunt Bridie always kept a separate loose box where she could isolate a sick animal. That one would be ideal as it is away from the main sheds.'

Paul was pleasantly surprised to find Peter so adept with his hands. He had forgotten about the wooden toys he had made for him when he was a boy, and which probably still languished in one of his granny's cupboards. Peter was

31

pleased with Paul's approval but he was keenly aware of Ryan's uneasy silence.

'I need to talk to you, Paul,' Ryan said as soon as Peter had left them.

'You don't approve of Peter renovating the old buildings? Is it the money for materials?' Paul didn't really like the idea of using Ryan's capital to improve his farm, and yet he knew this was all part of their partnership and their agreement. Perhaps he hadn't discussed it enough . . .

'Nothing to do with the buildings,' Ryan said shortly.

'All right.' Paul frowned, his heart sinking as he wondered what to expect. 'What's wrong?'

Four

Ryan frowned and moved from one foot to the other, his jaw clenched.

'Well? What have I done, Ryan?' Paul demanded. 'If it's . . .'

'You haven't done anything. It – it's . . . I've had an idea. But I'll not blame you if you don't agree . . .'

'Oh.' Paul's tone was relieved. 'Spit it out then? This idea of yours.'

'Molly's brother is having labour problems. His dairyman has fallen off a ladder and hurt his back and he has a broken leg. It'll be several weeks before he's fit to work again and they have a lot of heifers calving just now. Norman's looking for a temporary milker to help out . . .'

'So . . .?'

'I – er I was wondering about offering my services. He would pay well. But I don't want you to think I'm leaving all the repairs to you and Peter and not pulling my weight here. The truth is – well I'm not much good at all this handyman stuff. I'm a stockman, plain and simple . . .' Ryan finished unhappily.

'Is that all?' Paul asked with genuine relief.

'All? It means I shall be away most of the day.'

'Of course I don't mind if that's what you want to do, especially when you'll be getting paid. There's certainly no money coming in here. I'm trying to employ Peter as productively as I can until we can start milking our own cows. It's going to be a long while before we're making any money though,' he said unhappily.

'It's a good thing we didn't buy any lambs to fatten though. Molly's father said they took away the hind quarters of some

33

of their lambs for testing and they had to bury the rest of the carcasses. He says some of the land near the shore is still testing high since the Chernobyl accident.'

'Well, I'm glad we've managed something right but I hate drawing on your capital to pay Peter's wages. I thought that might be why you'd been a bit . . . quiet?'

'I never gave it a thought. Anyway it's "our" capital now. Remember!' He gave Paul a hefty thump on the back and a wide grin. 'I'll go and phone Molly's brother and see whether he wants me.'

'You'll soon have both feet under her father's table at the rate you're going!' Paul called after him.

'Oh-oh! I wish!'

Norman Nairne seized Ryan's offer and he started as temporary dairyman that very afternoon.

Peter felt easier with one young boss out of the way. He and Paul worked together on several repairs and saved money on the tradesmen. The most important thing was to make the existing cubicle shed wind and water tight and replace most of the metal, mushroom shaped cubicle divisions. It would have to make do until they could afford a new building, if ever that day came.

Peter had always had a deep affection for Paul. He had known him since he was born and as a boy Paul had followed him everywhere around Wester Rullion during school holidays and at weekends, always asking questions. Peter had felt like a surrogate father to the small fatherless boy, and later to the long-legged teenager Paul had become.

During the last three years however Peter felt they had grown apart. Paul's Aunt Bridie had insisted he should gain experience on a dairy farm up in Ayrshire and this had been followed by his years away at agricultural college. Peter had looked forward to Paul's return and the establishment of Wester Rullion as a proper farm again, with their own cattle and sheep and a proper continuity of births, rearing young animals, milking the cows and caring for lambs as they used to do when his father and grandfather had farmed Wester Rullion. But things were not going as smoothly as Peter had dreamed. He had forgotten there would be two young men

34

instead of just Paul. He liked Ryan well enough but now he had two bosses and in his opinion they were both too young for the responsibilities they were taking on.

Equally worrying to Peter were Paul's bouts of preoccupied silence and the sight of his clenched jaw and a throbbing pulse. To Peter, who knew him well, it was clear the lad was grappling with some inner problem. Peter wished he understood what was troubling him but he knew it was useless to ask. Even as a child Paul had bottled things up. Usually it had taken all his grandmother's skill and patience to get him to share his fears. He was a young man now and Mrs Maxwell was probably no longer in his confidence.

One Saturday lunch time when Ryan had been working for Molly's brother for nearly a month he met Paul's eyes across the table.

'I have a proposition to make . . .'

'Oh?' Paul asked warily. 'Are you wanting to stay with Norman and withdraw from our partnership agreement?'

'Of course not! Why do you never think of anything but work and the farm?'

'What else is there worth thinking about?'

'Life! We have to live and enjoy our lives, as well as work. What do you say to making up a foursome for the Christmas Eve Dance? Now that I'm earning I can afford to treat us all to the tickets.'

'All? If you're matchmaking again, Ryan, you can forget it. There's neither time nor place in my life for women.' Paul's tone was inflexible. Ryan grimaced.

'You'd be doing me a favour, and I'm not matchmaking. You know how friendly Kirsten is with Molly.'

'You mean cousin Kirsten?'

'My wee sister, yes. Anyway she's not your cousin really . . .'

'She's near enough.'

'It's our mum who is your cousin, even if it does seem strange, I mean the difference in ages and all that. My grandfather must have been a bit of a boy, eh?' He grinned. 'Anyway that makes Kirsten and me your half cousins or second cousins or something . . . Oh what the hell! What does that matter anyway? I'm only asking if you'll partner Kirsten to the dance. I'm not suggesting you make her your wife, though I'd think that was fine if you did.'

'Ryan . . .' Paul interrupted warningly.

'If you must know, it's Molly. She doesn't want to leave Kirsten out of things at Christmas when they're such good friends.'

'A-ah! Now I see it. You cunning rascal. If I don't agree to take Kirsten you're afraid Molly will refuse to go with you!'

'Something like that,' Ryan muttered.

'Now I understand,' Paul nodded mockingly. 'And have you asked Kirsten whether she wants me to take her?'

'Oh I know she will. She adores you anyway.'

'What's all this?' Joanne Williams asked as she placed a large dish of beef casserole on the table. She was smiling broadly. She had known both boys all their lives, and in fact she had known Ryan's mother, Lucy, since the day she was born and she herself had been a young evacuee.

'Who adores our handsome Paul?'

'Oh it's only Kirsten I'm talking about, Joanne. Though most of the girls run after him anyway, the great hulk that he is. I'm trying to persuade him to make up a foursome for the Christmas Eve Dance.'

'Sounds a good idea to me.'

Rachel had followed Joanne, bringing potatoes and more vegetables.

'A very good idea, laddie,' she said to Paul. 'You work too hard and now's the time you should be going out and enjoying yourself. Once you get the milking parlour finished you'll be too busy milking cows and getting up at the crack of dawn to want to go dancing very often.'

'Besides,' Ryan persisted, 'Mother will scarcely let Kirsten out of her sight but she'll agree if she knows you'll be looking after her.'

Paul gave an exaggerated sigh and looked round the table.

'It seems you're all against me. I suppose I may as well give in.'

'You will! Good-oh!' Ryan let out a whoop of joy. 'You're a sport!'

The two women smiled at each other, each feeling a small pang that their own youth was long past, but silently rejoicing in the happiness of the two boys they had watched grow into manhood, though they often behaved more like young puppies squabbling over a ball.

Paul had to admit he really enjoyed the dance. Molly and Kirsten were both attractive girls. Although they loved dancing, and it was evident to Paul that Molly was head over heels in love with Ryan, they were both determined to put their education before too much socializing. They had already had good results in their Higher examinations and were applying for university, hoping to go to Edinburgh after the summer. Paul wondered how Ryan would react to such a separation. Watching them, he found himself hoping Ryan would not hurt Molly too badly when he tired of waiting for her return. He had always been quick to turn his attention elsewhere when they were at college. His friendship with Molly had lasted longer than usual.

'You're a lovely dancer, Paul,' Kirsten smiled up at him. 'I think you must have the Maxwell music in you.'

'You're pretty good yourself,' Paul complimented truthfully, 'and I'm not the only one to think so either, judging by the way the lads are seizing you the minute I let you go. In fact you're pretty altogether. That dress really suits you.' She dimpled up at him.

'It's supposed to be my Christmas present from Grandma Maxwell but she gave it to me early when she heard about the dance. Mum says she always had good taste.'

'Mmm, I'd agree with her choice for you anyway,' Paul said, eyeing the dress and her slim figure appreciatively. The emerald green matched her eyes and brought out the lights in her reddish brown hair. It looked simple from the front, almost like a vest top with its low scooped neck and the neat bodice in some sort of soft, clingy material which accentuated Kirsten's slender figure. The slight V at the waist fell into a swirling skirt when he spun her around but it clung to her slim hips invitingly when she was still. The back of the bodice was no more than a series of broad horizontal straps and Paul was stirred by the feel of her warm smooth flesh as he put his arm around her to guide her from the floor.

'I'm really enjoying myself tonight. Much better than I expected, to tell the truth,' Kristen grinned at him, her green eyes sparkling. 'Cameron was a bit miffed because Ryan didn't get him a ticket, or even invite him.'

'He didn't need to be invited. It's an open dance.'

'Oh I know, but Cameron is so miserable when it comes to parting with money, and now that he's a student at university he's always pleading poverty and expecting someone else to pay. He thinks Ryan has loads of money because Grandfather is helping over the farm. Anyway he'd have been telling me what to do and who I should dance with so I'm just as pleased he didn't come with us. He thinks I'm still in kindergarten.'

'He would scarcely think that if he saw the way the lads are admiring his young sister,' Paul teased and enjoyed seeing the delicate colour mount her cheeks. It occurred to him that she looked more like his sister than Ryan's, with her long legs, slender figure and the green eyes which Uncle Conan, her mother, Kirsten and he had all inherited from Granny Maxwell. He liked Kirsten, really liked her. He was proud to have her as his partner, but he couldn't imagine her in the light of a girl-friend, or having a serious relationship. He'd known her since she was born. She was like an adopted young sister. Even so he found himself being unusually protective when one or two of the older lads made unwelcome suggestions as the evening wore on.

'Damn!' Paul stopped suddenly, staring across the hall. 'What in the name of . . . What can he be doing here . . .?'

Kirsten followed his gaze.

'Who? Who are you looking at?'

'Nobody you'd know, or want to know!' Paul said derisively. 'See the fellow over there in the royal blue suit and pink tie? He was in our year at college. He was about six or seven years older than the rest of us. His name is Nigel Kent, but we used to call him Lord Nog.'

'Lord Nog!' Kirsten laughed aloud. 'But why?'

'Dunno.' Paul shrugged and smiled down at her. 'Well I suppose we called him Lord because he was always trying to lord it over everybody. For some reason he believed he was better than everybody else, even the lecturers. That wouldn't have been so bad but he really slowed things up in lectures with his persistent questions and stupid comments.'

'I see,' Kirsten nodded. 'One of those who thinks he knows it all and really doesn't know much.'

'Something like that. He thinks he was born to rule anyway, though I can't think why. He lives near Glasgow but Ryan says he has an uncle down here. Mr Bardrop . . .'

'Oh I've heard of them. The son is horrible, or so I've heard.'

'I wonder if Lord Nog is visiting for Christmas. I believe he was in some sort of trouble with his father . . .'

'You're about to find out. Don't turn around! He's coming over and he's heading straight for you.'

'Damn! Can't we escape?'

'Too late,' Kirsten whispered.

'Well, fancy meeting you in this neck of the woods, Maxwell.'

Kirsten bit back a smile. Lord Nog had quite a swagger and he talked as though he had a plum in his mouth. She could imagine Ryan taking the mickey with someone like this.

'I live in "this neck of the woods" if you remember,' Paul replied evenly, but without warmth.

'A-ah yes, so you do, so you do, my good fellow. Are you going to introduce me to your attractive partner?' Paul frowned.

'What are you doing down here?'

'Working, dear boy, working.'

'What doing?' Paul was puzzled. 'The last we heard you were going to Australia to run about a million and one acres . . .' Lord Nog looked pained.

'There's no need to be sarcastic. As a matter of fact I'm working down here in an official capacity. With the government, you know,' he added pompously. 'Come to think of it

. . .' His small eyes narrowed. 'Mmm, I may well have your place down for an inspection.'

'Inspection? What can you inspect?' Paul laughed. Lord Nog had never been the brightest of students in any subject in spite of his own conceit. Everyone wondered how he had scraped through his exams, but he did have plenty of confidence to impress the examiners when it came to orals.

'Oh records and such,' he said airily.

'What records?'

'Haven't got around to finding out yet, but I'm sure I shall find something to put you on your toes. I've only been down here three weeks. You haven't introduced me . . .?' He looked at Kirsten.

Reluctantly Paul performed the introductions and he knew Kirsten was too polite to refuse Nigel Kent's invitation to dance but he felt irritated just the same.

'Don't forget the next dance is mine, then,' he said abruptly.

Kirsten returned to Paul at the first opportunity but Nigel Kent had done his best to hang on to her. She shuddered. He was one of those with hands all over the place and soft, sweaty hands they were at that. She was relieved to see Paul waiting, watching out for her and she greeted him with an eager smile which was not lost on the watching Lord Nog.

'Thank goodness you warned me, and waited for me. You should have heard the questions he asked!' she said indignantly.

'What sort of questions?'

'Oh, all sorts. He wanted to know exactly where you and Ryan were living and the name of the farm. When I got him off that subject he became personal. Wanted to know when he could see me again – like tomorrow night! I – er . . .' she blushed hotly. 'He was so persistent . . .'

'You didn't agree to meet him?' Paul stopped in his tracks.

'No. I – I inferred we were more than good friends, Paul. I'm sorry. I didn't know how else to put him off . . .'

'I'm glad you did. Don't worry, little Kirsten, I'll play along with it if he asks me any questions. He was always persistent and he was never popular with the opposite sex, or his own come to that. I'd better warn Ryan too.' He frowned and looked around the room. 'I haven't seen Ryan and Molly for a while . . . Aah, they're dimming the lights for the last dance. Come on . . .'

As the year 1986 drew to a close Paul and Ryan looked forward with a mixture of excitement and trepidation to the challenges ahead and to their first year in business.

Rachel envied their youthful optimism and tried to shake off the feeling that each new year brought her ever closer to the end of life. Earlier in the year the Duchess of Windsor had died amidst much speculation regarding the arrangements for her funeral and which members of the royal family would attend it. Now, at the very end of the year had come the death of Harold Macmillan. Rachel remembered how he had done his best to convince the British people that they had never had such good lives before.

'Perhaps he was right,' she said to Bridie as they waited for the church bells to herald in the New Year. 'But now there is so much unrest with threats of strikes and so many changes.'

'Mother, it's not like you to be in low spirits. You must remember both the Duchess and Lord Stockton were a decade older than you.'

'Aye, aye,' Rachel sighed and summoned a smile. 'I suppose I'm just tired. Pour out the drinks for the toasts please, dear? Sherry for me please, and bring in the trays of shortbread and the blackbun from the kitchen will you? It's almost midnight. I can hear the rest of them coming to join us. Then I suppose Ryan and Paul will be off first footing until dawn.' She stifled a yawn. 'Oh to have the energy of youth.'

'Just wait until they start milking cows at five o'clock every morning,' Max grinned as he joined them. 'Then they'll be glad to get to bed at night.'

'What about wee Iain?' his grandmother asked. 'Is he sleeping better at nights now?'

'He is,' Megan smiled, coming to join her husband, her glass ready to toast in a new year and hopefully a bright future for all of them.

* * *

41

On the first of April Paul and Ryan began their first milk production at Wester Rullion. This was the beginning of the new milk marketing year. Their herd was small, consisting of the cows which Max had brought over from Glens of Lochandee and a bunch of bought-in heifers which Bridie had recommended they buy at an average cost of five hundred pounds each. They saw their precious capital dwindling and they grudged the amount they had been forced to spend on buying milk quota, especially for such a small amount. At least they were in real farming again.

'The fertilizer spreader will have to do for another year at least,' Paul said anxiously, 'but it's worn out. Then there's insurance for the stock, and third party cover, the house and buildings, as well as our old truck and the tractor.'

'Maybe we could risk skipping the insurance for this year, do you think?'

'I'm not sure about that,' Paul said uncertainly. 'I agree with you that it seems a lot of money to pay out for no return.'

'Well we've always planned we'd have a pedigree herd,' Ryan persisted stubbornly.

'We can grade up the best cows to pedigree status later,' Paul said. 'I think that's what my grandfather did.' He saw the disappointment on Ryan's face. He knew it was his main ambition in life to run a pedigree herd. 'We'll buy an odd pedigree animal once we start getting a decent milk cheque each month,' he promised, 'but surely our main aim has to be producing as much milk as we can as soon as we can. We have to fill the quota now we've bought it, but we shall need to budget to buy or lease more each year until we've built up an economical allocation. That's a blow the Nairnes and our own relatives never had to contend with.'

Reluctantly Ryan agreed. His dreams of marrying Molly Nairne seemed to be receding. It was all very well to spend money on improving the buildings, he thought irritably, but they would always be part of Wester Rullion farm and it belonged to Paul. A good herd of pedigree cattle was move-able and could be divided between them. Was that what was in Paul's mind? Even as the thought entered his head Ryan knew in his heart that Paul had no ulterior motive. The buildings had to be kept in good repair if they were to use them for housing animals.

Even so it was a bitter disappointment to find Paul was not as dedicated to having a pedigree herd as Ryan had always believed. Deep down he felt the first seeds of doubt about their partnership agreement. Could it possibly last a lifetime as they had both believed?

He loved his animals, he was a stockman through and through, as his father had been, according to Aunt Christine, his father's sister. Paul, on the other hand, thought like a businessman as well as a farmer. He was a Maxwell, with his father's and his grandfather's blood in him.

When he mentioned this to his mother, Lucy smiled.

'It seems to me that farming is becoming more and more of a business, and not an easy one at that with all the European rules and regulations. I'm sure Paul does want a pedigree herd, like his grandfather, but I suspect he feels it wiser to build up gradually.'

'You're taking his side . . .'

'No, I'm not taking anyone's side, Ryan. You have Maxwell blood in you too. Your grandfather built up the Rullion Glen Coaches from nothing. He was very ambitious when he was young, I remember. That's why he and Uncle Nick couldn't agree to stay in partnership. They each wanted different things from life. Nick loved your Aunt Bridie and his children. Max and the twins meant everything to him.'

'But Grandfather loves Grandma, doesn't he? He said he'd never regretted marrying her.'

'Oh yes, he does love Fiona. They belong together. They have worked together all their married life and your grandfather knows he owes much of his success to Fiona's ideas and her grasp of business. By the way did you know they want me to give up teaching and join them at Rullion Glen?'

'No! When did they suggest that?'

'Oh, on and off for years now. But recently they have both been more persistent for me to take over some of the work, almost anxious that I should share the responsibility. I suppose they feel they're not getting any younger.'

43

'And are you going to do as they ask?'

'I'm thinking about it. Thinking seriously . . .'

'Does Cameron know?' Ryan asked. 'He's set his sights on taking over the company when he leaves university.'

'No, Cameron doesn't know.' Lucy frowned. 'I shall tell him when I've reached a decision.'

Five

As the year progressed Ryan and Paul worked hard to build up the farm. Only a few parishes were still affected by the Chernobyl fallout now so they had invested in a small flock of ewes, with lambs. The number of calves was increasing too. Ryan excelled when it came to helping the heifers bring their calves into the world. Paul admired his patience and expertise and he was generous in his praise.

Peter Forster was happier too. Wester Rullion had animals again, animals which belonged to the farm and would stay generation after generation, instead of the mixed bag of grazing animals he had been forced to care for over the years of letting. He and Shep, his gentle natured collie dog, enjoyed walking round them on Sunday afternoons. The spring corn had clothed the fields with a bright carpet of swaying green stems. His old pride at being part of Wester Rullion returned. He would never leave. Mrs Maxwell and Paul were the nearest he had to family and the animals were his life. He had the little house which Mrs Forster had left to him in gratitude for his company and help in her declining years, and he loved his garden. He asked nothing more than to end his days here in the peaceful glen which had become his home at the end of the war.

At the beginning of May a new silage pit had been constructed to hold enough grass for the winter. Regretfully Ryan and Paul had to agree it was impossible to buy the machinery they would need to harvest the crop themselves.

'I think we must bring in a contractor,' Paul sighed. 'What do you think?' He was trying hard to consult Ryan about all the decisions, but there were so many, and Ryan's mind was usually concentrated on the cows and which bull to select for artificial insemination. He had been on a training course and he was now competent to inseminate the animals himself.

'Most of the contractors bring their own men,' Ryan frowned. 'That willna please Peter. He's so set in his ways.'

'It's years since he made silage. The machinery is bigger and more complicated than it was then. We must find Peter other jobs. He's never idle.'

'All right. You talk to him then. It would help if he washed up the milking equipment, cleaned the parlour and took the cows to pasture. That would let both of us get on with the silage earlier in the mornings.'

'And the same again after evening milking?' Paul nodded. 'All right.'

'I could ask Molly's elder brother, John, about the contractor he uses,' Ryan offered.

'I thought the Nairnes had their own machinery?' Paul said in surprise.

'Norman and Molly's father share equipment and men, but John has more silage so he say it's faster if he gets a contractor. They get it done in a few days.'

'Will you be seeing them soon? You don't seem to have been out with Molly as often lately.'

'She's been doing exams. She's already been accepted for a place at university though,' Ryan added gloomily.

'But you've always known that's what she intended to do,' Paul said reasonably.

'It doesn't mean I have to look forward to her going though, does it!' Ryan snapped.

'Surely you weren't hoping she would change her mind?'

'She might have done, if I could have asked her to marry me. But I can't afford to, as you know damned well!' He strode away without waiting for a reply. Paul arched his dark brows. I hope that doesn't mean three years of moods to suffer, he thought. Maybe Ryan would take up with a new girl-friend when Molly went away. Their friendship had lasted a lot longer than Paul had expected. But marriage! Paul shuddered at the thought. Surely Ryan couldn't have been serious? Molly was so young. Her parents would never agree, even if Ryan could have afforded to keep a wife.

As things turned out Ryan accepted Molly's departure with good grace although he was quieter than Paul had ever known him in the weeks following the start of the academic year. At least twice each week there was a letter for him and Paul suspected he replied just as often, judging by the amount of time he spent in his room in the evenings and the acquisition of a dictionary and a thick wad of writing paper and envelopes.

Kirsten had gone to university too and Paul was relieved she was out of the way of Nigel Kent's pestering. She had confided that Lord Nog had telephoned her several times since the Christmas dance. The last time he had been very unpleasant when she still refused to go out with him.

'When he got it into his thick head that I meant what I said he started threatening to cause trouble for Ryan and you at Wester Rullion.'

'Blackmail!' Paul laughed. 'What a way to try and get a date.' But Kirsten didn't laugh. She was almost in tears.

'I think he meant it, Paul. He says he has the power to cause you some serious problems and he has a score to settle with you for the way you treated his uncle over the tenancy of the grass.'

'Power my foot!' Paul said derisively. 'All the officials from the Department have been more than helpful with anything we've needed since we started farming on our own. Except for the milk quota of course and there's nothing they can do about that. Europe rules. OK.'

'Are you sure Lord Nog can't do anything?'

'I'm certain, so don't you worry, little Kirsten.' He gave her a brotherly hug. 'Anyway he's not been there very long and he has no more qualifications than I have, or Ryan – not as good if the truth be known.'

'Well you'd think he runs the whole Scottish Department the way he talks,' Kirsten said.

'He always was a bag of wind.'

Even so Paul was glad Kirsten was away from the district. Maybe Lord Nog would get transferred, he thought hopefully, or more likely lose his job if his past record was anything to go by. Either way Paul forgot about him once Kirsten was safely out of his reach.

Life at Wester Rullion allowed Ryan little time to mope about Molly's departure. A visit from Bridie brought just the sort of news he had dreamed of. She knew of a small pedigree herd which was to be sold immediately. The owner, who had never been ill in his life, had died suddenly. His wife knew nothing about running the farm. His only daughter lived in Edinburgh and had no interest either.

'But Aunt Bridie, we could never afford to buy the whole herd, even a small one!' Paul exclaimed. 'Much as we would like to,' he added wistfully. 'Anyway we don't have any spare milk quota.' The monthly milk cheque barely covered the cost of cattle cake and detergents, wages for Peter and Joanne, housekeeping for Granny Maxwell. There was little to spare for their own spending, or other farm expenses. They both knew they needed to produce more milk but it was like boxing with one hand tied behind one's back. 'It's a vicious circle.'

'Mm, I thought money would be a problem,' Bridie frowned. 'I wouldn't suggest it if I didn't know you'd be getting a real bargain.'

Ryan surprised himself with his proposal.

'How about asking the bank for a loan, a short term one, I mean. I can understand why Mrs Turner doesn't want any trouble preparing the young stock to sell at the market but I'd enjoy getting them into top condition and we'd certainly make a profit for our labour.'

'Do you seriously think you'd get a bank loan?' Bridie asked. 'Should I be encouraging you to borrow more money so early in your business, I wonder . . .'

'We'll not know if we don't ask,' Paul said simply. He didn't like the idea of a loan but he knew Aunt Bridie would never have suggested they buy the herd if she hadn't believed it would be a good deal.

'Once we got them here,' Ryan said excitedly, 'we could study the pedigrees and decide which animals we really want to keep. The rest we could clip and groom and shampoo – you know, Aunt Bridie – bring them out really well for sale . . . We'd soon get some of the money back.' Ryan's enthusiasm was infectious.

'It would be a lot of extra work but we'd get the benefit

of presenting them at their best and selling at auction,' Paul agreed. He arched his dark brows at Ryan. 'There will be even less spare money for pleasure for a long time if we do get a bank loan.'

'Pleasure! What's that?' Ryan scoffed. 'Anyway Molly's away for the next three years! It's now or never.'

'Right then, I'm game if you are, Ryan, and so long as we can persuade the bank manager.'

'Joanne would help you sort through the pedigrees,' Bridie suggested. 'She used to enjoy doing them for your father, Paul.' Yes, Paul thought bitterly, but what had his mother done to help? Just squandered everything. We shouldn't have been in this mess if it were not for her.

It was a very nervous pair who kept the appointment with the bank manager. Rachel had heard all their plans, she had seen their eagerness to buy the herd and she trusted Bridie's advice, but she couldn't help worrying.

'Don't be anxious Granny.' Paul smiled at her, his green eyes sparkling with enthusiasm. 'Anyway now that we're so short of cash Ryan will not be able to buy Molly an engagement ring for Christmas,' he teased. Rachel and Paul glanced smilingly at Ryan but they were amazed to see hot angry colour suffuse his ruddy cheeks.

'I was only teasing! Don't tell me you were thinking about it?' Paul exclaimed. 'Not seriously?'

'What if I was,' Ryan muttered defensively. 'I haven't asked for any extra money. I've been saving up. Anyway we've known each other for two years . . .'

'A-ah laddie . . .' Rachel said softly. 'Two years! That's nothing out of a lifetime. If Molly really loves you she'll wait for you – with or without a ring. If you're afraid she'll take up with one of her fellow students then an engagement ring wouldn't keep her.'

'I know that.' Ryan hung his head. He missed Molly dreadfully.

'Well there's nothing wrong with telling her what you had in mind, laddie. Explain what you and Paul have done and that it will mean a better future for all concerned. At least I hope and pray it will,' Rachel added fervently.

49

'Oh it will! I'm sure it will,' Ryan insisted, cheering up at his great grandmother's philosophical view. 'The milking cows are even better than we expected, aren't they, Paul?'

'Yes,' Paul nodded, 'but we must sell some of the heifers to repay the first instalment of the bank loan as we agreed. We've decided to calve them first. Ryan's good with them and we shall get their calves to build up our own herd.'

'Aye, well don't count your chickens before they're hatched, or at least your calves,' Rachel cautioned. 'You'll have a lot of work to get them all reared.'

'Well there's two of us and Peter seems happier now we're actually farming. Between us it makes the work a lot easier,' Paul assured her.

It was true Peter fussed over the young calves like a mother hen with her chicks. He understood they were the foundation for the future Wester Rullion herd and he was as keen for success as if Paul and Ryan had been his own sons. Peter knew his limitations with modern machinery but he made up with his care of the animals.

It was Joanne who pointed out the letter informing Paul and Ryan of a wages inspection.

'I can't imagine why they're coming to Wester Rullion when there's only Peter and me employed,' she said, 'especially when you're such a new business.'

'It's probably just a formality to keep another of the bureaucrats in a job,' Ryan said. 'I'll leave all that to you and Paul.'

'Well the man is coming on Thursday afternoon and he wishes to speak to all your employees during his visit – all two of us!' Joanne laughed.

'Are you sure it's not the health and safety?' Paul asked.

'No,' Joanne glanced down at the letter in her hand. 'It says wages inspection here. Mr Nigel Kent will call at 2 p.m. on Thursday. Please make sure all your employees are available.'

'Nigel Kent!' Ryan exclaimed. 'It can't be Lord Nog.' He looked at Paul and burst into a roar of laughter. 'Is that the sort of job he's landed himself? Well, well.'

Paul was silent, frowning. Obviously Kirsten had never

mentioned Lord Nog to her eldest brother, and neither had he. He hadn't seriously believed Nigel Kent had any authority to cause problems for them. Now he began to wonder.

Six

Nigel Kent was charming when he met Joanne but she was not fooled. She had seen surface charm many years ago in her fickle fiancé. She was instantly wary.

'I am surprised your employers can afford a farm secretary,' he remarked pleasantly enough.

'Och, I'm a general jack o' all trades.' Joanne smiled. 'Wester Rullion is my second home. I came here as a farm secretary years ago but now I spend a lot of my time helping Mrs Maxwell. I enjoy helping with the young animals and keeping the pedigrees though. I'm only on the farm books for the sake of keeping the record straight with the income tax and national insurance people.'

'I see.' He began to question her about her hours and her rates of pay but Joanne was too intelligent to be taken in by his leading questions. Eventually he realized he wouldn't get what he wanted out of Miss Williams. She was far too loyal. He had examined the books. There must be some fault he could find and exaggerate but everything was paid according to the agricultural wages schedule, including the supply of free milk and protective clothing. Then he noted there was no provision of housing for the single male employee.

Peter Forster became quite agitated when Nigel pompously introduced himself as a government inspector and asked to speak with him in private. It never occurred to him that the man's questions were aimed at tricking him into providing the information Kent desired. Anxiously Peter did his utmost to justify his employment while half forgotten memories of his youth in Poland raced around his brain. The checks, the searches, questions, questions . . . Had the man come to tell him he was no longer worthy of employment in Britain?

Peter grew increasingly nervous. It had troubled him that he had been unable to help his two young bosses to make the silage. In truth the huge machines terrified him the way they gobbled up grass at one end and spewed it out at the other, all chopped up into little pieces. Peter always hoped none of the wild animals and birds would get caught up by the powerful monster. He shuddered and looked at Mr Kent's plump face.

'So on Sunday you walk around the fields? You observe the animals?'

'Y–yes, Sir.'

'Are you paid for this?'

'Of course not!'

'And if an animal is sick? What do you do then?'

'I would bring it inside for attention, or fetch Master Paul.'

'I see. Good man.' Nigel Kent nodded his satisfaction and smiled encouragingly. 'And in the summer you do the same in the evenings.'

Peter hesitated. 'Not every evening,' he admitted unhappily, but with his scrupulous honesty. 'Sometimes I'm working in my garden. But I always supply Mistress Maxwell with potatoes and vegetables,' he added quickly, hoping this would help justify his continued stay in the country he had come to regard as his homeland. He felt his stomach churning. His early memories flooded back – men inspecting homes and people, drafting men off to war or to some other service for the good of the country, or so they had said.

It had never happened to him in Britain since Mr and Mrs Maxwell had given him a place and work at Wester Rullion and vouched for his good conduct. He began to tremble with nerves. Then he saw Mr Kent smile. It was a strange smile. He had all the information he needed. In relief Peter headed straight for his cottage and the toilet. He felt ill with anxiety.

Nigel Kent anticipated his interview with Ryan and Paul with smug satisfaction. Typically hospitable to all and sundry Rachel had made a tray of coffee and shortbread and Joanne carried it into the small room they used as an office.

'Ryan and Paul will be with you in a few minutes,' Joanne said. 'I've told them you wish to ask them some questions.'

53

'Indeed I do,' Nigel said pompously, but he did not inform Joanne of the nature of the questions as she had hoped. She handled the tax and national insurance herself and she was sure there was nothing amiss with the wages records. Nigel ate three pieces of shortbread and drank his coffee almost before Joanne had taken the first sip of her own. She hoped the boys would not be long.

They came in together and Joanne escaped, leaving them to it. Afterwards she was sorry she had.

Nigel promptly launched into a lecture about the penalties of underpaying their staff and contravening the agricultural wages regulations.

'But we don't contravene anything,' Paul said indignantly. 'Joanne doesn't come under the Wages Act for Agriculture, and if anything, we pay more than the minimum as far as Peter is concerned.'

'You pay the wage for an ordinary week's work but this man works almost twice as many hours as laid down in the schedule.'

Paul and Ryan stared at him incredulously and then looked at each other, brows raised in disbelief.

'You're talking out of your hat, Nigel!' Paul said.

'Mr Kent, if you please,' Nigel corrected coolly. 'I expect you thought I wouldn't question your man outside but we had a good talk. I'm satisfied you are grossly underpaying him for the number of hours he works each week. This is a serious matter and you . . .'

'Now just a minute!' Paul interrupted. 'You're just stirring up trouble. We pay Peter for a good week's work. He's happy and so are we.'

'That is not the point,' Nigel Kent said stiffly. 'You are not paying him for the hours he works.'

'We are paying him for the hours we have asked him to work,' Ryan said, puzzled by Nigel's attitude. 'If he works longer it is by his own choice.'

'I have looked into this thoroughly and I'm satisfied your man is underpaid. It is my job to report such cases and you will be required to pay compensation in full for all the hours the man has done since you two took over.' Ryan and Paul stared at each other. They were paying Peter the proper wage and there was no way they could afford to pay any more, even less any back pay. Moreover Paul knew this was some ruse of Nigel's to cause trouble, and he knew the reason.

'We'll get Peter in here and hear what he has to say.'

'There's no need for that. I've made a careful note of the hours and times and the work he described.'

'Then you'd better tell us too. Peter is not given to telling lies,' Ryan said.

'Nor to exaggerating,' Paul added tightly, his expression grim now. 'Not like some people,' he added pointedly. Nigel's small eyes narrowed.

'I'd advise you to be civil, Maxwell. You're in serious trouble . . .'

'I don't believe a word you say. We'll get Peter in here.'

'These are the times he gave me, and you said yourself he doesn't lie.' Nigel looked down at his notes. 'There's Sundays for a start, and remember it's overtime rate . . .'

'Peter doesn't work on Sundays!' they said in unison.

'Oh? Then what about the Sundays he looks around the cattle and sheep? Can you tell me he has never had to bring in a sick animal on a Sunday afternoon?'

'He doesn't work! Oh, he goes for a walk with Shep most Sundays, and quite often in the evenings in summer, but he's not working.'

'Can you deny he brought in a calving heifer two Sundays ago?'

Paul wrinkled his brow. 'He might have done, but . . .'

'Then that's work.'

'In your case it bloody well would be!' Ryan spat out angrily. 'But Peter doesn't consider that work.'

'And neither do we,' Paul insisted. 'If Peter had been the kind who wanted paid for every minute he set foot in the yard then we would never have kept him on here when we took over. As it is we made a job for him because . . .'

'You can't wriggle out of this, Maxwell. I have the facts here in black and white.'

'Well if you're saying that's what we have to pay Peter

every week he's here then we can't afford to keep him on. Do you want the man to lose his job?'

'You can't sack him. He's done nothing wrong. You will have to give him compensation of course and I shall report you to—'

'Now wait a minute!' Paul said between his teeth. 'I'll see what Peter has to say about all this. And then I want the name of your superior, Mr Kent.' There was no doubting the scorn in Paul's tone as he addressed Nigel and Ryan could see the pulse throbbing in his lean jaw as it always did when he was in the grip of strong emotion. Right now Ryan knew they were both tempted to take Lord Nog by the scruff of his thick neck and stuff him in the water trough.

'I'll be back in a minute,' he said and made his exit before either of the other two could object. He hurried across the yard just as Peter emerged from his garden gate.

'Ryan, Ryan,' he called anxiously. 'Will it be all right? I am able to stay? Britain is my country now? I try to answer the questions. He ask so many. What I do on Sundays? I do nothing wrong . . .?' Peter wrung his hands. Ryan stared at him. Understanding dawned.

'Bloody hell! He's put the fear of death into you! Now I understand his little game!' Ryan let out a long breath.

'He p–play game?'

Ryan looked into Peter's honest eyes, saw his worried face. 'You've done nothing wrong, Peter,' he said gently.

'I stay here then?'

'Of course you'll stay here. It's your home. It's where you belong. Always.' He actually patted the older man on the shoulder and saw his eyes shine with relief. Ryan almost ran back to the house and burst into the little room just in time to hear Paul hiss angrily, 'You tried to blackmail Kirsten into going out with you and when that didn't work you're trying to cause trouble for us. Well I'm going to speak to your boss in Edinburgh, or wherever he is . . .' Ryan didn't understand what Paul was talking about but he chipped in anyway.

'Oh yes, we definitely need to speak to his boss. He has put the fear of death into Peter. The poor sod thinks he might be sent back to Poland if he's not doing enough work every week. And you, you rotten rat, you put words into his mouth to make up your blasted figures.'

'Don't you dare speak to me like that, Greig!'

'I'll speak to you how I damn well like. You're not fit to be in such a job. You'll give the rest of 'em a bad reputation if they keep you in their offices.'

'He's got it in for us, that's why he's using Peter. It's all because he can't get a woman,' Paul informed Ryan. 'He's been pestering Kirsten since the dance last Christmas. She refused to go out with him and he blames me so he's using his job to get at us this way.'

'Kirsten?' Ryan said incredulously. 'My wee sister, Kirsten?' He stared at Lord Nog, his eyes travelling over the heavy jowl and thickening waist. Oh boy!' he began to laugh. 'You're joking!'

'No, I'm not,' Paul said seriously. 'If necessary I shall ask Kirsten to prove it to his boss. If I remember correctly the names of farms due for wages inspections are supposed to be drawn at random by computer, unless there's been a complaint. Seems strange that we should be selected for an inspection when we've only been in business a short time, and even stranger that it should be Lord Nog that should undertake it.'

Nigel Kent began to splutter with anger. Paul's green eyes narrowed.

'Either you hand over those notes and get out of here right now or we report you to your superior. Which is it to be?'

'Oh come on now, I was only playing a prank on you two.' Nigel Kent tried hard to sound convincing and failed dismally.

'Whatever you were trying to do you've made a mess of it, as usual,' Paul snapped. 'And you've wasted enough of our time. We'll relieve you of your notes.' He held out his hand. Nigel hesitated then handed over the pieces of paper attached to his clipboard.

'Nigel . . .' Ryan held him by the shoulder and turned him face to face, 'I can't believe you would go after a young girl like my sister, but you leave her alone in future. Right?' Nigel didn't answer and Ryan's grip tightened. 'I mean it or you'll have me to answer to. Got that?'

57

'Oh all right!' Nigel answered sullenly and jerked himself free and out of the door like a frightened rabbit.

As soon as he was out of earshot both boys heaved a sigh of relief and then began to laugh. 'Poor old Nig-Nog. He never did manage to do anything right. No wonder his father was so disappointed in him he tried to send him to Australia.'

When Molly came home for the Christmas holidays Ryan was jubilant. They were almost inseparable. Mrs Nairne knew how Molly felt and she was relieved Ryan seemed a nice young man from a decent family. She asked him to join them for Christmas dinner when all the family would be there. Ryan desperately wanted to accept but he knew his mother would be hurt if he didn't go home on Christmas Day.

'I understand, Ryan,' Mrs Nairne said gently. 'I would feel just the same if Molly deserted our family gathering. But if you're free after the evening milking perhaps you could join us for supper instead?'

'Thank you! That would be splendid.' Molly and Ryan looked at each other with stars in their eyes. When they left Mrs Nairne turned to her husband.

'I believe it's serious between those two. I don't think they'll want to wait long before they get married once Molly finishes at university.'

'What they want and what they can afford to do are two different things,' Mr Nairne said gruffly. 'Norman says the laddie is a grand worker and a first class stockman, but he has no money to keep a wife. He doesna even have a house o' his own for her to live in. Molly's a grand lassie, she's our lassie, but we've got to admit it, we've spoiled her a bit, her being the only lassie and so much younger than the lads . . .'

'I know . . .' Mrs Nairne sighed. 'I know . . . They're so young, and so much in love . . .'

Ryan and Paul were just finishing milking and washing the parlour on Christmas afternoon when a shiny blue car drove into the farmyard. It took them both a few seconds to recognize Molly behind the wheel.

'Goodness, Molly! I didn't recognize you. Where did you

get that smart chariot?' Paul asked. Ryan simply stared in astonishment.

'It's my Christmas present from all the family.' Molly chuckled at their surprise. Ryan's heart sank like lead. He and Paul could only afford the battered old pick-up truck between them. He must have been mad to think he could ever ask Molly to be his wife.

'You're awfully quiet, Ryan,' she said anxiously. 'Don't you like it? Aren't you pleased I've come to collect you for supper?' Ryan didn't answer. Paul looked at him sharply. He knew immediately what was in his mind. His heart ached for his cousin, but not nearly as much as Ryan's ached for Molly.

Paul strode away to the house, leaving them alone together.

'I could never marry you, Molly,' Ryan said, his voice choked with emotion. 'How could I ever have imagined I could ask you to be my wife?'

'Ryan! Wh–what do you mean . . . ?' Molly's voice trembled.

'Just this. It will take me years before I can buy a car – any old car,' he said bitterly. 'I must have been mad to dream of buying you an engagement ring.' His face flamed as he thought what a fool he would have made of himself in front of all the Nairne family, presenting her with a cheap little ring. He turned away. Molly cried out.

'Don't go!' She grabbed his arm, tugging at his sleeve. 'P-please, Ryan . . . Listen to me. Mother knows how much I miss you when I'm away at university. She – she was afraid I wouldn't settle without you. Maybe I wouldn't have stayed away if you hadn't written back to me every time, and – and phoned me sometimes. Even so Mummy understood I might give up before the finish. The c–car was her idea. She persuaded Daddy that if I could drive home at weekends – well some weekends – and s–see you then I'd be more likely to stick it to the end of the course and get my degree. Oh please, Ryan . . .' Molly was almost in tears. 'I hate being away from you . . .'

'I hate it too,' Ryan said gruffly. He turned back to her. 'But it will be years before we can afford to marry,' he said dully. 'I see that now. I doubt if I'll ever be able to afford all the things your parents buy for you.'

'There's only one thing I really want,' Molly said softly, shyly, 'and my parents couldn't buy it for me, not if they had all the money in the world.'

'How's that?'

'Because all I want is for you to love me. Ryan . . . ?' In the dim light streaming across the yard from the house she gazed up at him beseechingly.

'Oh, Molly!' Ryan seized her in his arms and held her tight, forgetting he had just come from the milking parlour and his clothes smelled of cows. Molly didn't care. She clung to him as though her life depended on it.

It was a good five minutes later before Ryan realized Molly must be getting cold. He sighed, but still he held her close, reluctant to let her go. 'I can't imagine what kind of future I'll ever be able to offer you, Molly. All I know is I don't want any future without you.'

'I'm glad to hear that, Ryan Greig,' she said tremulously, 'because I don't intend anyone else to have you.'

'You're getting cold. Come on into the house and meet my great granny while I get washed and changed.'

'Would she mind? Your granny, I mean . . . if she knew we loved each other?'

'She's guessed how I feel already. Come on. You'll like her. Everybody does. She's a wise and kind old lady.'

Megan and Tina corresponded intermittently, usually depending on news of family and mutual friends. Megan had spent most of her schooldays near the village where Tina and her father now lived and she looked forward to hearing local news, especially since Tina wrote such delightful letters, with humour or compassion as the subject required. She was interested in people. She cared about them and she made time to listen.

Although the locals had been less than welcoming to Tina and her father when they first arrived from Ireland they had gradually become accepted as part of the community and she often regaled Megan with amusing anecdotes. Tina was in her final year of studies and with the spring well advanced Megan knew her friend must be fully occupied between home and work so she was not really surprised when the weeks passed by without any letters.

So it was a surprise when she received two letters in less than a week. The tension in the first was clear but even so Megan was unprepared for the devastating news which Tina's second letter brought.

Seven

It was clear that exams were the last thing on Tina's mind and Megan was dismayed and saddened as she read on. Tina had not had an easy life. She didn't deserve more trouble.

I have suspected for the last few months that Daddy was not well. I sensed he was hiding something from me. I have been doing as much as I could to make the farm work easier for him because he seemed so drained of energy. Then I overheard some gossip in the village. One of the salesmen had called at the farm in the middle of the morning and found Daddy lying stretched out on his back as though sleeping in the hay shed. When the man approached him Daddy told him he was gathering up the energy to start on the next job. The salesman told me that himself when I confronted him. He said he had felt concerned, but he didn't know what to do in the face of Daddy's stubborn refusal to admit there was anything wrong.

Somehow the tale started rumours that he's taken to drink, or drugs. One man confronted me himself. He said Daddy was bone lazy and why hadn't he got his bullocks fed before mid afternoon last Tuesday.

Oh, Megan, I can't tell you how worried I am or how unpleasant some people can be once they get hold of gossip – and truly it is gossip. Daddy just kept saying there was nothing to worry about when I kept asking him. He said it was my imagination. I knew my instinct was right. My fears have been confirmed. I managed to persuade him to see the doctor at last. He is to have tests. Don't doctors always say that when they don't know what is wrong? I think they do. Or when they suspect some-thing really serious and are reluctant to say so without confirmation. At least Daddy admits now that he has not been himself since he had the influenza in March. He has such a peculiar sort of cough, not like a cough at all really, more of a whistle which seems as though it will never end once it has begun. The perspiration pours from him then. I am so worried, Megan. In my heart I know it is no trivial illness. He looks so haggard and he is dreadfully pale. I cannot think to leave him during the week when I am supposed to be at college. What does education matter if the most important person in your whole life is ill? I can't bear to leave him. I simply can't.

There was a little more with Tina enquiring for baby Iain, as she never failed to do. Megan was worried. It was not like Tina to imagine trouble or to exaggerate. She was always so cheerful and practical.

'Telephone her tonight,' Max suggested when she told him and showed him Tina's letter. 'It's a great pity it has happened just before her final examinations. Have a talk with her. Sometimes it's easier than writing.'

Megan did telephone but Tina sounded strained and she said it was not convenient to talk, but she would write if there was any news.

'I think her father must have been near and able to over-hear our conversation,' she told Max.

In the next letter Megan learned there were to be more tests. She sensed her friend's desperate worry, and she appeared to be working far too hard trying to look after the farm almost single-handed. Tina made no mention of her studies. They would seem of secondary importance to her just now, and yet they were so important for Tina's own future.

'I just wish I didn't live so far away. There might have been something I could have done to help,' Megan fretted.

'Dearest Megan, I suspect anxiety is Tina's biggest burden until the doctor can come up with some results from all the tests they are doing. Waiting and worrying is almost worse than knowing, however bad things are.'

63

'But everything seems to move so slowly. Each time there is another few weeks to wait for an appointment. Tina takes the rest of her exams in less than two weeks.'

It was much later when Megan learned Tina had kept an appointment with their own GP the day before she was to take her most important exam. He had told her that her father had cancer in his wind pipe, close to his lung and too far advanced to operate. Although the doctor said it was usually their policy to tell patients when they had a terminal illness he felt her father was not in a suitable frame of mind to be told the truth.

'I think he does know.' Tina, white faced and tense, confronted the doctor. 'In his heart I think he has known for some time, but he is hiding it from himself, from me, and from the world. He doesn't want to accept it after seeing Mummy . . .' She choked on the words. Later, when confiding in Megan she said the doctor spoke kindly to her, but there was just nothing he could do.

'We can try other treatments,' he said. Tina had showered him with questions but there was no hope of cure, only of prolonging her father's life, perhaps for months, maybe a year, depending how well the treatment worked. Tina did not take her examination the following day.

'I felt it was all so futile. I had already neglected my studies. Daddy needed me. I need to treasure every day, every moment of every day, for whatever time I can have with him. He is all I've got. Later . . . later there will be time for other examinations.'

Megan could only murmur words of sympathy which she felt were pitifully inadequate, especially on the other end of a telephone line.

During the summer Tina strove to keep things going as normally as possible so that her father would not give up hope. Their dairy herd was small in comparison to their more affluent neighbours but this only made the work twice as hard. The farm was less modern and less well equipped with labour saving systems than larger dairy farms, and they were entirely dependent on their own labour. During these months she exchanged a few letters and occasional telephone calls with Megan. Many of the people she had got to know in the village were kindly but there was little in the way of practical help.

It was mid September when she telephoned Megan. Her father had had a particularly bad week due to the effects of a new treatment the consultant was trying.

'If only we could talk about it, Megan. There are changes here, at the farm, we need to make. I think Daddy believes if he doesn't mention the dreaded word cancer then I shall never think of it. But I'm not a child to be shielded from the truth this time.' Megan could hear the tears in her friend's voice. She sensed the utter weariness and despair.

'If only there was something I could do . . .' she said help-lessly.

'There is,' Tina said. 'You can give me a bit of information, and maybe a bit of advice. I can't go on like this any longer, Megan. I have enough sense to realize I must keep up my own strength to see Daddy through this, however long it takes. I can't give up the tenancy of the farm just yet. That would mean moving out of the house and the upheaval of looking for another. It would really upset Daddy. He would realize the end is in sight. He would worry about my future too. But I have made up my mind that the cows must be sold. They're not pedigree or anything special, as your father's were, but I thought you could tell me who to approach. You knew the auctioneers. When would be the best time? Though choice is not an option any longer. I need to cut down the outside work if I'm to give Daddy the care and attention he needs.'

'Oh, Tina. I'm so sorry you're having all this on top of everything else. I can give you the name of the auctioneers who handled our farm sale and I will ask Max for any suggestions which might help. I'll telephone you back.'

'Make it tomorrow night then please, Megan. I'm dead on my feet. I'm going up to bed. Daddy is so restless most nights.'

Max realized how upset Megan was on Tina's behalf, and she had often told him how kind the Donnellys had been when she needed help.

'Megan, I have a suggestion. What do you say if we ask

Mother and Father to come and stay at Glens of Lochandee to oversee the farm and look after Iain for a few days. We could go down and stay in a bed and breakfast place somewhere near Tina's. Richard can manage the cows here now the harvest is in and things are a bit quieter. I'll ask one of the other men to give him a hand.'

'You would do that?' Megan's eyes shone and she flew into Max's arms. 'Oh, Max, you're so good. No wonder I love you. It would comfort me no end if I felt I had done some small thing to help Tina after all her father did for me.'

After several more telephone calls Tina contacted the local auctioneers and a date was fixed to sell most of the Donnellys' cows. Max and Megan were to travel in time to help Tina get the cows sorted out and groomed ready for the sale. Tina's relief and gratitude were evident, even over the telephone, and Megan's heart swelled with love for her husband.

'I know it is not the time to tell Tina that many a cloud has a silver lining,' Megan said. 'But I thought the end of my world had come when my father had his heart attack and we had to sell up everything, but then it brought you to see our herd, dearest Max.'

Max drew her into his arms and kissed her tenderly.

'And I got the best bargain any man could wish for,' he said softly.

Megan was shocked at the sight of Tina's father and it was all she could do to hide her dismay. Tina watched her reactions closely and she was not fooled by Megan's assumed cheerfulness. Her heart was heavy but she was deeply thankful to have Megan and Max beside her. They were true friends when she needed a friend most and they understood what needed to be done.

The morning after the cows had been sold at auction Megan and Max were preparing for the journey home. Tina popped in briefly at the guest house to bid them goodbye and to thank them one more time.

'It's such a relief to know I don't have to get out at the crack of dawn to get the cows milked in time for the tanker to collect the milk. I can manage the feeding of the rest of the animals when Daddy is sleeping, as he does more and more these days. He has never mentioned the cows. I don't think he realizes they've gone. He hears the noise of the other animals in the yard and he seems content. I couldn't have managed without you two.'

'You would have managed, Tina. But I'm glad we came,' Megan said simply.

'What about the tenancy?' Max asked. 'How long notice do you need to give?'

'I'm not sure whether it's a year or six months. I have made up my mind to discuss it with the agent and give notice.' Her mouth trembled. 'Six months from now . . .' She chewed hard on her lower lip. 'N–nothing on this earth will worry Daddy any more . . .'

Megan hugged her young friend in silence. What was there to say that would bring comfort?

'You must come up and stay with us for a while before you rush to find another house, Tina,' Max said. 'I know Megan is always pleased to have your company and Iain is becoming quite a handful. It would be good for both of you.'

'Thank you, Max, you're very kind.' Tina summoned a wan smile. 'I'll think about it if . . . when . . .' She broke off. Max squeezed her hand in silent understanding. 'Well you know where we are and that you're always welcome.'

It surprised Megan, and even Tina herself, when Mr Donnelly managed to hang onto life well into January of 1989.

A few weeks before his death two events occurred in Megan's life which temporarily pushed Tina's troubles aside.

The first was the realization that she had not had a period since her visit to Hereford with Max. That, coupled with the queasiness she was feeling each morning, made her realize she was expecting another child. The prospect filled her with joy, but also some trepidation, knowing the problems she had had with other pregnancies and how much she would hate to be parted from Iain if she had to go to hospital for any length of time.

She completely forgot her own worries when the most devastating tragedy occurred just before Christmas.

Megan had cleared away the evening meal and washed the dishes. She tiptoed upstairs to see whether Iain was asleep. She was alarmed to hear a sound like thunder, and yet not thunder . . . Had the house trembled? Or had she imagined it? Iain slept on, his chubby hand grasping his favourite teddy-bear, his cheeks clean and flushed from his bath. Megan turned and ran downstairs. Max had gone out to check on a newly calved cow with milk fever. She met him coming in the back door. His eyes were round with disbelief, his face white.

'Did ye hear that? It's raining fire. Look! See, the glow in the sky over there!' He tugged Megan outside. They stared in dismay. 'I think two of the low flying jets must have crashed head on.'

'It's so close! It must be very near to Lockerbie surely?' Megan whispered hoarsely. 'Please God there's nobody hurt, whatever it is.'

'It's certainly not far away.'

At Wester Rullion Rachel was watching the television. Suddenly the programme was interrupted. There was an urgent newsflash.

'An air crash? Over Lockerbie!' She couldn't take in what the announcer was saying. Paul and Ryan were still sitting at the kitchen table discussing the day's work. She called to them.

They stood together, staring at the television, open mouthed with shock. Such things did not happen in this small quiet corner of the British Isles.

'They think the plane has crashed into the petrol station!' Ryan repeated. 'There's houses all round there . . .'

'Listen.' Rachel held up a hand. 'They're appealing for all the doctors and nurses who are off duty to report for work immediately.'

Half an hour later Joanne arrived, her face pale.

'Have you received an appeal to make sandwiches,' she asked, 'for the rescuers?'

'No. What . . . ?'

'Bridie is making some. And Megan and Lucy. We're to take them to a collection point. I came to help here. I haven't much at home anyway but I've brought bread and butter . . .'

'We've plenty more bread, and tins of meat,' Rachel said and led the way into the kitchen.

'They say it's a jumbo jet,' Paul reported, unable to take his eyes off the television.

'Right over Lockerbie,' Ryan muttered in disbelief.

Joanne and Rachel made a big box of sandwiches and Joanne took them to her car.

'They've closed all the roads into Lockerbie except for medical staff, police and such like,' Paul told her.

'That makes sense,' she nodded. 'I've to drop these off. Someone is organizing a combined delivery. I think they're opening the school. It's closed for the Christmas holidays.'

Doctors and nurses assembled ready for duty. They moved patients. They made beds. They waited for survivors. None came. There were none.

In the days which followed reports began to filter through. The enormity of the tragedy was an inescapable fact. The horror of it was over and around the little town and beyond.

Helicopters and planes circled over Lockerbie and Langholm and all the villages and farms, including Wester Rullion and Lochandee, scrutinizing far and wide in their search for debris and clues of any kind. Soldiers on foot combed the hills and woods. Limbs, luggage, debris, were discovered in fields and woods over several miles in and outside the town. All two hundred and fifty-nine passengers had been killed. In addition eleven Lockerbie residents had died as their homes vanished in smoke.

'Thirty-eight of the passengers were students at university,' Rachel said sorrowfully. 'So young. On their way home for Christmas . . .' She shuddered. 'Just the same age as you two boys . . . Dear God, how could such a thing happen?'

'Doesn't it make you wonder if there is a God, Granny?' Paul said, and wished immediately he could recall the words. Ryan shot him a startled glance. They both knew Rachel was a devout Christian and her faith had strengthened with the years.

'This is devil's work, Paul,' she said quietly.

In the days which followed floral tributes were laid on the

main street in Lockerbie. It seemed the only way many could express their sympathy to the bereaved families. One such tribute was to 'the little girl in the red dress', fondly remembered by a fellow passenger who had been fortunate indeed to leave the flight at Heathrow.

The air crash was widely reported and Tina was quick to try and contact Megan, knowing that Lockerbie was her nearest town and that part of the aeroplane was reported to have come down in a village three miles away. The telephone lines were jammed. Like thousands of other anxious friends and relatives she had to wait. When she did get through the following day she was relieved to know that Megan, and all the Jones and Maxwell families, and their friends, were safe.

'It makes me feel ashamed the way I have railed against my own troubles,' she said. 'and the way I've fought against the hand fate has dealt to Daddy. We are nothing compared to so many. It makes me feel so small and insignificant when I hear of all those people killed. Lives snuffed out like a candle.'

'I know what you mean, Tina,' Megan said gently. 'But your father belongs to you. It is your life, and his, which are affected. You're allowed to grieve for those you love. There's nothing wrong or selfish about that.'

'I know, but I feel selfish all the same, and helpless and . . . Oh I don't know, Megan. My only plea is that I can keep him with me, at home to the end. I know he can't last much longer and I think the pain is getting worse. Am I being selfish to want to keep him here, do you think?'

'Does your father want to go to hospital?'

'Oh no! Definitely not, he's made that very clear, and I've promised to try . . .' Her voice broke.

'Then you're certainly not selfish, Tina. You're just doing your best to grant his last wish.'

Eight

It was the end of February and Joanne shivered as she hurried into the doctor's surgery. It was only her routine check for hypertension and a repeat of her prescription so she was not concerned for herself but she could see immediately that the waiting room was fuller than usual and she guessed the doctors would be running late. There were coughs and sneezes all around. She thought most of the patients would have been better at home beside the fire with a hot drink instead of coming out on such a cold day. She had told Mrs Maxwell she would be a bit late getting to Wester Rullion but at this rate it would be nearly lunch time before she arrived.

At Wester Rullion the postman opened the back door as usual and called a cheery greeting as he placed a neat bundle of letters and the daily paper on the kitchen unit. These days Rachel usually left the bundle for Joanne to sort. They were mostly bills anyway, or forms to be filled in for the farm, or unwanted circulars advertising products none of them wanted or holidays they couldn't afford. Today she glanced idly across at the bundle and saw the top letter was a thin blue airmail. Curiously she looked closer. She was surprised to see it was addressed to her. She picked it up, puzzled. She didn't know anyone abroad, not since John Allan had died. He was Paul's maternal grandfather and one of the nicest men Rachel had ever met.

What he had done to deserve a daughter like Gerda it was hard to tell. After Gerda's marriage to Ewan her selfishness and self absorption had continued, and even increased. Rachel could still picture John Allan shaking his greying head sadly.

71

'I couldn't have wished for a better laddie than Ewan for a son-in-law if I'd had him made to measure,' he had said sincerely. 'If that lassie o' mine canna pull herself together now and consider someone besides herself, then I wash my hands of her.' He had given his only child all he could afford and still she demanded more.

John Allan had despaired of her and taken what little happiness he could with a second wife called Dolly. Gerda had been furious when her father sold his house and went abroad to live. Rachel had met Dolly once and found her a cheerful little woman who was determined to give her new husband the happiness he deserved. They had shared several contented years in Spain until John Allan's death.

Dolly had sold the Spanish villa and returned to her native Dundee. She always sent Rachel a card and a letter at Christmas but the last two years it had deteriorated to a few sentences on her card, telling Rachel her hands were so crippled with arthritis she found it painful to write much these days. Now as Rachel stared at the airmail she wondered if Dolly had returned to a warmer climate to help her arthritis.

Frowning she turned it over to see whether the sender had included a name. Her heart gave such a thump she slumped on to the kitchen stool and grasped the edge of the unit for support. The blood drained from her face.

'Gerda!' she whispered hoarsely. 'Paul's mother! After all this time . . .'

Rachel had no idea whether she had married the man she ran away with, the scoundrel who had helped her cheat her young son out of his inheritance. She couldn't remember his name. Her brain seemed to be reeling. Her knuckles gleamed white with the effort of holding on to the kitchen counter top. She forced herself to take slow deep breaths. Gradually her world steadied. She reached for a knife and slit open the thin paper.

The only address was a post box number in a place Rachel had never heard of.

The letter was brief. It was not even a letter really, Rachel thought later. It was more a demand.

To Mrs Rachel Maxwell or the person opening this letter.
I need to contact my son, Paul Ross Maxwell.

Rachel's heart beat at an alarming rate.

'Oh Paul . . .' she whispered. She read the stark sentences again, and then again. They seemed to dance before her eyes but she forced herself to read the rest.

I have tried to contact my father, John Allan. According to the Spanish authorities he is dead. If my son is still living at the farm, or if you know his address, ask him to contact me at this address.
Gerda Fritz-Allan (Maxwell).

Footsteps approached the back door and Rachel stuffed the letter into the pocket of her skirt.

'Hello, Granny.' Paul looked at her in surprise. 'Why are you sitting there?' He frowned, seeing the way her fingers were grasping the edge of the counter. 'You're dreadfully pale. Do you feel faint?' Without waiting for a reply he kicked off his wellington boots on the mat and moved to her side, putting his strong young arm around her shoulders. The sight of his grandmother looking so ill had given Paul a shock but he would not let her see that. 'Come on, let me help you on to a proper chair,' he said gently.

'Och, I'm fine, laddie.' Rachel strove to keep her voice steady but even to her own ears it sounded faint and wavery. 'I – I th–think I'm needing my mid-morning cup o' tea. J–Joanne hasna come yet.'

Paul glanced at the clock and then at the empty cup and saucer on the draining board. Certainly Joanne was later than she had expected but he could see his grandmother had had her usual cup of tea already. He didn't argue. He pushed the big kettle on to the hot plate of the Aga and reached for the tea-caddy.

'Let me get you to a proper chair,' he said and helped her to her feet. He was dismayed to realize how slight she was these days. She almost fitted under his arm. He thought of all the times he had run to her for comfort and how she would scoop him up in her firm strong arms, hugging him, comforting, always reassuring. His grandmother had always been the centre of his life. He couldn't imagine Wester Rullion without her there to welcome him with her warm, wry smile. She was the rock on which his very existence depended. But her strength was ebbing after the years of responsibility, trying to hang on to Wester Rullion until he was of an age to take over the farm.

He felt the stab of anger he had begun to feel whenever he thought of the unknown woman who had been his mother. She had brought so much grief into his grandmother's life as well as making his own attempt to farm Wester Rullion so much more difficult. He didn't care for himself. He would win through however long it took and whatever problems he had to overcome, but it was different for his grandmother. He glanced at her pale face and his heart sank. Time was running out for her and he desperately wanted her to see the farm restored to the fine place it had been in his grandfather's care.

Paul hovered uncertainly long after he had made them both a cup of tea and drunk it. Granny seemed to have withdrawn into a world of her own which was not like her at all. He didn't want to leave her alone. It was a relief when he heard Joanne's little car drawing up outside the back door. He hurried outside to meet her.

'I don't think Granny is very well,' he said in a low voice. 'I found her slumped on the stool in the back kitchen. I've made her some tea but she seems to be staring into space, hardly aware I'm there . . .'

'Oh dear, that doesn't sound like the Mrs Maxwell I know,' Joanne frowned. 'And it had to be this morning I had such a long wait at the surgery.' She bit her lip. Now was certainly not the time to tell Paul, or Mrs Maxwell, that the doctor had advised her she must slow down and reduce her working hours. She couldn't believe her blood pressure was as high as he said. It was probably the frustration of waiting too long to see him. She turned to Paul. 'I'll see to things now. I'll call you if I need anything. Will you be around?'

'Yes, in the barn probably. I'm grinding corn for the cows. I'll come if you give me a shout.'

Rachel had heard Joanne arrive. She had probably given Paul a fright. She must pull herself together and think clearly. Why did Gerda want to contact Paul after all these years? What did she want? Money? That seemed most likely. She had never had enough money for her many cravings. Should she tell Paul? Gerda was his mother after all. Shouldn't he have the right to make his own decisions? He was a man now. Wasn't it up to him whether he contacted his mother or not? Did she have the right to deny him that? She brushed a hand across her brow just as Joanne entered the kitchen.

Joanne knew at once that Rachel had received some kind of shock but she also knew she must wait for the older woman to confide in her if she wished to do so. Even so her brow creased with worry at the sight of the bowed shoulders which were always so erect, the pale lined face, devoid of the warm smile with which Mrs Maxwell greeted everyone. The best thing was to continue the usual routine and hope things would return to normal, Joanne decided, but she couldn't help wondering what had happened to upset her employer.

'Have you heard from Bridie today?' she asked conversationally.

'Bridie? Oh . . . er . . . no.' Rachel frowned. Should she tell Bridie about the letter? She was one of Paul's trustees until he was twenty-five. What would she advise? Rachel knew instinctively Bridie would be furious and tell her to burn the letter. But no, she couldn't burn it, at least not yet.

'I – I think I'll go upstairs, Joanne. I – I haven't made my bed yet.' Joanne knew Rachel always made her bed every morning before she came downstairs to breakfast, except on Mondays when she changed the sheets and turned back the blankets to air. It was all a part of her unchanging daily and weekly routine, just as she clung to her blankets and refused to try a duvet.

'All right,' Joanne nodded. She knew better than to offer to help. Rachel Maxwell was fiercely independent. Instead

75

she busied herself in the hall until she was satisfied Rachel was safely at the top and into her bedroom.

Once there Rachel slumped on to her bed and put her head in her hands. The past was racing through her mind as clearly as if the events had happened yesterday. Ewan's death, the debts, Gerda running away with that actor man, stealing the money from the farm account, having to sell the Wester Rullion cattle . . . The demands for money, the shame of it all. Rachel shuddered as the memories flooded into her mind. Paul, so young, so frightened and then so upset with all the events in his turbulent young life.

'No!' Rachel murmured aloud. She sat up straighter. She took the thin blue paper out of her pocket. She smoothed it out, staring at it as though it might tell her more. Why did Gerda need Paul after all these years? She had abandoned him. Surely she had forfeited her rights as his mother. No, she decided, I will not add another burden to his young shoulders. Carefully she folded the letter. She lifted the paper lining of her underwear drawer and slipped the letter beneath. She straightened and pulled back her shoulders. That was the end of that. But it could never be the end.

Rachel tried to put the letter out of her mind as well as out of sight but when she went to bed that night her thoughts returned to Gerda, Ewan's widow, her own daughter-in-law, Paul's mother . . . Her conscience was troubled. Did she have the right to come between a son and his mother? Had she the right to deny him the opportunity of meeting Gerda?

'Please God help me to make the right decision,' she prayed fervently.

In her heart she felt Gerda Fritz-Allan could not have changed her old habits. She had been utterly selfish from the beginning and truly wicked in the end with her scheming and stealing. Surely it couldn't be wrong to protect Paul?

As the days passed into weeks, and then into months Rachel still pondered the rights and wrongs of her action to hide away the letter. It lay in her drawer as a flimsy bit of paper, but its message lay on her conscience like a heavy weight, almost too much to bear alone.

Nine

Tina stayed alone at the farm in Herefordshire after her father's funeral. She felt utterly drained but the remaining animals had to be cared for and the tenancy did not end until May. In any case she had nowhere else to go. Max and Megan had repeated their invitation to stay with them until she decided whether she wanted to repeat her final year at university and continue with teacher training. She valued their friendship but she could not burden them with her presence or her problems, especially now that Megan was expecting another child.

She would have to look for a cottage to rent somewhere when the farm tenancy expired. Before then she must sell the rest of the stock and implements. Beyond that she could not think or plan. Her life seemed empty and devoid of meaning now. She had no one of her own.

It was the beginning of May when Tina finally knew what she wanted to do. Ever since she was fourteen she had tried to take her mother's place and look after her father. She needed someone to care for, she realized now. She was not the sort of person who craved a high powered career, and it would be wrong to go into teaching unless she felt dedicated to the work.

I am not going to rent a cottage, nor shall I buy one for now, she wrote in her letter to Megan. *I shall put all the money from the farm sale into a decent bank account or maybe a bond. I have decided I need a job where people matter. I think I may decide on nursing but in the meantime I shall look for employment as a carer – either privately or in a home for elderly or handicapped people. I think I might enrol for evening classes on first aid and anything else which may help.*

I feel so much happier now that I have finally decided what I want to do. I realize I have been living in a sort of limbo and avoiding any decisions since Daddy died.

Megan telephoned Tina as soon as she received her letter.

'Tina, your letter came this morning. If you really mean what you say about caring for people I desperately need your help.'

'You do? You need help, Megan? Is something wrong?' Tina asked anxiously.

'It's the baby. You know I had two miscarriages before I had Iain? Well the doctors are afraid I may lose this baby too. They keep telling me I must rest. I try, Tina, I really do, and Max does his best, but it isn't easy with a toddler running around all day. Max's mother is very good but I don't like to keep asking her to look after Iain when his father is not very well.'

'Mr Jones? Is he ill then?'

'It's his arthritis. It seems to have got much worse recently. He's in considerable pain but there's such a long wait for hip replacements.'

'Well I'm more than willing to help in any way I can,' Tina said. 'I shall be free once I clear the house at the end of May. I shall sell most of the furniture but there's a few pieces I really want to keep. I will start looking around to see where I can put them in store then I'll let you know when I can come. Will that do?'

'Oh, Tina, you don't know what a relief that is. I've been dreading having to leave Iain if they take me into hospital. I shall not mind quite so much if you're here to look after him.'

'Well that will be easy. He's a little darling.'

'Not always! He's growing big and bad these days.' Megan chuckled. 'And, by the way, you could easily bring your furniture with you instead of putting it into store. The old bothy is clean and dry and you might want to have any

78

smaller pieces in your room here. That is if it won't cost too much to bring them up?'

'Are you sure? That would be super, Megan. I could hire a van to bring all the furniture I want to keep, and my own things will go into the car. I'm keeping it of course.'

'A-ah, Tina, you'll never believe what a relief it is to know you're coming. I'll go and tell Max right now. I know he's been worrying about how we'll manage.'

Lucy felt her house was too quiet at weekends now that both Kirsten and Cameron were away at university, and Ryan living and working at Wester Rullion. In her heart she knew she was missing the buzz of the classroom and school life in general. Conan had finally persuaded her to give up teaching altogether so that she could help Fiona more often with the Rullion Glen Coach Tours. She was kept busier than she had anticipated with the holiday bookings and learning to do the accounts the way Fiona liked them done, but she still missed the children.

So on a lovely Sunday at the beginning of June she persuaded Ryan and Paul to come to lunch and bring her grandmother with them. As an afterthought she phoned to ask Bridie and Nick to join them, as well as her father and Fiona. Lucy enjoyed cooking and they were all replete as they carried cups of coffee out to the long garden which stretched down to the little burn at the back of Lucy's house.

Bridie was concerned about her mother. She sensed there had been something troubling her for quite some time now but no one seemed able to discover what was wrong. She'd had a talk with Joanne but she had been unable to enlighten her. She was so preoccupied it was a while before she saw Nick and Conan and Fiona had been sitting down by the big chestnut tree for some time. They seemed to be deep in conversation. She went to join them.

Fiona greeted her warmly. They had been good friends since schooldays.

'We're arranging a trip to Australia, Bridie. Conan has persuaded Nick the climate might be good for his arthritis. Will you come with us? What do you think?'

79

Bridie stared at them all, wide-eyed. Then her eyes met Nick's. She could see he would like to go. He would do anything if it would give him some ease from the constant pain he had suffered in recent months. She hesitated.

'It depends when you plan to go . . .' she said uncertainly. 'I'm sure there's something the matter with Mother but Joanne says she never complains about her health and she still does the cooking every day. I don't know what to think but she seems to have aged all of a sudden . . .'

'Yes, I said the same thing to Fiona,' Conan nodded. 'But you can't stay at home indefinitely, Bridie. Mother wouldn't want you to and if there was anything wrong I'm sure she would tell one of us.'

'Are you? I'm not . . .' Bridie frowned. 'I'm certain she's worried about something, but it may just be the boys and their bank overdraft. I know she was not in favour of that and now that the bank base rate is up to 13 per cent it means a hefty payment in interest.'

'But they seem to be doing reasonably well.'

'They're doing all right considering the way farming's going at present.'

'Oh, come on, Bridie!' Conan laughed teasingly. 'When did any farmer ever admit times were good?'

'Not often,' Bridie smiled back ruefully, 'but you have to admit the milk quota business has hit hard, especially for young folks just starting off on their own. Anyway I'm not worrying about Paul and Ryan. I just can't help wondering if that is what's bothering Mother, or if it's something else entirely. I just know there's something. Then there's Megan . . . I don't like to go away before the baby is born. Megan is having problems already and it's not due until the end of August. It's worse this time because she has Iain and she'll hate it if she has to go into hospital.'

'But I thought she was getting that girl, what's her name . . .?' Conan said.

'Tina Donnelly. Yes, she arrived last week and she's very capable and a hard worker. Megan says she's wonderful with Iain,' Bridie said slowly. 'But I still feel I ought to be here. How long are you planning to be away?'

'Six weeks, maybe eight or nine . . .'

'Six weeks! Oh, I . . .'

'Perhaps we could wait until August to go to Australia?' Nick suggested quickly.

'Well September would suit us all right,' Fiona said thoughtfully. 'Lucy will be well into the way of the business by then and bookings will be quietening down.'

'I'd have preferred to have gone at the end of June,' Conan said, 'but I see I'm outnumbered. September it is then. I'll see to the bookings. I would like to do some market research in various areas but if you two want to stay in some of the places for longer we can always arrange to meet up again.'

'Surely you're not thinking of arranging tours in Australia?' Bridie asked incredulously.

'We'll have to see about that,' Conan grinned. 'We can't allow the business to stand still. Lucy's dynamic pair will soon be joining us. Cameron already has ideas.'

'I'd have thought Conan would have been preparing to retire, or at least take things easier,' Bridie said to Fiona as they left the two men to themselves.

'Well I must admit I'm looking forward to having things a bit easier as Lucy takes over more of my work,' Fiona smiled, 'but I can't imagine Conan ever retiring so long as he's in good health.'

As things turned out Megan was kept in hospital on account of some alarming symptoms during a routine health check at the beginning of July. The weather had been unbearably hot and it aggravated Megan's tiredness even more. She fretted terribly but Tina did her best to comfort her and visited almost every afternoon, taking Iain with her to see his mummy. Megan was tearful and Tina didn't know whether it made things better or worse to know that he was quite content at home when she was not there herself.

'Of course he misses you terribly, especially at bedtime,' she said, hoping to comfort her friend but she only succeeded in bringing the tears to her eyes and that upset Iain too.

Max had entered several cows for the Dumfries Show at the beginning of August but the day before the show the doctors decided they must operate immediately for Megan's sake as well as the baby's. Max wanted to be with his wife and he put the show out of his mind. Rachel reported the Lochandee news to Paul and Ryan at tea time. Immediately they telephoned Max and offered to help Richard Green, the Lochandee stockman, prepare the cattle for the show while Max was away at the hospital.

'By tomorrow the operation will be over and if Megan and the baby are all right you'll wish you'd had the cattle ready,' Ryan said. He was desperate to have cattle of his own to show.

'Well Richard will be very disappointed if we don't go,' Max said slowly, scratching his head as he pondered what to do.

'He told me last week the entry for the young cow class is one of the best Lochandee has had,' Ryan said

'Yes, she's a beauty,' Max conceded. 'All right then. You youngsters can get them ready, but I'm not promising we shall be at the show tomorrow. Everything depends on how Megan is. We've quite a number of cattle entered. You'll have a busy day getting them all clipped and shampooed.'

'We'll come over as soon as we've finished milking in the morning,' Paul said firmly. 'Peter will finish off for us and check the other stock.'

'All right then. I could ask Mother to come up and look after Iain if you like. I'm sure Tina would be happy to lend a hand. She's a dab hand at washing cattle. She prepared all her own animals for sale. Even though they weren't pedigree she presented them really well. I take my hat off to that girl. I don't know what Megan and I would have done without her these past few weeks.'

'Tell her if she helps us we'll take her to the Show dance,' Ryan grinned, 'if everything's OK here of course,' he added hastily as Paul quirked an eyebrow at him.

'I thought you'd be taking Molly to the Show dance?'

'Of course I am,' Ryan said, 'but that doesn't stop us taking Tina, does it?'

'Us?' Paul murmured blandly.

'Oh, come on! It'll not do you any harm to take the lassie

out. You heard Max say how hard she works. And Kirsten's away staying with a university friend.'

'We'll see,' Paul said grimly, 'but I wish you'd remember you're not running an escort agency and I'm never likely to be one of your clients even if you were.'

Ryan grinned unrepentantly.

The following day Tina was glad to have some hard physical work to do to take her mind off her friend and her unborn baby. The doctors were sure it would be a reasonable size on account of Megan having had to take bed rest but it was fully four weeks premature and they had warned Megan and Max that this must be the last pregnancy if they valued Megan's health.

Paul and Ryan and Richard Green kept up such lively banter that it was impossible to remain in low spirits for long. They vied with each other to carry the buckets of hot water for her and it made her feel quite cherished. If only they knew what she'd had to do back home, she thought.

Back home . . . Home? She had no home now. Her only living relative was an aunt of her mother's back in Ireland. Great Aunt Augustine had disapproved strongly when her father left Ireland with his fourteen-year-old daughter. They had scarcely heard from her since. Tina had written to inform her of her father's death but her great aunt had not offered to come over for the funeral, nor had she invited Tina to Ireland to visit. She had sent a stiff little note on a stiff white card. It had brought no comfort at all.

'Cheer up, Tina,' Ryan teased, seeing her melancholy look. 'Paul's taking you to the dance tomorrow night, after the show. It's not good for a girl to have all work and no play.' Tina looked startled and glanced at Paul uncomfortably. Trust Ryan to put his big foot in it, Paul thought wryly. He smiled reassuringly at Tina, the slow smile which gradually moved to his eyes and made them sparkle like green pools in sunlight. Tina wondered if he had any idea what a transformation that smile made to his usual serious expression, or if he'd any idea how attractive it was.

'Don't take any notice of Ryan, Tina. You're more than welcome to come to the dance if you can escape from young

Iain, and if you want to go, but we'll have to wait and see how Megan is before we make any plans.'

'Yes.' Tina was grateful for his understanding. 'I hope and pray everything will be all right, with both Megan and the baby.'

Bridie came out to inspect the cattle they were preparing, regretting that she was no longer actively involved in the farm and the showing herself. She had always enjoyed the excitement of getting cattle ready for a show.

'You've made a good job of that heifer, Tina,' she remarked. 'Did you help your father show?'

'We didn't have a pedigree herd, but he always made the best of them when he was selling at the market. I never learned to clip though. Richard and Ryan have done most of that today,'

'But we've had the slave's job of holding them still,' Paul said, 'haven't we, Tina?' She smiled and nodded, feeling her spirits lighten. Paul and Ryan always seemed to create an atmosphere of warm camaraderie. Richard Green took his cattle very seriously, she knew, but even he seemed more relaxed and cheerful in their company. Bridie had brought Iain in his push-chair and he was tired of being ignored.

'Want up, Tina. Want out . . .' He struggled with the straps of his push-chair.

'Tina is busy washing the cows,' Bridie told him. 'When you're a big boy you'll help Daddy wash the cows too.'

'Want to help now,' he protested. Then curiously, 'Do the cows cry if they get soap in their eyes, Tina?'

'I don't put soap in their eyes,' she laughed, 'and I never put it in yours either when you get bathed.'

'I no like hair washed,' Iain told her seriously.

'I know you don't, but the cows don't mind. See how nice and clean and shiny their coats are now.'

'Go see Grandad now, Granny,' he demanded suddenly, looking up at Bridie. Bridie laughed. 'He's a bit young to be giving commands, but he's a typical boy, I suppose,' she said resignedly and pushed him away in the general direction of the house with a detour to see the calves and the few hens which still scratched around at Glens of Lochandee.

She was trying to keep him outside to give Nick a bit of peace. He loved his little grandson but he soon got tired these days and Bridie blamed the pain killers the doctor had prescribed for his arthritis.

When Bridie got back to the house she could hear the telephone ringing. Max had said the operation should be over by three o'clock and it was not yet midday. Even so some sixth sense made her hurry indoors in case Nick had not heard it.

'Mum . . . ? It's me – Max.' Bridie clutched the receiver, her heart pounding. She could hear the waver in Max's voice. Every instinct told her there were tears amidst the huskiness. If only she'd been at his side to give him support . . .

Ten

'Oh, Max . . . Wh–what about M–Megan? Is she going to be all right?' Bridie asked fearfully.

'She's still unconscious. They say she's come through very well considering . . .'

'Thank God for that,' Bridie breathed.

'Oh, Mum, she doesn't know yet.' The waver was back in Max's voice. 'It's a wee girl . . .'

'A wee girl! Is – is it a–alive? Is she alive?' she amended quickly, hardly daring to hope.

'Yes! She's in an incubator. But they let me see her for a few seconds.' Bridie could hear the emotion and the wonder in Max's tone. She still couldn't believe.

'Is . . . Will she be . . .?' Please God, let her be all right . . .

'They say she will need to stay in hospital for a few weeks. It's early days yet and they're very cautious. But, Mum, she looks so perfect . . .'

Bridie smiled. And there speaks one very proud daddy, she thought. A huge wave of relief swept over her. She uttered a prayer of thankfulness. She could feel her own eyes moist as she went to tell Nick he had another wee grand-daughter. He often complained they didn't see enough of the twins and their children but neither of them lived near enough to pop in every day, as Max could.

'Well, so long as things go on all right we can look forward to going to Australia now then?' Nick said.

'Yes we can. You do understand, Nick, I couldn't have gone all that distance until I knew Megan would be all right?' she said anxiously.

'Of course I do, cariad,' Nick said softly and reached for

86

her hand. 'As a matter of fact I wouldn't have been very happy being away from home either. Megan's a good girl. I'm glad she's come through this all right.' He hesitated, frowning.

'What is it?'

'Just . . . I hope they'll have the good sense not to have any more children,' he said with feeling.

'Oh I think they understand that now. The doctors have made it very plain. I think the surgeon is going to make sure Megan can't have any more.'

Tina did not go to the Show dance. She was staying at Glens of Lochandee because she was Megan's friend but she never forgot she was also there to work. Max looked deadly tired after his sojourn at the hospital and she guessed he would not want a disturbed night with Iain while she was out enjoying herself. Besides she was certain Paul would not have asked her to the dance if Ryan had not pushed him into it. She didn't want a reluctant escort, even though Paul was far too polite to make that obvious.

Instead she paid a brief visit to the hospital to let Iain see his mummy, or rather to let Megan see her toddler son. She was tired and tearful after the previous day's trauma. So far she had not seen her baby daughter. She hugged Iain tightly, reluctant to let him see her tears.

'I'm m–missing you so much . . .' she said huskily, kissing his chubby cheeks until he squirmed and wriggled off the bed.

'I'll leave you to rest, Megan,' Tina said gently. 'Max said you wanted to see Iain though, and I've brought your clean washing in case you need anything. I just hope we haven't exhausted you . . .'

'Oh no, you haven't, Tina.' Again Megan's chin wobbled and her eyes filled. She dashed a tear away impatiently. I don't know why I'm being so soft!' she said, impatient with herself. 'I was longing to see you both.'

'We'll come again tomorrow afternoon,' Tina promised.

'Thank you,' Megan said huskily. Then she held out a hand to Tina. She took it between her own, thinking how soft it had become during the weeks in hospital and how rough her own were in comparison. 'I just don't know how we would have managed without you, Tina. I shall never be able to thank you enough. You won't go rushing away the moment I get home, will you?' Megan sounded unusually anxious, Tina thought.

'Of course not. You'll probably have to kick me out!' She laughed softly. 'It's such a beautiful part of the country. So clean, so green and fresh, and yet the hills are never far away. And I love the view of the Solway Firth sparkling in the sunshine. I can see it sometimes from my bedroom window at Glens of Lochandee.'

'Yes, you can see it when the tide is in,' Megan nodded. 'I remember feeling much the same the first time Max brought me to stay up here after my father died.'

'I think I've fallen in love with it. Perhaps I'll look for a job not too far away and then I can visit you all when I get some free time.' She smiled and pulled Iain on to her knee, giving him a hug. 'I'm going to miss this young man more than I thought possible.' Iain didn't understand but he beamed at her anyway.

'Oh, Tina, it would be wonderful if you could.' Megan looked excited at the prospect. 'I'm sure there must be lots of carers and nurses needed up here, just the same as everywhere else. No one seems to look after their families at home these days. It's such a shame.'

'We'll see what the future holds, as Daddy used to say,' Tina said, 'but we must go now or the nurse will be chasing us.'

Megan had another operation, a minor one this time, before she was allowed home but her baby had to stay a while longer so Megan was torn between her longing to be back at Glens of Lochandee with Max and her reluctance to leave her baby, Mhairi.

In view of the doctors' warnings they had decided before her birth that she should be christened immediately and the Reverend Duncan, from their own Lochandee Kirk, had willingly carried out the simple ceremony at the hospital. They had chosen the names of her grandmother and her great grandmother, Mhairi Rachel, Mhairi being Bridie's middle name. Both women were delighted.

Bridie was reluctant to leave the newest member of her family to travel across the world but she knew how much Nick was looking forward to the holiday in Australia and she would do anything which might ease his pain.

So towards the end of September Rachel bid her daughter and son and Fiona and Nick goodbye. Just before they left she had been tempted to confide in Bridie about the letter. Although weeks had passed with no further communication from Gerda it was never far from her thoughts and it troubled her conscience. Instead she tried to stifle her feelings of guilt and deceit.

Ten days after Bridie's departure Joanne sorted the morning mail and smilingly handed Rachel an airmail letter. She was astonished at Rachel's reaction. The colour drained from her face and her hand trembled so violently the flimsy paper slipped through her fingers.

Hastily Joanne pulled out a chair from the kitchen table and helped her employer on to it.

'Are you all right?' she asked anxiously. 'I'm sure Bridie's letter will be telling you how much they are enjoying themselves . . .'

'B–but Bridie said she would phone . . .' Rachel whispered faintly.

'And so she did. That was just to let you know they had arrived safely. This will be describing the things they've seen and done, though she'll probably phone again too. It was a great idea of Conan's to get one of those mobile phones so that we can keep in touch if . . . well if we needed to. Now I'll make a cup of tea while you read Bridie's letter then you can tell me how their holiday's going.'

'Thank you, Joanne,' Rachel said gratefully. 'I don't know what we should do without you.' Her voice was still a little wavery and she could feel her heart racing.

Joanne bit her lip. She had grown very fond of Rachel Maxwell. So far she had been unable to bring herself to tell either Paul or his grandmother that she would have to give up her work at Wester Rullion.

'But it's not hard work,' she had protested when the doctor had informed her that her second check up and the blood test results were causing concern.

'It may not be physically heavy but it is constant,' Dr Little insisted. 'Perhaps if you cut down to mornings only and make sure you take a good rest after a light lunch. Every day,' he had added emphatically.

Joanne frowned now as she made a pot of tea for herself and Mrs Maxwell. She knew she was getting slower at her work, but she was getting older after all. She gnawed furiously on her lower lip. Paul couldn't possibly afford any more help for the house. There was no profit in that. In her heart she knew he and Ryan would be better off financially if they were left to manage on their own, even if the house did get rather rough and their meals somewhat sketchy. But she knew Mrs Maxwell was totally opposed to living with Bridie and leaving Paul on his own at Wester Rullion. In fact Joanne suspected both Paul and his grandmother would be extremely upset if she were to mention such a solution.

'You look worried, Joanne. I'm sorry if I gave you a shock,' Rachel said, glancing up from her letter as Joanne set the tea pot on the table. 'It's just as you said, a lovely letter from Bridie telling us all about the sights. They've even been to the Sydney opera house.' She pushed the airmail towards Joanne. 'You read it. It's very interesting.'

A few years ago, even twelve months ago, Rachel would have sensed there was something serious troubling Joanne, but her mind was too preoccupied with the rights and wrongs of life, and in particular her own moral duties. Her reactions were slower. She was not the alert and intuitive woman she had been. She realized her physical limitations and lamented the fact but she didn't realize it was her subconscious worrying about Gerda's letter which was sapping her energy.

'I wouldn't want to live until I was a hundred and one,' she had remarked with emphasis after reading of the death of Irving Berlin. 'But he did write some lovely songs.'

I wonder whether any of us realizes when we've come to the end of the road, Joanne pondered, and even if we do, there's not much we can do about it. She pushed Dr Little's report to the back of her mind. She would think about it again when Bridie returned from Australia at the end of October.

On a Sunday evening, a few days after the incident with the airmail letter, Lucy dropped into Joanne's for a chat, as they had both been in the habit of doing over the years. On the spur of the moment she mentioned Rachel's extraordinary reaction to Bridie's airmail letter.

'It was almost as though your grandmother was anticipating bad news,' she said. 'And it's so unlike her to be pessimistic, or jump to conclusions. But she hadn't even opened the letter. Just the sight of it really upset her . . .' She tailed off as Lucy stared at her in silence, her thoughts going round and round.

'Lucy . . .? Is something wrong?' Joanne asked tentatively.

'N–no. Well, not exactly. But I do wonder . . .'

'What? I mean what do you wonder? You think I'm imagining things? I'm not!' Joanne was indignant. 'I assure you it was . . .'

'No, no I don't think that, Joanne. You know my grandmother as well as any of us after all these years. It's just,' Lucy frowned thoughtfully. 'I didn't really want to discuss this until Bridie returned, so please promise you'll not breathe a word to – to Paul, or to anyone else.'

'Of course I promise, but I don't see . . .'

'I had an airmail letter myself. It came a couple of weeks ago. Now I'm wondering whether Granny Maxwell has had a similar letter. It – it was from Gerda.'

'Gerda!'

The name dropped into the silence like a stone in a very deep well.

'Gerda . . .' Joanne repeated in a whisper. 'Paul's mother . . . I – I can't believe it. After all these years . . . And you think when your grandmother saw the blue airmail she believed it was from Gerda too?'

'If she's already had one, it's possible,' Lucy said. 'And you know how much store Granny sets by morals – telling the truth, not being deceitful, and that sort of thing. Supposing she's heard from Gerda and doesn't want to tell Paul . . . I – I

f–feel rotten about it myself but that's what Gerda wants –
to get in touch with Paul.'

'Get in touch with Paul . . .' Joanne knew she was repeating
Lucy's words stupidly. But she was shattered. None of them
had ever expected to hear from Paul's mother, ever again.'

'She – she says she's desperate, but she doesn't say why.'

'She doesn't need to say why!' Joanne said, bitterly
scathing. 'The only thing she was ever desperate for was
money – and men and clothes of course, but they came with
the money.'

'I – I know that. So I haven't replied – yet.'

'I should think not!' Joanne said.

'That's how I felt when I got the letter. It was a shock.
So you can imagine how Granny Maxwell would feel if she's
had one. When she saw Bridie's blue airmail she would
assume it was from Gerda.'

'I see . . .' Joanne breathed. 'We all felt she was worrying
about something.'

'Exactly. Bridie concluded it must be Paul and Ryan with
their massive overdraft. That's certainly reason enough to be
worried, especially with the bank rate going up again. I can't
help worrying about them myself. The base rate's 15 per
cent now so they must be paying nearly 18 per cent interest.'

'That's true,' Joanne conceded. 'They work so hard too
but it's like running the wrong way on a roller coaster.'

'I know. And I'm sure Granny does worry about them.
And yet . . .' Lucy frowned. 'She's been through those sort
of worries herself so I don't think she'd make herself ill
over them. She has a lot of faith in Paul's judgement and
she knows if the absolute worst happened they could still
sell Wester Rullion land and have enough to cover their
debts.'

'Oh yes, but that would be terrible!' Joanne said in horror.

'Better than some of the poor souls who can't pay the
mortgage on their own homes, and can't sell them either,'
Lucy said. 'That must be an awful worry to couples with
young families.'

'Mmm, negative equity they call it I believe. Not an envi-
able situation to be in, I agree,' Joanne nodded. 'But you

think Mrs Maxwell is worrying more about Gerda than the boys?'

'Could be a combination, I suppose. She would jump to the same conclusion as we have – that Gerda wants money, and of course Paul has more than enough debts of his own.'

'That would certainly worry her – Paul having his mother to support on top of everything else,' Joanne said glumly.

'Granny has probably been brooding about it, as I have myself for the past fortnight. Do any of us have the right to prevent her getting in touch with her own son?'

'She gave up any rights she had as a mother when she ran away and left Paul!' Joanne said darkly, but with absolute conviction.

'I'm inclined to agree,' Lucy admitted, 'but on the other hand do we have the right to deny Paul the chance of meeting his mother? Maybe he would like to know her? She is his own flesh and blood after all. Part of me feels it should be his decision? His choice. I just wish Gerda hadn't written to me and put me in this predicament . . .' Lucy stared unhappily into space.

'Well I don't have your qualms about denying Gerda anything,' Joanne said decisively. 'I learned to be tough after my own ghastly experience. He was a cheat and a liar, but Gerda was worse. You couldn't possibly think of burdening Paul with a mother like that, Lucy? Not a second time! He's already paying a high price for her greed and dishonesty.'

'That's what I've been telling myself,' Lucy said, 'but it doesn't stop me feeling guilty. I can imagine it would really upset Granny. After all, who are we to play God?'

'I can see what you mean about Mrs Maxwell,' Joanne said slowly, biting her lip. 'It's not the sort of moral dilemma she would easily resolve. But surely she would have told Bridie?'

'I suspect Bridie would share your convictions, Joanne. Oh, if only she hadn't written! If she'd given any details about her life even . . . or why she's so desperate to see Paul. I mean now! Why now? Obviously she doesn't know he's started up the farm again or she would write to him directly.'

'Well, I'm still convinced it'll be money she's wanting,'

Joanne said sternly, 'and if Paul was my grandson I'd do everything possible to keep her away from him.'

'Let's change the subject for now,' Lucy said wearily. 'But I'd like to know whether Granny has heard from Gerda . . .'

'I'll make some tea,' Joanne said. She laughed. 'We'll talk about something nice.'

'Like what?'

'Well Bridie and Nick are really enjoying their trip to Australia. They'd been to the opera. Do you remember how lovely it was to hear them sing together at the village concerts?'

Lucy and Joanne enjoyed a good half hour of reminiscing about the way life in Lochandee used to be. Somehow Joanne found herself confiding in Lucy about the report she'd had from the doctor, and his advice.

'Oh, Joanne! You must do as he says,' Lucy said immediately. She was stunned. Joanne always seemed so healthy and energetic.

'Mmm . . .' Joanne frowned. 'I hadn't meant to tell anyone yet. You're a good listener, Lucy. Somehow it just popped out.'

'But something will have to be done . . .'

'I thought I'd wait until Bridie comes back. Surely a few more weeks will not make any difference.'

Eleven

At Glens of Lochandee Megan felt her strength returning at last. Baby Mhairi was beginning to get into a routine. Tina had volunteered to deal with the 4 am feed and Megan was immensely grateful.

'It won't be for long,' Tina smiled. 'She's getting stronger every day now she's home and thriving.'

'I know you're right,' Megan admitted, 'but I expect I shall worry about her until she's toddling around like Iain.'

'And then until wee Mhairi is having babies of her own,' Tina grinned. 'Seriously though, Megan, you'll not be needing me much longer. I think it's time I started looking around to see what sort of jobs are going locally, and what sort of pay and whether or not I shall need to look for accommodation. All that sort of thing.'

'Oh, Tina, don't start job hunting yet,' Megan wailed. 'We shall miss you terribly if you leave us. Max was just saying how fortunate we are to have you.'

'That's nice of him but I can't keep taking wages unless I earn them,' Tina said firmly. 'We're almost at the end of October. Anyway I'm not going tomorrow. I only said I must start looking. I've no real qualifications except the first aid courses, and the psychology I did at university if that counts for anything. I really fancy having a go with an agency providing care to people in their own homes. You know . . . cancer patients and stroke victims. Something rewarding where I'm really needed. If I like it I may decide to study for some qualifications.'

'You're very patient, Tina, and I imagine for work like that you'd need to be practical and have some common sense. I'd say that was far more important than paper qualifications. I think you'd be good at it.'

'I suppose everybody likes to be needed,' Tina sighed, 'and I've no one else likely to need me now that Daddy's gone.'

'Don't you believe it! You're a giver, Tina, but there's plenty of people in this world who are takers.'

The week before Bridie and Nick were due to return from Australia Tina received a letter from Ireland. She was puzzled by the name of the solicitors stamped across the top. She turned it over twice before she opened it.

'Goodness!' She frowned as she read on, then gasped audibly.

Max was sitting at the kitchen table drinking his morning coffee.

'Not bad news surely, Tina?'

'We-ell, it depends how you look at it,' she said slowly. 'My great aunt has died.'

'Oh, I'm sorry. I . . .'

'The solicitor has waited until her funeral is over to let me know. What do you make of that?'

'I don't know. Seems strange . . .'

'We weren't close but she was the only relation I had. I'd have gone to her funeral.'

'Of course you would,' Max said gently, 'but maybe her solicitor didn't know how to get in touch with you?'

'Great Aunt Augustine had this address. I wrote to tell her when I left Hereford.' Tina lowered her eyes to the letter again. 'A-ah . . . he says it was her wish . . .' Her voice cracked, 'her wish to be laid to rest as quietly as possible and to c–cause no one any inconvenience or expense.'

'Maybe she thought it was a long way for you to travel when she was no longer there to greet you,' Max consoled.

'Maybe she did.' Tina frowned. 'But Mr McNaught, her solicitor, still wants me to go over there. It seems a bit point-less when she's no longer there . . .' Her eyes skimmed over the page. 'He says it was her wish that I should be there to dispose of her personal effects. Gracious me!' she said indignantly. 'He has enclosed a cheque! He says it is to enable me to make the journey! He must think I'm some kind of feckless pauper. Certainly Daddy and I never had much money to spare when we were at the farm, but we would always have made sure we could visit her if we had thought she wanted us.' Tina gave a hollow laugh. 'I'm not exactly wealthy but I have more cash in the bank now than Daddy ever had. He used to say the only time he would ever have money in the bank would be when he sold up the farm and retired.' Her voice cracked. 'He didn't live long enough to reach retirement.'

'No, but he is at peace,' Max comforted. 'No more worries. How soon does the lawyer want you to go?' Tina scanned the last of the typed pages, reading odd sentences aloud to Max.

'He suggests I should go to Ireland as soon as possible to sort out her personal belongings and empty the cottage.' She snorted. 'I expect he means it needs a jolly good clean before the landlord can let it again. She was a very old lady after all, and a bit eccentric as far as I can remember. I don't suppose she improved with age. He suggests next Thursday. He says he will meet me off the boat and drive me down.'

'Well that's considerate of him at least,' Max soothed.

'I suppose so . . .' Tina sighed. 'Perhaps I should have gone over to visit her as soon as I left the farm. But she always gave the impression she didn't want to be bothered with visitors. And she made it clear she regarded us as visitors the moment we "ran away to England". That's always the way she put it. Daddy always felt she'd never forgiven him for leaving Ireland.'

'Does Mr McNaught say whether she had been ill for long?'

'He says she died in her sleep. She had been at a concert in the village the previous evening. The local people were shocked when they heard the news of her death.'

'It's a good way to go,' Max said quietly.

'Yes. Yes, you're right, Max. I'm glad she didn't suffer or lose her independence. It meant so much to her. If I sound vexed it's at myself. I ought to have gone over to see her, whatever she said in her letters.'

Joanne did not go to work at Wester Rullion on Saturdays so, as usual, Rachel retrieved the letters from the postman herself. So far she had received three airmails from Bridie and she thoroughly enjoyed reading the descriptions. Bridie had always been good at English when she was at school and she wrote colourful descriptions of the sights and experiences they were enjoying in Australia. Rachel almost felt she was there with them. Today there was another one and she carefully slit it open with a sense of pleasurable anticipation. She pushed the kettle on to the hot plate ready for a cup of mid-morning tea and settled herself in her usual chair at the end of the kitchen table.

The sentences were short and stark. The demand for contact with Paul more urgent.

'Gerda!' Rachel gasped in shock – a shock every bit as bad as the first one had been all those weeks ago. Her heart bumped erratically. 'Gerda.' So she had not given up. What was she to do? Suddenly Rachel's fingers clenched convulsively on the thin paper. It offered no support. She slid to the floor.

Ryan had been attending to a heifer with a particularly difficult calving. The calf was dead but he had saved the heifer. Stripped to the waist and covered with blood and mucus he hurried to the house intending to wash off the worst of it in the back scullery before going to the bathroom. Not for the first time he wished they could afford to install one of the electric showers like they had had at college. He glanced in the kitchen window as he passed.

'Gran! Granny!' For a moment he gaped open-mouthed in shock. His beloved great-grandmother was lying on the kitchen floor.

Twelve

'Granny!' Ryan gasped. His stomach churned as he real-ized Rachel was unconscious. He glanced down helplessly at his bloodstained torso and filthy hands. He felt panic rising. Swiftly he rinsed his hands and, without both-ering to dry them, he dialled his mother's number. Lucy heard the urgency and fear in his voice. It was so unlike Ryan.

'It's Granny!' His voice was more of a croak. He gulped. 'She – she's lying on the floor. Come over! Phone the doctor! Oh, Mum. I – I th–think she may be dead.'

'Ryan!'

'Just phone, then come, Mum! Please. We need you. I'm in a mess from a calving. I c–can't touch anything until I clean up. Just come.' He put the phone down and went to the door. He roared Paul's name at the top of his voice. It was Peter who came hurrying over the yard. Ryan was already giving himself a hasty wash at the scullery sink.

'What's wrong, Ryan?' Peter panted.

'It's Granny. In the kitchen. I'm just coming.' He pulled on an old T-shirt from the wash basket to cover himself, knowing he was still streaked with blood and slime in places but too anxious to get back to the kitchen and his grand-mother to care.

Peter was on his knees, holding Rachel's wrist.

'Is – is she . . .?'

'No, laddie, she's not dead. I think she's had a stroke. Have you phoned the doctor? We'd better not move her. Get me a small cushion or something to put under her head.' Peter felt sick at heart. Rachel Maxwell and her husband had befriended him and become his protectors and guide when

99

he was younger than Paul and Ryan were now – a friend-less stranger in a foreign land.

'Please, God, don't let her die,' he whispered, praying for the first time in his life as far as he could remember.

Dr Little and Lucy arrived almost together. The doctor was confirming Peter's fears when Rachel opened her eyes. She tried to speak but the sound was an unintelligible jumble and Lucy felt sick to see her beloved grandmother so stricken.

Dr Little said he would make arrangements for an ambulance to take her to the hospital in Dumfries but Rachel became agitated. She tried even harder to make herself understood. The sound was heart-rending and Lucy saw that her mouth was twisted slightly.

'I'm sure she's trying to tell us she doesn't want to go to hospital,' she said. 'She's always said she never wanted to leave Wester Rullion . . .'

'You are probably right, but there is the possibility of another, more serious stroke occurring.'

'Perhaps that is a risk she would rather take . . .' Lucy said uncertainly. Rachel groped for her hand, almost as though she understood, Lucy thought. She wished with all her heart that her father and Bridie had been here. They were due back from Australia in three days.

'She needs twenty-four-hour care, at least for the next few days . . .' Dr Little broke off as Paul came rushing in.

'Peter says Granny is . . . Oh no! No . . .' Lucy saw her grandmother twitch convulsively and in the same moment she glimpsed the flimsy blue paper of an airmail clutched in her other hand. She understood at once what had happened. She fell to her knees beside her grandmother, briefly shielding her from Paul's view. Gently but swiftly she removed the letter and stuffed it in her sleeve as Paul came forward and dropped to his knees beside her. Was it her imagination or had her grandmother relaxed when she knew the airmail had been removed from her grasp?

She tried again to make herself understood.

'If you'll show me the telephone I will phone the hospital,' Dr Little said.

'No!' Paul twisted round and looked up at the doctor. 'She

100

has always said she didn't want to leave here, however ill she might be. Joanne will take care of her. She can move in here . . .' Paul broke off as he felt the doctor's hand on his shoulder and the insistent pressure of his fingers. Dr Little inclined his head, indicating Paul should follow him out of the kitchen and out of Rachel's hearing.

'Hospital really is the best place for Mrs Maxwell just now,' Dr Little began. Paul began to protest but the doctor silenced him abruptly. 'There is always the possibility of another stroke. All strokes are serious but as far as I can tell, without the back-up facilities, I think your grandmother may make a reasonable recovery, provided she is given proper attention early on in her treatment.'

'But Joanne will . . .'

'I believe you mean Miss Williams? Joanne Williams?' Dr Little wrinkled his brow in concentration.

'Yes of course,' Paul nodded. 'She has helped my grandmother for as long as I can remember.'

'Yes, so I believe. Obviously Miss Williams has not yet had the opportunity to discuss her own health with your grandmother, but you can take it from me, young man, she is not in a fit state to undertake the sort of nursing your grandmother will require, especially in the first few weeks.'

'Is Joanne ill? She said . . .'

'I'm afraid I cannot discuss a patient's health, Mr Maxwell. Miss Williams may discuss it with you herself in due course, but I assure you she should not be doing any lifting, as in home nursing of a stroke patient.'

'I see . . .' Paul's face went even paler than before.

'Mother would stay . . .' Ryan began.

'I think not at this stage,' Dr Little said firmly. 'Now I have given Mrs Maxwell medication,' he added briskly, 'but I am relying on you and your cousin,' he glanced across at Ryan's troubled face, 'to give her support and above all to keep calm yourselves. When I have telephoned the hospital I shall do my best to make her understand that we are taking the best course of action for her future recovery. Believe me, it is vital that your grandmother gets the very best care and observation during the next twenty-four to forty-eight hours. Understand?'

Paul and Ryan nodded glumly, accepting the doctor's advice with the greatest reluctance.

Lucy had promised to meet Bridie and Nick, Conan and Fiona at the airport. They had spoken briefly on the telephone on the night of Rachel's stroke but Lucy was anxious about their reactions to the way she had dealt with the crisis in their absence. As she drove the seventy miles to Glasgow her mind went round in circles. Would they blame her for allowing Granny to be taken to hospital? Would Bridie feel she should have vetoed the doctor's instructions? What would they say when she told them she and Joanne believed Gerda's letters might have caused the stroke?

She had always felt responsible for introducing Gerda Fritz-Allan to the family when they were at college but she had never dreamt that Ewan, her friend and confidant from childhood, would become so besotted with her charm and glamour that he would marry her. Surely no one could have foreseen the tragedy which would follow?

All these thoughts churned through Lucy's mind as she drove. Now she felt doubly guilty. She ought to have guessed Gerda would contact someone else besides herself, especially when she received no response. She wished she had replied immediately now. The letter, like her grandmother's, had been clearly marked 'Please forward. If undelivered return to sender.' The letters had not been returned to sender, but neither had they elicited a reply. What conclusion had Gerda drawn from their silence, Lucy wondered. She was certainly persistent. I should have guessed she would be, she thought.

Gerda would have no way of knowing whether or not Rachel Maxwell, her mother-in-law, was still alive. Certainly she would not have expected her, or Paul, to be living at Wester Rullion after the way she had stolen most of the cattle and drained the money from the bank account. She had not cared that she was destroying a good farming business as well as her own son's inheritance.

As her mind went over and over the letters Lucy felt her fury and frustration rising against Gerda as it had on the day her grandmother was taken ill. She regretted sitting down and writing in anger now, but she could not recall the letter. Would her father and Bridie blame her for that too? She had not slept well since Rachel had been taken to hospital and she knew she was working herself into a state. The traffic was heavier as she approached the city.

'Concentrate on your driving,' she told herself sternly, and gritted her teeth.

It was a very agitated Lucy who waited to welcome the travellers. Fiona saw at once that Lucy was both tired and tense and the dark shadows around her lovely green eyes told their own story. Bridie hugged her warmly but her first words were for her mother's health.

'Not wonderful,' Lucy said carefully, 'but not as bad as I feared. I visited her yesterday afternoon and she knew who I was. She said my name.' Some of yesterday's relief showed on Lucy's face.'

'Thank God she has not had another,' Conan said.

'Yes, that's what they seemed to fear,' Lucy said. 'Although she sounded very slurred and sleepy the nurse said it could be due to medication. It is her left leg which seems to be worst affected and her arm and hand a little, but they think her speech will come all right. Th–that's as m–much as I can tell you at the m–moment.' She turned and Fiona caught her in her arms and held her tightly as Lucy burst into tears.

'Hush, hush, Lucy,' Fiona said gently, holding her close, comforting her as a mother would her child. Fiona had never felt, or acted, like a stepmother to Lucy. Lucy's own mother had died when she was barely into her teens and she had entrusted her only child into Fiona's care. Lucy had been like a favourite younger sister and their affection and friendship had deepened over the years. Lucy had been the catalyst which had brought Conan and Fiona together. Now Fiona looked at her husband over the top of Lucy's head but her words were for Lucy. 'You've had too much strain and responsibility all on your own,' she said softly. 'But we're home now. You'll not be alone any longer.'

'B–but you d–don't know everyth–thing,' Lucy stammered, fishing frantically for her handkerchief, feeling stupid and annoyed with herself for bursting into tears like a child. Bridie wanted to ask what else they should know. She was desperately anxious about her mother. Every instinct had told her there was something troubling her. Now she wished she had never gone to Australia.

'Fiona's right, lassie,' Nick said, quickly, forestalling her questions. 'Let's all go and get ourselves a hot drink somewhere.' He looked at Conan.

'Yes, I'm dying for a cup of coffee,' Conan said quickly, though they all knew he wanted nothing more than to get home.

'I slept well on the plane,' Nick said. 'I'll drive home, Lucy.'

'Will you?' Lucy said with relief. 'I – I've had such a job concentrating this morning. I took a wrong exit from the motorway and had to make a detour.'

Usually Lucy liked plenty of milk in her coffee but she asked for it black. Fiona's eyes widened in surprise.

'Is there something else bothering you, Lucy? Something else you want to tell us?' she asked gently. Lucy looked at her and chewed hard on her lower lip. Nick set a scone and butter in front of her. She hadn't eaten any breakfast but she felt the food would choke her.

'Best get it off your chest, lassie, whatever it is,' Conan said.

'I – I blame myself for Granny being s–so upset. She – she . . .'

'You can't blame yourself, Lucy!' Bridie said. 'If anyone is to blame it's me. I knew she was worried . . .'

'I know b–but . . . Joanne and I . . . we think we know the reason now, why she's been so worried. We believe she'd had an airmail letter from Gerda . . .'

'Gerda!' Bridie and Conan exclaimed in unison.

'That bitch?' Nick's eyes narrowed. He rarely criticized anyone but he had never liked or trusted Gerda and he had never understood why his young brother-in-law had been so taken in by her charm when he was such a level-headed young fellow in every other respect. Lucy nodded and bit her lip. She told them about her own letter, how she and Joanne had confided in each other, and Rachel's own reactions to Bridie's first airmail.

104

'Joanne and I now believe Granny had already had an airmail from Gerda, and she would think it was another one when your first one arrived.'

'I see . . .' Bridie said slowly. 'And Mother may have received one the day she had the stroke? I can imagine that would be a shock if she opened it thinking it was from me . . .'

'Yes.' Lucy nodded unhappily. 'If – if only I had replied she – Gerda – wouldn't have written to Granny a s–second time. Don't you see?'

'We don't know that, Lucy,' Bridie said gently. 'After all she can't have waited very long for your reply. You can't blame yourself. I'd have burnt her letter if she'd written to me.'

'I suppose she's needing money,' Conan said dryly.

'That's what Joanne said, but she didn't ask for money,' Lucy said. 'All she asked for was to make contact with Paul.'

'So she thinks she'll get her claws into him now, does she? I wonder how she knew he was at Wester Rullion?'

'She doesn't, otherwise I suppose she would have written to him direct. I don't think she was sure where Granny would be either, or even whether she was still alive. She asked for her letter to be forwarded or returned to sender.' Lucy gulped. 'She – she seems to be clutching at st–straws. Granny had her airmail clutched in her hand.'

'Does Paul know about his mother then?'

'No. I took it away before he saw it. I smoothed it out. I – I read it. It didn't say any more than mine had done. All she wants is to contact her – her s–son! I was s–s–so angry with her. She's caused such an awful thing to happen to Granny . . . I – I sat down and wrote her a h–horrible letter. Now I feel more guilty than ever over everything . . .'

'It's probably what we would all have done,' Fiona said gently.

'Fiona's right,' Bridie said. 'I just wish mother had told me about Gerda's first letter instead of bottling it up. Lucy, my dear, you are so like my mother. You both have far too much conscience and far more Christian spirit than most of us would have in the circumstances.' She patted Lucy's

105

restless fingers. 'Come on, we need a smile to welcome us home.'

Lucy was grateful for Nick's insistence on driving. Squeezed in the back seat between Fiona and Bridie she felt herself begin to relax. Only now did she realize how tense she had been. It was an enormous relief to share her burden and she was eternally grateful that neither her father not Bridie held her responsible for Granny's stroke. She felt drained of energy and emotion. The warmth and the hum of voices was soporific. Before they were halfway home her head was resting on Fiona's shoulder and she was catching up on some badly needed sleep.

Bridie and Conan couldn't wait to visit their mother and they went together to the hospital almost as soon as they had unloaded the luggage. They both knew they would not rest until they had her for themselves. Rachel was sleeping in bed when they arrived and Bridie was dismayed to see how pale and frail she seemed.

There were four beds in the room and it was bright and airy and had a lovely view over Dumfries and the River Nith. Two of the other patients were younger than Rachel and they were making good recoveries from strokes themselves. They were cheerful and full of optimism. They both assured Bridie that her mother was making progress. The other bed was occupied by a tiny woman who could neither speak nor walk and she had very little sight.

'There's always somebody worse, as Mother would say,' Bridie whispered to Conan.

'I suppose so,' he said grimly. 'I think I'll see if I can speak to a doctor.'

'You'll be lucky, hen,' the women in the next bed told him cynically, but Conan strode off anyway and Bridie pulled up a chair and sat beside her mother's bed. She stroked one of her wrinkled hands where it lay motionless on the pristine white sheet. Rachel opened her eyes. For a moment she seemed disorientated and Bridie's heart sank, but then she tried to smile.

'Bridie,' she whispered. She closed her eyes again as though it was an effort to lift her eyelids, but moments later she opened them. 'Safe home,' she whispered.

Lucy's right, Bridie thought. Her words are slurred and her voice seems terribly weak, but at least she's making sense and we can understand her. When Conan returned she greeted him exactly the same but the nurse had warned him she needed rest and soon became tired.

'I feel better now we've seen her,' he said when they were outside. 'But it's going to be difficult knowing how to handle this.'

'Yes, as soon as Mother does begin to feel better, and when she's less sedated, or whatever it is, she'll want to come home,' Bridie said.

'I didn't see a doctor but the nurse said she would be in for at least a month. They hope to start some sort of physio-therapy soon.'

'Well I suppose that makes sense.'

'Yes, the muscles soon waste lying in bed. I suppose it depends how much power she has in her left side.' Conan frowned. 'They don't seem very sure what effect the stroke has had yet. Or if they do they're not saying.'

'Shall we call round by Wester Rullion and tell Paul and Ryan we're home and that we've been to visit?' Bridie suggested.

'All right. I wonder how Joanne is managing the pair of them?' Conan grinned.

But Joanne was not at Wester Rullion and both Bridie and Conan were dismayed when Paul told them Joanne's own health was causing problems.

'She thinks she may have to have a heart by-pass. We've suggested she should just come if and when she feels like it,' Paul said. 'And then only for office work. We're doing our own cooking and . . .'

'You mean I'm doing the cooking!' Ryan chipped in with a grin, pushing the kettle on to the hot plate to make a mug of tea for everyone.

'Mmm, well I get all the washing up to do afterwards, and the clothes to wash.' Paul defended himself. 'It's a good job Granny invested in an automatic washing machine. So?' His smile died and Bridie saw the anxiety in his eyes. 'You said you'd been to see Granny. What do you think?'

'I doubt if she'll get home for Christmas,' Bridie said slowly.
'Oh but . . .'

'The nurse said it would be a month at least and maybe longer at her age,' Conan told them. 'Though they don't know for sure how long. Once she's thinking straight your grandmother will be one determined lady,' he said. 'The thing is she's going to need looking after when she does get out of hospital.'

'Mother will come to us,' Bridie said. 'I'm glad we insisted on a downstairs bedroom with an *en suite* bathroom, even if it is small.'

'Granny willna want that!' Paul protested indignantly. 'She's always said she never wanted to leave Wester Rullion. We shouldn't have let the doctor send her away . . .'

'Now Paul,' Bridie said gently, but her voice was firm. 'When something like this happens we all have to change our minds.'

'Anyway we can't make any decisions for a while,' Conan added, seeing the determined set to his nephew's young face. Paul has probably spent more time in my mother's company than any of us, he reflected. She had been mother, father and friend as well as his grandmother. No wonder they were close. 'We'll come to whatever arrangement suits your grandmother best, laddie, never fear.'

Paul had to be content with that but he felt very troubled. He and Ryan didn't have any spare money to afford a house help, far less a nurse. Granny Maxwell had looked after him all his life, now it was time for him to take care of her and he was certain she wouldn't want to stay anywhere else. Wester Rullion was her home.

Recently Ryan had hinted frequently that he wished they had more free cash, but Granny was not Ryan's responsibility. Apparently he had enough problems of his own. He hated Molly being away at university. He couldn't wait for her to get her degree, but she had to spend months in France as part of the course. She was going straight after Christmas. He was dreading the separation. At least when she was in Edinburgh she could drive down for a weekend once a month, and they talked regularly on the telephone.

Ryan was beginning to resent the fact that all their money was tied up in the farm and stock. There were always bills waiting to be paid for feed or fertilizer, repairs to this and repairs to that, or water or electricity.

The elderly couple who lived in one of the cottages were always grumbling about the new poll tax which the government had brought in to replace the rates in Scotland. Mr Bates was talking of moving south and he had refused to pay the poll tax so far. Ryan didn't believe they could avoid it indefinitely but the situation had awakened ideas. If only he could afford to buy the cottage he and Molly could get married as soon as she finished at university. After all he would be nearly twenty-five by the summer. He was getting old, and he was tired of waiting.

Of course Molly would have to get a job at first but if the Bateses did sell the cottage it could be a bargain. They had done nothing to maintain it during the last fifteen years so it might not attract many buyers, especially when there were so many new houses for sale due to the repossessions by the mortgage lenders. The cottage was structurally sound and as near as he could get for convenience to his work. Surely Molly wouldn't mind making do so long as they were together? He would make it like a palace for her when he had made some money. If only they could breed a really fantastic bull and sell the semen for thousands and thousands of pounds like some lucky breeders seemed to do. It would be better than winning the football pools. These were the dreams which occupied Ryan. So far he had not plucked up the courage to share all of them with Molly.

Thirteen

Megan was disappointed when Tina wrote from Ireland to say she would not be able to join them for Christmas as she had planned. She sent gifts for both the children and Iain was full of excitement already.

'So what is Tina doing for Christmas?' Max asked. 'This will be the first without her father . . .'

'Yes, I know. I suspect she wants to keep busy and she is grateful for the warm welcome she has received over there. I believe Tina is really enjoying working at the nursing home in Ireland. She says Mrs McTeir is an excellent teacher and working with her is just like having a one-to-one tutor in home nursing, and in first aid.'

'Has the solicitor managed to sell her aunt's cottage yet?'

'No. He doesn't seem to get on with things very fast if you ask me. I don't think that's the only thing keeping Tina in Ireland at Christmas time though. She says most of the staff at the nursing home want time off to be with their families for some part of the holiday. I can imagine her feeling she ought to stay there and help but she sounds quite cheerful about the arrangement. Apparently they have all sorts of entertainment for the residents and her aunt always took part in the local carol concerts.'

It was true Tina was getting on splendidly, both with Jacquie McTeir and with the rest of the staff and residents at Mount Angelica Nursing Home. In spite of some of the difficulties of old age there was a happy atmosphere which Jacquie said was on account of it being small and therefore more personal but Tina felt it had a lot to do with her own cheery personality, her watchful eye and careful organization. She had given Tina a room in the home and she slept there while she was working and returned to the McNaughts for the nights she was off duty.

'Tina says the McNaughts are disappointed she will not be spending Christmas with them but they've agreed to join in the Christmas Dinner at Mount Angelica. My word! Mrs McNaught is taking the Christmas puddings for the whole lot of them . . . and she's ordering a huge basket of fruit and making little gifts for all the residents.'

'Very generous of her.'

'The McNaughts can't be bad people at that rate. Maybe they really do have Tina's best interests at heart. After all it was a surprise to her to discover her great-aunt was the owner and not the tenant of the property.'

'Mmm,' Max said over a mouthful of toast, 'and it was very good of Mrs McNaught to advise her about getting the antique dealer in to look at her aunt's old furniture.'

'Dearest Tina,' Megan sighed. 'She writes that she had dreaded the thought of Christmas without her father but this year she has had three genuine requests for her company. She says how much she appreciates our invitation to spend Christmas at Lochandee, especially with Iain being at such an adorable stage . . . I'm so lucky.'

'It's not luck,' Max said gruffly. 'Tina is a caring person with a cheerful nature. People sense that and they're drawn to her.'

It took a heated discussion between Lucy, her father and Bridie before they could decide whether or not they should mention Gerda's letters to Rachel. Conan thought they should forget about them and hope his mother had done the same.

'I don't think Granny has forgotten,' Lucy said with conviction, 'even though she hasn't mentioned them to us. You must remember she doesn't know I've had a letter too.'

'Well I think there's something holding her back from recovery,' Bridie said slowly. 'I don't know what. It's just a feeling I have, an instinct.'

'This isn't one of your animals we're talking about,' Conan said irritably. 'This is our mother, for God's sake.'

'Don't blaspheme. She wouldn't like that,' Bridie snapped.

'Please,' Lucy said unhappily, 'please don't quarrel. Everybody is so tense and walking on eggshells. But I believe Granny is doing the same thing.'

'Have you heard any more from Gerda?' Conan asked abruptly.

'No, but that doesn't mean there won't be a letter sooner or later. Suppose she sends it to Wester Rullion and Paul takes it in to her? I think it would be better to talk things over with her, tell her the burden isn't hers alone.'

'Burden! It isn't a burden . . .'

'Well that's what it feels like to me,' Lucy said with some asperity, 'and I'll be very surprised if Granny doesn't feel the same. And another thing, I think we should tell Paul his mother has been in contact. He's a man now and he's proved himself responsible and level headed since he took over Wester Rullion, and even more so since Granny has been in hospital.'

'I think Lucy is right about Paul being told. It should be his decision whether or not he wants to see his own mother,' Bridie nodded.

'Oh yes?' Conan exclaimed angrily. 'And have her come back and rob him a second time! Don't forget half the money in Wester Rullion belongs to my grandson now, and it came from me! Gerda is not getting her greedy paws on one penny of mine. Not after what she did to Ewan.'

Lucy went pale. She had always hated quarrels and she had never seen her father so angry.

'I think you should discuss all this with Fiona,' Bridie said quietly.

'Fiona? What has this to do with Fiona? It's my mother we're discussing.'

'Of course it is, but Fiona might see things more clearly than any of us because she's not a blood relation.'

'And she does have a lot of affection and respect for Granny,' Lucy said. Conan frowned at them in silence.

'Oh, very well. I'll talk to her tonight.' He strode away, leaving Bridie and Lucy feeling as though a whirlwind had just whipped them up and dropped them down again.

'Come into the kitchen and I'll put the kettle on,' Bridie

sighed. 'Fiona is the only one Conan will listen to when he's set his mind against something.'

'I know.' Lucy tugged at a corner of her handkerchief. 'I agree with you that something is holding Granny back though. The trouble is if we mention the airmails, or even Gerda's name, and it caused her to have another stroke . . .' She shuddered.

'I know,' Bridie nodded. 'Conan would never forgive us. Well let's hope he comes round to our way of thinking, because I'm convinced that if Mother doesn't get things off her chest she'll never make a full recovery. Her heart's not in it as she is right now.'

'I agree,' Lucy said slowly. 'I wonder what Paul's reaction will be if we tell him . . .'

'That's anyone's guess. He's bound to be a bit curious about his mother I think, but he never mentions her or asks questions, not as far as I know.'

'Ryan says he avoids any mention of mothers.'

Bridie brought the pot of tea to the kitchen table.

'Get the cups and saucers, will you, Lucy?' Bridie asked as she delved into her tins and produced gingerbread and fruit scones.

'It's a bit early for afternoons, isn't it?' Lucy remarked. 'I don't think I could eat a thing.'

'Yes you can,' Bridie said firmly. 'You're far too thin, Lucy. Fiona was just remarking how much weight you've lost recently. As a matter of fact I think you'll feel better once this business with Gerda is out in the open, with both Paul and my mother. Yes, come to think of it, I'm sure Fiona will think that too. Let's hope she can make that brother of mine see sense.'

'You may be right. It has been bothering me,' Lucy admitted, 'especially when I can't get to sleep at night. I do wish Kirsten was not going to Germany after Christmas, but that's part of her course. I know Ryan hates the thought of Molly being away in France too.'

Bridie nodded, accepting that Lucy wanted to change the subject, at least for now.

Conan agreed, with some reservations, that Lucy should

try to introduce the subject of Gerda's letters to Rachel. He had taken it upon himself to talk to Paul about them. His nephew's reaction had surprised him and reminded him instantly of his own father. Ross Maxwell had been a man who made up his own mind and frequently kept his thoughts to himself.

'I thought the day would come when some of the family would mention my mother,' Paul said coolly. 'There was a time when I wanted to know, now it's one subject I have no wish to discuss.'

Conan stared at him. He felt like a schoolboy being dismissed by his headmaster. He was suitably deflated. Suddenly he realized he had been on the point of acting the part of a rather pompous uncle, all prepared to deliver warnings and advice.

'B–but . . . She has contacted your grandmother. She wants to get in contact with you.'

'I have no desire to be in contact with her.' Paul's mouth snapped shut. His green eyes held his uncle's steadily.

'I see.' Conan pursed his lips. He frowned.

'We think the letters upset your grandmother. Lucy thinks she may be worrying about them still. She's had letters too. Airmails. She's going to try to get your grandmother to talk, to – to share her anxiety. We – er . . . we hope it will help her . . .'

'And if it makes her worse?' Paul's eyes sparked green fire.

'It's a risk we've got to take.' Conan bit his lower lip. 'Believe me, Paul, the decision was not taken lightly. But I'm outnumbered. All the women in the family believe the burden of guilt is holding your grandmother back from a real recovery.'

'Well if anything to do with my mother causes Granny's death, or even makes her worse, then I'll never, ever forgive her!' Paul turned on his heel and strode away, leaving Conan staring after him.

'You're just like your namesake – Paul Ross Maxwell,' Conan muttered aloud. For the first time he noticed that Paul was no longer a boy. He was every inch a man and he might very well be a force to be reckoned with before long.

* * *

114

The doctor patted Rachel's hand as though she was a child. Her health had improved dramatically since he had last seen her and he put it down to the fact that she was hoping to get home for Christmas.

'I expect you're looking forward to Santa Claus coming,' he said. Rachel looked at him pityingly and lowered her eyelids. He's so young, she thought, what can he possibly know of life? She couldn't tell him it was a talk with Lucy which had relieved her of a nagging secret and eased the burden of guilt which had been weighing her down. It had renewed her old enthusiasm for life.

She was impatient to get home now and she worked hard to follow the instructions of the physiotherapist, determined that she would walk unaided and return to Wester Rullion.

When the nurse told her she was not to get home for Christmas after all her disappointment was almost too much to bear. Her indomitable spirit crumpled and for the first time in years she felt like weeping.

Peter Forster longed to see Rachel but so far he had not had the courage to visit her in hospital. He was not sure whether it might be presumptuous for a mere worker like himself. However, Christmas was almost upon them and he had an urge to see her.

He had never visited the infirmary before. He spurned the lifts and climbed the stairs to the floor where her ward was situated. He was incredibly nervous and unsure. He would have turned around and left but a young nurse asked him whom he was visiting. She escorted him to the room where Rachel was sitting in a chair beside her bed.

The other patients had all been discharged or transferred elsewhere in preparation for Christmas so the other three beds were empty. As soon as Peter saw how lonely and forlorn Rachel looked his steps quickened and he hastened to her side. She looked up and her eyes widened in surprise then filled with tears. She lifted her good hand and brushed them away. A wobbly smile curved her lips and she held out her hand in greeting.

Shyly Peter produced a large bunch of grapes and a magazine. She thanked him warmly.

'But it's you I'm pleased to see, Peter. Draw up a chair and tell me what's going on at Wester Rullion. Nobody tells me anything these days. They all think I should be kept in a glass case.'

'I expect they want to protect you from any worries,' Peter smiled. 'Everybody is missing you, but especially the laddies.' His smile broadened. 'I don't think either of them is used to cooking.'

'No,' Rachel sighed. 'They're not. If only I could get out of this place I could at least tell them how to do things.'

'Aye, aye,' Peter sighed. 'We'll all be pleased to see you home, Mistress Maxwell.'

'Thank you, Peter. Bridie thinks I should go to live with her and Nick,' she said slowly, as much to herself as to Peter for there was nothing he could do about it. 'It's good of them to offer but Wester Rullion is where I belong.'

'Of course it is,' Peter agreed simply. 'How long do you think you'll be here . . .?'

'They want to see me walking on my own. I can't seem to manage that however hard I try.' Rachel bit her lip and lowered her eyes, unwilling to let Peter see how much her incapacity distressed her. Peter understood her feelings and turned his gaze on the empty beds.

'Surely they could let you come home for Christmas Day – with your wheelchair?'

'Do you think they would?' Rachel seized at the idea eagerly. Much as she hated having to be wheeled around like a baby in a pram anything would be better than staying in hospital at Christmas.

'There's no harm in asking,' Peter smiled. 'That's what you always say to me.'

'Y–es, so it is, Peter. You rarely ask for anything though. You've been a good man all these years. But you're right, I will ask. You tell Paul I intend to be back at Wester Rullion for Christmas Day. I expect he and Ryan will have a bit of tidying up to do.'

'B–but I er . . .' Peter frowned, wondering if he had made a big mistake with his suggestion. 'Wouldn't Mrs Jones be expecting you to stay with them in Lochandee?'

'Probably, but I want to go home, Peter.'

'Yes, yes I can understand that. But Miss Williams is going to Glasgow for an operation so she doesn't come to Wester Rullion very much at present. We're all bachelors. Mrs Jones will be afraid there'll be no one to help you.'

'I expect she's right.' Rachel sighed heavily. 'Oh, but I'd dearly like to go to Wester Rullion. I have a little money of my own set aside for emergencies like this. I'll ask Bridie to advertise for someone to help in the house.' She sounded confident and determined and Peter's heart sank. He hoped the family would not blame him for encouraging her.

The following day Peter saw Bridie striding across the farmyard towards him. He felt like running and hiding away but it was too late.

'Peter! Just the man I want to see.' He waited nervously until she reached his side. 'You've given Mother a new lease of life with your suggestion. They've agreed she can come home for Christmas Day so long as we take her back by seven o'clock. She was so depressed when the other patients left but yours is a brilliant idea.'

'A-ah.' Peter breathed a sigh of relief. 'I'm glad I did no harm then.'

'You did a world of good. The only thing is, my mother is just so stubborn. She's insisting we all have Christmas together, here at Wester Rullion. Of course I haven't room for the whole family at my house and I did wonder if it might be too tiring for her anyway, but she insists.' Bridie raised her dark eyebrows comically. 'I don't know whether it's a relief, or an even greater worry, when my mother starts organizing us again. You've to join us for Christmas dinner as usual, Peter.'

'Oh but this year . . .'

'It's a command, from Mother.' Bridie smiled. 'She wants everything as it has always been, in spite of her wheelchair. Lucy and I will bring the food here on Christmas Eve. I'll get the turkey ready and ask Ryan to put it in to cook.'

'I'm sure everything will be fine,' Peter said, smiling broadly in his relief. 'I've been thinking a raised bed for her gardening might give her something to think about and plan.

Er . . . Mrs Maxwell did say she means to come back here to live . . .'

'Yes, so I gather,' Bridie said dryly. 'I really don't know where we shall find suitable help but she's determined. She'll need nursing care to begin with. She is an old lady after all, apart from the effects of the stroke.'

Peter was jubilant at the prospect of Wester Rullion having its mistress back again, however frail she might be physically. He discussed his idea for a raised bed with Paul and was surprised at his enthusiasm.

'I think two raised beds would look even better. One on each side of the backdoor would be ideal,' Paul said. 'Granny has always enjoyed gardening and she can sit in her wheelchair and plant and weed whenever she feels like it. You're a genius to think of it, Peter.'

'They would have to be narrow enough for her to reach to the middle,' Peter said thoughtfully. 'I could make a start with the foundations this afternoon. How about two crescent shaped beds? They would look better than rectangles beside the door, don't you think?'

'I leave that to you, Peter,' Paul grinned. 'But I'll order the materials and if I've time before milking I'll go and get them this afternoon. Everything will be shut down for a fortnight over the holidays. Granny will be pleased. As you say, it'll give her something to look forward to.'

'I don't think your Aunt Bridie is quite so enthusiastic,' Peter cautioned. 'She's worried about getting suitable help. I suppose it would have been easier for her if Mrs Maxwell went to stay at Lochandee, especially when her husband is not too fit either.'

'Mmm.' Paul frowned and bit his lip. 'I'm forgetting just how much help Granny will need . . .'

'Talk to your aunt about it, laddie.'

'This is her home, Peter. This is where she belongs!' Paul said vehemently. 'There has to be a way . . .' He bit his lip. He couldn't confide in Peter about money being so tight.

Granny was his responsibility and no one else's. He wondered whether he could get a personal bank loan in addition to the business loan. It was proving far more difficult

118

to pay off than they'd expected, but they hadn't bargained on paying interest at seventeen per cent. His shoulders sagged. He doubted if any bank manager would consider a loan to pay for a nurse or a house help.

Such mundane subjects as money and bank interest were the last thing on Paul's mind as he helped Bridie get his beloved Granny Maxwell out of the car and wheel her into the house at Wester Rullion on Christmas morning. Her eyes lit up at the sight of Peter standing beside the one completed raised bed, with the foundations of the second already taking shape.

'That's a wonderful idea! Peter, so thoughtful . . .' her voice was husky with emotion, but she reached out and touched his hand in a gesture of gratitude which needed no words to bring a surge of joy to Peter's heart.

Rachel's happiness at being back in her own home, even for a day, was plain for all to see.

'I feel like a queen on my throne instead of an old woman in a wheelchair,' she said, beaming at them all as she looked at her assembled family seated around the long table at Wester Rullion.

Fourteen

Inevitably the flu epidemic which had hit Britain by mid December was now affecting most parts of the country and doctors and nurses did not escape. Many hospital wards had had to be closed, except for emergency admissions.

Bridie was never quite sure whether it was her mother's idea or the doctors', but she was discharged far earlier than they had anticipated. There were vague mentions of some support from the social services and attendance at the physiotherapy clinic. Rachel was so relieved to get out of hospital than she agreed to stay with Bridie and Nick without argument.

'But I shall go home to Wester Rullion as soon as you can find me a suitable helper,' she reminded Bridie sternly.

'If you stay here with Nick and Bridie at Lochandee, Granny, I can come in to help,' Lucy suggested gently.

'I thought you had a job to go to, lassie,' Rachel said.

'I have but we're not so busy just now, and by the Easter holidays I'm expecting Cameron will make himself available. He's spent long enough getting degrees at university. He'll be leaving in the summer but it's time he earned some money for himself.'

'Easter! Summer! I'm expecting to be back at Wester Rullion long before then.'

'Mmm, well we'll see,' Lucy murmured pacifically.

'Of course I shall, lassie. I'm getting along fine with two sticks and soon I'll manage with one – you see if I don't.' Lucy nodded meekly but she had to control her expression as she met Bridie's eyes and saw her shake her head in mock despair. Almost as though she had eyes in the back of her head Rachel half turned towards her daughter. 'Have you put that advertisement in the paper yet?'

'There hasn't been time,' Bridie said. 'Anyway we're discussing what arrangements would be best.'

'What is there to discuss? Who is discussing?' Rachel demanded.

'We are. The family.'

'They're thinking of putting me in the wheelchair instead of you,' Nick intervened with a grin at his mother-in-law. His ruse succeeded in distracting her as he had intended and Bridie flashed him a grateful glance.

It was true Rachel was managing far better than any of them had believed possible a few weeks earlier. She had never lacked determination but the prospect of getting home had given her an added incentive to persevere with the exercises. Even so she would need help for some time, and possibly indefinitely, considering her age. As Conan had pointed out, their mother had little idea of present-day wages, especially with inflation so high. Her own savings would soon dwindle and that would cause her renewed anxiety.

'If she insists on returning to Wester Rullion we can't expect Paul to pay for the care she'll require,' he added. They mulled over the problems but so far no adequate solution had presented itself.

'I think it will be up to you and me to pay for someone to care for her,' Bridie said. 'If you agree I'll discuss it with Max. Most of my capital is still tied up in Glens of Lochandee. I'll ask him to pay some of it out now that he's had several years to find his feet on the farming ladder.'

'There's no need for that!' Nick interrupted their discussion. 'There's the capital from my business lying in the bank. We can use that for our share of your mother's care . . .'

'No, that wouldn't be fair, Nick,' Bridie protested. 'You don't know what you might need yet, especially if you have to wait much longer for your hip replacement. Maybe we should enquire about getting it done privately.'

'That would cost a fortune,' Conan whistled. Bridie scowled at him. 'Of course it would be worth it when you're in pain all the time,' he added quickly.

Later he said to Bridie, 'It might be a good idea for Mother to go to Wester Rullion if we can get someone reliable. You have enough to do looking after Nick. He's got a lot worse this winter.'

'Yes he has,' she said crossly, 'and you almost put your big foot in it. I'm doing my best to persuade him to pay for an operation if he can get it done earlier, preferably before his other hip gets any worse.'

'Oh. I see. Sorry.' Conan shrugged. He was still in the best of health himself. He rarely suffered aches and pains so it was hard for him to understand how Nick was suffering.

Max readily agreed to pay his mother a monthly sum from the farm.

'I'm surprised you've let me keep all of your capital for so many years, Mother,' he grinned. 'We've got a bit set by in case you needed it urgently, haven't we, Megan?'

'Of course we have,' Megan smiled and Bridie gave a sigh of relief.

'I'm glad it's not going to restrict you too much with your farming plans. Conan is going to pay half so a set sum each month would be ideal.'

'Are you sure? Certainly we could manage a monthly payment more easily,' Max assured her.

'Getting someone reliable and honest to live in at Wester Rullion will be a greater problem,' Bridie said glumly. 'It would be so much easier if Mother would agree to stay with Nick and me. She has her own room after all . . .'

'What about Tina?' Megan said. 'She hasn't mentioned when she's returning to Scotland but I know she's had two offers for her aunt's cottage. She thinks that rascal, Mr McNaught, was only using that as an excuse to keep her in Ireland over Christmas because his wife is missing her own daughter and grandchildren. I'm sure he could have posted the documents here for her to sign.'

'You think Tina would take a job like that?' Bridie asked eagerly. 'She would be absolutely ideal, but I thought she was going to get some qualifications and take up nursing as a career?'

'Well I could always ask her what she plans to do. Even if she is going in for nursing she wouldn't be starting just now, would she?'

'I don't know,' Bridie said, 'but do ask her and let me know what she says. Getting someone reliable has been worrying me more than anything, and I know it bothers Lucy. She even talked about giving up her job and moving into Wester Rullion herself. Conan got quite upset about it. I think he wants her to take over the running of the company eventually.'

'I thought Cameron had plans to do that?' Max grinned.

'Cameron probably thinks so too,' Bridie said darkly, 'but he has a lot to learn about the real world. All the degrees in the world won't prepare him for the harsh realities of business and real people and their problems.'

'But he is going to work for Uncle Conan when he leaves university this summer, isn't he?'

'Oh yes, he's supposed to be. I think that's why Conan wants Lucy to have a good grasp of the way things are run before Cameron joins them and tries to take over.' She shrugged. 'Maybe I'm doing the laddie an injustice but he is the most confident of Lucy's three children, and he's a different nature to Ryan and Kirsten.'

Tina received the letter from Megan asking when she was returning to Scotland and whether she would consider taking on the care of Max's grandmother, at least until the new term started next autumn. She knew at once she would accept, though not until she had given Jacquie McTeir time to find someone to take her place.

Mr McNaught had hummed and hawed about which of the offers she should accept for her aunt's cottage but she told him she needed to return to Scotland and she would prefer to sell to the couple who planned to live in the cottage and use the two small paddocks.

'Even if their price is a little less I shall be richer than I ever dreamed of being,' she told the elderly solicitor with a smile.

'But 'tis hardly a fortune, child.'

'It is enough to buy a house and still have some capital left. I shall be more than satisfied and I'd like to think of Great Aunt Augustine's house being lived in. I didn't like the idea of it being knocked down by the other man who is offering.' Reluctantly Mr McNaught agreed to follow her instructions and conclude the sale.

Fifteen

Bridie and Lucy were both relieved when Megan told them Tina was returning to Scotland before the end of January and she would take on the job of caring for Mrs Maxwell if they all agreed.

'I'm sure my mother will be happy with Tina,' Bridie said. 'Although she's so young I feel instinctively that she's reliable and caring, and she's already coped with illness in her own family.'

'She has a cheerful personality too,' Lucy chuckled, 'and Granny could never stand long faces around her, even when Ewan and I were children.'

'I . . . er I didn't mention money,' Megan said tentatively, 'and Tina didn't ask. I have a feeling it will be just as important to her to be with people she likes as quibbling over pay.'

'Even so we must sort it out properly,' Bridie said quickly. 'If you give me her address, Megan, I'll consult Conan and then we'll put everything in writing for her.'

'I think it makes a big difference that she will be living at Wester Rullion and not having to pay for accommodation and food. At least that's the impression I got when Tina phoned,' Megan said. 'I must say we'll be pleased to have her living so close. Iain can't wait to see her again.'

Paul was delighted when Bridie told him they had arranged for his grandmother to return to Wester Rullion by the end of the month and that Tina had agreed to look after her, at least until the autumn.

'Of course my mother will need to use the downstairs bedroom,' Bridie said. 'I suggest Conan and I pay to have a shower installed in the cloakroom. There's plenty of room and the door is conveniently across the passage for her. It's almost as good as *en suite*.'

'Oh it'll be better!' Paul grinned. 'Because it's here, at Wester Rullion.'

'O-oh, I'm sure you're right there, dear nephew.'

'I've been thinking about it,' Paul said slowly, serious now. 'You know we never use the dining room these days. Don't you think we should take the furniture out and fix it up for Tina so that she's in the next room if Granny needs anything during the night?'

'Yes! I think that's a splendid idea, Paul,' Bridie said in surprise. He was head and shoulders taller than she was but she gave him an impulsive hug round his middle. 'You're a good laddie, Paul. No wonder my mother thinks the world of you.'

'I owe her several times over, Aunt Bridie.' His mouth tightened. 'Lucy told me about the airmail letters you know. I'm sure she's right about them causing Granny to take the stroke. I'm glad she's somewhere abroad. I hope I never run into her because I could never forgive her for the trouble she's caused! Never.'

'Oh, Paul,' Bridie said softly. 'Don't be like that. Life's too short to be bitter. It was because Mother thought she was shielding you from being pestered, and yet she felt guilty for keeping you and your mother apart. Then she bottled it all up inside herself. That's what probably caused her stroke, but we'll never know for sure. Anyway she feels better now it's all in the open and it's not just her decision anymore. She really is making a remarkable recovery. I believe she'll live until she's ninety yet.'

'I hope so,' Paul said fervently. 'It isn't the same without her here.'

Once the furniture had been removed Ryan and Paul both thought the room looked rather dark and shabby for a young woman like Tina.

'It's good thick paper,' Paul said, running his fingers over the raised pattern. 'Maybe we could paint over it? We could ask Peter's advice. He does all his own decorating.'

'It would certainly be cheaper if we did it ourselves,' Ryan agreed, ever conscious of the need to save money wherever possible.

Sometimes he wondered whether he would ever be able to afford to get married to Molly. A-ah, Molly, he sighed inwardly. The very thought of her made his body ache with longing.

It had been a terrible wrench for both of them saying goodbye when she left for France just over a week ago. His face burned at the memory of those last few days before she left. Desire had got the better of him but Molly had responded with a passion that astonished and delighted him. He had been full of remorse after that first time. The following evening, the last time they would be alone together before she left, he had been desperately afraid she would regret having given herself so completely, so unreservedly. He was sure she would blame him – as he blamed himself. Instead Molly had run into his arms immediately, instantly rekindling their passion. Indeed he had taken her more tenderly. There was less urgency and even deeper love bringing them together. It had all been so perfect. But it had made it even harder to part from each other, knowing Molly would not return until June – six long months. Ryan groaned inwardly at the prospect.

'You haven't heard a word I've said!' Paul interrupted his thoughts. Ryan shuddered and came back to earth with a thud.

'Er . . . you said we'd paint the walls . . .'

'I said that ten minutes ago! Oh, never mind. I know your mind's in France with Molly.' Paul grinned.

'Just you wait until you're in love!'

'That'll be the day! Actually I was asking if you thought cream would look all right but I think I'll consult Peter and see if he knows how much we'll need.'

'Mmm, he might offer to help us in the evenings,' Ryan nodded.

In fact Peter volunteered to tackle the woodwork and advised them how much emulsion paint to get for the walls.

'No skimping, mind,' he warned sternly. 'It will need two coats to look right and don't leave any streaks.'

Ryan and Paul did their best. It was not a perfect job but they hoped Tina might overlook their mistakes.

'At least it looks brighter and it's clean and fresh,' Paul said with satisfaction. 'I only hope Tina will cope all right.'

'Megan says she has enjoyed looking after old people in Ireland,' Ryan reminded him, 'and our granny isn't cantankerous or one of those who moans all the time.'

'Of course she isn't. What I mean is will Tina get bored and will she stay until granny can manage on her own again,' Paul explained anxiously.

Lucy was surprised when she saw the boys' efforts.

'I'm sure Tina will approve too,' she smiled. 'New curtains would just finish off the transformation. In fact . . . I'll just measure the window while I'm here. I'll make them as my contribution to welcoming Tina to Wester Rullion, but I'll wait to see what colour she likes. She strikes me as being a home-loving sort of girl, and I know she has some pieces of furniture of her own.'

Towards the end of January hurricane winds swept the country, causing several deaths in England from falling trees, collapsing roofs and overturned motor vehicles. Railways and roads were blocked, and the damage at the famous Kew Gardens was devastating.

Tina postponed her journey across the Irish Sea for another two days but eventually she arrived at Wester Rullion. Almost before she had had time to collect her own bits of furniture and unpack her possessions at Wester Rullion, Rachel was insisting on returning to her own home.

The day before Bridie brought her, Peter had proudly added some finishing touches to the two raised flower beds he had built for her. He had bought pots of purple and white winter heathers, and two pots of *helleborus niger* with their buds just waiting to burst into bloom. A gold-leaved euonymus added a bright spot to each of the beds. He had lifted clumps of snowdrops from beneath the shrubs in the garden with the greatest of care. Their heads nodded shyly, adding a note of white perfection. He knew Rachel adored the snowdrops. She had once told him they brought hope and new life to the world after the trials of winter. Later the miniature daffodils and crocuses would bloom and after that Peter hoped his beloved mistress would find the strength and the will to choose the flowers herself. For Peter it was a labour of love and the best he could offer the woman who had befriended him in his time of need.

Rachel's reaction was everything he had hoped for, but she had difficulty in thanking him adequately because of the lump in her throat. Tina was equally moved by the efforts Ryan and Paul had made to make her feel welcome. Bridie and Lucy had played their parts too by filling the huge chest freezer with every home-cooked dish they could cram in.

'Just so that you won't starve if the boys forget to do the shopping,' Lucy told her cheerfully.

'Oh but I don't mind doing the shopping and the cooking,' Tina said. Then she stopped, hesitated and looked at Rachel. 'Of course I shall not neglect my patient. We'll just have to see how we get along . . .'

'We shall get along just fine, lassie.' Rachel nodded her satisfaction. 'I'm not an invalid you know. I just need a bit of help now and then.' She threw Bridie a challenging look as though daring her to contradict. 'When you've brought your car over from Lochandee I'll maybe go shopping with you, even if I do have to sit in the car and wait.'

Lucy and Bridie looked at each other with raised eyebrows.

'I think this patient may take a bit of managing,' Bridie said. 'You'll have to be firm with her, Tina.'

'Tina and I will manage very well without any interference,' Rachel declared firmly. 'I'm tired of being treated like a piece of fragile glass in a heap of cotton wool. It's time I took control of my life again.' She gave Tina a very definite wink and Tina knew they were going to get on well. She liked an old lady with courage and spirit.

Paul, watching anxiously, detected the wink. He saw Tina's gentle smile in answer and heaved a sigh of relief. Granny wouldn't be his Granny Maxwell if her spirit had been quenched.

By the end of February it was so mild it could almost have been mid-summer but just before March actually began more stormy weather reminded everyone that spring was not guaranteed just yet.

The long cubicle shed was where the cows were housed during the winter. At each end there were heavy sliding doors of corrugated steel. These opened wide for ease of cleaning and feeding, and also to allow plenty of fresh air to circulate when the weather was mild. This had been needed just a few days previously but they always closed one of the doors at night. Now, as the wind howled down the chimney and through the keyhole Ryan remembered he had left the other big doors wide open. He was well aware that high winds rushing into the shed, and unable to get out the other end, might easily lift off the roof. That would be a catastrophe they could not afford. In addition there was always the danger that falling roof sheets or even the girders could kill or injure some of his precious milking cows.

Silently he left the fireside and went out to the utility where he had left his waterproofs and wellingtons. In the hall he met Tina who had been seeing Rachel off to bed and taking her the drink of hot chocolate which she favoured as a nightcap.

'I'm just going out to check all the doors are shut and everything is battened down for the night. The storm's getting worse,' he explained in answer to her questioning look. 'I'll not be many minutes.'

'Take care then. I can hear that old beech tree in the garden creaking and groaning. There will be slates and chimneys off somewhere or other by morning.'

'Well let's hope we escape the worst of it,' Ryan said with his warm slow smile. Tina thought if she'd had a brother she would have liked him to be just like Ryan. Although he and Paul were such good friends they were very different.

Tina found it much harder to talk freely to Paul and she was never sure what he was thinking. He kept his feelings well hidden but sometimes Tina saw a tiny pulse beating in his jaw and she was fairly certain it was a sign of tension, or was it disapproval? She hoped he did not disapprove of her, because she was beginning to enjoy being at Wester Rullion and her affection for Rachel Maxwell was growing

130

daily. More importantly, she sensed the feeling was mutual and that reassured her considerably. Jacquie McTeir had felt it was vital that patients should have trust in their carers and feel at ease in their company.

Tina's thoughts were on her work at Wester Rullion as she joined Paul in the television room. He looked up and smiled but he was evidently engrossed in a current affairs programme and Tina snuggled up in a corner of the old settee and allowed her mind to wander over the daily minutiae of her life here.

Rachel did not really need, and certainly did not want, to have someone constantly hovering over her. Tina had sensed this from the beginning.

'You know I am here and perfectly willing to help with anything you ask,' Tina told her on their second morning, 'but I suspect you want to have a go at doing most things yourself, even if it takes twice as long. Am I right?'

'A-ah, lassie! You are right. What a relief that you understand an old woman's whims.'

'I respect your desire to be independent,' Tina said, 'but will you promise me you'll not be too proud to ask for help when you need it?'

'I promise,' Rachel agreed.

'I don't think looking after you is going to keep me busy at all,' Tina smiled. 'Do you think it will be in order for me to cook for all of us? You don't think your daughter will consider I'm neglecting you if I do things around the house?'

'So long as I'm happy Bridie will be happy too,' Rachel assured her. 'I shall enjoy helping you in the kitchen, and having somebody to talk to at the same time. I can still peel the vegetables while I'm sitting at the table, you know. Oh, I may be a bit slower than I used to be, but I like to think I can still be useful.'

'In that case I think we understand each other and we'll get on splendidly,' Tina nodded. Rachel eyed her curiously.

'You sound very mature and sensible, Tina. Yet Bridie tells me you're a year younger than Paul. Maybe you've had too much trouble in your young life? I hope you'll not spend all your time working while you're here, lassie. Everybody deserves some pleasure.'

131

'Thank you,' Tina responded with a warm smile. 'But already I feel I'm among friends and that gives me the greatest pleasure of all.'

The television programme finished and Paul tossed the zapper across to Tina.

'Is there anything you want to see? I'm sorry I was engrossed. I don't watch television often, but that was interesting.' He smiled apologetically and Tina thought how much younger, and how attractive, he was when he smiled like that.

'Ryan said he was going outside to check everything was secure, but he's been gone quite a while,' Tina said. 'Do you think there's anything wrong?'

'I don't know.' Paul rose to his feet instantly. 'It's certainly a wild night. I'll just take a look out and see what Ryan's up to.'

Paul donned his coat and wellingtons and opened the door, holding on to it against a sudden gust of wind. There was a brief lull.

'Ryan . . .' he breathed. He'd heard a single shout for help but everything else was drowned by another onslaught of wind and rain.

Sixteen

Fortunately Paul had the foresight to call out to Tina, telling her Ryan must be in some kind of trouble, then he ran, head down against the wind and rain.

'Oh dear heavens!' he gasped as he rounded the corner of the cubicle shed and found the massive steel door lying on the ground and Ryan trapped beneath it.

'I c–can't get out.' His teeth were chattering and he was soaked to the skin. 'C–can you lift it, Paul?'

'I doubt it, but I'll have a go. Can you move? I mean maybe you shouldn't move. We need to call an ambulance . . .'

'No! J–just get me out of here.' Ryan was almost sobbing in pain and frustration. He had had a nightmare vision of lying here until morning when Paul came out to milk the cows.

Paul tried to lift the door but it was far too heavy for one man. Even if he lifted it enough, what if he let it fall again before Ryan could get out. He might injure him worse than ever.

'It would have killed you if it had fallen on your head.' He spoke his thoughts aloud even while his mind was frantically grappling with the situation. 'I'll bring the tractor and loader. I'll lift one side of the door with the forks.'

'Can I help?' Tina was running towards them, battling against the wind.

'Yes,' Paul shouted in relief. 'Wait with him 'til I bring the tractor.' He was running further up the yard now, towards the implement shed. He wondered whether they would need Peter to help lift Ryan. Should they even attempt to move him? He felt his own teeth beginning to chatter and knew it was shock.

'Oh, Ryan!' Tina gasped. 'Oh, my dear, are you badly hurt? Can you feel . . .'

'My arm's the worst – I think. If only Paul can lift off the weight of the door . . .'

'He will. I can hear the tractor. He's coming now . . .'

Paul manoeuvred the tractor slowly and carefully. He was afraid of hurting Ryan even more. He needed to get the iron prongs of the manure loader far enough under the door to lift it safely, but without injuring Ryan with the sharp points. He had to be able to lift the door and hold it steady. Slowly, bit by bit, he edged the tractor in, depending on Tina for guidance when he could no longer see over the bonnet of the tractor.

He saw her hold up her hand, indicating that he had gone far enough. Thank God she's not one of those squealing women who panic at the sight of a worm, he thought gratefully. Tina lifted her arm slowly and he followed her instructions, lifting the huge forks inch by inch until she indicated he must hold it there. To his horror he saw her lie down in the rain and mud and disappear from his view. He realized she must be wriggling under the door to help Ryan.

Ryan was stiff and chilled and at first he didn't think he could move after all.

'I wish I knew more about dealing with emergencies,' Tina muttered despondently. But she was thankful for her evening classes in first aid and the brief refresher Mrs McTeir had given her.

'Dear God!' Ryan groaned. 'It's my arm. I think it's broken.'

To Paul, holding the loader steady in position and unable to see what was happening, it seemed an eternity.

'Try not to move your arm then, Ryan,' Tina said as calmly as she could, wishing there was enough space for her to bind it against him. She was afraid if Paul lifted the door any higher to give them room it might wobble off the two mechanical prongs of the fork and crush them both. Ryan was moving his limbs cautiously, one by one, until the blood flowed again and feeling returned. Tina helped as much as she could and together they wriggled out from under the massive door. She scrambled to her feet and signalled Paul to lower the door to the ground again. He did so with a sigh of relief and then jumped off the tractor and ran to Ryan.

'We think he's broken his arm,' Tina said. 'We ought not to move him though. There may be internal injuries.'

'I think I'm all right except that every inch of me feels as though it's been beaten. Help me up, Paul.'

'Are you sure we should?' Paul asked anxiously.

'Yes.' Ryan was already struggling on to his knees. 'Bloody hell!' He bit his lips hard as the pain in his arm almost made him faint.

Between them Paul and Tina helped him slowly to the house. Once there, Tina immediately telephoned for an ambulance while Paul covered him with the travelling rug from the back of Granny's chair.

'They're sending an ambulance right away,' Tina said with relief. 'I'll not make you a hot drink, Ryan, because I think you'll need an anaesthetic. They'll probably keep you in overnight at least. They'll want to make sure you don't get pneumonia or any other delayed reactions.'

'You're soaked yourself, Tina,' Paul said with concern. 'Go and get changed into some dry clothes. We can't afford to have you ill.'

'What about yourself?'

'I'll change when you come back.' He frowned as he looked down at Ryan. He looked young and pale, lying there with his eyes closed and his hair dark with rain. 'Please God, let him be all right,' he prayed silently.

It was the following evening when Paul collected Lucy and they visited Ryan in hospital. He explained what had happened.

'I knew it was risky to leave the doors open at one end of the shed with the wind coming in such terrific gusts. I thought it might lift the roof off. When I got there the door had come loose from the bottom guides. I was just trying to jerk it back into place when it swung out as though an elephant had rushed at it. One of the top pulleys must have snapped off, I reckon. The next thing I knew it was lying on top of me.' He grimaced.

135

'And what do the doctors say?' Lucy asked, more anxious about his health than explanations.

'They're keeping me in for another night and I may need to come back once or twice for them to check it. They say it's broken in two places. But I'm sure I'm fit to go home with you now.'

'Better do as they advise,' Lucy cautioned.

'But how are you managing, Paul?' Ryan asked anxiously.

'We'll manage, dinna fret.'

'But you must be missing me,' Ryan protested.

'Oh, Ryan, you sound like a small boy,' Lucy chuckled. He glared at his mother indignantly.

'I think I work bloody hard. You must be missing me, Paul? Most of the cows are newly calved. It takes longer to get them all milked at this stage, and all the young calves need fed.'

'Well there's nothing you can do about it, old boy, so just flirt with all the pretty nurses and make the most of your chance to have a rest.' Paul grinned but he saw the anxiety in Ryan's eyes and knew he was thinking about his beloved cows. He relented.

'Of course we're missing you, but you could have been killed. Don't you realize how lucky you are? Anyway Peter turned out at five o'clock this morning and helped me with the milking, then we both fed the calves together afterwards. We were a lot later getting finished for breakfast of course, and by the time we'd cleaned up and fed all the young stock and checked the ewes it was nearly time to start milking again. Thank goodness the ewes have not started lambing yet . . .'

'But it'll be weeks before they take this bloody plaster off,' Ryan said in frustration. 'And we still have the spring barley to sow.'

'Ryan, please don't swear,' Lucy protested. 'As Paul says, it could have been a lot worse than a broken arm.'

'But you don't understand, Mother. There's a lot of work at this time of year with all the animals inside. They're all to feed and muck out and bed, as well as the milking.'

'I understand better than you think, my laddie,' Lucy said

sternly. 'Who do you think did the milking, and all the other chores, when you were a small boy and your father was so ill?' Her voice held a tremor at the memory of those dreadful months.

'I'm sorry, Mum. I forgot.' Ryan's cheeks were hot with shame. How could he have forgotten how his mother must have struggled, while his Grandfather Greig was too miserable to offer a man to help, or even his support.

'Yes, well, there's always a way.' Lucy nodded. 'And Paul's already proved himself a capable organizer.'

'Mmm, that's all very well but Peter is getting old, remember. He'll get scunnered, or knock himself up, if he has to keep getting up at five o'clock every morning. He must be at least seventy . . .'

'Sixty-four or -five according to Aunt Bridie,' Lucy corrected.

'Well, he's not young, is he?'

'Don't worry, old boy,' Paul grinned. 'I'm making a list of all the jobs you can do with one hand – like pressing the keys of the computer to do the bookkeeping . . .?'

'Oh no!' Ryan groaned aloud. 'Can't we get Joanne back to do that for a few weeks?'

'It would be good for you to have a go, Ryan,' Lucy said seriously. 'And it would relieve Paul a little bit. You're lucky he usually does all that sort of thing.'

'Well, I do other things. We're a good partnership, aren't we, Paul?'

'Of course we are. Seriously though, Ryan, you are looking a bit pale and shattered. Just think about getting yourself well again for the next few days.' He grinned again. 'At least it's your left arm that's hurt. You'll still be able to write those long letters to Molly.'

'Thank goodness for that!' Ryan said fervently. He frowned. 'Molly's letters haven't sounded quite right somehow recently. I think something's bothering her . . .'

'I expect she's bound to feel a bit homesick,' Lucy comforted. 'Kirsten hated being in Germany to begin with and having to speak in German all the time, but now she admits it's the very best way to get to grips with another language. I'm sure Molly must feel the same and of course she'll be missing you, Ryan, as well as her parents.'

'Do you think that's what it is? The language I mean . . .'

'And missing you, old boy,' Paul teased. 'I think that's the bell to let us know visiting is over. It's time to leave.'

'I'll drive in to collect you, Ryan,' Lucy said. 'Give me a ring when the doctor has done his rounds.

'OK,' Ryan nodded but he looked solemn and forlorn. 'This year's started badly, what with Molly having to go to France, and now this bloody fracture.' He caught his mother's reproving eye. 'Sorr-eey,' he shrugged, 'but I hope the rest of it improves pretty damn soon.'

As they walked back to the car park together Lucy turned to Paul.

'I know you were making light of the work, Paul, for Ryan's sake, but it is going to make things very difficult. Is there anyone you could get to help out temporarily?'

'No one that I know of.' Paul frowned. He held the car door open and when Lucy was settled he slid into the driver's seat, but he didn't start the engine. He turned to look at her. 'I can manage the milking myself if need be, but it would certainly take longer and the milk tanker comes in at seven o'clock to collect the milk.'

'Which means if you're on your own you'd need to be out at the parlour by four o'clock every morning to get the milk into the tank and cooled before then.' Lucy shook her head. 'It's all right for a short time but this is going to be for a couple of months at least, I'd say. You've other work to do during the day. You can't go to bed after breakfast like some of the full-time dairymen do. No,' she shook her head, 'don't knock yourself up, Paul, if there's any other solution.'

'Peter wouldn't leave me to it anyway.' Paul shrugged. 'You know how conscientious he is.'

'Mmm, I do. He'll be out every morning whatever time you start. Could Max spare any of his men to help, do you think?'

'I haven't had time to think about that. Tina says she did the milking when her father was ill. She's volunteered to help me in the mornings so that Peter doesn't over-tax himself, but she's worried the family might feel she's neglecting her

138

job of caring for Granny. She won't consider coming out to the milking parlour unless Granny promises not to get out of bed until she returns to the house. What do you think, Aunt Lucy? Even if Granny agrees, could we rely on her to keep her promise? Tina would never forgive herself if she fell, and neither would I.'

'Tina is worth her weight in gold,' Lucy said with conviction. 'There's not many would offer to take on extra work, especially milking. As to Granny Maxwell . . . she certainly has a mind of her own but I think if Tina makes her understand the situation I believe she would keep her word.'

'We'll see what Granny says then. I certainly don't want Peter insisting on starting at five every morning and working through until six or seven at night. He says they all did that during the war but he's older now. It's too much for him.'

'Of course it is, I agree,' Lucy said emphatically. 'A-ah, but Paul! We're forgetting. Ryan will be at home. He would be there for Granny if she needed anything while Tina is outside.'

'But he wouldn't be able to help her, not with one arm in plaster.'

'He could make her a cup of tea. He could talk to her, keep an eye on her.'

'Why, yes, so he could! We never thought of that. That would reassure Tina; me too. We'll wait until Ryan gets home then, before we mention it to Granny.'

They drove the rest of the way home in silence, each mulling over recent events. Lucy was on the point of telling Paul she had received another letter from his mother, but she decided he had enough problems to contend with at present. In any case Gerda had said she was moving to London for an operation and she didn't know where she would be staying after that.

At least the letter had been more normal this time, almost as though Gerda had overcome some sort of problem, or reached a decision. She even mentioned the man she had run away with, telling Lucy he had cleared out as soon as the money was finished and his creditors began to catch up on him.

'You will never believe this. I've been teaching. English in a Spanish school would you believe.' Knowing Gerda, Lucy could almost hear the bitter mockery behind her written words. She was right though, it was difficult to believe. Gerda had hated teaching even when she was in Britain. In fact she had hated work of any kind. 'Now I can't even do that,' she had written, almost with resignation, or maybe relief? It was hard to tell in a letter, Lucy felt. 'So I have agreed to go to London and have an operation. I've nothing to lose after all.'

It was this last sentence which made Lucy wonder, and worry, and feel guilty all over again.

Her mind was so preoccupied she didn't notice until Paul had drawn up at her own garden gate. He obviously believed her thoughts were on Ryan.

'Don't worry, Aunt Lucy. Ryan will be fine, you know. And the weeks will soon pass.'

'Oh! Y–yes, of course. Thanks for the lift, Paul. Good night.' She watched the tail lights disappear.

'And I still haven't mentioned Gerda's letter to her only son,' she sighed.

The whole family rallied round to help at Wester Rullion. Bridie and Lucy brought casseroles ready to pop in the oven to save Tina cooking. Megan was kept busy with her two lively children but she brought over batches of scones, pancakes and sponges whenever she had been baking. She knew Granny Maxwell usually had a rest in the early after- noon so she often called in the mornings and brought the children. Sometimes Iain would snuggle up on the old sofa next to his great-granny. It frequently brought a lump to Tina's throat to see them together, Iain with his head resting on her lap while she gently stroked his soft curls.

'They both look so happy and contented together,' she said to Megan when they went into the kitchen together to make some coffee.

'I know. It's rather wonderful how love can bridge the widest gap, even age and generations.'

'Everyone has been so helpful. You know, Megan, I feel

as though I've known the family – even been a part of it – for years, and yet it's so short a time.'

'I'm glad you're happy here, Tina,' Megan said simply. 'How are you getting on helping Paul in the milking parlour?'

'Well, apart from the fact that I wish I was a foot taller,' she grinned, 'I mean so that I can reach the cows' udders with the milking machine clusters. I'm really enjoying it. Paul couldn't believe it when I told him it was so much easier than milking in a cow shed. He says milking parlours are already much improved since they installed this one at Wester Rullion.'

'That's true,' Megan admitted. 'Max has installed computers in ours and it makes feeding the cows so much quicker and easier. You just press in the number of the animal as it comes into the parlour and it measures out the correct amount of feed for each individual cow. It's connected to the house computer and we can get a printout of the milk yield for each cow for that milking. It's marvellous.'

'Oh, you'll be telling me next the cows will be milking themselves!' Tina teased.

'Well they are working on it,' Megan said seriously. 'Robotic milkers they're called, but they're not perfected yet. Anyway they'll cost the earth I expect.'

'We shall soon not need people any more at this rate,' Tina laughed.

'The world will always need people like you, Tina,' Megan said with sincerity. 'The carers, the helpers, the kindly folk. I can't tell you how relieved everyone is that you've come to look after Max's granny. We all think the world of her and we all owe her so much.'

'Yes, I can understand that. I feel she's my friend already.'

'We're all your friends. You've got yourself a whole new adopted family. Honestly! Don't look so disbelieving.'

'Mmm, well I'm not so sure about Paul . . . Oh, we get on splendidly when we're working together. In fact it's fun. He has quite a sense of humour. But then . . . Oh, I don't know. It's as though the real Paul withdraws behind a blackout curtain or something. He seems so . . .' Tina frowned. 'Wary . . . No, not that exactly . . .'

141

'I know what you mean but I can't put my finger on it either. Paul's a very complex sort of man. I don't know all his story but from the little I've heard he may have reason to be wary, cautious maybe, moody even . . .' Megan shrugged. 'I'm no good at analysing people's personalities, but I believe there's a reason for Paul being the way he is from what Max has said. I just hope for his sake that he can learn to trust, perhaps even find love one day. At the moment the only person who really matters to Paul is his grandmother.'

'Yes,' Tina nodded. 'I know what you mean, but it's good that he does appreciate all she's done for him. It can't have been easy for her when he was orphaned so young.'

'Oh but he's not an orphan! His mother is still alive, wherever she is.'

'His mother is alive? Goodness gracious! He never mentions her. No one does. I assumed . . .' She shrugged. 'I should know by now, never to assume anything. Let's change the subject and take this coffee in or it will be dinner time before I know where I am.'

Two weeks later it was Fiona who drove Ryan into the outpatients for one of his check-ups.

'Your mother is a bit tied up today,' she said. 'Your grandfather wants her to meet some of the people we do business with when we're arranging the tours. I have to go into Dumfries anyway to pick up some brochures. I hope you don't mind me driving you instead.'

'I don't mind at all,' Ryan grinned, 'just so long as somebody can get me there and back. It's just a nuisance having to come at all.'

'Well at least they're keeping an eye on you so we should be grateful.'

As they walked together from the car park Ryan was surprised to see Molly's brother, Norman, walking towards them, deep in thought. He flushed, almost guiltily, when he saw Ryan. They exchanged greetings and introductions. Norman straightened his shoulders as though reaching a decision.

'I expect you're wondering what I'm doing here at the

hospital at this time of day.' Ryan had wondered but he was too well brought up to display his curiosity. 'I've just been seeing my father . . .'

'Your father's in hospital?' Ryan's eyes widened. 'Molly never said . . .'

'That's because she doesn't know. We're not telling her. Mother doesn't want her upset. She would want to come home to see him. He's had a heart attack.'

'A heart attack! B–but surely . . .'

'The doctors say it's not a bad one, or we would have had to tell Molly, of course. They say it's a warning to him to take things easier . . .' Norman grimaced and raised his eyebrows. 'I don't know how you get a man like my father to do that. Myself, I think he's been worrying over this BSE problem. That's six cows he's had with it, and two of them his favourites – really well bred.'

'Isn't that always the ones you lose,' Ryan grimaced.

'I suppose so. The thing is the scientists seem to think it's the way the cows have been fed but how are we to know the suppliers have been making up compounds from weird ingredients. Father thought the big firms must be trustworthy when they're so well known. Now we're not so sure. They tell us it's 16 per cent protein, or 18 per cent for winter rations, or whatever. We take their word for it. I always assumed they used soya beans and peas with a bit of fish-meal for the best quality cake.'

'Yes, that's what they told us at college,' Ryan agreed. 'But it seems some of the big firms have been cutting corners. There's rumours they even processed feathers to make up the right protein analysis.'

'I wouldn't put it past them,' Norman said grimly, 'but they still charged high enough prices for their cattle cake.'

'We only buy from the local merchant,' Ryan said. 'I don't think they have the big machines for processing feathers, or offal, or whatever they're supposed to have used. So far we've not had any affected animals anyway. Of course we bought in most of our milking cows and we don't know what they were fed on when they were young.'

'And now there's rumours it can be passed on to humans

143

who eat beef,' Norman said glumly. 'The French have banned British beef imports and the bottom has fallen out of the market. It's enough to give anybody a heart attack, and my father does worry about these things.'

'But the government says it's perfectly safe to eat beef,' Fiona said. She had been following the conversation intently. Norman turned to look at her and smiled apologetically.

'I'm sorry for ranting on. I'm afraid it's given us all a bit of a shock, my father having a heart attack. I've never known him to be ill in his life.'

'Don't apologize,' Fiona said gently. 'It's natural to be concerned. This warning may make him realize none of us is immortal. He won't want to risk another.'

'You may be right,' Norman said slowly, 'but farming is his whole life. I can't imagine him retiring.'

'Are you sure Molly doesn't know?' Ryan asked. He was convinced there was something worrying her.

'Oh, I'm certain. It only happened the day before yesterday.'

'I see.' Ryan frowned. 'I almost wish I didn't know either – just in case I let anything slip . . .'

'Yes, well . . .' Norman flushed again. 'I wasna going to tell you . . . But meeting you like this, Ryan . . .' he shrugged. 'I decided it was only fair to say why I'm here. Anyway we all know you wouldn't hurt Molly so I'm relying on you to keep this to yourself until she finishes in France. Hopefully Father will have made a good recovery by the time she sees him again. I'll keep you posted now you do know.'

'Thanks . . .'

As they walked on Fiona looked at Ryan's frowning face.

'It's not going to be easy keeping this from Molly,' she said, 'for any of her friends and family. It's so easy to let things slip. I wonder if they're wise.'

'I think they should tell her,' Ryan said with conviction. 'Molly's not a child any more. She's grown up . . .' He blushed bright red and Fiona's brows rose in surprise, but he went on hurriedly, 'She's twenty-one but they still treat her as though she's ten because she's a lot younger than her brothers. I wonder . . .' he frowned, then he glanced uncertainly at his grandmother. 'Do you believe in telepathy? I don't really. But I do know something's bothering Molly, and I don't believe it's anything to do with her studies, or living in France. I just wondered whether she . . . well, sort of guessed in advance.'

'I suppose it's possible. In a way.' Fiona smiled. 'She's bound to be thinking about everyone back home . . .'

Ryan was always in high spirits when he had received a letter from Molly. Paul knew he'd had one that morning because he had sorted through the letters himself, mainly in the hope of receiving an overdue cheque from a man who had bought two tonnes of barley. So why was Ryan so preoccupied and short with everyone, even Granny Maxwell? Suddenly Paul stopped in his tracks. Surely his beloved Molly had not met someone else? Only something like that in a letter would upset Ryan, surely?

Seventeen

Ryan followed Paul out of the house as soon as lunch was over, leaving his pudding half eaten and abruptly refusing Tina's offer of coffee or tea. Paul turned to him.

'What's biting you, Ryan? You were barely civil to Tina just now.'

'I've a lot on my mind. I . . . er, I need a word with you.'

'Oh? Make it quick then. Peter and I are tackling some de-horning this afternoon. I'd like to finish the biggest batch of calves before milking time.'

'I know how busy you are, you don't need to keep reminding me.'

'For goodness' sake, Ryan, what's got into you? You know I'm not reminding you, nor am I grumbling. You're like a bear with a sore head. Spit it out, man, whatever it is!'

Ryan frowned and chewed his lip.

'Sorry,' he muttered. 'I – I . . . Molly wants me to go to London.'

'London?' Paul's green eyes opened wide. 'When? Why – I mean what for?' His eyes narrowed. His lean face softened. 'She hasn't met someone else, has she?' he asked gently.

'God, I hope not! No, no it can't be that . . .' Ryan gave a stricken look. 'All she says is, can I meet her in London next weekend. She knows I'm not much use here and she can get across for a long weekend. She wants to see me. She says it's important, but she doesn't answer any of my questions. I've thought for a while there's something bothering her . . .'

'Well then . . .?' Paul frowned. 'I don't really see why you're asking me? Do you need some extra cash?'

'I hadn't thought of that! Yes, I shall need to pay for the

146

bed and breakfast. Molly is going to book us in. But I'm supposed to be keeping an eye on Granny until after breakfast, and checking the cattle and suchlike. It's not much, I know, but I feel bad about taking off like this and leaving you with everything.'

'Oh, Ryan. There's no need to feel bad. If you want to meet Molly this is as good a time as any to do it, when you're laid up anyway.'

'That's what Molly thought, but . . .'

'She's right. Granny is co-operating really well over staying in bed until she hears Tina is in the house again. Anyway Tina says she hardly needs her help with anything now, except bathing and washing her hair and a few odd things like stockings and shoes.'

'I know. Mother and Aunt Bridie are really pleased with the way she's improved since she returned to Wester Rullion.'

'And Tina is a grand help with the milking, especially since Peter fixed the duck boards in the bottom of the parlour for her. She can reach a lot easier now. We're managing better than I dared to hope the night I saw you lying under that door. You get off to London and enjoy seeing Molly.'

'There's the barley still to sow. It's time it was in now.'

'I know, but Max has promised to send two of his men over from Glens of Lochandee to do the drilling as soon as he's finished sowing his own. He says we can keep one of his men long enough to spread the fertilizer on the remaining grassland as well. So don't worry . . .'

'All right. Thanks, Paul.' Ryan looked relieved.

'Do you want a lift to the railway station?'

'I thought I might ask Mother if I can borrow her car . . .'

'Drive you mean? With one arm! Aunt Lucy will never let you do that.'

Paul was right about that. Lucy did offer to pay the train fare though but Fiona had a better idea. She discussed it with Conan.

'They're young and in love and desperately short of money to enjoy life,' she said.

'So? What have you in mind, you scheming woman?' He

chuckled, and seized her around her waist. He nuzzled her neck. 'I may not be as young as they are, but I'm still in love . . .'

'So you'll understand how frustrated they must feel then.' Fiona smiled up at him and returned his kiss. 'I bet they'd think we're too old for this.'

'I expect they would. I remember being quite shocked when I discovered my mother was expecting Ewan when I was seventeen,' he smiled reminiscently.

'I like Molly very much, and so does Lucy.' Fiona gently brought his attention back to the subject she had in mind. 'Ryan's a lovely lad, and he does work hard. He deserves a treat.'

'I agree with that, Mrs Maxwell,' Conan teased. 'So . . .?'

'I've been checking our tours to London. He could travel down with this one. Look . . .' she pointed her pencil at one of the charts, 'and there's spare bookings for bed and breakfast for both of them. Then Ryan could travel north as far as Gretna on this other one on the Tuesday . . . There's just one spare seat. What do you think? One of us could meet him at Gretna.'

'Sounds ideal to me,' Conan nodded. 'You phone Ryan and suggest it to him. You know how proud he is though. Tell him we're treating Paul and Tina too – to a dinner and theatre in Edinburgh, or something. If we give them both a treat, he won't feel so bad.'

'And are we? Treating Paul and Tina, I mean.'

'We'll think of something when Ryan is back to work. Tell him it's to be a surprise though, then we're not committed to a time or place.'

'You're a lovely grandad,' Fiona said, half teasing but mainly serious.

'Aren't I a lovely husband too, then?'

'Of course you are, and you're still an attractive flirtatious man, but I hope that's only with me.'

'You know it is,' Conan said softly. 'There's no one in the world like you, Mrs Maxwell.'

'We've been so lucky.' Fiona snuggled against his chest. 'Sometimes Paul reminds me very much of the way you were when I first knew you. I do hope he learns to trust and finds real love one day.'

'Yes,' Conan sighed. 'So do I. In his case his mother has a lot to answer for,' he added darkly. 'I can't understand Lucy feeling so guilty about her after what she did to Ewan.'

'Lucy has your mother's Christian soul, that's what it is.'

This was true. When Lucy found out Ryan would be in London for the whole weekend she telephoned the hospital number which Gerda had scribbled at the bottom of her letter. All she wanted was the hospital address and to know which part of London it was in but she was prepared to invent some story about sending a get well card if she had to. As it was she received the full address and instructions without any trouble at all.

It was only after Lucy put the receiver down and studied the details she had written that she began to wonder. Surely the name of the hospital was familiar? Didn't it specialize in cancer treatments, or was it heart transplants? She was sure it was well known for something like that.

She gave the details to Ryan.

'I know you and Molly will want to spend all the time you can together but if you're on your own after Molly returns to France on Monday you might see whether you can find this place. I haven't mentioned it to Paul, or to Granny Maxwell yet, but his mother is in London now, for an operation. Don't ask what for because Gerda only tells people what she wants them to know, and she didn't go into details.'

'But Mum . . . I don't even know her!' Ryan protested.

'Oh all right then, it doesn't matter if you haven't time,' Lucy sighed. 'It was just a thought. I can't help feeling she must be pretty desperate about something when she wrote again, especially after the horrid letter I sent her when Granny Maxwell had her stroke.'

'I'll see then.' Ryan tucked the piece of paper in his wallet but he had no intention of searching round London for a hospital. All he wanted was to find out what was troubling his beloved Molly.

Eighteen

Most of the tourists on the coach seemed to Ryan to be middle-aged or older. He was the only one who was in any hurry to get off and into the hotel and he curbed his impatience with an effort.

Eventually he found himself entering the automatic doors. Through the glass he could see Molly already there, anxiously scanning the new arrivals. He wanted to push the heavy doors to make them move faster. He wanted to shout her name. Then she caught sight of him. Her face lit up, but only briefly. As Ryan escaped from the revolving door and hurried towards her he felt a stab of dismay which was almost a physical pain to his heart.

Molly's face looked pinched and pale and her eyes were dark ringed and wide with anxiety. Her hands were twisted together and he clasped them with his one good hand, noting her tension. He thought she must have had a long wait, or perhaps a traumatic crossing on the ferry.

'I'm here now, Molly,' he breathed, 'I'm here my dearest, darling girl.' He wanted to hug and kiss her but he remembered how shy Molly had always been in public. Even after her time at university, and here amongst strangers, she still withdrew a little, gazing at him with fearful, searching eyes.

'I'll get my room key in a minute and we'll go up there. Oh, but Molly, you don't know how good it is to see you! How much I've missed you.'

'H–have you, Ryan? You really mean it?' She gave him a wan smile, a mere shadow of the radiant greeting he had hoped for. He clasped her shoulder and looked into her face. A frown creased his brow at the sight of her pinched, pale face.

'You've lost weight, Molly. Isn't the food good in France? Don't you like it?'

'The food's fine. Look, it's our turn next. They gave their names to the receptionist and she handed them each a card and security number and explained how to use them.

'Oh good, we're right next door to each other. That's very convenient.' Ryan grinned wickedly at Molly but there was no answering smile and her eyes looked dull with misery. He had hoped they wouldn't occupy separate rooms. He felt a sickening pang. Could Paul be right? Had Molly found someone else? Had she brought him here to tell him so? He knew she was not a coward to take the easy way out and write him a dismissive letter. She was the kind of girl who would feel she had to tell him face to face. He fumbled with the card. Molly took it from him and opened the door. He thought she looked like Marie Antoinette must have looked when she was going to the guillotine, and he certainly felt that way.

As soon as they were safely into the bedroom he turned to her, his own face pale now, his whole body tense.

'What is it, Molly? What's wrong? You've got to tell me now I've come all this way.' He hadn't realized his voice was stern and sharp until her eyes filled with tears.

'D–don't be mad at m–me, Ryan. P–please . . .'

'I'm not mad at you, Molly. B–but you've got to tell me what's wrong . . .?'

Molly chewed her lip. She gulped hard. But she didn't seem able to find the words.

'You . . . you've met someone else. Is that it?' Ryan said flatly and sat down heavily on the edge of the huge bed.

'No! No! Oh no, Ryan. There could never be anyone else . . .' Molly was staring at him aghast.

'There isn't?' Ryan was on his feet again in a flash. In one stride he was standing in front of her. He wanted to seize her in his arms. 'Oh this damned plaster! So long as you've not fallen for someone else nothing else matters. There's nothing in the world we can't work out if we're together, Molly!' His voice rang with conviction. 'Come and sit beside me on the bed. This side so that I can hold you close with

151

my good arm, and kiss you 'til you call for mercy.' He was grinning widely now. Molly moved with him, but even when he kissed her he could feel her tension.

'Dearest Molly, what's bothering you? It can't be so bad you can't tell me, can it?'

'It is. Oh, Ryan it is. A–and it's all m–my fault . . .'

'What is?' Ryan was genuinely puzzled by her distress. 'You're not ill, Molly? Are you?' He heard the fear in his own voice. His father had died with leukaemia and he had been young. A girl in his class at school had had it too . . . His imagination ran riot. 'Tell me, Molly!'

'I – I'm p–pregnant. I – I'm going to have a baby. Oh, Ryan, I'm s–so sorry . . . I – I know we've no money and – and . . .'

'A baby! You're having a baby . . .' Ryan gazed at her with a mixture of relief and wonderment. 'Oh, my darling Molly,' he said softly, and held her close, desperately wishing the stupid plaster wouldn't get in the way of his pressing her close to his heart.

'I – I know I sh–should have taken the p–pill,' she whispered. 'Most of the other girls at uni are on it. I'm such a f–fool . . .'

'A-ah, Molly. You're not a fool. I know how shy you are about things like that. It's one of the things I love about you. Anyway I'm just as much to blame. I should have been prepared too. We both got carried away when you were leaving. Don't blame yourself, my darling girl.' Ryan's voice was husky and he kissed Molly with infinite tenderness, almost reverence. This time Molly's response was everything he'd dreamed of. Tenderness swiftly turned to passion. It was a hunger which could only be satisfied with complete and magnificent surrender for both of them.

Later, much later, Molly touched Ryan's plastered arm. It was the only part of him hidden from her sight.

'I hope we haven't injured it.'

'It's a damned pest for a job like this,' he grinned, 'but I'd willingly have it broken all over again for such a reward.' A delicate flush coloured Molly's cheeks at the look in his eyes.

Lying in the curve of his arm a little while later Molly whispered, 'I've been so afraid, Ryan. I – I didn't know what to do. I – I know neither of us has any money to keep a baby. I know how hard you work and how much you want to farm . . . B–but I couldn't think to have an abortion. I just couldn't . . .'

'God, no! No, Molly. D–don't you want a baby?'

'Oh yes. I want your baby, Ryan. It's just . . . I don't know how I'll manage . . . I don't know what Mother and Father will say.' Her small face took on the pinched look again. 'I know you weren't reckoning on anything like this . . .'

'But I was, Molly.' Ryan raised himself up and looked down into her face. 'Oh I admit it was mostly in my dreams. You don't know how many times I've imagined asking you to marry me. How I've wondered what you would say? Even if you'd agreed I worried about your parents. What would they say to their only daughter marrying a penniless farmer . . . ?'

'Oh, Ryan!' Molly smiled, really smiled this time. 'Did you really have dreams like that too? I wished and wished we could be married . . .' She blushed bright pink and half turned away in embarrassment. Ryan chuckled triumphantly.

'So you'd have said yes? Truly?'

'Of course I would. I love you, Ryan.'

'And I love you, my dearest Molly . . .' Ryan said huskily. He lay back on the mound of pillows, his good arm behind his head. 'It's the money that's the problem. I even thought of trying to buy one of the cottages so we could be married as soon as you finished at university. The old couple who live near Wester Rullion were going to sell it when the poll tax came in. They planned to move south of the Border, but now they have the poll tax in England too so they changed their mind. I comforted myself with the thought that it wasn't meant to be. I thought you might despise me for asking you to live in a cottage anyway.'

'Oh no! Ryan, you know I'd never despise you if we had to live in a caravan.'

'You'd do that? If we could be married?'

'I'd do anything if we could be together,' Molly answered

153

fervently, 'but I know you have so many plans for the farm . . .' Her voice tailed off forlornly. She had gone over and over all the problems in her mind these past few months. But at least she knew now that Ryan had always planned to marry her, that he loved her. He was not just marrying her because of the baby. He was not the least bit angry about it either.

'Well, now I'm going to have a wife – and a baby . . . Imagine that – a baby . . . Our baby,' he said softly. 'That's far more important than my plans for breeding cows. It doesn't solve the money problem though. I don't think your parents would consider a caravan to be a very good place to bring up a baby. In fact I think your father might have something to say if that's the best I can offer you.'

'I hadn't thought of that,' Molly said in a small voice.

'We'll work something out. I know Paul wouldn't mind if we all had to live at Wester Rullion but I don't want to ask you to do that if we can find any other way. It wouldn't be fair to you with a young baby. Or to Great-Granny, I suppose. She needs peace now, or at least I suppose she does . . .'

'I'd live anywhere so long as we can be together,' Molly said.

'Well, we'll work something out,' Ryan promised recklessly. 'Peter reckons the old couple are still thinking of selling their cottage and moving into sheltered housing. It needs too many improvements to let me get a mortgage I could afford. But if I asked Grandfather to lend me enough to buy it, maybe we could do the improvements a bit at a time . . .' He looked earnestly into Molly's face. 'It's not the sort of home I dreamed of for you, Molly. I don't know what your father will say.' He stared glumly into space at the thought of approaching Mr Nairne. The prospect had been daunting enough in his daydreams but this grim reality was ten times worse. 'He'll blame me for this situation of course. I would if I were in his shoes.'

'Of course he can't blame you, Ryan, at least not any more than he'll blame me for being stupid enough to get pregnant. But I don't want him to know yet, Ryan,' she added urgently and struggled to sit up in the big bed. 'Father has had a heart attack, but I'm not supposed to know about it.'

'You've heard about that?' Ryan asked incredulously.

'So you knew too? And you didn't tell me?'

'I daren't. I met Norman at the hospital and he told me then, but he swore me to secrecy in case you wanted to come home.'

'Well in other circumstances I would have wanted to see him immediately,' Molly admitted, then blushed. 'But now I don't want to go home until I've finished my course and got my degree.'

'How did you know? About your father, I mean?'

'My sister-in-law. You know – John's wife, Patsy. She often writes to me. We get on well in spite of the difference in our ages. She's always felt the family still treat me as a child. Over this she felt I ought to know, just in case Father had another heart attack.'

'You don't blame Patsy for telling you then?'

'No, she's right. Imagine what a shock I'd have got if I'd had no warning he was ill. I've never known him have a day in bed before.'

'I thought it might be something like that which was upsetting you, Molly. I knew there was something wrong from your letters. It's a tremendous relief to clear the air. Whatever problems we have – and I do know we shall have a lot in the circumstances – promise me we'll have no more secrets in future. I can't stand not knowing what's wrong.'

'I promise,' she said softly, and hugged him tightly. 'It's a wonderful relief now you know, Ryan. And it's an even greater relief that you've taken it all so well. I – I thought you might w–want me to g–get rid of the baby . . .'

'Never! You surely didn't think that, Molly?'

'In my heart I didn't think so, but when I was alone and worrying all the time . . . all sorts of things crossed my mind.'

'My poor darling. I wish you'd told me sooner.'

'I didn't want to tell you in a letter. I needed to see your face . . .' She stroked his cheeks tenderly.

* * *

155

It was the following morning, when Molly insisted on helping Ryan to dress, that the piece of paper fell out of his wallet. She bent and picked it up.

'This is the name of a London hospital.' She frowned and handed it back to him, clearly puzzled as to why he should have such a thing. 'Your arm is all right, isn't it, Ryan? I mean there's nothing else wrong, is there?' she asked anxiously.

'Of course not.'

'So why are you carrying the address of a London hospital?' Molly was not entirely reassured.

'Oh that's just an address Mother gave me. She says Paul's mother has come over to London for an operation.' He grimaced. 'Mother thought I might make time to go and see her while I'm here, but I don't even know her.'

'Paul's mother . . .' Molly mused. 'You know . . . I don't think I've heard either of you mention Paul's mother before. In fact, I suppose I assumed she was dead.'

'Nobody in the family ever mentioned her either until recently. I don't think anyone knew where she was. Paul certainly didn't. He refuses to talk about her. When we started farming Wester Rullion together there were a few spiteful comments from disgruntled tenants. One especially made nasty remarks about her to Paul. He was furious. I doubt if he remembers her any better than I do. We'd be about five when she ran away with another man and drained Uncle Ewan's bank account.'

'What a dreadful thing to do!'

'I believe she left lots of bills too, and secretly sold a lot of cattle. Or at least her boyfriend did. I believe they could have gone to jail, but as far as I can gather Great-Granny Maxwell refused to pursue matters. I suppose she was right really. Paul would have found it even harder if his mother had been in jail.'

'Oh yes, I'm sure he would. Poor Paul. No wonder he has that sort of wary bit about him. I think I might understand him better now. I was a little in awe of him before. It must be awful to know your own mother ran off and left you when you were a child.'

156

'Yes, I suppose it could give a person a complex . . .' Ryan reflected. 'I've never really thought about it. I've always known Paul and we've always been good friends. It was my mother who introduced Gerda to Uncle Ewan. She still feels responsible, even after all this time. I expect that's why she hopes I'll find out what's really wrong with Gerda. I suppose she wonders whether she's telling the truth this time. Apparently she was quite an actress and she could act the drama queen when she was young, at least according to Uncle Nick. He couldn't stand her apparently. I vaguely remember her being very slim and glamorous with long blonde hair . . .'

'Oh do you, Ryan Greig? You were eyeing up glamorous women when you were five years old then, were you . . .?' She punched him playfully.

'You wait until I get rid of this damned plaster, Miss Nairne, and I'll teach you not to box with me!' Ryan threatened teasingly and seized her with his good arm, holding her prisoner while he kissed her thoroughly. Gerda was forgotten.

It was almost lunch time at Wester Rullion when Paul answered the telephone. He was surprised.

'The milk recorder is coming this afternoon,' he announced as soon as he entered the kitchen and saw Tina. 'It's a new girl. She's very late letting us know,' he frowned, feeling irritated.

'Oh? What's happened to Rosie? Is she off ill?' Tina asked.

'I don't know. Rosie always phones straight after breakfast.'

'Mmm, she hasn't given us much warning right enough,' Tina agreed. 'I'll put clean sheets on the bed after lunch.'

'Did your father have his cows officially recorded?' Paul asked.

'No. Our cows weren't pedigree so he didn't think it was worth paying for the service. He just kept his own records for managing them, you know?'

'Yes. I'd do the same if we didn't need the official records for the pedigrees, I think. Sometimes it's not very convenient having the recorders to stay overnight either, but it's so they're here at five o' clock for the morning milking. There's talk of changing their routine so they can travel. They may get more married women to do the job if they can stay at home at nights.'

'I see. They'd need more money then, especially if they didn't get their evening meal and breakfast as they do at present.'

'Yes, I'm afraid they would,' Paul agreed, 'but it would be easier for you.'

'It's no problem, so long as I know she's coming.'

'You're very good, Tina. It is short notice. Perhaps she didn't realize she should have phoned earlier. Mind you, they're not supposed to give too much warning of an impending visit. Most farmers know roughly when they're due though. Time has gone so quickly I can hardly believe we're due another test already.'

'Why haven't they to give much notice?'

'It's so the farmers can't cheat by milking earlier the day before, and that sort of thing. The records give a truer picture of the cows' real potential for breeding. It's important to breeders wanting to sell pedigree cattle at high prices.'

'Do many breeders really cheat?' Tina asked curiously.

'I've heard lots of stories,' Paul grinned. 'You ask Max sometime. He'll tell you some of them try to influence the milk yields, or the quality, or maybe both! I can't see the point myself, and neither can Ryan. We want to know what our cows are really capable of if we're going to breed from them ourselves.'

'Mmm, that makes more sense, I'd say,' Tina nodded.

'Dare I ask you another favour?' Paul asked diffidently.

'You can always ask.' Tina smiled. 'I don't have to say yes.'

'I feel we've asked you to do so much already and you're not paid to do any of it.'

'I'm enjoying myself here at Wester Rullion,' Tina said truthfully. Her smile faded and she grew pensive. 'In fact I shall be really sorry to move on to a new job, but I don't think your granny will need me much longer.'

'Oh she will!' Paul exclaimed in dismay. It suddenly struck

him how much he would miss Tina if she were to leave. She was such easy company.

'What was the favour?'

'The fav— Oh yes. I wanted to ask if you would help with the afternoon milking today, as well as the morning milking as usual. Even though our cows all have a freeze brand number Peter gets a bit flustered when there's something different – like the milk recording going on. Usually it's Ryan and me doing the milking so he never needs to be involved. If you're willing I'll phone and ask Aunt Bridie if she'll pop in – just to keep an eye on Granny and prevent her trying to make the evening meal – as she used to do.'

'I'm perfectly willing to help,' Tina agreed, 'but you're right, it's just the sort of thing Mrs Maxwell would attempt to do if we're all outside working.'

Nineteen

Ryan and Molly were content just to be in each other's company. Neither of them had much money to waste so they had explored the parks and shops and lunched on fruit and cheese sitting on a park bench in the intermittent spring sunshine.

In the evening they had dinner in the hotel dining room.

'I could scarcely eat any lunch after such a big breakfast,' Molly laughed, 'but I'm famished now. It's very generous of your grandparents to arrange such a lovely hotel for us. The food is delicious. If I'd known we would be having posh dinners I'd have brought a smarter dress.'

'You're lovely just the way you are,' Ryan assured her.

'I never believed I could be so happy,' she said softly, stretching a hand shyly across the table.

'I swear you've put on six pounds since yesterday,' Ryan teased. Then his smile faded. 'I was so worried when I saw how pale and thin you looked, waiting in the foyer.'

'I haven't been able to think about food for worrying,' Molly admitted. 'By the time I come home I shall be huge. Will you mind if I look like a barrel?'

'I shall love you just the same.'

'I can't help feeling sad for my mother and father,' Molly said, her eyes pensive. 'I didn't want to hurt them, and I know they will be disappointed in me when they realize . . .'

'Are you sure you don't want me to break the news to them before then, Molly dearest?' Ryan asked. He was dreading having to face Mr Nairne. 'Perhaps if I told your mother first . . . Maybe she would break it to your father more gently . . .' he said diffidently.

'We'll not tell either of them until we have to,' Molly said firmly.

'Surely we ought to tell them we want to get married as soon as you get your degree, Molly?'

'We-ell yes, I suppose we ought to prepare them for that . . .'

'We'll wait until we have some definite plans. After I've asked Grandfather about a loan. If we can't buy the cottage I'll have to look for another one not too far away from Wester Rullion.'

'Yes, that would be best,' Molly said more positively. 'If we can present them with our own arrangements they'll realize we really mean it. Otherwise Mother will want to organize us.'

On the Sunday afternoon it was Molly who suggested they should take a tube to the hospital where Paul's mother was.

'When we're so happy ourselves it seems only right we should go and cheer up someone who is ill. It would probably please your mother too, Ryan, otherwise she wouldn't have given you the address.'

'Are you sure you want to do that, Molly?' Ryan was surprised.

'I feel so happy, and so relieved, I want all the world to be happy too,' Molly chuckled, squeezing his arm. 'And we can't make love all day, as well as all night,' she whispered wickedly.

'Mmm, I don't see why not . . .' Ryan murmured blandly.

They found the hospital without difficulty but they had to ask directions to the ward where Mrs Gerda Maxwell was.

Ryan had only the vaguest of childhood memories but he knew he could never have recognized Paul's mother if she'd been in a long line of patients. As it happened she was in a room on her own.

'She will be moving into the ward tomorrow,' the nurse informed them as she ushered them along the corridor to the door of Gerda's room. There she left them. Ryan was shocked by the appearance of the figure in the bed.

Her skin was the colour of yellow parchment and her hair was short and fine and pure white. She had several tubes attached and she appeared to be sleeping.

Ryan and Molly stood close together in silence, over-whelmed at the sight of a woman who looked too ill to survive the night, let alone move into a ward.

'She's resting,' Ryan whispered uncomfortably. 'I think we should go . . .' Molly bit her lip, wishing she hadn't persuaded him they ought to visit.

'Donald . . .' Gerda said sleepily, staring at Ryan. Her eyes were the only thing Ryan remembered. Eyes so pale it was hard to tell whether they were grey or blue.

'I . . . er . . .' He cleared his throat and stepped closer to the bed. 'I'm Ryan. Ryan Greig.'

Gerda stared at him for a moment and tried to lift her head.

'You look just like your father . . .' Her voice was weak. She slumped back against the pillows.

'My father is dead.'

Gerda's brow puckered as she tried to remember.

'Yes . . . Yes he is, isn't he . . .' She closed her eyes again. 'Is this your little sister?' she asked without opening them. 'I – I've forgotten her name.'

'My sister's name is Kirsten, but this is my fiancée, Molly.' He drew Molly close to his side, holding firmly to her arm, whether to give her support or because he needed it himself he wasn't sure. He simply couldn't believe the pathetic figure in the bed was Paul's mother. He thought of his own mother. She seemed young and fit in comparison, and yet they had been at college at the same time.

'So you're going to be part of the family, Molly?' Gerda lifted her eyelids briefly. 'I wish you luck.' Molly looked puzzled. Ryan bit his lip.

'The nurse said we shouldn't stay too long . . .' he said awkwardly.

'Makes a change having a visitor.' Gerda made an effort to open her eyes and look at them both. 'I haven't got long anyway. It's cancer of the liver.'

'Oh dear,' Molly murmured involuntarily.

'Doesn't matter any more . . . nothing they can do. Not much to live for anyway.'

'I – I'm so sorry,' Molly said softly. She moved closer to

the bed and took one of the pale limp hands. Gerda let it lie there and focused on Molly's face. She gave a little grimace.

'You're probably the only one who is sorry.' She turned her head slightly to look at Ryan. 'Tell Paul . . . tell him I'm sorry.' She closed her eyes wearily.

'I – I'll tell him,' Ryan said thickly. 'When I go home. I'm only here for the weekend.'

'Yes.' Gerda closed her eyes wearily. They waited a little while.

'Perhaps we should leave now,' Ryan said gently. 'I think we've tired you.'

'They say I'm getting better.' Gerda didn't open her eyes. 'I know I'm not. The other doctor told me the truth. Six weeks . . . six months if I'm lucky he said. If I'm unlucky . . .'

'Please don't say that,' Molly pleaded. 'Life is so precious.' Gerda opened her eyes at that.

'Mine isn't. I don't know where I'll be when they send me out of here, but I'd like to have seen Paul . . .' She closed her eyes again. 'Just once . . .' The words were barely audible. Ryan gnawed his lip. He knew only too well how bitter Paul felt about his mother. Would he feel the same if he saw her like this?

'We had better leave now,' he said. 'But I will tell Paul.'

'Goodbye,' Molly said softly. In answer Gerda raised her hand slightly, but she neither spoke nor opened her eyes again as they left the room.

On the way out they saw the same nurse.

'Are you relatives of Mrs Maxwell?' she asked. Ryan hesitated, frowning.

'She's . . . she's my aunt – well sort of. My great-aunt I suppose.'

'Doctor would like a word if you wouldn't mind?' She led them to a small room at the end of the corridor.

'I may as well come straight to the point,' the doctor said. He looked harassed and in a hurry. 'There is nothing more we can do for Mrs Maxwell. I believe she knows this and accepts it.'

'Yes,' Ryan said.

'We can't keep her here indefinitely, I'm afraid. Once she recovers from the operation she will be fit to go home – say in two weeks or so. Naturally she will need someone there, but she could be moderately well for a time. It's impossible to say how long.' The doctor shrugged. 'It could be six weeks. It could be six months, though I doubt that. She has lost the will to live and there is only so much we doctors can do. The point is,' he sighed heavily, 'she refuses to discuss any plans for when we discharge her. The only contact name we have is a person in Scotland – a Mrs Lucy Greig.' He didn't notice Ryan's start of surprise. 'Apparently she is not a relative. However, we may have to depend on her providing us with instructions if Mrs Maxwell cannot – or will not – make arrangements herself.'

'I – I see. I know Mrs Greig. I'll tell her when I return to Scotland,' Ryan said non-committally.

When they got outside Molly turned to Ryan.

'Why didn't you tell the doctor Mrs Greig is your mother?'

'Well they're not exactly bosom friends after the way Paul's mother treated everybody,' Ryan said dryly. 'I don't want to be responsible for involving Mother.'

'What about Paul? Surely he will want to know how ill his mother is? It doesn't sound as though she will have very long, does it?'

'No. I'll tell Paul we've seen her. I think he has enough problems being responsible for Granny though.'

'Ye-es . . . I suppose he has,' Molly nodded slowly. 'She looks so frail and pathetic though. I wish there was something we could do for her.'

'Mmm,' Paul sighed. 'I know what you mean, but then even I don't know the whole story of her treachery. It's hard to forgive someone who has stolen your birthright, not to mention deserting Paul while he was still a toddler.' Ryan turned to look at Molly. 'Would you ever desert your own child?'

'Oh no!' Molly was aghast at the thought.

'I'm sure you wouldn't,' Ryan said warmly, 'however many

164

problems we have. It would be better to have an abortion now than bring a child into the world and then neglect it.' He shuddered. 'I couldn't bear to do that.'

'Neither could I.' Molly slipped her hand into his. He squeezed it and gave her a warm smile.

'I hated seeing her like that,' he mused, 'and I don't know what can be done about her situation if she has no money and nowhere to go, but all the same, I'm glad you persuaded me to go.'

'So am I. She didn't say much, I know, but I got the feeling she was pleased we've been. It's strange her mistaking you for your father. Do you look like him?'

'Everyone says I do. I can hardly remember him except from photographs. I know he was short and square like me.'

'You're not short! It's a good thing you're no bigger, Ryan Greig, or I'd have only been able to reach far enough to kiss your chest.'

'A-ah, that would never do,' Ryan laughed. 'Paul and my kid brother are both a lot taller than I am though.'

'I don't know Cameron very well.'

'You soon will. Grandfather says he's been at university taking degrees long enough. He's finishing this summer and he's coming back to run Rullian Glen Coach Company, or at least he thinks he is. I don't see Grandfather giving up his business yet though. I expect Cameron will be working there for his Easter vacation.'

'I suspect you and Cameron don't see eye to eye?'

'You're right there. You wouldn't think we were full brothers. We're not a bit alike.'

'It's strange. I've always got on well with Norman and John, even though they're so much older than I am, and even though they do tease me about being Daddy's spoiled brat sometimes.' She smiled fondly, but the smile faded and she stopped walking. Ryan looked down at her questioningly.

'What is it, Molly.'

'I do hope they don't hold it against me . . .' She put a hand against her stomach. 'I mean the way things are, and – and if we upset Mother and Father because of it.'

'I think your brothers will understand,' Ryan said slowly. 'My main concern is that we don't upset your father. I'd hate them to blame us if he had another heart attack.'

Twenty

It was Fiona who met Ryan off the coach at Gretna Green, late in the afternoon of his return. She was cheerful as ever but Fiona was always perceptive and she knew as soon as Ryan was settled in the car that he had things on his mind.

'We'll go somewhere for tea, I think. You must be ready for a cup after all that travelling, Ryan?'

'But we'll be home soon . . .'

'And when you get there you'll be going to do the milking?' Fiona smiled and eyed his plastered arm.

'Well no . . . I can't, can I?' He shrugged lightly. 'So I suppose there's no hurry, unless you . . .?'

'Oh, they'll be pleased to keep me away from the office,' his grandmother chuckled, 'or at least Cameron will. He has a month off for Easter and he's supposed to be helping out.'

'Of course, I'd forgotten he'll be started already. Aren't we going for tea in there then?' He nodded to where the rest of the passengers were still alighting from the coach to stay overnight on the first leg of their Scottish tour.

'It'll be busy booking them all in. We'll find somewhere quieter. There's plenty of hotels to choose from in Gretna, that's for sure.'

While they waited for tea to be brought Fiona asked if he had enjoyed his weekend.

'Oh yes! And thanks for arranging our accommodation. It was super. Really good food.'

'That's what we like to hear. We should send you sleuthing more often, Ryan.'

'Mmm. That would be OK, if I'd nothing else to do anyway.'

'And Molly? Is she well?'

167

'Er . . . yes, yes she's very well.' Try as he might Ryan couldn't hide the telltale colour which flooded his ruddy cheeks. 'She enjoyed it too.'

'So she's not homesick any longer?'

'No.' Ryan bit his lip. 'Can you keep a secret, Granny?'

'I certainly can. But don't confide in me unless it's what you really want to do.'

'Well I can't tell Mother because we don't want to say anything to Molly's parents until our plans are made. We intend to get married as soon as Molly gets her degree in June.'

'You do? Well, I can't say I'm surprised. Neither of you has had eyes for anyone else for the past three years. But where do you plan to live, Ryan?'

'That's the problem. We don't know yet. I . . . er . . . I would like to ask Grandfather's advice first. I . . . Oh hell. I need to ask him for a loan. There! Now you know.'

'Yes, now I know. And you'd like me to pave the way? Is that it?'

'Oh no! Well . . . that's not why I'm telling you. Honestly.' He looked at her earnestly and Fiona was reminded of Lucy when she was a vulnerable teenager. 'But . . . well I suppose you could warn him. If he can't help us I shall ask Paul if we can stay at Wester Rullion until we can afford something else, though we'd rather not if we can avoid it, in the circumstances.'

Fiona didn't enquire which particular circumstances but she eyed him shrewdly. Marriage was obviously of paramount importance to them, and without too much delay. That, plus the fact that Molly had needed to see Ryan so urgently, made her draw her own conclusions.

'Speaking of Paul . . .' Ryan grimaced slightly, 'I think he'll probably be really mad at me. We went to see his mother in hospital.'

'You saw his mother? You saw Gerda?' For once Fiona's usual calm deserted her. 'In hospital you say?'

'Yes, didn't Mother tell you? She gave me the address. She didn't know she was so ill though. She's dying, Granny. She looked awful . . .' He shivered at the recollection.

168

'I see . . .' Fiona frowned.

'Oh I know she did some wicked things. Unforgivable things. But she says she would like to see Paul. I said I would tell him. He's not going to be pleased though.'

'No, I don't think he is,' Fiona said morosely.

'The thing is the doctor asked to speak to us. I don't think anyone else has visited. She won't tell them where she's going when she's discharged from there. He says there's nothing more they can do. She could live six weeks or it could be six months. You wouldn't think she could survive six days if you saw her . . .'

'I see,' Fiona said again. Her mind was mulling over Lucy's possible involvement.

'My mother's name is the only contact they have. I don't think Paul's mother has anywhere to go. I think that's why she won't tell the hospital her plans.'

'I know it sounds harsh, Ryan, but Gerda was a cheat and a liar, as well as a thief and she only has herself to blame if she finds herself destitute and friendless in her hour of need.'

'I know . . .' Ryan said in a small voice. 'I suppose you think we shouldn't have visited her . . .'

'Molly went with you? What impression did she have of Gerda?'

'She thought she looked pathetically frail. I thought she looked like an old woman. Not a bit like Mum. You wouldn't believe they were the same age. Her skin is so yellow too . . .'

'My main concern is that your mother doesn't get lumbered with her, but I can just see it happening if Gerda has nowhere to go. In spite of everything she's done . . . all the hurt she's caused.' Fiona was silent for a moment or two, then she murmured almost to herself, 'It would be just like Lucy to take her in. I can see it now.'

'You . . . you don't think Paul will help her then?' Ryan asked anxiously.

'Can you blame him? I can't.'

'But I have to tell him. And Mother will want all the details . . .'

'Yes. They have to know, I suppose,' Fiona conceded reluctantly. She glanced at Ryan. 'Am I right in thinking you felt sorry for her yourself? You think someone ought to help her?'

'I . . .' Ryan bit his lip and frowned. 'Maybe I'd think differently if she'd been my mother and deserted me, and stolen my inheritance . . . but all the same she looks so ill, so pathetic . . .'

Fiona didn't say anything but in her heart she knew already that Lucy would offer Gerda a refuge if none of the other members of the family would take her in. Fiona knew she would always feel fiercely protective of Lucy, as protective as if she'd been her own flesh and blood.

Ryan lost no time in making a proper appointment to see his grandfather. He wanted to appear as businesslike and responsible as possible. Conan, already warned by Fiona, agreed to see him at the office the day before Ryan was due back at the hospital to have his plaster removed.

The first person Ryan saw when he entered the main office was his brother Cameron.

'What are you doing here?' he demanded.

'I've come to see Grandfather. Do you mind,' Ryan said coolly. Inside he was feeling nervous enough already without any interrogation from someone like Cameron. In fact he'd forgotten he might be here. He had specifically arranged to come when he knew his mother would not be working. He had not mentioned his plans to her, or to anyone else, except Grandmother. Cameron would be sure to tell their mother he had been at the office. Naturally she would be curious that he had come during business hours.

'Well? Aren't you going to let me past?' Ryan asked when Cameron continued to stand four square in front of him with no inclination to move.

'No. Grandfather is busy this morning. Other people have to make appointments to see him, you know.'

'I do know. I have an appointment.'

'You . . .?' Cameron stared at him suspiciously. 'Why would you want an appointment?'

'That's between Grandfather and myself,' Ryan said, his

170

lips tightening. At that moment the inner door opened and Conan put his head out.

'I thought I heard your voice, Ryan. Come on in here. Cameron, ask Jennifer to bring us some coffee and biscuits, will you?' He ushered Ryan before him into his own office and shut the door firmly. Cameron stared after them, open mouthed with surprise. Coffee and biscuits indeed! For his brother too.

'Did I hear your father asking for coffee?' a middle-aged woman asked. 'I'll just make it.'

'Yes, do that,' Cameron said curtly. 'That's my brother in there. I'll take it in.'

'Very well.' The woman frowned. She was disappointed in the attitude of Mr Maxwell's grandson. Rumour had it that he was going to be taking over the running of the company. He had told Judy so himself and Judy was personal assistant to Mrs Maxwell and Mrs Greig in accounts. She was not just a young impressionable girl from the typing pool. Jennifer had been at Rullion Glen for the past ten years but she was beginning to wonder whether she would want to continue if Cameron was taking over the running of the offices.

Conan faced Ryan across the desk. He had already decided what he would do but he had no intention of making it easy for Ryan. He remembered how stern and implacable his own father had been when he had wanted to set up his own business away from Glens of Lochandee and farming. As he grew older he knew he had a lot of Ross Maxwell in him. He hoped he was always as fair as his father had been, but it didn't pay to be too soft in business. Ryan would need to learn that too.

'Your grandmother tells me you and Molly intend to get married as soon as she finishes at university in June? So what plans have you made?'

'I expect you'll think I've an awful cheek to ask you for any more help, Grandfather, when you've been so generous with help to get going at Wester Rullion, but I want to buy one of the cottages down the road from the farm. It needs a lot of repairs. I wouldn't get a mortgage unless I had an official survey done and agreed to do all the things they ask straight away. That would cost a fortune.'

'I see.' Conan frowned and steepled his fingers, surveying his grandson thoughtfully. He wished Ryan had been the one who wanted to join him in the business. 'And would Molly be willing to live in such a cottage?'

'Oh yes! Just so long as we can be together . . .'

'And how do you know the present owners will sell?'

'They've been thinking about it for a while.' Neither Conan nor Ryan heard the door open just a crack. 'They're an elderly couple. I think they'd sell if I could make them a reasonable offer and if they didn't have any hassle with people looking round. But I haven't approached them yet. There's no point if I can't get a loan from you and I do mean a loan. I will pay you back . . .'

'A loan!' Cameron pushed the door wide open now and rushed in with the tray of coffee, slurping it into the saucers in his haste and anger. 'You can't have any more money from this firm! You've already had more than your share. You used it to buy your stupid cattle!' he accused, glaring at Ryan. 'Tell him, Grandfather! Tell—'

Conan had risen to his feet the moment Cameron entered the room. His mouth was a tight line, a pulse throbbed in his jaw, but it was the glitter of his cold green gaze which stopped Cameron's tirade.

'Pack your things. Get out of here. Now!' Conan had not raised his voice. Indeed it was deadly quiet. Cameron stared at him in disbelief.

'But . . .'

'Out! Now! You'd better start applying for jobs.'

'Applying for jobs!' Cameron's voice rose indignantly.

'You heard me. There's no place for you here. You have a lot to learn, Cameron. You go out and learn somewhere else. Now go.' Cameron stared at Ryan accusingly but Conan stopped his accusations before he could utter them. 'Close the door behind you. I have business to discuss.' There was such icy finality in his tone Cameron dared not linger.

Ryan stood up, his face white, his eyes wide and troubled.

172

'I didn't mean to cause trouble. I'd better go now. Th–thank you for seeing me.'

'We haven't finished our discussion yet, Ryan,' Conan said firmly. 'Sit down and drink your coffee, what's left in the cup,' he added dryly. Ryan sat down but he couldn't take the cup.

'Mother will never forgive me for causing a rift between you and Cameron. And she didn't even know I was coming to see you . . .'

'Let me put you straight first,' Conan said. 'No one would cause a rift between me and anyone else unless there was good reason. Cameron has been trying my patience, yes, and the patience of some of my most loyal workers, these past weeks – and he isn't even a member of the team yet. He's just a student doing a holiday job.' Conan gave a harsh laugh and shook his head in amazement. 'Cameron has a lot to learn. I knew that of course. It was one reason I wanted your mother to take an active part in the running of the business. I knew it would be some time before Cameron could be trusted not to throw his weight around unless there was someone to keep him in order. I'm meaning to be around myself for a long time yet, but we never know.'

'But he's probably right. I didn't want to ask for more money . . .'

'Who else can we turn to if we can't ask our family for help in time of trouble, laddie?' Conan sighed. 'I disappointed my own father terribly. He felt I'd let him down because I didn't want to farm. It made me all the more determined to prove I could be a success. I'm hoping Cameron will learn a few lessons. When he has, then we'll consider whether there's a place for him here. Time will tell.'

'Now back to your affairs, Ryan. I will loan you the money to buy the cottage – and maybe one day I'll call it a gift – but I have two conditions . . .'

'Oh?' Ryan said nervously. 'What are they?'

'Firstly that you go and tell Molly's parents what you plan to do before you even ask the old couple to sell their cottage. From what I've seen of Mr Nairne he is not the kind of man to enjoy being presented with a *fait accompli*, especially not when it concerns his only daughter. You must take them into your confidence and tell them what you hope to do, not what you have already done, irrespective of their wishes. Molly needs them on her side.'

'Yes, I see that . . .' Ryan said slowly. 'I wouldn't want to cause any more family quarrels . . .'

'You haven't caused any yet,' Conan reminded him. 'Cameron did that himself, with his attitude. He thinks he should take charge. Make sure you don't do the same with the Nairnes, but in your case by being too independent, rather than grasping at money.'

'You don't think Cameron was jealous of me, then? You believe he was grasping at your money?'

'And authority. He wants to be in charge. He wants power. It's his nature, but it's not his God given right and he needs to learn that. Forget about him for now. You can tell the Nairnes you have the money to buy the cottage. If they agree to Molly living there that's fine, you can go ahead. It's possible they may want to give her some money to modernize it, or even to help you buy a better one together. I don't know how they'll react, but I do know what I'd do if she was my daughter. I'd want to help, and not feel shut out. Consult them and see what happens.'

'Very well, I will. Thanks, Grandfather.' For the first time Ryan smiled. 'I should have thought of their point of view myself. Er . . . what was the other condition?'

'A-ah, you may find it even harder . . . Now that you're aware of Cameron's attitude you will understand why I want your mother to spend as much time as she can in this business. So . . . I don't want her getting involved with Paul's mother again. Gerda Fritz-Allan always knew how to use people and your mother was far too gentle to deal with the likes of her.'

'B–but mother is already involved,' Ryan said in alarm. 'She gave us the address of the hospital. She wanted us to visit.'

'I know that. But from what you told your grandmother it sounds as though she's homeless. I don't want her taking advantage of your mother again.'

174

'Then you don't know Paul's mother is going to be transferred to Dumfries Infirmary by ambulance?' Ryan asked, his eyes wide with apprehension.

'How do you know that?'

'Mother told me yesterday. I think it's worrying her a bit. She can't stay in hospital indefinitely, but she has nowhere to go.'

'So your mother is likely to get landed with her . . .' Conan's brow darkened. 'I was afraid of something like this. Your mother needs someone to protect her from herself . . .'

'But what can I do?' Ryan asked despairingly. He was the eldest of the family. It was his duty to protect her, but how? 'She seems to feel she's doing it for the sake of Uncle Ewan. She says he was almost like a twin brother to her when they were young.'

'Yes . . .' Conan said slowly. 'I suppose that's true.' He sat up straighter. 'But that doesn't mean she owes Gerda anything. She was another grasping, manipulative character. Well, between us we must do our best to prevent your mother becoming her nurse. You'll have to tell Paul about her.'

'I already have,' Ryan said unhappily. 'He says as far as he's concerned he hasn't got a mother. But her only request was to see him . . .'

'I'll bet it was!' Conan said harshly. 'He's her next of kin. The authorities will regard him as being responsible, I suppose.'

'I haven't told him she's being transferred back to Dumfries yet. I've a feeling he'll blame me for that, because we went to see her in hospital.'

'Well the sooner you tell him the better,' Conan said firmly. 'Now that your great-granny is so much improved perhaps Tina would agree to nurse Paul's mother. Bridie can't be expected to keep on paying half of Tina's wages of course, but I'd pay her. I'd rather do that than have your mother take on the job of nursing Gerda. You can tell Paul I'll see to the expenses if he'll keep his mother at Wester Rullion . . .'

'I don't think it would be just the money. Paul doesn't

want to upset Great-Granny all over again. He told me I'd not to mention seeing her in London.'

'I hadn't thought of that aspect,' Conan admitted. 'None of us wants that. Though I've a feeling it will upset her just as much if she knows Gerda is sponging off Lucy . . .' He frowned thoughtfully. Then he looked Ryan in the eye. 'Do you honestly believe Paul's mother is dying? It's not just another of her dramatic performances?'

'Oh no! If you saw her you'd know. Anyway the doctor said there was nothing they could do. They've stitched her up again and he said she would improve for a little while, once she got all the tubes out, but he didn't expect she would have more than six months to live, and probably a lot less.'

'I see . . . Well, you leave Mother to me. I have a feeling I know what was really troubling her regarding Gerda and if I'm right she'll not be upset about Tina caring for her at Wester Rullion. But I'm relying on you to persuade Paul.'

'Then I think you should talk to Great-Granny first,' Ryan insisted. 'I don't know if I can even persuade Paul to see his mother, let alone have her to stay in the same house. Certainly he'd need convincing Great-Granny wouldn't be upset at such a suggestion – and really so would I after the effects the letters had.' He shivered as he relived the moments of finding her unconscious on the floor.

'Fair enough,' Conan agreed. 'My mother is tougher than you think though, once she understands the score. She's faced plenty of troubles in her lifetime but her common sense and wisdom have always seen her through. I think they will this time too. Just don't mention any of this to your mother until we see how things can be worked out.'

'All right,' Ryan nodded, and stood up. He reached out his good hand to grasp his grandfather's across the desk. 'Thank you. For everything.' Conan took the outstretched hand and held it between both of his. For the second time that morning he wished Ryan had been the one to join him in the business. There was something honest and trustworthy about him, a strength of character he had not yet seen in Cameron.

Twenty-One

Paul was puzzled by the letter which bore the name of an Edinburgh solicitor. He turned it over twice before he slit it open, but he was just as bewildered when he had read the contents.

He picked up the letter and went in search of his grandmother.

'She's still in her room,' Tina told him. 'She's getting dressed. It takes a long time but she prefers to be independent. Better knock first.'

'Thanks, Tina.'

'I'm dressed now, Paul. Come on in,' Rachel called in response to his knock. She turned from her chair to look at him. During the period when Tina was helping in the milking parlour she had formed the habit of having her breakfast before she began the laborious process of dressing herself for the day. Even though Ryan was back to work, and Tina no longer went out early, Rachel had continued with this routine. It worked well for both herself and Tina. 'Is something wrong when you want to see me so early in the day, Paul?'

'No, nothing wrong. I've just opened the mail and I've received a puzzling sort of letter from a firm of Edinburgh solicitors. Do you know anyone called Wright – Mrs Dorothea Wright – formerly Sturgeon?'

'No . . .' Rachel wrinkled her brow thoughtfully. 'I don't think so.'

'She died recently, apparently. The solicitors are wanting to contact Paul Ross Maxwell. There can't be two of us, surely?'

'I hardly think so,' Rachel said, puzzled. 'Not with all three names. What do they want?'

177

'This letter simply says they are holding a letter for Mr Paul Ross Maxwell of Wester Rullion farm. It was left by their client, along with her last will and testament, and will I please get in touch with them as soon as possible.'

'I knew a Dolly once . . . but she was your Grandfather Allan's second wife. Her full name may have been Dorothea, but surely she would have been Mrs Allan . . . I usually get a card from her at Christmas. This year I was still in hospital myself and I can't remember who sent cards and who didn't.'

'Oh well, there's only one way to find out,' Paul shrugged. 'I'd better telephone and speak to Mr Findlay, since he's signed this letter. Maybe he can tell me more.'

Paul was put through to the solicitor without delay. After a series of questions, mainly concerning his own identity, Mr Findlay told him Dorothea Wright – known as Dolly – had specifically stated the letter must be handed to him in person and not sent by post or handed to a third person.

'She must have had doubts about it reaching you, Mr Maxwell. Would it be possible to call at our Edinburgh offices?'

'Well yes, I suppose I could come up to Edinburgh. Was Dolly Wright, or Sturgeon, ever Mrs Dolly Allan?' Paul asked.

'No, they were never married. But she did live in Spain for some years with a Mr Allan, or Fritz-Allan,' the man replied without hesitation. 'Perhaps the letter will give you more information. We would appreciate it if you could attend to the matter as soon as possible. There is a small legacy and we should like to clear up the matter without delay.'

Paul found his grandmother in her favourite chair beside the living room fire by the time he had finished on the telephone. He sank on to the old settee while he gave her the rest of the news from the firm of lawyers.

'I always thought they were married,' Rachel mused. 'It was usually Dolly who wrote letters, and when you were a wee boy she never forgot your birthday, or Christmas. She was genuinely fond of your Grandfather Allan and she felt it deeply when he died. I'm sure the feeling was mutual. It's strange they didn't make their union official.'

'Each to his own, I suppose,' Paul said. 'Maybe one

marriage had made him wary of total commitment too. I'll need to make arrangements to go to Edinburgh sometime next week. It shouldn't be so difficult now that Ryan is back to work. The ewes are finished lambing and the barley is all sown.'

'You should make a day of it, Paul. You've had a busy winter. It would do you good . . .'

'What would do him good?' Conan grinned, tapping on the door and coming to join them. He had already spoken to Tina in the kitchen and confided that he wanted a word with his mother, without Paul.

'I think he'll be going outside anyway, but he hasn't had his morning coffee yet. He's not usually in the house at this time of day. He's been busy on the phone,' Tina said.

'Are you making coffee then?'

'I am,' Tina smiled. 'Shall I put on an extra cup?'

'Please. And if you've time to join us you can help me get Paul out of the way afterwards. OK?' Conan gave her his charming smile. Tina nodded, thinking how alike he and Paul were on the rare occasions when Paul was relaxed enough to smile in her presence.

'Well . . .?' Conan looked from his nephew to his mother questioningly.

'I'm suggesting Paul has a day off,' Rachel said. 'He has to go to Edinburgh on business and I thought he should make a day of it.'

'I think that's a splendid idea,' Conan said, standing to take the tray of coffee from Tina so that she could arrange a small table at his mother's side. 'And it would be even better if you took Tina with you. As far as I know she never gets much time off either, except for the odd visit to Megan at Glens of Lochandee, and there'll be no peace for her there.'

'Oh but I'm fine,' Tina said, blushing furiously. She looked across at Paul in embarrassment but he was smiling broadly.

'I think that's an excellent idea,' he agreed. 'A day in Edinburgh wouldn't be much fun on my own. But have you noticed, Tina, how my family do like to organize everybody . . .?' He winked at her.

'Oh but, Paul,' Rachel protested, 'I was only wanting what's best for you. And Conan is quite right, Tina has worked incredibly hard these past months.'

'I'll have a word with Fiona,' Conan said, turning to his mother for support. 'When Ryan went off to London we agreed we should treat Paul and Tina to dinner and the theatre – partly for doing Ryan's work while he was off, but also because both of them have worked so hard since they started up at Wester Rullion. We weren't sure they would stick it out but they seem to be doing fine.'

'Of course we are,' Paul said indignantly. 'We wouldn't have started if we hadn't known it was what we both wanted to do with our lives.'

'All right! All right, don't jump down my throat – not until I've drunk my coffee anyway,' Conan teased. 'You're just like Ewan was at the same age,' he added reminiscently.

'Mmm . . . Well it's past time I was outside or Peter and Ryan will think I've gone back to bed for the day.' Paul drained his coffee cup and stood up, all in one lithe movement.

'So I'll ask Fiona to book dinner for the pair of you one day next week, shall I?' Conan called after him.

'If Tina's willing to risk it,' Paul answered, then put his head round the door again to add, 'and thanks very much, my wicked uncle.' Conan just grinned at him and Tina gathered up the coffee cups and shut the door, leaving Conan and his mother alone together.

Immediately they were on their own the laughter died from Conan's eyes and he grew tense. Rachel had always been able to read his face like an open book and she knew the banter had been all on the surface, but she was pleased he and Fiona were so generous to Paul, as well as to Ryan.

'Is something bothering you, Conan?' she prompted.

'Yes . . . yes it is . . .' He frowned. The last thing he wanted was to cause his mother to have another stroke. She'd made a remarkable recovery and it would be a tragedy if he set her back. Suddenly he was not sure it was wise to mention Gerda's name.

'You might as well get to the point, laddie. It's not like

you to beat about the bush,' she said with some asperity.

'It's Lucy,' he blurted out, which was not what he had rehearsed at all. 'She told you she'd had letters from – from Gerda, didn't she?' He saw his mother tense and his heart sank.

'She did tell me, yes. Does she know Gerda is very ill?'

'You know that?' Conan asked incredulously. 'But how? Who . . .?'

'I may be an old woman, but I still have all my senses,' Rachel said dryly. 'As a matter of fact I've been hoping to talk to Lucy but I haven't seen her on her own for a while.'

'So how did you know Gerda is ill?'

'I overheard Ryan talking to Tina. He was asking her advice. He said he was plucking up courage to tell Paul he had visited his mother in hospital, while he was in London. According to Ryan, Paul refuses to mention her, or to acknowledge he has a mother. I blame myself for that. I never talked about Gerda to him. I was always afraid I might let my bitterness colour anything I told him . . .' Rachel sighed. 'It's so hard to know what's best sometimes.'

'Paul truly appreciates everything you've done for him, Mother,' Conan said. 'But even though you didn't mention Gerda there would be plenty of other people who did, boys at school and that sort of thing. Remember she caused such a scandal at the time, and what people don't know for sure they make up. Besides, he has every reason to be bitter, as we all have.'

'Yes . . .' Rachel sighed heavily. Conan glanced anxiously at her, and hoped he hadn't worried her too much already. 'So why are you worrying about Lucy?' she demanded. 'She's not ill too, is she?'

'Oh no, nothing like that. It's just that Lucy has your forgiving nature – Christian spirit, Fiona calls it.'

'She's a good lassie, Lucy.' Rachel smiled fondly. 'One of the best.'

'Mmm, too charitable for her own good sometimes,' Conan said darkly. 'Gerda always used her. She twisted Lucy around to get what she wanted, just as she did with Ewan in their early years. I'm afraid she might get involved in caring for

Gerda. Ryan talked to one of the doctors. They give her anything from six weeks to six months to live. They think it will be shorter rather than longer. They won't keep her in hospital until – until nearer the end. If she has nowhere else to go . . .' Conan grimaced. 'You know Lucy . . .'

'You think Lucy might agree to take her in? And nurse her?'

'It's just the sort of thing she would do . . . I can't think why in Gerda's case.'

'I can see why you're concerned. No, it wouldn't be right for Lucy to look after her . . .' Rachel nodded. 'You'll have to give me time to think about this, Conan.'

'I don't want to upset you over Gerda again, Mother,' Conan said urgently. He took her wrinkled hand where it lay on her lap.

'But she is dying . . .?' She looked up at Conan sharply. 'There's no pretence this time? No dramatics? I couldn't bear Paul to be used, or to be hurt again.'

'According to Ryan she's a very sick, very frail woman who looks twice as old as Lucy.'

'I see . . . If that's the truth, and if she really has nowhere else to go, this is the place she should be. Give me time to think about it, Conan.'

'So long as you don't allow it to upset you . . .'

'I need to talk to Paul. I must choose the right time, and the right words. Perhaps I should wait until he has been to Edinburgh . . .'

'Please don't worry about it, Mother.'

'I won't.' She gave him a wry smile. 'Gerda can do him no harm if she's dying. It was the old Gerda, the spendthrift, the cheat, the woman who was a stranger to truth and decency, without conscience – she was the one that worried me. I couldn't bear the possibility of her destroying Paul's happiness, as she did with Ewan. I thought she wanted to use Paul, drain his meagre resources. I allowed myself to get worked up at the possibility of her cheating him again. I should credit Paul with more strength of character and common sense. I see that now. Instead I tried to protect him from his own mother. Believe me, Conan, that made me feel so guilty.'

'Yes,' Conan nodded. 'I know. But the circumstances are

different now.' He had hoped his mother might see things this way. 'If Paul does agree to bring her here, I'd be willing to go on paying my half of Tina's salary, if she will agree to stay on and nurse her to the end.'

'You'd do that for Gerda?' Rachel looked at him in surprise.

'No,' Conan smiled sheepishly, 'I'm doing it to protect Lucy from herself.'

'A-ah, I understand that.' Rachel smiled at him and patted his hand with her free one. 'You were never a bad laddie, Conan.'

'That makes me feel about six instead of sixty,' he grinned.

'Sixty plus a few more years . . .' Rachel reminded him with her old dimpling smile. 'A mother never forgets when her first child was born, you know. But you don't look your age, Conan. Fiona must take good care of you.'

'She does. But I could say the same for you now, Mother. Tina has really put you back on your feet.'

'I couldn't have wished for a better, or more thoughtful girl,' Rachel nodded.

Conan went away feeling greatly reassured by the way his mother had accepted Gerda's possible needs. All the same he wondered whether she would feel quite so philosophical about it when she saw Gerda again. That could be the biggest test of her inner strength.

Lucy was in Fiona's office at Rullion Glen, getting on with her work, when he got back. He told her he had been to see her grandmother and they had talked about Gerda.

'You have?' Lucy was astonished.

'Yes. Now she knows Gerda is no longer a threat to Paul's future she's taking it very calmly.'

'But do you really think she accepts the fact that Gerda will need to come back here? I've been so worried about telling her.'

'I think so.'

'Thank God for that,' Lucy said fervently. 'The hospital telephoned this morning. They have made arrangements to transfer Gerda by ambulance to Dumfries Infirmary the day after tomorrow. They expect her to stay there about a week. After that I shall . . .'

'After that,' Conan interrupted sternly, 'I think she should go to Wester Rullion.'

'That's impossible!'

'No it's not, but time is shorter than I thought. Your grandmother is a stronger character than you realize, even now. She is going to find an opportunity to discuss it with Paul. After all, it is his house. And Gerda is his mother. It has to be his decision. Of course he'd need to ask Tina if she is willing to stay on at Wester Rullion, and if she'll nurse Gerda. She may refuse.'

'I don't think she would . . .' Lucy said slowly, 'but there's not much time to make arrangements.'

As usual, when she heard the various problems, Fiona took charge with her calm efficiency and compassion.

'If Paul could arrange to see the solicitor at the end of this week, I could book two rooms for him and Tina for Friday night. They could stay overnight and have more of a break. There is usually Scottish dancing on a Friday night at the hotel I have in mind. Or they could go to the theatre if they choose.'

'That would certainly give Mother more time to talk him round. She seemed to think a little relaxation might mellow him.'

Ryan made up his mind to visit Molly's parents before Paul went to Edinburgh. He had to break the news that he and Molly planned to marry as soon as she finished university in June and he was dreading telling them on his own. Each evening he had found an excuse for procrastinating.

So Thursday evening found him sitting nervously in the Nairnes' elegant sitting room and wishing desperately that Molly was at his side. He had already enquired after her father's health and he didn't know what else to say, or how to bring the talk round to Molly.

'It's good of you to take the time to call on us, laddie,' Mr Nairne beamed, 'especially when Molly's not here as the attraction.'

'Don't embarrass the laddie,' Mrs Nairne chided her husband. 'Have you heard from Molly recently, Ryan?'

'Oh yes,' Ryan nodded eagerly. 'We write at least once a week . . .'

'Of course they do,' Mr Nairne chuckled. 'That's a daft question, Annie.'

'I . . . er . . . We want to get married,' Ryan stammered.

'Well that's no surprise,' Mr Nairne nodded. 'I expect Molly will want to work for a year or two first though, to put her education to good use, save up a bit and suchlike . . .'

'No, er – I mean we want to get married in June as soon as she's finished her degree.'

Mr and Mrs Nairne sat up straighter. They both stared at him.

'Molly's never said anything about a wedding in her letters,' Mrs Nairne said.

'She wanted me to ask you in person . . . She wanted to be sure Mr Nairne was keeping better before we mentioned our plans.'

'You told Molly I'd had a heart attack?' Mr Nairne demanded.

'No, I didn't tell her,' Ryan said truthfully. 'She corresponds with a lot of friends and relations while she's in France. I believe one of them had mentioned that you'd been in hospital,' he said, deliberately vague about the identity of Molly's informant. 'I was able to tell her you were making a good recovery when I saw her in London.'

'Oh that's all right then,' Mrs Nairne said with relief. 'A June wedding . . . That's very short notice – just a couple of months away. I don't know whether I can arrange it all in such a short time . . .'

'Oh we don't want any fuss, just a quiet wedding. Surely that would be better anyway when Mr Nairne is still recovering,' he added with a flash of inspiration.

'Well . . . there is that. Surely a June wedding next year would be better though . . .'

'No! I mean, n–no, we don't want to wait any longer . . .'

'I see.' Mr Nairne was looking at him shrewdly. 'And where do you propose to live if you get married?'

'One of the Bevandale cottages is coming up for sale,' Ryan said. 'It will need a lot of repairs, damp proofing, heating – things like that, – but Molly says she doesn't mind so long as we can live there together. Grandfather Maxwell has promised to help me buy it. That is, he'll help if you agree to the – the wedding . . .' Ryan was doing his best to be diplomatic.

'I see . . .' Mr Nairne said slowly, stroking his chin. 'I see . . .' There was more to this than he could fathom at the moment. It was all the drugs they were giving him. He felt his brain didn't function as quickly as it used to do. He wished he didn't get tired so easily . . .

'I've been going to bed early since I got out of hospital, laddie. I'm better in the mornings – always was, mind you, always was.' His wife looked at him anxiously and Ryan rose quickly to his feet.

'I – I'm so sorry. I didn't mean to tire you . . .'

'Och, it's not that late yet,' Mrs Nairne protested.

'Maybe it's not, but I shall feel better in the morning,' Mr Nairne insisted stubbornly. 'Give us time to think about it, Ryan. It's a bit of a bombshell – losing our wee lassie so soon.'

'Of course we'll not be losing her,' Mrs Nairne said briskly. 'We shall be gaining a son. Isn't that right, Ryan?' She smiled at him. She had always liked Ryan Greig since the first time Molly brought him home. She just wished young folks didn't want to do things in such a rush. It would take time to plan the wedding of her only daughter. Twice Molly had been a wee bridesmaid for her brothers, now it would be her turn to be the bride. Oh she'd be a lovely bride . . .

'I'd better be going, Mrs Nairne,' Ryan said, interrupting her daydream.

'I'll see you out,' she said. In the hall she lowered her voice. 'William will come round, you know. It'll be all right.'

'I just hope I haven't upset him,' Ryan frowned anxiously. He dreaded to think what either of Molly's parents would say when they knew all the circumstances.

'It doesn't take much to upset him these days. I think the heart attack has been a shock to him. It reminds us we're not indestructible, and we are getting older.'

Ryan felt he had not achieved a very satisfying conclusion.

He and Molly were going to get married anyway but he knew Molly would be upset if her parents disapproved. He was supposed to be preparing them and making things easier for her, instead Mr Nairne seemed to assume they would only go ahead with their plans to marry if, and when, he agreed. He didn't realize Molly's father would put him in an even worse dilemma the next time they met.

Twenty-Two

Paul had had no difficulty getting an appointment with the Edinburgh solicitor for Friday afternoon at two o'clock but he had been taken aback when Fiona arrived at Wester Rullion the previous day. He and Ryan, Tina and Granny Maxwell had all been sitting at the kitchen table having tea and scones before starting milking.

'I have booked you both into this hotel for dinner, bed and breakfast,' she announced with a wide smile. 'It's one we use regularly so I get favourable terms and I can recommend it.'

'B–but . . .' Paul looked from Tina to Ryan.

'You'd better take up the offer,' Ryan said. 'Granny promised to treat you two when she arranged my trip to London. It's only fair you should have a bit of free time too after carrying the can for me all those weeks.'

'Well, I don't know . . . What about it, Tina?' Paul looked at Tina with some embarrassment. Supposing she didn't want to spend the night in a hotel with him?

'If you're game, then so am I,' she grinned, quoting back his own comment. 'As a matter of fact I've never been to Edinburgh so if you're sure it will be all right . . .?' She looked anxiously at Rachel.

'Och, don't worry about me, lassie,' she said. 'I'm not an invalid any longer. In any case,' she added dryly, 'if I know Lucy and Bridie they'll both be popping in on the pretext of bringing this or that. I know well enough they're just checking up on me. So you go off to Edinburgh and enjoy yourself.'

'There's some lovely shops,' Fiona told her. 'Even if you only window shop while Paul keeps his appointment.'

'Paul will drag you round the museums and all the historical places if you don't put your foot down,' Ryan warned
with a grin.

'I haven't been to Edinburgh that often myself!' Paul
protested indignantly.

'No, but I remember you dragging us round the castle and
to the Museum of Childhood,' Ryan reminded him.

'Well, naturally I shall be the perfect gentleman as usual,'
Paul grinned, 'when I'm away from your bad influence. I
shall consult Tina on every detail.' He turned to Fiona.
'Thanks for being so generous, Aunt Fiona.'

'It's a pleasure, Paul. You and Tina both deserve a break.'

The following morning Tina felt her spirits rise as she
and Paul climbed into the car.

'We'll go by Moffat and the Beef Tub and we'll come
back by Biggar tomorrow,' Paul suggested. 'How does that
suit?'

'I'm in your hands.' Tina smiled.

'Edinburgh, here we come then!' Paul smiled back. She
felt her heart give a leap. He was an attractive man, but when
he smiled like that he had a magnetism that would be hard
to resist. More importantly he didn't seem at all conceited,
yet he must be aware of his attraction. She had rarely seen
him in a suit and tie, but today he had dressed for his appointment with the city lawyer. His cream shirt showed off his
tanned skin and the muted greens of his silk tie reflected the
green of his eyes. In his well-cut jacket his shoulders seemed
broader, and with his slim hips and long legs, Tina felt her
emotions were in danger of flying out of control.

As they drove up through the wide main street of Moffat
she gazed around with pleasure.

'It's such a pretty town and a beautiful part of the country.
What is the Beef Tub you mentioned and where is it, Paul?'

'Och,' he chuckled, 'it's just a bit further along the road.
We'll stop and have a look. It's where the Border raiders
used to hide their cattle. I suppose the tales about it are a
bit like the old American western films where the ranchers
rustled cattle from each other, or fought the Indians. Here it
was the Scots and English – Raiders and Reivers.' His smile

189

faded and he glanced at her. 'Mind you, there's a bit of sheep rustling even in these modern times.'

'Are you serious?'

'Oh yes. A few beef cattle have mysteriously disappeared from fields, never to be seen again recently. There was a notice in the papers warning farmers to keep a close check on their stock, and to lock up small tools.'

'That's terrible. I expect they slaughter the animals and sell them privately?'

'Well, that's what the police think. Until recently there's never been anything worth stealing at Wester Rullion so we haven't had that worry.'

'I'm pleased to hear it,' Tina said fervently. 'I wouldn't like to meet any thieves on my way across the yard on a dark night!'

'It usually happens after someone has had a chance to snoop around the place. I'm always a bit suspicious of these transit vans wanting to sell things off cheaply, or supposedly wanting to buy scrap metal or machines, or antiques.'

'Mmm, I never thought of that . . .' Tina mused, 'though I suppose some of them are quite legitimate salesmen.'

'Oh yes, of course, they're not all bad. The thefts seem to happen in waves in various areas, up and down the country. I suppose the thieves move on when the police get on their trail. The latest craze in this area is for cattle trailers – the sort that hook on to the back of the pick-up trucks or Land Rovers, like ours. I did hear of one farmer who had his pick-up stolen as well, while he was at the market. He hadn't bothered to lock it so it was partly his own fault. The police never found it. Apparently there are some organized gangs who buy them to respray and sell them abroad. A-ah, look, this is the Beef Tub. Look out for a lay-by and we'll get out so you can see.'

As they stood side by side looking down the steep sides of a green ravine, Tina shivered. The air was crisp and cool after the warmth of the car. Paul automatically put an arm around her shoulders and drew her closer, shielding her from the breeze. It seemed so natural. She looked up at him.

'It's all so peaceful now,' she said softly. 'It's hard to

190

imagine people fighting down there. The farms and cottages along the bottom of the glen look like toys from here.'

'They do now,' Paul agreed, 'but I believe some of the feuds and fights were very bitter. And in the winter this can be very bleak, even dangerous. Further along there's a monument to a postman who died in a blizzard while doing his daily work.'

'Oh . . .' Tina shivered and instinctively snuggled closer. Paul's arm tightened for a moment and he looked down on to the shining red gold of her hair. She fitted so neatly under his arm. It felt right, and comfortable, and . . .

'Come on, Tina, we'd better get back into the car and we'll remember it as a green and pleasant place.' He shepherded her round to her side of the car and opened the door for her. He has such nice manners in such a manly sort of way, Tina thought happily.

'I'm really glad I came today,' she said, speaking her thoughts aloud, 'but I do hope nothing goes wrong with your grandmother while we're away.'

'Och, she'll be fine. Don't worry, Tina. She's almost back to her old self. It's amazing really.'

'Yes . . . yes she is.' Tina was glad Mrs Maxwell had made such a good recovery but her spirits sank a little and the sunshine didn't seem quite so bright. How much longer would she be at Wester Rullion, she wondered. She really didn't belong anywhere anymore. Perhaps she should have kept Great-Aunt Augustine's cottage after all. At least she would have had a base, a home to call her own. But no, that was not the place where she wanted to spend her life. At least she would have enough money to buy herself a house as well as some left over once everything was finalized.

There had been a hold-up because the buyers were having problems with the sale of their own property but surely it couldn't be long now before Mr McNaught had everything signed and sealed. She still couldn't believe she would inherit seventy-five thousand pounds. She hadn't told anyone, not even Megan – partly because she wouldn't believe it until the money really was in her bank, but mostly because she felt it would be boastful to mention it. But money was not

191

everything, she thought sadly. If only they'd had a little more while her father was still alive . . . It would have made his life – and his death – so much easier. He had been so worried about her future.

Even the old corner cupboard, incorporated into the cottage from the time it was built, had been valued at a thousand pounds. The antique dealer had had it carefully removed with the thick wooden plugs carefully kept intact. He was exporting it to America. Aunt Augustine would have been tickled at the idea, Tina was sure. A small smile curved her lips.

'I'm pleased to see that smile again,' Paul teased and lifted a hand from the steering wheel to pat her knee. 'I thought you'd gone all solemn on me since the gory stories of the Beef Tub.'

'Oh, I'm sorry. My thoughts were miles away. I was thinking of Ireland and Great-Aunt Augustine and wondering what my future will hold when I leave Wester Rullion . . .'

'Oh.' Paul frowned slightly. 'Let's just enjoy the present for now, shall we? At least for our next couple of days of freedom. Is that a pact?' He glanced at her. 'Yes?'

'All right.' Tina smiled suddenly and her spirits rose again. 'We'll let the future come to us.'

'That's better,' Paul said with relief. He didn't like the idea of Tina leaving Wester Rullion, and yet he knew she was right. Granny no longer needed a nurse, or even a carer, except for one or two things, but they did need a house-keeper at Wester Rullion. Granny Maxwell would never be fit to do that again. Tina had been remarkable the way she had turned her hand to help with everything, but they couldn't ask her to stay on as a housekeeper. Megan had told them she was planning to go back to university in the autumn and get some nursing qualifications.

'Now you have gone back into your own solemn world, Paul,' Tina teased.

'A-ah! I'm sorry. I must take my own advice and let the future take care of itself. Right now we're coming into Edinburgh and I'd better watch the traffic. Can you follow the directions Fiona gave us for the hotel, please? They're in the glove compartment. If we book in we may be able to leave the car and make our own way from there.'

'Here we are,' Tina said and bent her head to concentrate on the piece of paper.

'Will you mind window shopping while I keep my appointment, Tina?' Paul asked. 'We'll have lunch first of course and we'll arrange where to meet up.'

'That's fine.' Tina smiled. 'I think I'm going to enjoy this. Maybe I'll do more than window shop. I haven't bought myself any new clothes since . . . not since Daddy died.'

'Then you deserve to treat yourself,' Paul said. 'I'll bet your father would have wanted you to be good to yourself occasionally.'

'Yes, yes, you're right. He would.'

They found the hotel without difficulty with Fiona's explicit directions and Tina's guidance. Their rooms were on the same corridor directly opposite each other.

'This is lovely,' Tina said, 'I didn't expect anything as luxurious as this.'

'Mmm, trust Aunt Fiona to do us proud. Shall we lunch here too? I'm quite ready to eat.'

'All right.' Tina looked down at her jeans and the fluffy green jumper which was one of her favourites. 'I think I ought to change though. I feel quite scruffy in these surroundings, and you're so smart today.'

'Thank you, madam.' Paul grinned and gave a little mocking bow. 'You look fine to me but I'll wait if you'd feel better. Give a tap on my door when you're ready.'

Tina had brought a trouser suit which she had intended to wear with her yellow silk shirt for the evening but she decided she would put it on now. It was in a dark brown which she felt matched her eyes and didn't clash with her auburn hair. The jacket was short and fitted neatly into her narrow waist, accentuating her figure. It made her feel good as she twirled in front of the mirror.

Paul opened the door as soon as she knocked.

'Oh my!' he said and gave her a very definite wink and a nod of approval, bringing the colour to Tina's cheeks. He chuckled when he saw her confusion and took her hand, leading her down to find the dining room.

They both chose a light starter of smoked salmon mousse served with freshly made crisp oatcakes and butter curls.

'Mmm, that was delicious,' Tina said. 'I wonder how it was made?'

'I'm glad you came with me, Tina,' Paul said, surprising himself as much as her. 'I mean it's more fun if you have good company, don't you think? Someone to share.'

'Yes, I know what you mean. I'm glad I came too. And I'm looking forward to looking round the shops while you attend to your business. Shall we meet back here?'

'If you're going shopping I reckon we'd better. I . . . er expect you'll end up with loads of packages if you're true to your sex,' he murmured blandly, but with a teasing glint in his eyes.

'Ugh! Cheeky!'

'I know,' he grinned and dodged a playful fist. 'It'll be warmer meeting here though, if one of us happens to be delayed. I've no idea how long I'll be.'

On the way out they stopped to look at the various brochures in the vestibule.

'Oh look! There's a ceilidh tonight,' Tina said eagerly. 'I think I'd rather stay here than go to the theatre. What about you, Paul?'

'I'm at your service.' He smiled down at her, enjoying her enthusiasm. 'I really don't mind how we spend the evening. It'll be nice not having to rush home to milk the cows for a change, or in your case to prepare food.'

'Yes, so it will. If you think there'll be dancing it will be an excuse for me to buy a dress – if I can find one that doesn't clash with my hair.' She pulled a wry face.

'Oh Tina! You've lovely hair. I thought that the first time I saw you, but I was a bit frightened of you then – in case you had a hot temper. Come to think of it you're the first redhead I've met who doesn't fly off the handle at the least excuse . . .'

'Oh? And you've known a lot of "redheads", have you, Paul Maxwell?'

'Ahem . . .' He frowned thoughtfully, then raised his brows in surprise. 'Only one, come to think of it, but she had a temper bad enough for half a dozen.'

'You didn't like her then?'

'I never took the trouble to get to know her,' Paul shrugged.

'So do you have a bad temper, Tina?'

'I think you'd have known if I had. I'm sure it's just a story about people with my hair colour. But I must admit I do get very angry if I'm provoked and, as Daddy would have told you, I don't mince my words then.'

'Then let's hope I'm never unfortunate enough to provoke you,' Paul chuckled. 'I'd hate to be hit on top the head with a frying pan.' Tina looked up at him, her eyebrows raised.

'I think I'd need to grow a bit to reach.'

Paul found the solicitor's offices without much difficulty. It was quite a long walk from the hotel but he welcomed the exercise after sitting in the car and then enjoying a richer lunch than usual.

Mr Findlay didn't keep him waiting long but he settled him in a small ante-room and handed him a letter.

'Perhaps you would care to read this first, Mr Maxwell? You may have some questions when you have read it. I have no idea of the contents. It was sealed when Mrs Wright brought it here. Take your time. I would like to return a telephone call to another client.'

Paul nodded and thanked him. Once alone, he slit open the envelope. There were three pages but the writing was large, round and childlike. Paul frowned as he read. He could imagine the writer being rather anxious and at pains to make him understand her situation, and her feelings for the grandfather he had never known. His mouth tightened as he read.

Apparently Dolly Wright had lived in a small cottage on the Fife coast. It had once been part of a row of fishermen's cottages but she had bought it in 1970. She had paid two thousand pounds for it. She was almost apologetic and at pains to tell him it was a very humble abode. But it was her own and she had made it a cosy home.

His grandfather had also owned a house but Dolly had not

wanted to move to the city. After a serious quarrel with a member of his family he had been extremely upset.

'I'll bet that was with the woman who is supposed to be my mother,' Paul muttered bitterly under his breath. He read on.

His grandfather had decided to sell his own house and move to Spain. He had asked her to marry him. She had agreed to go with him, and to live as his wife, but she had refused to marry him.

> He had only one daughter, and you'll know who that is if you're reading this. Although he vowed he wanted no more to do with her I was afraid she might come back into his life, maybe demand more money, or sell the house, and cause more misery for both of us. So I kept my wee cottage by the sea and let it to tenants.

Paul had the feeling the woman was trying hard not to blacken his mother's name. He read on.

> I didn't know until your grandfather died that he had bought the villa in Spain in my name. I learned later he was protecting me, making sure his daughter couldn't touch it. We were very happy together. Please believe me. We were truly content. Then he died. I couldn't stay there without him. I sold the villa. Please believe me,' she repeated. 'I did feel guilty about you. He would have loved to enjoy his wee grandson – but he said it wasn't to be. He didn't make any conditions. He simply left all he had to me. I was not his widow legally so I could not share his pension. I have been using the money from the villa to live on. I'm sorry, truly I am, but I fear most of it has been used up, even as I write this. I've not much to leave now. I'm giving instructions to Mr Findlay to sell my wee cottage and send the money to you. I think it's what your Grandfather Allan would have wanted me to do. I wish it could have been more.

There were another couple of sentences. Paul folded the letter neatly and slowly slipped it back into the envelope. He put it in the inside pocket of his jacket. He felt a peculiar sadness for the unknown woman. So her cottage, or its proceeds, were the small legacy the solicitor had mentioned. He guessed it had taken Dolly Wright a long time, and a great deal of effort, to write the letter, trying to explain her predicament without blackening his mother's name.

It was as Paul had thought and apart from some legal preliminaries Mr Findlay proceeded to tell him more or less what Dolly Wright had already told him in her letter.

'The cottage has not been put on the market yet. I was not sure whether you might wish to live in it?'

'No. I already have a house,' Paul said briefly, then he surprised himself by asking if he could see the cottage before it was put up for sale. The solicitor went away to get directions and Paul wondered how he could fit in a visit to the cottage. What had possessed him to want to see the home of a woman he had never known? Yet, somehow, he felt he wanted to know something of her. Deep within him he felt a pang of regret that he had never known her, or his grandfather. It was all due to that woman of course – the woman who had borne him but who had never been a mother to him. It only added to the bitterness he felt for her. He could never call her Mother, whatever sad – or sob – story Ryan might tell him.

Twenty-Three

Tina had not returned from her shopping when Paul reached the hotel. He removed his suit and shirt and hung them carefully on a hanger ready for dinner later that evening. He donned the towelling robe provided and relaxed on the bed, hands behind his head as his mind went over the day's events and the letter from the woman he had never met. He felt instinctively he would have liked Dolly Wright.

Half an hour later there was a light tap on his door.

'Come in,' he called. Tina came in looking pink and tousled.

'Oh . . .' she drew back uncertainly at the sight of his long bare legs stretched down the bed.

'It's OK, Tina,' he grinned, 'I'm perfectly decent.' He saw her colour deepen and realized that under her calm competence she was probably quite shy when it came to relationships with the opposite sex. He sat up and swung his legs to the floor. 'These robes are a bit skimpy,' he said pulling at it ineffectively. 'I was just relaxing. I thought I'd better preserve my suit for this evening. I didn't want you to be ashamed of me if you've been buying up half of Edinburgh.'

'I didn't do that, but I have bought myself a new dress. Have you been waiting long?' she asked apologetically.

'No, not long. Am I to see the new dress then?'

'I didn't think you'd be interested in such things.'

'A-ah.' Paul held her gaze with his green compelling eyes. 'I am interested if you're wearing it. Very interested.' She blushed and bit her lip, her heart pounding. Paul in this mood, in these surroundings, was far too attractive for her peace of mind.

'Sure, I – I'll wear it tonight then, for the ceilidh. Will that do?'

'All right,' Paul nodded. 'In that case I'll pull on my jeans and a sweater. What do you say if we have afternoon tea then a walk in the gardens? Or are you too tired?'

'I'm ready for a cup of tea.'

As they walked in Princes Street Gardens Paul took Tina's hand, swinging it as they walked and talked. He felt perfectly relaxed in her company, just as he did with Ryan. His usual wariness of the opposite sex seemed to have deserted him, at least for today.

Suddenly he made his mind up.

'We don't have to rush back home in the morning. How do you feel about driving into Fife?' He chewed his lower lip, but he went on, 'I've been left a cottage. I didn't know the old lady who owned it. She's not even a relative . . .' He flushed slightly. 'She was a close friend of my late grand-father apparently. Anyway it's rather a surprise. I just feel I'd like to see the cottage and perhaps discover a little about her. What do you think, Tina? Are there other things you'd rather do in Edinburgh?'

'No. I'd like to go with you. Do we go over the Forth Road Bridge?' She felt warmed towards him for wanting to see the old lady's home.

'Yes, and then along the coast on the other side of the Firth of Forth. The next-door neighbours have the key. I'd need to telephone and make sure they would be there.'

'Do you think everything will be all right at Wester Rullion?'

'You mean will Granny be behaving herself?' he smiled down at her. 'We'll telephone Ryan to make sure and we can warn him we shall not be back until late.'

Later Tina enjoyed a soak in the luxurious bathroom before she dressed for dinner. The dress had been in the window of a boutique which she had wandered across quite by chance. She had tried on several others before she asked diffidently if she could try on the one in the window. As soon as she came out of the changing room the assistant nodded emphatically.

'It fits you perfectly. Several clients have tried it but none of them have fitted into it so well, and the colour is absolutely right.' Tina smiled but she knew she had to make up her own mind. The dress was a lot more expensive that anything she had ever owned and sales talk was rarely sincere she felt. In this case she was wrong. As she twirled in front of the mirrors the door opened and the owner of the boutique came in. She stopped short.

'I knew that dress would look really special if only it had the right person inside it!'

'I was just telling madam that no one else has fitted into it so perfectly,' the assistant nodded, bending to tweak an imaginary thread.

'You're right. You can knock twenty pounds off, Miss Sinclair, if madam decides to take it.' She swept past them and disappeared behind thick velvet curtains. The assistant raised her eyebrows in surprise.

'It's not often that happens,' she said quietly, 'but it was one of her favourites, and you really do it justice.'

So Tina had bought the dress, as well as a pair of court shoes and a small matching evening purse. Later she had purchased a pair of smart cream trousers and a cashmere sweater. Never in her life had she spent so much money in one day. She thought she ought to feel guilty but she could only feel exhilaration. After all she had not spent any of the money she had earned since she came to Wester Rullion and she had not touched the capital her father had left her. Even if the sale of her aunt's property did fall through – and she half expected it might – she still had more money than she'd ever had before. Besides, she wanted to look special tonight. She didn't stop to ask herself why it was suddenly so important.

Paul had showered and dressed before he telephoned Ryan.

'You make the most of your leisure,' Ryan chuckled on the other end of the line. 'Granny is enjoying being in charge and she's in great spirits. Er – there is one thing though . . .'

'Oh? Something wrong outside?'

'Oh no, nothing like that. It's Molly's parents. They want both of us – you and me – to go there for dinner tomorrow evening. I told them you were away. Mrs Nairne asked if we could make it Tuesday or Wednesday. You will come, Paul?' Ryan sounded anxious.

'I suppose so . . .' Paul frowned at the telephone, 'but why do they want me there?'

'I don't know. I expect they're trying to push me into making arrangements for the wedding. Molly keeps telling them we don't want a proper wedding but we can't convince them. I suppose they'll be expecting you'll be my best man. You will, won't you, Paul?'

'If you say so, old boy. All right,' Paul chuckled, 'I'll come with you on Wednesday night and hold your hand . . . Oh my!' he gasped, his eyes widening as Tina opened the door and came into the bedroom.

'What's wrong?' Ryan demanded.

'Everything's right! Very right! You should just see the beautiful vision that's come to take me to dinner!' he teased. But the gaze he fixed on Tina was filled with admiration. 'We'll see you tomorrow, Ryan,' he said, quickly replacing the telephone receiver. He took Tina's hands, eyeing her approvingly from top to toe until she blushed beneath his scrutiny.

'Do – do you like it?'

'Mmm . . . I like the whole delightful package . . .' Paul murmured, twirling her round so that the skirt of the dress fluttered out like the petals of a flower opening in the sunshine. At first glance the emerald green shot silk looked like a neat fitting sheath showing off Tina's figure to perfection, but below the hips the skilfully cut skirt swirled gently as she moved. The bodice was simple and sleeveless with a deep V both back and front but Tina wore the matching swathe of fine silk around her shoulders. It's watery transparency only added to the allure of her creamy skin beneath it. 'You're truly beautiful,' Paul said sincerely.

'Thank you.' Tina's voice was soft and tremulous. It was only now that she realized how important it had been to her to have Paul's approval.

As soon as they entered the dining room Paul saw it was almost full but immediately a young man appeared at their side to escort them to a secluded table. He was dark haired, possibly Italian or Spanish, Paul thought as his flashing dark eyes rested too long on Tina. Instinctively Paul put his arm behind her, his hand resting lightly on her hip. The young man smiled. The message was as clear as if Sir had shouted it from the roof top, 'She's mine, eyes off her.' As he held Tina's chair, Paul remarked, 'It seems busy tonight?'

'Yes. It ees the danceeng. They do not sleep tonight here. They come many times. They enjoy. This night the music very good.' He smiled widely. 'Scotteesh, Ireesh . . . they dance, they sing, yes?'

'I see,' Paul nodded. 'Thank you.'

Much later Paul leaned across and filled Tina's wine glass for the third time.

'He was right. It's an excellent group. It must be very popular, but a lot of the diners are not so young.'

'No, but they're all good dancers,' Tina observed, watching an elderly couple enjoying the Gay Gordons with all the gusto of people half their age. After that a group of Scottish dancers performed a more intricate dance followed by a tenor singing an Irish ballad and then 'The Rose of Tralee'.

'He's good,' Tina beamed, clapping enthusiastically.

'It's our turn now,' Paul grinned, standing up and coming round to take her hand and lead her on to the oval dance floor at the far end of the dining room. 'We need to dance off some of this excellent dinner.'

'Mmm, it was delicious. I must remember and thank Fiona when we get back.' Tina had almost said back home, but Wester Rullion was not her home, however much she felt she belonged there. She pushed away the darkling spirits which threatened to spoil the evening and allowed herself to be guided through the steps of an energetic jig.

'Phew, I enjoyed that,' she gasped as it ended. 'But where do all these people get their energy? I thought everybody went to discos now.'

'We'll stay on the floor for the next dance,' Paul said, already drawing her into his arms. 'It's a Scottish waltz.' He was aware that the wine had swept aside some of Tina's inhibitions, and he felt relaxed and happy himself. 'I think we should do this more often,' he said softly to the top of her head.

'Mmm . . . Where did you learn to dance, Paul? I remember you and Ryan are both very good.'

'Oh Aunt Lucy, Ryan's mother, saw to that. Anything musical and Aunt Lucy encouraged it. Aunt Bridie too. She used to sing at all the village concerts, and Uncle Nick often sang with her. But it's Aunt Lucy who inherited Grandfather Maxwell's musical talent for instruments. She taught us all to dance and she tried to teach us to play the piano but Kirsten is the only one who is good. Cameron's not bad on the accordion, mind you . . .' He stopped talking and enjoyed the dance. Tina was so light on her feet he felt he could have swept her away.

They were both tired, and more than a little hazy from the wine by the end of the evening. Paul put an arm lightly around her shoulders as they spurned the lift and climbed the wide stairs to their rooms. He paused outside her door but he did not remove his arm as he waited for her to find her card and open it.

Her heart began to beat faster. Did Paul intend coming in with her . . .? Would he . . .? Her knees felt weak, in fact she felt weak all over. As Paul drew her into his arms she knew, for the first time in her life, she would offer no resistance if he wanted to make love to her. She trembled and his arms tightened. He tilted her chin with a gentle finger and looked down into her eyes. She saw the question in his green gaze. She had no resistance to offer. She closed her eyes and leaned against him. Her lips parted as he kissed her. It was a gentle butterfly kiss. He kissed her eyelids. 'Open them, Tina,' he whispered, his lips already moving back to her mouth. Paul was dismayed at the swift, uncontrollable desire which shot through him as he felt her mouth, sweet and soft and yielding beneath his own. He knew Tina must be aware of his arousal. She did not draw away. His kiss deepened. It was almost more than he could endure to withdraw from her now. But he must. He had to . . . He groaned softly as he reluctantly drew his mouth from hers.

'Good night, my beautiful witch . . .' he murmured gruffly. Even then he knew if Tina gave him the slightest sign he would lift her in his arms and make wild and passionate love

203

to her. But Tina offered only a low, muffled 'g' night', and disappeared behind the door like a moonbeam slipping behind a cloud – hidden from sight and completely unattainable.

Paul lay for a long time on the cool sheet, stripped naked, waiting for the sleep which would not come. He had been unprepared for the swift shaft of desire he had experienced with Tina tonight. He had always prided himself on his control. He had always been a little aloof. Ryan kept telling him his attitude only attracted the girls even more, but he was not playing games with them. It was his innate caution which made him wary.

Tonight all thoughts of caution and distrust had been swept away. Tina was different, but her situation was also different; she was his grandmother's carer, employed by his family and living under his roof. She couldn't simply run away or shun him if he took more liberties than he ought. Even the first night he and Ryan had met her they had known she was not a flirt, out to catch a partner at any price, or ready for a one night stand.

Thank God he had managed to salvage a vestige of control. He respected Tina . . . he . . . Paul's thoughts stopped short. He not only respected her – he believed in Tina's integrity, he trusted her . . . Trusted . . .? He who had vowed never to trust a woman, not as his father had trusted his mother, and suffered cruel betrayal. His mind went round and round. But there was no getting away from the way he felt about Tina Donnelly. He could not forget how she had felt in his arms, so perfect . . . how she had responded to his kisses, how he . . . He punched viciously at his pillow. For the first time in his life he understood how Ryan must feel when he and Molly were apart. He understood now what it meant to be burdened with debts. He was as tied to Wester Rullion as if he had been shackled to its gate posts. He had nothing to offer Tina, he thought bitterly, nothing but a huge bank over-draft. His thoughts returned to the woman who had deprived his family of their wealth. She was responsible for his present handicap.

Sleep did not come easily to Tina either. Her cheeks burned and she wondered how she would face Paul tomorrow. He must have been aware of her yielding traitorous body leaning into him. Would he think her cheap? Would he despise her now? And yet . . . and yet he had not been immune . . . Her face flamed anew as she relived the feel of him against her. Her stomach muscles clenched with desire for fulfilment.

They both slept late the following morning. Tina dressed slowly. She could not bring herself to knock on Paul's door. She packed her dress and her overnight bag. She sat miserably on the edge of a chair and wondered whether he had gone down to breakfast without her.

It was not in Paul's character to shun awkward situations. He straightened his shoulders and strode across the corridor to tap on Tina's door.

'May I come in, Tina?'

'Y–yes, of course.' She stood up nervously. He moved into the room, seeing her packed holdall and shopping bags.

'I see you're all ready for leaving.' He looked at her steadily, searching her face with his shrewd green gaze. 'I'm sorry about last night . . .' Tina bit her lip and struggled to lift her eyes to his. He frowned. 'No! I'm not sorry, damn it. I enjoyed last night. I enjoyed your company and dancing with you, and – and everything else! The only thing I'm sorry about is if you think I took advantage when you're living under my roof . . .'

'Oh, Paul, I never thought of that – not at all. And – and you didn't take advantage.' Silently she admitted she almost wished he had. 'I – I . . .We were both a little drunk – I think,' she said in a low voice.

'Mmm . . . Maybe.' Paul knew he had been more drunk with desire than with wine but he let it pass. 'It was a heady atmosphere,' he agreed wryly. 'Now we'd better get down to breakfast before they clear it all away. Then if you'd prefer me to take you straight home . . .'

'No.' Tina raised her eyes to his face. 'Let's go to Fife and see the cottage as we arranged.'

'Splendid!' Paul responded and seized her hand, feeling his spirits rise in spite of the many lectures he had delivered to himself in the small hours of the night. 'We'll come back for our luggage.'

As they drove along the Forth Road Bridge Tina gazed at the wide stretch of water below them. She was fascinated too by the fine structure of the railway bridge.

'I believe by the time the painters get to one end they need to start painting all over again at the other,' Paul told her. His easy teasing had reverted to his usual pleasant manner but Tina missed the easy camaraderie of the previous day. Away from Wester Rullion Paul had been relaxed and happy but now she knew he was remembering his responsibilities, not least that she was employed to care for his grandmother.

They made their way along the coast to the small fishing village and the address which Mr Findlay had given Paul. They found it easily and the woman next door had obviously been looking out for them. She greeted them with a friendly smile.

'Would you like a cup of tea before you look round? I have it ready, and a freshly made scone.' Paul guessed she had probably made the scones specially for them. It would be churlish to refuse, although he suspected the woman was probably consumed with the curiosity of most country people, or perhaps it would be kinder to call it interest.

'We're not prospective purchasers, Mrs Crosbie,' he told her, to save her asking questions.

'Oh, you're not?' She looked disappointed.

'The cottage has not been advertised for sale yet. Did you know Mrs Wright?'

'Och aye, I'd kenned Dolly for years. She was a grand neighbour, aye ready to help. She lived next door when I came here as a young woman, then she went to live in Spain and the cottage was rented out. Some of the tenants were decent folks. Some o' them left the place in a tip,' she said in disgust. 'There now, help yourself to a scone and butter, dearie,' she pushed the plate towards Tina, 'and here's home-made strawberry jam.' She turned back to Paul. 'Now where was I? Oh yes, Dolly went to Spain with Mr Allan. Sad it was, when he died. Really sad. She thought the world of him and they got on so well together. Dolly was never the same after he'd gone. Did ye ken her?'

'No, we never met,' Paul said.

'Then . . .?' Mrs Crosbie frowned. 'If ye're not here to buy the house . . .'

'I just wanted to see where Mrs Wright lived and to hear a little about her,' Paul admitted. 'You see she left instructions for the cottage to be sold and whatever money is left from her estate has to come to me. It seems strange when we never met.'

'Ah, then you'll be Mr Allan's grandson?' Her expression cleared as understanding dawned. She looked across at Tina. Paul hid a smile at her curiosity, but he obliged.

'This is my friend, Tina. She is staying with us, nursing my grandmother back to health, and making a good job of it too.'

'I see. Dolly would have liked to meet you both, I'm sure. Sad the way life turns out. She'd only been married a year when her first husband died. She'd no family of her own.'

'Did she suffer? Before she died, I mean?' Paul asked.

'No. We must thank the guid Lord for that. Just ill a couple of days, she was, with pneumonia. The doctor sent her to the hospital but she died the next day.'

'I see. The scones are delicious,' Paul said, charming as only Paul could be, Tina thought with a pang. 'But we really ought to look at the cottage now and then be on our way. We must get back down to Dumfries this afternoon.'

'I'll just get the key,' Mrs Crosbie said and bustled into the tiny hall. She handed it to Paul.

'I suppose it needs a lot of repairs . . .' Paul remarked.

'Oh no. Dolly was real proud o' her wee hoose. Kept it in good condition she did. It's the same as this. They all are in this wee road, except that Dolly built on a glass porch – a conservatory she called it – after she came back from Spain. She liked to sit in there in the evenings and look out to sea and watch the sun setting.' Mrs Crosbie sighed. 'Aye we shall miss Dolly.'

Paul and Tina made their way up the short garden path and into the cottage. It was in excellent condition and spotlessly clean.

'Mrs Crosbie is making a good job of looking after it,' Tina said. 'That should help with prospective buyers.'

Like Mrs Crosbie's, it had a reasonable sized living room and two small bedrooms but at the end a larger, more modern kitchen had been added on.

'This is lovely,' Tina said. To the side of the cottage the conservatory led into a long narrow garden which reached almost to the cliff top, except for a narrow field where some sheep were grazing. 'It's a beautiful view.'

'Yes.' Paul frowned. 'I feel guilty just being here, let alone accepting whatever money it might bring. When Mr Findlay said she had left me a small legacy I thought he meant a hundred or two. This is far more than I expected. Mrs Wright bought the cottage for two thousand pounds in 1970.'

'That was before decimalization,' Tina said. 'The price of everything jumped sky high after that, according to Daddy. Great-Aunt Augustine's cottage was almost derelict but her solicitor said the ground it sits on has value too. What do you think this will make? I could live here very happily myself . . .'

'Oh Tina, you're not serious?' Paul stared at her. He didn't like the thought of her moving away anywhere if the truth be known.

'Not really I suppose. But everyone should have a base, don't you think, a place they can call home and where they truly belong . . .'

'B–but . . .' Paul wanted to tell her Wester Rullion was her home, but of course it wasn't. He knew she had more ambitious plans for her life.

'I'd like a cottage not too far from Megan, I think,' Tina said firmly, trying to convince herself she must leave Wester Rullion soon. Instead she succeeded in convincing Paul her plans had no place for him in them – and who could blame her when all he could offer was a huge bank overdraft and unrelenting work.

'We'll take the key back and head for home, shall we?'

'If you've seen everything you wanted to see.'

When he handed the key back to Mrs Crosbie Paul asked if the solicitor was paying her to take care of the cottage.

'Och, bless you, laddie, I'm doing it for Dolly's sake. She asked me to take her clothes to the Red Cross so we've done that, but everything else is just as she left it.'

'Well, if there's anything you can use please take it,' Paul said. 'Mr Findlay will be arranging for a house clearance and I shall tell him to see you're properly paid for all your trouble.'

'Oh, Dolly would have loved you, laddie,' Mrs Crosbie said warmly and Tina felt like echoing her words. Paul could be so thoughtful and he certainly didn't grasp at every penny he could lay his hands on. She had heard him and Ryan discussing the farm often enough to know they were constantly short of money for all the improvements and repairs they needed to make, so he could certainly put a legacy to good use. Neither she nor Paul, or even Ryan, could have guessed that it would take a far larger legacy than Dolly Wright's to ease the financial burden which was about to be heaped upon Paul.

Twenty-Four

Rachel knew there wasn't much time to waste if arrangements were to be made to bring Gerda to Wester Rullion. The day after Paul's return from Edinburgh she told him she wanted to speak to him alone. Paul assumed Granny Maxwell wanted to hear about his interview with Dolly's lawyer and the outcome of it.

Before she had time to ask he told her he had visited Dolly's cottage.

'It's in an excellent state of repair. She must have looked after it well. Mr Findlay thinks it could make anything from thirty to forty thousand pounds, less any legal expenses of course.' Paul had thought she would be as astonished as he had been considering Mr Findlay's mention of a small legacy.

He frowned. Granny didn't seem to have taken in what he had said. She fiddled distractedly with a piece of thread she had plucked from the sleeve of her woollen cardigan.

'Paul, I believe Ryan told you he and Molly had visited your mother while they were in London?'

'Yes.' He stiffened and sat up, alert, tense.

'You know she is dying?'

'That was Ryan's opinion.'

'The doctors have confirmed it. It's true.'

'It is not something you need to worry about, Granny.'

'I'm not worried, laddie. Not now I know the reason for Gerda contacting us, after all these years. It may sound cruel . . . but now that she's dying Gerda no longer presents a threat to you, or to any of us. We are alive and well, we have a lot to be thankful for . . .'

'No thanks to her,' Paul reminded her. 'Her letters caused your illness.'

'Yes,' Rachel sighed, 'if only she had said what she wanted, why she needed to contact you. But we can afford to be charitable now.'

'What do you mean?' he asked sharply.

'She has been transferred up to Dumfries Infirmary . . .'

'And you want me to visit her? No! There is no way I can regard her as a mother after all these years . . .'

'I'm asking you to do more than that, Paul,' Rachel said quietly, but her voice had a ring of steel Paul had not heard since he was a teenager. He frowned, wondering what she could possibly expect him to do for a woman he did not even remember.

'She can't stay in hospital indefinitely. They do have a special unit there though and they will take her in when the end is nearer,' Rachel said. 'She is using the name Gerda Maxwell. You are her next of kin. You must arrange for her to come here to Wester Rullion.'

'No! Never!'

'I would like you to ask Tina if she will stay on here and nurse her as long as possible,' Rachel went on as though she had not heard Paul's refusal. 'Conan is willing to continue paying his half of Tina's wages . . .'

'Why should he do that? She's nothing to him.'

'Conan knows Lucy will take Gerda into her own home, if we don't bring her here. He wants to protect her from herself. Those were his words. Lucy is a good Christian, but Conan thinks Gerda will use her again, as she did when they were young. Lucy is too kind for her own good sometimes.'

'I don't want her here.' Even to his own ears Paul knew he sounded like a spoiled child.

'At least discuss it with Tina. We can do nothing without her help anyway. Or the help of someone to nurse your mother if Tina feels she cannot stay.'

'Mother? I haven't got a mother!' Paul's lip curled derisively.

'I know how bitter you must feel, laddie,' Rachel said more gently. 'But we have all done our best to make it up to you. Even Dolly Wright . . .'

Paul frowned at the mention of Dolly. If his Grandfather

Allan had survived her, would he have left the money to his daughter? Or to himself as his grandson?

'Are you saying I owe her a home because Dolly Wright has left me money to provide for her?'

'No. It's ironic. Money was the only thing Gerda craved at one time, but all the money in the world is no use to her now. She needs a home and family. But at least you will have the money to pay for her care, without it affecting your partnership with Ryan and Wester Rullion.'

Paul's mouth tightened. The way Granny Maxwell put things made him feel guilty, unless he did as she asked. He planted his elbows on his knees, clasped his head in his hands and stared at the carpet. They were both silent for some time but eventually Rachel spoke softly.

'At least discuss it with Tina, Paul. If she can't stay and nurse Gerda then perhaps we should look for a private nursing home . . .'

Paul raised his head and stared at his grandmother.

'Are you saying Tina must leave if she doesn't want to nurse her?'

'I shall miss Tina very much when she moves on, but I don't need a nurse any longer, Paul. We're all using Tina. She does everything for us. We're taking advantage of her willingness. You know as well as I do, Tina is an intelligent and capable young woman. In the autumn she will probably go back to university. I believe that was her original intention?'

'Yes.' Paul nodded glumly.

'Well at least ask her if she will nurse Gerda for the next few weeks. When all this is over we must look for a housekeeper. I know I shall never be fit to manage Wester Rullion on my own again, but that's our problem, not Tina's.' Rachel was watching the expressions flitting across Paul's face. She knew how much they would all miss Tina, but she felt Paul would miss her more than he realized. He had to face facts. Nothing in life stayed the same for ever.

'Very well,' he said stiffly and rose to his feet. 'I will discuss it with Tina. But don't ever expect me to call her Mother, or even to see her. Not even if she comes here . . .' He closed the door behind him.

212

Rachel stared after him. How very bitter he was. Dear God, where have I gone wrong? What else could I have done? Should I have talked to Paul about his mother? What could I have said that was truthful, without poisoning his young mind even more? Rachel sighed and put her head back wearily against her chair, silently praying for some sort of solution, some kind of guidance.

Paul was so deep in thought as he strode out of the house he didn't see Tina leaning against the garden wall with a small pair of binoculars in her hand. His jaw was rigid and his whole expression grim. Tina shivered. Paul would make an implacable enemy.

He had paced almost the full length of the garden and back again before he lifted his head and saw her. Tina saw his eyes widen, and for a moment she thought his expression lightened, but if it did it had gone in a flash.

'I didn't see you there. What are you watching?' Even his voice was grim, although the question was normal enough.

'I was watching a pair of great-tits. Look, over there. I think they're nesting.' Normally Paul would have taken the binoculars and looked himself, relishing sharing a few moments of closeness with Tina, but his mind was in a turmoil and even his stomach seemed to churn. He frowned at her without even focusing on her face.

'You look as though you have a problem,' she said at length.

'I have.'

'Can I help?'

'Nobody can. It's that woman! That . . .'

'Which woman?'

Paul stared at her uncomprehendingly for a moment.

'Who? Mrs Gerda Maxwell, that's who.'

'Your mother . . . Then why d—?'

'I haven't got a mother!' Paul almost snarled and Tina drew back a pace. 'She's never been a mother. I wouldn't even recognize her if I saw her in the street. So why should I treat her as a mother now? Tell me that!'

'B–because she gave you life . . .' Tina offered tentatively. 'Because she needs you ⸴. . .?'

'No, she doesn't need me. She never has.' He looked at her then. 'Never needed – or wanted – me, her own flesh and blood! But she does need you. Or at least she needs someone to look after her. Even after all the heartache she's caused this family, Granny Maxwell thinks she should come here . . .' He shook his head, angry and bewildered.

Tina looked at him in silence, chewing her lower lip. She didn't know what to say. She was aghast at his bitterness, the hardness in him. This was the complete opposite of the teasing, generous, loveable man she had known in Edinburgh. Had she been mistaken? Was it possible to love a man who felt so bitter about his own parent? Tina had loved both her parents deeply. She found it hard to understand how anyone could be so devoid of feeling.

'I need a walk.' Paul stared down at her morosely. 'Do you want to come?'

'If you want me to . . .'

'I wouldn't be asking if I didn't, would I?' As soon as the words were out Paul drew a hand across his brow. 'I'm sorry, Tina, so sorry. There's no need to take out my ill temper on you. Will you come? I need you. I need to talk to you.'

'Very well,' Tina gave a small smile, 'so long as you promise not to bite my head off again.'

'I promise,' Paul said with a grimace. 'I just can't understand why everyone is so bloody forgiving and eager to be charitable to Gerda Maxwell after all these years, and after what she did. Not that it's of any interest to you, but how would you feel about nursing her, if I agree to have her here?'

'Well I would do my best.' Tina frowned. 'But you know I'm not a qualified nurse, don't you?' Paul looked down into her upturned face and his own relaxed a little. He took her hand and swung it as they walked.

'According to Granny you have far more common sense and compassion than most of the nurses at the hospital with all their paper qualifications.'

'Thank you. I believe Ryan said your moth—, er . . . Gerda has cancer. I did nurse my father but I had a lot of support from our local doctor, and the district nurses were very good too, at the end.' Her voice tapered away as memories came flooding back. Paul stopped and took her other hand. She saw again the concern in his green eyes. It was hard to believe that moments ago they had been as hard as granite pebbles.

'I shall understand if you feel it is too much of an ordeal for you, Tina,' he said gently.

'No. No, I'll be fine.' She blinked rapidly then looked up at him with a watery smile. 'It's just that Daddy and I were so close. It's hard for me to understand that you have no feeling, no feelings at all for your own parent.'

'I can't remember either of my parents . . . well only the vaguest memories of my father.' His face was bleak again. 'There is one thing you must understand, Tina, if you agree to nurse her.'

'What's that?'

'Don't expect me to see her or refer to her as my mother. She will be just a woman who needs to stay in the same house and who needs your care.'

'I see . . .'

'So think about it. Let me know when you've decided. Arrangements will need to be made to move her by Friday. There's not much time. On Wednesday evening Ryan and I are invited to the Nairnes for dinner.' He grimaced. 'I never felt less like helping anyone make wedding plans but Ryan wants me to be his best man.'

'Of course,' Tina said simply. 'You're good friends. And Paul, I have made up my mind. I will do my best to take care of Gerda Maxwell for as long as possible. But do you mind if I visit her at the hospital before then – just to meet her and to see what sort of treatment and nursing she will need?'

'That's all right with me, so long as you don't expect me to accompany you.'

'No, you've made that perfectly clear,' Tina said coolly. 'I might ask Ryan, or his mother, to go with me though, if you've no objections. I'll arrange it before Wednesday evening.'

'Fine,' Paul nodded.

* * *

215

Mr and Mrs Nairne welcomed them warmly but Paul was surprised to see Ryan so ill at ease and jumpy. Ryan had been sorely tempted to confide in him about Molly and their baby, and gain his support for a quiet wedding, instead of the grand affair Mrs Nairne had set her heart on, but he had promised Molly he would not tell anyone until she had had an opportunity to break the news to her parents herself.

'Well, Ryan, laddie, you haven't eaten much of a meal,' Mr Nairne said, 'and you're as fidgety as a cat on hot bricks. So we'll tell you why we wanted you both here tonight . . .'

'I know it's to do with the wedding,' Ryan said quickly, 'and Paul has agreed to be best man, but Molly really, really doesn't want a proper wedding. She only wants the closest family members. She . . .'

'Och, women never know what they want.' Mr Nairne brushed aside Ryan's protests. 'That's why I thought we men were better to get together – all together – to discuss what I propose to do. I expect you'll have heard the doctor told me to take things a bit easier?'

'Yes, Norman told me. But that's all the more reason not to have a big wedding . . .'

'I'm not talking about weddings! I'm talking about my farm. It's not in me to give it up all together. There'd be nothing to live for. So I've had an excellent idea, and it suits Annie very well too, doesn't it dear?' He stretched an arm towards his wife.

'Very well indeed, but you'd better tell them both what you're talking about.' She smiled. Ryan and Paul looked at each other and shrugged in bewilderment.

'Aye well, you know, Ryan, how much it upset me losing some of my best cows with this BSE business – and it may not be over yet by all accounts. And now the government's bringing in hundreds of new regulations. Every animal born alive has to have two ear tags, and a passport that has to move with it wherever it goes. It's more palaver than registering babies . . .' He shook his head despairingly. 'It's all to do with tracing every animal from the day it's born until the day it dies.' He grunted irritably. 'That's more than they can do with all the men, women and children who live in Britain, not to mention the rest of the world . . .'

'Do come to the point, dear,' Mrs Nairne prompted.

'Aye we-ell, as I was saying. All this paper work, it's getting beyond me. It needs a younger man. So this is what we'd like to do. Annie and me . . . we've seen a nice wee bungalow about three miles down the road. Just being built they are, five of them in a wee crescent. We'd like to buy one and retire – well sort of semi-retire.'

'I see,' Ryan said, frowning, because he didn't really see what this had to do with him.

'Aye we-ell, this is what we want you to do, lad. Instead of buying that cottage you talked about you could use the money, plus your share of Wester Rullion, and you could buy a third share in this place instead – land, stock, machinery – everything. I've had a rough valuation. It's about six hundred thousand, including the land and stock, but you're welcome to have your own valuation done if you want. You'd be a partner with me and Annie.'

Paul stared from one to the other in stunned dismay. Ryan opened his mouth to protest but Mr Nairne was in full flow now. 'The bungalows cost around ninety thousand so we could buy one with some of the money you'd be paying us for your share and we'd have a bit of capital to spare, for changing the car and emergencies. You and Molly would have this house of course and you'd get on with the farming. Of course I'd keep coming back to lend a hand and see what's going on. After all I'm not ready to give up altogether yet, and I shall only be three miles away. It would be better than Molly starting married life in a run-down old cottage, and this will all be hers some day. The sooner you start getting to know the farm, and taking over from me, the better. What d'you say?'

'I – I . . . I d–don't know what to say. I . . .' Ryan looked helplessly at Paul but Paul was staring at Mr Nairne, his face pale with shock.

In fact he felt sick in the pit of his stomach. How could he possibly manage to pay Ryan his share in Wester Rullion? So soon? They hadn't been farming long enough to build up any capital. What little profit they had made had all been needed for repairs and improvements and buying the bloody milk quota. That had been like a stone around their necks from the beginning . . .

Twenty-Five

'I c–can't do that,' Ryan stammered. 'I appreciate your offer, but . . . Paul . . .?' His eyes pleaded with him to say something but for once Paul's usual eloquence had deserted him. He could find no words which were adequate to describe the way he felt.

'P–please . . .' Ryan stammered. 'This is not what I expected. I – I mean I really appreciate your offer . . . But . . .'

'But you want to think it over?' Mrs Nairne suggested tactfully. 'Maybe you want to discuss it with Paul and . . .'

'I must discuss it with Paul,' Ryan said, pulling himself together as his mind began to function more clearly. 'We're partners. Apart from anything else we have an agreement, a minimum of a year's notice on either side. My grandmother insisted on it. Even if she hadn't, I wouldn't leave Paul just like that!' He snapped his fingers. 'In any case my capital and the money for the cottage would never come to the two hundred thousand you're asking. And there's my favourite cows . . .'

'Well you could bring some of them as part of your share,' Mr Nairne said amiably. 'It's the chance of a lifetime, laddie. The place will be yours and Molly's some day, but Wester Rullion can never be yours alone, now can it?'

He made it all sound so reasonable and right – and it was – from his point of view, Paul thought. Of course if all went well for Molly and Ryan it was a wonderful opportunity for them too, he admitted, trying to be fair.

'Say something, Paul . . .?' Ryan pleaded.

'We need to discuss it,' Paul said. 'On our own.'

'Now, lad, there's no need to be difficult . . .' Mr Nairne began.

219

'I am not being difficult, Mr Nairne.' Paul stood up, drawing himself to his full height. 'Ryan and I are good friends as well as partners in business. I would never stand in his way. But you must understand you're pulling the rug right from under my feet with your proposal. Our partnership is binding, on both of us, for a year, but that's no time at all in farming. Your proposal needs some serious consideration. Where do you think I'm going to get the money to pay out Ryan's share of Wester Rullion? Most of the capital for the stock was his. Then we had to take out a bank loan to buy milk quota before we could start. We haven't been farming long enough to make much money.'

'It's not so easy to make money from farming these days, not with all the changes and bickering between the buyers and the power of the supermarkets,' Mr Nairne conceded. He sighed heavily.

'Give them time to talk it over, dear,' Mrs Nairne said.

'Yes, yes . . .' Her husband rubbed his brow. He had had it all planned so well in his own mind . . . 'I suppose you're right, Ryan. But if you can't raise the two hundred thousand, we could settle for a quarter share. What do you think, Annie?'

'I'm sure we could,' his wife agreed, 'and if we gave Molly a share for her wedding present we'd all four be partners together.'

'Now that's an idea!' Mr Nairne nodded vigorously, 'and a generous offer. You've certainly got my women folk eating out of your hand, lad. But we'll need to know your decision soon if we're to put a deposit down on one of the bungalows. Or will you postpone the wedding for a year?' He looked at Ryan.

'No!' Ryan said sharply, then more calmly. 'No, but I do need to discuss all this with Molly.' His heart sank. Her parents might not be so generous, or so amiable, when they knew about the baby and the reason why Molly couldn't be persuaded to have the kind of wedding they would like.

'Och, Molly will agree so long as she knows you're happy, laddie. And you'll be together. Besides this is her home, it's what she's been used to having. Think about her too.'

Paul was driving home but the roads were quiet and Ryan

expected him to be keen to talk but he was silent and pre-occupied.

'There are things the Nairnes don't know yet,' he said slowly. 'Things they might not accept. They might withdraw their offer.' Still Paul didn't answer. In truth his mind was in a whirl. Too many things had happened within so short a time.

There had been the letter from Dolly Wright, the possibility of a legacy he could never have dreamed of having. The prospect of a brighter future at Wester Rullion for all of them.

Then there was Tina. For the first time in his life Paul knew he was in danger of casting aside all his assertions that he would never trust any woman enough to marry. But he couldn't get Tina out of his mind. Somehow she had got under his skin. If he was honest he knew he would never have agreed to take her to Edinburgh at all, let alone stay overnight, if he hadn't enjoyed her company – more than enjoy – he yearned for her . . .

Life was never smooth, he thought cynically. It had been a shock to learn Gerda Maxwell was already in Dumfries, and worse, that his grandmother believed it was his duty to give her a home and care at Wester Rullion. After all the years when none of his family had wanted to talk about the woman who had given birth to him, he felt slightly aggrieved that he was the one who felt wrong-footed now.

But this busines with the Nairnes . . . This was the worst blow imaginable. He would have to sell up at Wester Rullion to pay out Ryan's share . . . or go back to letting the fields to other farmers again and take a job. This was a setback from which he felt he and Wester Rullion might never recover.

'You didn't hear a word I've said, did you?' Ryan demanded.

'Er – sorry, no,' Paul admitted. 'My mind was on other things.'

'Well I'm just telling you I had absolutely no idea Molly's parents had anything like this in mind when they invited both of us. There's a lot they don't know and I wouldn't be surprised if they withdraw their offer.'

'What makes you think that?'

'Oh . . . I must speak to Molly, then I'll tell you. I'll telephone her . . .'

'It's too late to phone tonight,' Paul said flatly. 'And I think it would be better if we don't mention all this to Granny until we've sorted something out. There's no use worrying her.'

'I agree. It might never happen anyway. I wouldn't leave you in the lurch, you know, Paul.'

'I know you wouldn't if you could avoid it, but Molly's father is right, it's a good opportunity – at least it is if you can put up with him interfering until he gets too old to be bothered.'

'Mmm, I hadn't considered that. I think this heart attack has really shaken him up though.'

Late or not, Ryan went straight into the little office to telephone Molly in private. She was getting ready for bed but one of the other girls got her to come to the phone. He told her about her parents' proposal.

'Even if Paul and I can come to some sort of arrangement, I couldn't accept unless they knew about the baby, Molly. They will probably change their minds then. As it is, your mother has set her heart on a proper wedding and she would like us to wait at least until August.'

'We can't do that, Ryan.' Molly was dismayed. 'The baby will be born in September. They'll just have to accept that we don't want a wedding.'

'Couldn't you telephone and speak to your mother, Molly? Or let me tell them. I hate deceiving them like this. Besides, if they are very angry and want nothing more to do with me I need to know. I ought to be putting in an offer for the cottage to make sure we've somewhere to live. There's not going to be much spare room here either. Paul's mother is coming to stay. Tina is going to nurse her.'

'Is she?' Molly's surprise was evident. 'I thought you said Paul didn't even want to talk about her.'

'He doesn't. The word "mother" is anathema to him. He refers to her as "that woman" or Gerda Maxwell, if he mentions her at all. I think Tina is finding it hard to understand that he can be so hard and unforgiving to his own mother, but she doesn't know how badly she treated him. Anyway we've enough problems of our own. What are we going to do, Molly?'

'I'll telephone Mother tomorrow. The problem is the telephone here is so public. Everyone can hear so I'm not promising to tell her over the telephone, but if the right opportunity occurs I – I'll try to break the news about the baby. If only we didn't live in such a small community where everybody gossips. They'll be sure to say I caused Dad's heart attack, you know.'

'Well we know better, and that's all that matters,' Ryan comforted her. 'Will you let me know if you do tell them?'

'Of course I will, Ryan,' she said softly and blew him several kisses down the telephone.

'If only they were real,' he groaned.

'Only six more weeks, then we'll be together . . .'

As it happened one of the lecturers who had become a friend and mentor to Molly in her early weeks in France offered her the use of her private room at the university and Molly asked her mother to phone her back.

'I'll not need to speak in French to get through, shall I?' her mother asked anxiously.

'No, the number I've just given you is a direct line.'

After a few preliminary greetings Annie Nairne moved eagerly to the subject of the wedding and Molly's heart sank. She understood now what Ryan meant. They couldn't let her parents go on making plans – even in their heads.

'Mum, I'm sorry to tell you this over the telephone, but there's no other way. I really want to stay over here until I finish my course. At least I shall get my degree and I hope you'll be proud of me for that at least.'

'Molly, we're always proud of you . . .'

'Please listen, Mum,' Molly pleaded, feeling suddenly near to tears as she visualized her mother's eager loving face. 'I'm afraid you're going to be very disappointed with me over the wedding and – and other things.'

'What other things, dear?'

'We don't want a big white wedding because . . .' Molly took a deep breath and expelled it as though it was her last. 'Because Ryan and I are going to have a baby in September.' There she'd said it. She could almost see the stunned expression on her mother's face. 'Mum . . . are you still there?'

'Y–yes . . .'

Molly could tell she was struggling to take in what she'd said.

'Mum, I'm so s–sorry to tell you over the telephone like this.'

'Oh, Molly . . .' Annie Nairne fumbled for her handkerchief and blew her nose, trying to come to terms with her daughter's news. 'I . . . I can't believe it. Babies are such a big responsibility and you're so young . . . You'll have no time to enjoy life . . .'

'Mum, Ryan and I are going to be married. We shall be together. That is what I want from life – to be with Ryan. He – he wanted to tell you himself. He thinks Father will withdraw his offer of a partnership now. We shall understand if he does. Ryan will try to buy the cottage near Wester Rullion and we'll live there. So long as we're together, that's all that matters. I – I'm sorry you're so disappointed in m–me . . .'

'Oh, Molly . . .' Her mother was weeping openly now. 'Just give me some time to get used to – to the idea. I had such plans for you . . . It seems only yesterday you were a baby yourself . . . a–and now . . .'

'Mum, I'm twenty-one. Lots of girls have babies at seventeen – and younger. They manage . . .' Molly lifted her chin defiantly. 'And so shall we. Ryan and I will be together.'

'Y–yes. Can I telephone you later?'

'Not on this number, it's a private line. You have the hostel number?'

'Y–yes. I'll telephone tonight. And, Molly . . .'

'Yes, I'm still here, Mum?'

'Are – are you k–keeping well? Have you plenty of money? Are you eating enough good food?'

'Yes, Mum . . .' Molly smiled tremulously at the telephone receiver. Whatever her father might have to say, she knew now that her mother would accept things, when she had had time to recover from her initial surprise and disappointment.

Her father might be a different matter. Molly loved him dearly but she was aware he had always held rigid views about the way people should behave. She set her mouth firmly and thrust out her small chin. She would hate to quarrel with her parents, but there was no going back now. The baby, hers and Ryan's, was well on the way. He would have to accept that things were different to when he was young. At least we're going to be married, she consoled herself, that's more than a lot of young couples do.

Tina had received another letter from her great-aunt's solicitor. The money from the buyers had still not come through, so the sale could not be concluded. Mr McNaught still felt they should hold on, rather than put the cottage on the market again. Surely his advice was sound? After all her aunt must have trusted him. She had heard all sorts of stories about lawyers embezzling their clients' money, or putting it in their own bank accounts to gain interest as long as possible. The McNaughts had been so kind and hospitable towards her she couldn't believe they weren't trustworthy. Even so she had considered asking Mrs Maxwell if she could make a visit to Ireland just to see for herself what was happening, but now that Gerda Maxwell was arriving in the morning she knew it would be impossible to leave Wester Rullion.

Lucy had accompanied her to the infirmary to meet Gerda. In spite of Lucy's efforts to prepare her Tina had still been shocked at how ill and frail her prospective patient looked. On the way home afterwards she remarked on this to Lucy.

'She looks too ill to be discharged from hospital. Don't you agree?'

'Yes.' Lucy sighed and glanced at Tina before returning her eyes to the road. 'I think time is running out faster than the doctors thought for Gerda. I'm almost sure she has insisted on them discharging her. I think she's still hoping to see Paul and make her peace with him. Did you notice how eagerly she looked towards the door when we entered, and how she seemed to sag when she saw there were only the two of us?'

'You think she was expecting Paul to visit?'

'Maybe not expecting, but I'd say she was certainly hoping he would be with us.'

'He's adamant that he doesn't want to see her. He says he doesn't regard her as his mother,' Tina said in a troubled voice. 'Did you know that he insisted on changing bedrooms. He is sleeping downstairs next to Mrs Maxwell now. I'm to sleep in his room so that I shall be next to Gerda Maxwell.'

'But why?' Lucy asked, bewildered.

'The reason he gave to me was that I couldn't attend to both of them. He says he will hear his grandmother if she gets up during the night. But I think the real reason is so he doesn't need to see Gerda. Now that I've seen how weak she is I don't think there's any likelihood of her going downstairs and bumping into him, do you?'

'Oh no. She could never make it. I expect Ryan told Paul how ill she is. I do hope you will not find it all too difficult, Tina,' Lucy said anxiously. 'Please give me a ring if there's anything I can do. If you need me to sit with Gerda or something like that . . .'

'Thank you. I'll remember. But it troubles me that Paul can be so unforgiving and so harsh with his own parent.'

'It troubles me a little too.' Lucy frowned. 'It's not good for anyone to bottle up so much anger and hurt inside. Yet I can understand how bitter Paul must feel after the way Gerda behaved, and especially when she still ran away and left him, even after Ewan was killed. I know Granny Maxwell has thanked God many times that she's been given the health and strength to look after him until he was able to take care of himself.'

Molly's mother was almost afraid to break the news to her husband about the baby. She feared he might fly into one of the uncontrollable rages which had so beset him during the weeks before his heart attack. She didn't want to cause another. Since his return home from hospital he had reverted to his former calm and reasonable self. He still liked to organize everyone of course, she thought with a little smile, but he had always been like that. It was his nature and part of his success as a farmer.

226

When they had finished their meal that evening he looked at her with that penetrating stare which had turned her bones to jelly when they were young and courting.

'For goodness' sake, Annie, sit down and stop messing about. Come and tell me what's on your mind.'

'Why should I have anything on my mind?' she countered warily.

'I don't know, but after all these years I know something's bothering you.'

'Well, promise me you'll keep your temper and not work yourself into a state then. I couldn't bear you to have another heart attack, and Molly would blame herself . . .'

'A-ah,' he nodded. 'So it has something to do with Molly, then? I hope it's not this damned wedding again. If they don't want a fuss, why should we worry? Look on the bright side, at least it'll cost a lot less . . .' He grinned at her.

'I know you're not so miserable that you'd grudge the money, William Nairne.'

'So what's wrong then?'

'I – I've found out why they're so set against a proper wedding. They're expecting a baby . . .'

'They're what?' William Nairne stared at his wife for several seconds. Then he grimaced. 'Well, it's not the first time it's happened, and it'll not be the last,' he said resignedly. 'I'm sorry it's done you out of arranging the wedding of your dreams for your only daughter though, Annie lass.'

'Oh, the wedding's not important now . . . We-ell, I admit I'm a bit disappointed the way things are. There'll be plenty of gossip in the village.'

'Times are changing, lass. We've got to face it. At least they are meaning to get married, I take it?'

'Oh yes, definitely.'

'Well, that's something these days. I suppose the bairn will be due about September, eh?'

'September?' Annie stared at him open-mouthed. 'How do you know that?' she demanded almost accusingly.

'It's not hard to figure. At Christmas it was plain to see Molly was taking it hard because she wouldn't be seeing Ryan for so long when she'd to go to France. If you put a young bull with a bunch of heifers you'd expect to get calves, wouldn't you . . .'

'Oh, William! Don't be so crude!'

'Well, it's true, lass. It's only nature. They've gone together a while now. They love each other. They were going to be separated . . .' He shrugged. 'I suppose we might have expected something like this, except that I thought most young folks took precautions these days.'

'Well, they obviously didn't,' Annie said crossly. 'Anyway, Ryan told Molly he wouldn't even consider your offer of a partnership until they'd told us. They seem to think you'll withdraw now. That's why Molly had to tell me over the phone.'

'I see . . .' William Nairne frowned and sat deep in thought. His wife watched him anxiously. She had really set her heart on one of the new bungalows. But whatever William decided she would go along with it, as she always had since they were married.

'The way I see it,' he said at length, 'yes, the way I see it is this. If Molly's going to have a baby to care for, so soon after getting a husband to look after, then she's going to need a decent house to live in, not some old cottage that needs lots of work to make it habitable. We might be a bit disappointed by the way the pair of them have carried on, but I'll tell young Ryan the least he can do now is to give my lassie a good house to start off their married life. By that I mean I expect him to find the money to become a partner with us, and get himself moved in here as soon as he can come to an agreement with Paul Maxwell.'

'You mean you do still want Ryan to become a partner with us?' Mrs Nairne said jubilantly.

'That's what I said, didn't I?'

'Yes, William, I suppose so, in your usual roundabout way. Shall I go and telephone Molly now then? I said I would phone her tonight.'

'All right, you go and do that first. When you come back I reckon we ought to invite Ryan's family here for a meal and discuss things round the table.'

'You mean his mother?'

'Yes, and his grandparents. After all they helped him start up in partnership at Wester Rullion. Maybe we should ask Paul and old Mrs Maxwell along as well. They're Ryan's family too, and they're involved in all this.'

'All right.' Annie Nairne went off to telephone Molly with the news that her father had taken everything in his stride but he was going to insist Ryan must become a partner now. He wanted to see them settled into the farmhouse before she had the baby.

'But Mum!' Molly protested. 'Ryan can't just walk out on Paul without his year's notice to dissolve their partnership. And Paul would need to find the money to pay Ryan's share.'

'Oh, Molly! I thought you'd be really pleased that your father has taken your news so well . . .'

'I am, Mum, really I am. But we have to consider other people . . .'

'Well your father proposes that I should invite all Ryan's family here for a meal so that we can discuss everything. Even if you're having a quiet wedding it still needs to be arranged.'

'Y–yes, of course,' Molly agreed wearily. Although she was relieved she felt desperately tired. She had worried all day about how her father would take the news of the baby and whether it would upset him or make him ill again. She hadn't been able to eat either. Now she felt faint and drained.

'So now we can put a deposit down for one of the new bungalows,' her mother said happily.

'Yes, Mum. Let me know how things go. I'll have to ring off. Someone else wants the phone.' That was not strictly true but Molly wanted nothing more than to curl up in bed and sleep for a week. It didn't occur to her that her mother would telephone Ryan's family immediately.

Twenty-Six

L ucy was surprised when she heard Mrs Nairne's voice on the telephone. Her first thought was there must be something wrong with Molly. She listened carefully, scarcely able to take in what the older woman was saying.

'Am I right in thinking you had no idea what they've been up to either?' Mrs Nairne said when Lucy's stunned silence eventually registered.

'None at all,' she said briefly. She felt incredibly hurt that Ryan had not had the courage to confide in her himself. Had he asked Molly's mother to break the news to her instead? Was she so much of a dragon that her own son couldn't tell her what was happening? Molly was expecting a child. My grandchild, she thought with a tumult of conflicting emotions. However will they manage? They would have so little money. Will Molly leave the baby and take up her career? But Mrs Nairne was talking volubly now and Lucy had to make an effort to listen. The shocks were not over.

'I'm sorry,' Lucy apologized, 'I must have misunderstood. Ryan is already in partnership – with Paul . . . at Wester Rullion. I thought you knew that?'

'Yes, yes, dear, we know that. But as I was saying William is ready to take things easier since his illness and now that Molly is going to have a baby we feel it's only fair they should move into the house here. We'll talk it all over if you can come to dinner. We thought next Thursday night at about seven. We'll see you then.'

Lucy was dumbfounded. Mrs Nairne had rung off before she had had time to gather her wits. What can she possibly mean? I must get to the bottom of all this nonsense, she thought, and dialled the Wester Rullion number.

230

As well as feeling hurt Lucy was angry with Ryan. Of her three children he had rarely been the one to cause her any anxiety – until now.

It was Tina who answered the telephone.

'I'm sorry, Ryan went back out to mend a fence after he finished his evening meal. Can I ask him to phone you back?'

'Yes, please do that, Tina. In fact if he doesn't phone in an hour you can tell him I'm coming right over there tonight.' Tina seemed so much a part of the Wester Rullion household Lucy forgot she was not speaking to a member of the family. 'Tell him I don't take kindly to getting the news of my own son's wedding and baby and various other things he's planning, from someone else . . .'

'I – I'm sorry, Lucy. You seem terribly upset.'

'I am. I feel very angry. Oh just listen to me! I shouldn't be taking it out on you, Tina. It's just . . . I've had Mrs Nairne on the phone and . . . oh, never mind. But don't forget to tell Ryan to phone me as soon as he comes in.'

Tina had no sooner put the receiver down than the telephone rang again. This time it was for Rachel.

'I will get her to speak to you on her extension,' Tina said. 'Can I ask who is calling please?' Tina nodded and went to ask Rachel if she would speak to Mrs Nairne on her bedroom extension.

Five minutes later Rachel called Tina back.

'The Nairnes have invited Paul and myself to dinner next Thursday,' she said with a frown. 'She says it's to discuss the wedding arrangements for Molly and Ryan. Apparently Molly is expecting a child. Did you know that, Tina?'

'No. Ryan has never mentioned it to me.'

'Nor to me. Lucy must have known of course. I wonder if Paul knew? She said something about Ryan going into partnership with Molly's father. I couldn't understand what she was talking about. Ryan is already in partnership – here, with Paul. Surely the Nairnes know that. When Paul comes in will you ask him to come in to see me, even if I'm in bed? My mind will be going round and round all night if I don't speak to him.'

'Oh, I do hope not,' Tina said in concern. 'It's not good for you . . .'

'I shall be all right, dear, don't you fret, but I shall sleep better once I know what's going on. My imagination is often worse than the reality these days.' She smiled at Tina.

When Fiona and Conan received a telephone call from Mrs Nairne with an invitation to dinner they were left feeling just as confused as Lucy and Rachel.

'She seems very excited,' Fiona said, 'but I couldn't understand what she meant about Ryan going into partnership with Molly's father.'

Before Tina could pass on the messages to Ryan and Paul the telephone rang again at Wester Rullion. This time it was Molly who had fully recovered from her earlier exhaustion.

'Ryan is just taking off his boots, Molly, I'll put him on if you wait a second.' She called through to Ryan to hurry, then asked, 'How are you, Molly?'

'Oh, Tina, I'm so happy now, I can't believe it. It's all such a relief! Everything is falling into place for us. Mum has even accepted that we must have a quiet wedding. Will you be my bridesmaid? I shall still need one, don't you think?'

'I don't know, Molly,' Tina chuckled. 'Only the bride can decide that, I believe. Here's Ryan . . .' She handed the receiver over. 'You're to telephone your mother afterwards. It sounds urgent,' she said in a low voice. Ryan looked strained and tense, but he nodded.

When Ryan said goodbye to Molly and put the telephone down he gave a great yelp of joy and whirled into the hall, just as Lucy walked in.

'Mum! What are you doing here? I've some great news for you . . .' He stopped in front of her, his grin fading as he saw her expression. 'There's nothing wrong, is there?' he asked sobering instantly. Lucy looked back at him, her lips tight, her green eyes, so like Paul's and Rachel's, were glinting with angry tears.

'How do you suppose I felt hearing about my own son's wedding – and his baby – from someone who is almost a stranger?' Lucy gritted her teeth and blinked back her tears, unwilling to let Ryan see how much he had hurt her.

'You know! But how? I've only just spoken to Molly. I've only just heard myself . . .'

'Only just heard!' Lucy echoed scathingly. 'Only just heard you're getting married in a few weeks' time! Only just heard you're going to be a father in a few months' time!'

'But, Mother . . . Look, come into the kitchen and I'll make you a cup of tea and . . .'

'I don't want a cup of tea!' Lucy said angrily, but Ryan was already propelling her towards the big warm kitchen. Tina turned from the cooker.

'I've just made a tray of tea, if you'd like a cup,' she said quietly. 'I'm going to bed now. Gerda is arriving by ambulance in the morning . . . Oh, and Ryan, I think Mrs Maxwell may want a word with you.' She gave him a sympathetic glance. 'She's talking to Paul just now, but Mrs Nairne phoned here too.'

'God! She must have been busy! Molly only told her about the baby this afternoon.'

'Oh . . .' Lucy said, feeling her anger begin to ebb away. Ryan was so like his father. She had always found it difficult to be annoyed with him for long. 'If Molly was telling her mother this afternoon why didn't you come and tell me?'

'Because Molly wasn't sure whether she would be able to mention it. What with her father's heart attack and one thing and another. I've been longing to tell you, Mum, honestly.'

'All right,' Lucy nodded, 'I'll believe you, but what's all this about going into partnership with Mr Nairne and living at the farm?'

'A-ah . . .' Ryan's face fell. 'Now that's another matter altogether. I'm glad everything is in the open now. Paul knows about Mr Nairne's idea. We were both invited there for dinner last week and he sprung it on us. He wants me to use my share of Wester Rullion, plus the money Grandfather Maxwell is lending me to buy the cottage, and buy a quarter share in his farm. It would include a share in the land as well as the stock. Paul admits it's a great opportunity but we both know there's no way we can take that amount of cash out of Wester Rullion and leave it as a viable business for Paul.'

'I see . . .' Lucy frowned. 'Poor Paul . . . He no sooner begins to find his feet than something happens to knock him back. First Gerda shows up on the scene again, and now this. No wonder he can't get over his bitterness. If Gerda hadn't stolen all the assets when she ran away with that horrible man, then Wester Rullion would have been just as prosperous as the Nairnes' place.'

'I know, Mum. But it doesn't solve anything now, does it,' Ryan said unhappily. 'Paul and I will talk it over, but I don't see how I can take up the Nairnes' offer.'

'Neither do I, not without it putting Paul out of business. But the way Mrs Nairne talks, it's clear they think you owe it to Molly to take up their offer so that she will have a decent home, especially now that she's expecting a baby.'

'Molly doesn't mind where we live, so long as we're together.'

'Maybe not, but she'll not want any ill feeling between you and her parents.'

'But surely they'll see I have to behave honourably towards Paul.'

'I have a feeling the Nairnes are used to making decisions and expecting everyone to fall in,' Lucy said dryly, 'though I don't doubt they mean well in this case,' she added quickly, in case Ryan felt she was criticizing his future in-laws, 'and if you could have accepted without it affecting Paul and Wester Rullion I would have been very grateful to them on your behalf. I'm sure your father would have been proud of the way you and Paul have worked since you left college.'

'I'll let you know, Mum, as soon as Paul and I have had a proper chance to discuss everything,' Ryan promised. 'And Mum . . . I'm sorry Mrs Nairne jumped the gun with our news, but we're both relieved they've accepted the baby and everything so well.'

'Yes, I suppose so.' Lucy sighed. 'Tell Tina I'll come over and help her settle Gerda tomorrow. I'll speak to Granny then too. It's getting late to disturb her now. Goodnight, Ryan.'

Paul stayed with his grandmother a long time that evening, much later than usual for Rachel. Although she was an old lady Paul was amazed at her grasp of the problems he would face if he and Ryan ended their partnership so soon. She talked to him about the struggles she and his grandfather had had when they first went to Glens of Lochandee, and how the war and the demand for home-produced food had helped them pay back their debt to the bank, and later to take yet another loan to buy Wester Rullion.

As she talked, Paul realized she was offering him encouragement to keep Wester Rullion going, even if he had to do it alone.

'It's impossible to look into the future, laddie. You can only do the best you can as each change comes along. Farming was different then. We had a bit of everything – eggs and pigs and sheep, as well as milking cows, and we had to grow corn whether we wanted to or not. The nation was desperate for it. Now everything is streamlined. If your main enterprise fails, the whole business fails, so you think carefully . . .'

'I will. I am,' Paul assured her, 'but it costs so much for equipment before we can even begin now – with milking parlours and bulk tanks, and we've still got a bank loan for the milk quota we bought. I feel I have no option but to use it all to the full.'

'I do see that, Paul. All I'm saying is I think you should spread your income if you can.'

'You mean I shouldn't expand the dairy herd as we had planned? I suppose I could make do with the quota we've got so far, at least for now, but I'd need to keep more sheep, and grow more corn to use the land to the full . . .'

'Yes, but even if you do have to go back to letting some of the fields to other farmers again it would be better than selling up completely and it wouldn't be for so long this time.'

'No . . . I suppose it's worth bearing in mind . . .' Paul frowned as he thought it over, 'and there would only be me to keep, instead of the two of us. By the way did you know, Granny, Peter will be sixty-five in August? He was telling me the other day he intends to draw his pension but he'd like to keep on doing a few jobs for as long as he's fit. Maybe if I keep fewer cows for a while we could manage between us . . .'

'Well, think about it carefully, laddie, work it all out as far as you can in this uncertain world. If you believe you could make it work you'll need to see the bank manager. I'd like you to do that before we go to dinner at the Nairnes' next week, if you can. Make up your own mind, then stick to it. I don't want Mr Nairne telling you what to do.' She set her lips in the way she used to do when she was young. His grandfather would have recognized that determined look very well indeed.

When Paul left her he realized he had expected Granny to be anxious and upset about the Nairnes' offer. He had felt they should protect her from any knowledge of it. Instead she had seen the whole thing as a challenge for him. She had faith in him too. At least if he was on his own he would have no one else to consider, or to blame, if things didn't work out. His mind was too active, considering possible solutions and rejecting them. Sleep eluded him until the early hours and in consequence he overslept and was tired next morning.

He saw the ambulance arrive but he didn't wait around to see the patient. When he and Ryan went in for lunch Gerda was already settled into the bedroom where she had first stayed as his father's girlfriend more than twenty-five years ago. She was very weak. Already she wondered what had possessed her to give in to her longing to return to Wester Rullion and to see the son she had abandoned all those years ago.

Lucy had arrived to help Tina settle Gerda into her new surroundings, but all she wanted was to go to bed. Later that afternoon Bridie arrived. She had never had any liking or respect for Gerda but she did not shirk from greeting her. More importantly she had brought a gadget for Tina which Megan had recommended.

'Megan says it will save you running up and down stairs to check how she's doing every five minutes,' Bridie smiled as she handed it over. 'She has one for the children so that she can hear when they waken up, or need anything.'

'Oh yes! I've seen Megan's baby listener. Thank you. Though at the moment Gerda doesn't seem to want anything except to doze.'

'Mmm . . .' Bridie looked cynical, 'that doesn't sound like the demanding Gerda we used to know, but time will tell. I hope you can cope, Tina, but please let us know if you can't. Has Paul been up to see her yet?'

'No. I have a feeling that is the only thing she really wants, and the one thing Paul has no intention of doing.'

Even Rachel made an effort to climb the stairs, with Tina's help. She made sure Gerda had everything she needed.

'Paul carried up this comfortable armchair specially,' she said, 'and he bought this table for rolling over the bed.' She hoped these small things might compensate Gerda a little for Paul's absence.

'Mmm, he's been making sure I shall stay out of his way, I see,' she responded dully.

Paul's mind was so preoccupied that he barely gave Gerda a thought. As soon as the evening meal was over he disappeared into the office. He did the same the next evening and several more after that. Tina believed he was making sure he didn't run into Gerda. Perhaps he didn't realize she hadn't enough strength to go up and down stairs anyway. Tina's manner towards Paul became short, her tone sharp.

She had felt respect for him . . . No, it was more than that . . . she had been in danger of falling irrevocably in love with him, she admitted honestly to herself. Obviously it had been just an illusion. She couldn't love any man who treated his own mother so harshly.

Paul noticed the change in Tina but he assumed she was probably tired too. He was preoccupied with facts and figures, and plans which he continually considered and discarded.

It was the morning of the Nairnes' dinner invitation before Paul eventually got an appointment with the bank manager. He explained what had happened, and the possibility of a change in the partnership at Wester Rullion. Mr Cranley knew William Nairne well and he nodded.

'Yes. Since his heart attack I can see it might be the best solution for William to have his son-in-law as a working partner,' he said after a short deliberation, 'but I do see how difficult this makes things for you, Mr Maxwell.'

'I have inherited a small legacy – possibly thirty to forty

thousand pounds,' Paul said, 'but that still leaves seventy thousand I need to borrow to pay out Ryan. I have drawn up plans for the next five years, and a cash flow as far it's possible, given the vagaries of the weather and the ever changing policies of politicians . . .'

'Yes, it is not easy to forecast what the future holds for farming at the present time. If you'll let me see your ideas please? You do still own the land at Wester Rullion, don't you?' He looked sideways at Paul.

'Oh yes, the land is mine, but most of the capital belonged to my cousin.'

'Land is one of the best securities the bank could ask for in this uncertain climate and we do need security with inflation soaring as it is. Even so I wouldn't like to see you needing to sell your farm to pay off a bank loan which should never have been granted to you in the first place. So draw up your chair and we'll go through these figures.'

When Paul came out of the bank he felt as though he had been through a milling machine. He stifled a yawn. Mr Cranley was willing to set up a loan for him with Wester Rullion as security, but the interest alone would make a huge hole in his budget. He felt ravenously hungry but he had a sudden urge to talk all this over with Aunt Fiona. She was the best person he knew when it came to finance and shrewd judgement. He would value her opinion and probably follow her advice.

Paul and Fiona went over his plans for the immediate and long-term future of Wester Rullion and Fiona asked him a lot of questions. When he was ready to leave Paul was surprised when Fiona thanked him for being so helpful.

'I think I'm the one who should be thanking you,' he grinned.

'No, you've helped me understand quite a few of the present problems in farming, Paul, as well as a few terms which were unfamiliar to me. We accountants may understand balance sheets and figures but we don't always understand the special problems which apply to some specialist businesses. You see in the city an accountant would never consider a business to be viable if it had so much capital tied up as you have in Wester Rullion, yet generated so little profit in return. Our discussion has helped me see that land is a different type of asset. I needed to know some of these facts before we join you all for dinner tonight.'

'Oh gosh, yes, I'd better hurry. But you've given me one or two ideas worth thinking about to improve my cash flow in the first year. Thanks.'

In his heart Paul knew keeping Wester Rullion was the most important thing in the world to him – or so he believed until he arrived back home, very late for lunch.

Tina was just coming into the kitchen carrying a tray. She looked tired and pale. His heart lurched at the sight of her and he had a sudden urge to gather her in his arms and protect her. Fiona agreed the bank loan was the most sensible way forward if he intended to let Ryan withdraw from their partnership. But if he went ahead with a large loan it would be years before he had any spare cash, or could afford to keep a wife. A wife! His train of thought brought him up short and he stared at Tina.

'Your lunch is in the bottom oven,' she said wearily. 'You'll have to help yourself. You're very late. It'll probably be all dried up by now.'

'I know, I'm sorry. I went to see the bank manager. Tina, You look dreadfully tired . . .'

'Your mother had a very bad night,' she said, deliberately using the word mother and half expecting him to flare up at her, but he barely seemed to notice. She blushed faintly under his scrutiny. He was looking at her almost as though he had never really seen her before and it made her insides tingle, in spite of her exhaustion and her resolution to smother her burgeoning love for him.

'I heard you up several times during the night,' he said. 'Her room is just above mine.'

'I know. She couldn't sleep. I telephoned the doctor this morning. He's calling in later. He'll probably leave another prescription for her. Would you be able to collect it from the chemist?'

'Yes, of course. Ask which one is doing late opening though, will you? I'll go in straight after milking.'

239

'Aren't you supposed to be going to the Nairnes' for dinner tonight?'

'Yes, but it's more important you have the prescription for her and it'll not take me long. Tina, if she sleeps this afternoon, couldn't you have a rest too? I hate to see you looking so exhausted.'

'I'll see how things go.'

'Do you want me to ask Lucy to come over and relieve you?'

'No thanks, not yet. I have a feeling there may be a lot of disturbed nights to come yet.'

'I see. Maybe we shall have to see about getting her back into hospital . . .'

'She really doesn't want to die in hospital. She wants to stay here. I'll manage a while yet.'

'All right, but . . .'

'Just leave it, Paul. She's where she wants to be now.'

'Strange, when she couldn't wait to get away,' he said almost under his breath. Tina looked at him sharply, but there had been no bitterness in his tone, and none of the usual derision on his face. Instead he seemed preoccupied, as he had been for days now. Was something else worrying him besides his mother being here?

Twenty-Seven

R yan began to fret about being late for the Nairnes' dinner party when he heard Paul had to go into the chemist's to pick up a prescription.

'Uncle Conan and Fiona are picking you up,' Paul told him. 'I'll bring Granny in the pick-up truck. That way we shall not all be late. Also Granny and I can come home earlier, if she's tired.'

'All right, but try not to be too late.'

Paul kicked off his wellingtons and yanked off his boiler suit.

'Which chemist am I going to, Tina?' he called as he washed his hands.

Ten minutes later he parked the truck in the small car park at the back of the shops and ran round to the front. He didn't pay much attention to the four men loitering in the square, but he did notice a child tugging at the trousers of the tallest man and hopping from one leg to the other, obviously desperate for the toilet. He had almost reached the door of the chemist's when he heard the child cry out. He could hardly believe his eyes as the tall man tossed the toddler in the direction of one of his three companions. Taken by surprise the man almost dropped the boy. He managed to grab him by the arm in time to prevent him crashing on to the cobbled square. With barely a pause he threw the screaming toddler on to the next man as though he were a rugby ball.

'Nige, catch the brat!'

But the man, who was standing with his back to Paul, was laughing drunkenly with the first man. He was short and square and there was no way he could catch the child, even had he been prepared for him hurtling towards him.

241

Instinctively Paul dashed forward, just in time to catch the screaming toddler before he hit the cobbles. As he turned he saw the assistant in the chemist's had pulled the door wide open.

'Bring the wean in here, Mr Maxwell!' she gasped, anger and indignation in every line. Behind her the pharmacist was hurrying forward to relieve Paul of his howling bundle.

'Bar the door, Jane,' he commanded swiftly. 'We don't want the drunken louts in here, even if this poor wee fellow does belong to one of them.' He held the child against him, oblivious of urine now streaming down the boy's legs, and tears and mud soiling his pristine white coat. He hooked a leg around a chair and sat down with the child on his knee but the little boy screamed in pain at the movement. The pharmacist frowned and gently felt the boy's limbs, telling him to shout if anything hurt. He certainly did that with an ear-splitting scream.

'I think he has dislocated his shoulder, or possibly torn the ligaments. Telephone for an ambulance, would you, Jane?' He frowned as two of the men hammered on the door, peering in. 'And alert the police while you're at it,' he said grimly. One of the men standing further back looked vaguely familiar to Paul, but he couldn't imagine being acquainted with such stupid scoundrels and they were all wearing woollen hats pulled well down their faces so it was impossible to be sure of their identities.

'I was in rather a hurry,' he said apologetically to the pharmacist. 'I'm sorry I was a bit late getting in . . .'

'Just as well you came when you did,' the man said grimly, 'or I fear this wee chap might have been seriously injured. He's in enough pain as it is but he would almost certainly have suffered a severe head injury if you hadn't caught him.'

'The police are on their way, and an ambulance,' the assistant reported. She was carrying the prescription which Paul had come to collect.

'Prescription for Mrs Gerda Maxwell?' she asked. 'Can you just sign here please?'

'Jane, I think you'd better take Mr Maxwell through the back and let him out of the other door. Are you parked in the car park, Mr Maxwell?'

'Yes, I am, but . . .' He glanced outside and saw the four men were still waiting, shouting, and bickering with each other.

'It would be safer.' The pharmacist nodded. 'They're like wild animals cheated of their prey.'

'I'm sure that tall fellow and the thickset one are on drugs,' Jane remarked contemptuously. 'This way, Mr Maxwell.'

The incident was banished from Paul's mind in the bustle of getting bathed and changed and helping his grandmother into the truck for the drive to the Nairnes'.

Mrs Nairne was an excellent cook and hostess and the dinner went smoothly with conversation flowing easily up and down the table. Lucy had been edgy since the day Mrs Nairne had phoned with the news that Molly was expecting a child. Gradually she began to relax as she realized Mrs Nairne was one of those people who were never happier than when they were organizing home entertainment. Later she was won over when Annie Nairne confided what a shock it had been when her husband had suffered his heart attack.

'It made me realize how sad you must have felt, and how difficult your own life must have been after losing your husband while you were both so young.'

'I've had a lot of help and support from my family,' Lucy said simply.

'Even so you have made a good job of bringing up your children. We've always liked Kirsten ever since she and Molly became friends. We're sorry she will be in Australia for the early part of summer but Molly says it was all arranged before Kirsten knew about the wedding.' She grimaced slightly. 'They did rather spring a surprise on everyone, but we couldn't have chosen a nicer boy than Ryan for a son-in-law. I do so hope he will manage to come to an amicable arrangement over the partnership.'

'Ah yes.' Mr Nairne had overheard the tail end of his wife's conversation. 'Have you reached a decision yet, Ryan?'

'I . . . er, I . . .' he looked at his grandmother uncertainly. Fiona had warned him on the way here what she intended to do.

'Before Ryan makes a decision, Mr Nairne, I wonder whether you would let me have a look at your accounts?' Fiona said pleasantly. 'I am his accountant you see and my husband and I are his guarantors.' Mr Nairne stared at her, his mouth slightly open in shock. Only his own accountant ever saw his books.

'I'm sure you would never buy a share in a sweet shop, or any kind of business, without looking to see what you were buying before you handed over your money?' Fiona smiled. Even Conan, who was so used to seeing his wife in action, had to admire the firm, yet gentle manner in which she handled Mr Nairne. She had such an air of calm and dignified authority that Mr Nairne could think of no reasonable way to refuse her request.

'W—well . . .' he stammered, 'when you put it like that . . . I suppose you are only looking after Ryan's interests . . .'

'Had his father been alive I'm sure you and he would have reached some agreement on behalf of the young couple,' Conan said. 'I assure you my wife is a qualified accountant and discreet in the extreme.'

'Oh, I've nothing to hide,' Mr Nairne said quickly. 'I'm just so used to making the decisions and nobody ever questions them. I'm beginning to see it might be different having to discuss things with a son-in-law, eh, lad?' He looked at Ryan who smiled back nervously. He hoped his grandmother wouldn't upset Molly's father.

'We'd better go through to the room I use as an office then, Mrs Maxwell. You'd better come too, Ryan.' As they moved away from the table Fiona caught Paul's eye and she gave him a broad wink.

'A-ah.' He let out a long breath, now he knew why she had asked him to explain so many points about farming and different methods and yields, earlier in the day. He stifled a yawn. It seemed to have been a very long and eventful day.

Fiona and Ryan were closeted in Mr Nairne's office for what seemed a very long time, but Mrs Nairne had moved them through to the comfort of the large sitting room and she kept the conversation going, asking Conan about his various package holidays, and discussing recipes with Rachel and Lucy. Even so, Paul was relieved to see the other three returning.

'Everything seems to be in excellent order,' Fiona said, 'so now I believe it's up to Paul and Ryan to reach an agreement over their own partnership.' Ryan looked at Paul uncomfortably.

'You know how awful I feel about us splitting up . . .' he said awkwardly.

'Yes,' Paul nodded. He looked across at Fiona and she smiled and gave a faint nod of encouragement. 'Well then – since you and Molly are rushing into a shotgun wedding,' he grinned wickedly at Ryan as Mrs Nairne gasped, 'I don't think you're going to be much use to me at Wester Rullion. You'll be too busy drooling over your wife and baby, and working to help your new father-in-law . . .'

'Hi, steady on!' Ryan protested, but Paul only grinned. Inside he didn't feel like grinning at all. He just hoped and prayed he could make a go of things with the hefty loan he would be taking on.

'This is what I thought. If you take your choice of ten of our cows, the ones you're always going on about, we'll have them valued. I'll make your share up to a hundred thousand in cash . . .'

Ryan gasped. 'Can you manage to do that, Paul?' he asked anxiously.

'Just wait until you hear the rest of my proposal,' he said and caught his grandmother's eye, her nod of encouragement. He gulped. 'As I said, you'll be wanting to spend your time here with Molly so I thought we could end the partnership in three months' time, instead of the year we originally agreed, but . . .' he looked at Ryan seriously, 'if you do that you'll have to wait until I get the thirty thousand or so for the cottage. That might take a while, depending on the demand for houses up there. If Mr Nairne wants his full whack before you move in here,' Paul shrugged, 'then you'll have to borrow the rest from the bank, as I'm having to do.'

'Oh, I don't think that'll be necessary,' Mr Nairne said

quickly, 'I can wait, so long as I know it's coming eventually. Within a year, say.'

'That's it then.' Paul looked across at Ryan and got to his feet. 'Now I think it's time Granny and I went home. It's been a long day.' Ryan followed him into the hall while Mrs Nairne found Rachel's coat.

'Thanks, Paul,' Ryan said quietly and squeezed his shoulder. 'You've always been the best friend I ever had. Molly and me . . . we'll not forget.' His voice was husky and Paul was alarmed he was going to get emotional.

'OK, pal,' he said briskly and thumped Ryan on the back. 'You'd better go and keep sweet talking your father-in-law,' he summoned a grin, 'at least until you've got your feet firmly under the table.'

Tina had given Gerda the medication as the doctor had recommended and for the time being it seemed to have eased the pain in her back sufficiently to let her sleep. She knew she ought to take the chance of an early night herself, especially as the doctor had warned her Gerda would require a repeat dose every four hours to keep the pain at bay. He had told Gerda herself she would receive more effective pain control in the hospital with the modern methods of administering medication, but she had become very agitated. She insisted she would suffer the pain so long as she could stay at Wester Rullion.

Tina sighed and settled down in Rachel's armchair beside the Aga to watch the news. She must have dozed for she sat up with a start. She checked the listener but there was no noise from Gerda's room. Then she realized it was the sound of an engine. Could it be Paul and Mrs Maxwell home? But the engine sounded more like a tractor than the pick-up truck, and not a very healthy tractor at that. Frowning she opened the back door and looked out into the yard.

She stared in astonishment. It was a tractor, but it was certainly not Paul or Ryan driving it, judging by the way it was being revved and weaving about as it came down from the upper yard where the machinery was always kept.

Tina turned back into the house and flicked the switch for the yard light. It illuminated the square in front of her and the buildings surrounding it but it did not reach around the corner to the oncoming tractor with its dazzling headlights. As it came closer she saw the cattle trailer was hitched on behind.

Something was wrong. The tractor was coming closer. Someone must be stealing it. Then she remembered Paul saying how a warning had gone out to farmers about the thefts of tools and trailers. The thieves must have thought there was no one at home with the house in near darkness and the pick-up truck gone. They would be gone before the police could get here – unless she could delay them . . .

She wished fervently she hadn't been in the house alone, but there was only one thing to do. She must shut the two heavy gates which blocked the entrance to the road, and which Paul and Ryan only ever closed when they were moving cattle around. She dashed across the yard, aware that she must be plainly visible in the pool of light, but the tractor and trailer were already coming drunkenly down the slope into the lower yard.

She swung one heavy gate closed but when she went to the other side the gate would not budge, then she saw the big stone propping it open and she bent to roll it away, just as the tractor started across the square yard. Using all the strength she could muster she managed to dislodge the stone. The gate swung free. She heard a man shouting something but she ran with the gate. Pulling the two together and slamming down the huge hook which held them shut. The tractor had put on speed. She realized the driver either could not stop it or he was intent on ramming the gates and running her down. Frantically she leapt to the side.

Out of the glare of the headlights Tina could see there were two men on the tractor, one driving, the other standing on the draw-bar behind. Just as Tina braced herself for a crash the driver managed to slew to the side, almost throwing the other man under the wheel of the trailer. Tina heard him swear, then over the noise of the engine he yelled furiously,

'I thought ye said ye could drive yin o' these bluidy things, Nige! Ye nearly haed me killed. Yer a bluidy fool.'

'It was that woman. Didn't you see her? She shut the gates. Wait 'til I get my hands on her . . .'

Twenty-Eight

Tina shrank back into the shadow of the dry stone wall which surrounded this side of the farmyard. Her heart was thumping wildly as she calculated whether or not she could sprint to the door of the house and lock it. Even if she did, would it be sufficient to keep the men out? They were bound to see her when she crossed the lighted square.

'Switch off the headlights, can't ye!'

'They'll help me find the girl.'

Tina gasped and edged further along the edge of the wall, but she dislodged a stone and knew she dare not risk moving again. She curled herself up as small as she could, pressing into the shadow of the wall and hiding her face and hands in case the man should see them pale against the darkness.

'Never heed the girl. Get the gates open and let's get this trailer away. Jock willna wait all bluidy nicht in the lay-by, not wi' yon Range Rover.'

'You open the gates yourself while I see where she's hiding. She didn't run back to the house, did she?'

'How the hell wad I ken! I wis hanging on for ma life. Ye damn nearly killed me the way ye drive that bluidy thing.'

'I didn't know Maxwell was living with a woman. When I find her it'll be better than stealing his trailer – even if it is for Jock and his horses.'

'What have ye agin the man? 'Twas my bairn he took. Bloody good job he did. Ye'd hae dropped him and spilled oot his brains 'stead o' his bladder. The police wad hae haed more tae rave aboot then.'

Tina's teeth were chattering so much she thought they would hear her as she huddled in a cramped-up ball against the wall. Her head was bowed against her knees so she didn't see the arc of light which swept across the gates but she heard one of the men swear.

'There's Jock coming to find us.'

'Got tired o' bluidy waiting, didn't he?'

'He can hook the trailer on himself now then and get it out of the way. Open the gates, Lanky, while I look for the girl . . .'

'Bluidy hell! That's no' Jock! It's a truck . . .'

'It's Maxwell! Let's get out of here . . .' Tina raised her head just enough to see the two men run off in the direction of the upper yard and the fields beyond. Then she heard the pick-up stop at the gate. She tried to get to her feet but her legs felt like jelly and she was stiff and cramped. In the light from the pick-up Paul began to open the gates, but the tractor was only a couple of feet away.

'Paul!' Tina called, almost sobbing in her relief. 'Paul . . .' she edged her way along the wall into the beam of light.

'Tina! What's going on . . .?' He hurried towards her and gathered her to him. 'You're trembling. What's happened? Why is the tractor . . .?'

She began to tell him but her teeth were chattering so much the words would barely come out. Paul had heard enough to guess she had foiled thieves attempting to steal the tractor or trailer or both.

'Never mind them now. They've obviously run off. We must get you back to the house. You're shivering . . .' He called to his grandmother to wait in the pick-up until he returned, then he scooped Tina up in his arms and carried her to the house. In the light and warmth of the kitchen he saw how pale she was and realized she was badly shaken.

'It's shock,' he said. 'Now sit in that chair and don't move until I return.' He grabbed a travelling rug from the back of the chair and wrapped it round her. 'I must get Granny inside. She's had enough excitement for one day.'

Tina nodded and huddled into the chair, trying to overcome her shivering. She knew it was just reaction. She had felt so terrified and then the relief of Paul returning had made her want to weep. How silly could she get . . .?

It took some time for Paul to move back the tractor and trailer away from the gates, bring the pick-up truck to the door and see Rachel to her room, and all the time he was longing to be with Tina. At last he returned to the kitchen.

'Granny has gone straight to bed. I don't think she realized we had had thieves about so I didn't enlighten her,' Paul said.

In fact the lights from the truck had clearly illuminated the closed gates, the tractor and then, to the edge of the beam of the lights, she had watched Paul gather Tina into his arms. For a few moments he had stood there, gazing down at her. Like a blinding flash Rachel saw what should have been so clear to her long ago. Paul loved Tina. She wasn't even sure whether he realized it or not yet, but to her, seeing the tenderness as he held her close, and witnessing the concern on his lean face, every instinct told her this was the case. She decided her own curiosity about the strange events could wait until morning.

'I'll make you a drink of hot chocolate and lace it with brandy, Tina,' Paul said. 'It will warm you up.'

'I – I'm not really cold . . .'

'Well you're still trembling. The brandy will calm you down.' Paul's voice was gentle and concerned and Tina ached for him to hold her, yet how could she possibly love a man who could treat his own mother so harshly he would not even acknowledge her existence? Resolutely she put aside the blanket and stood up. Paul had just put milk into a pan and set it on the hot plate. In two strides he was at her side, sitting her back into the big chair.

'It won't be long, Tina. You need it or you'll never sleep and you look exhausted.'

'No, no, I mustn't take the brandy. The doctor said I was to give Gerda her medication every four hours, no more, no less. I must stay alert.' She glanced at the clock on the wall above the cooker. 'She will be due soon.'

'Never mind that. You need this. You've had a nasty shock.' His face grew grim. 'You can tell me all about it in the morning. I think we must tell the police, but for now I insist you drink up.'

'But, Paul!' Tina protested as she saw him pouring in a generous measure of brandy.

'Drink it, and don't worry,' he commanded.

Tina felt too weary to do anything else, but as she cradled the hot mug in her hands and sipped it slowly she felt the warmth seeping into her and her trembling began to subside. She had almost finished when they heard the first stirrings from upstairs on the listening device, followed by a faint moan. Tina knew Gerda would be ready for her medication. She sighed inwardly. It could be several hours before she slept again. As though reading her mind, Paul looked at her, then his mouth set in a firm line.

'You administer the medication, Tina, then go to bed. I'll listen in case she needs anything.' Tina looked up at him, sorely tempted to do as he suggested. He looked so strong and manly. Her heart leapt. Yet there was no doubting the determined set to his features. He would never be easily influenced, however hard she tried to persuade him that his mother needed him now, more than he had ever needed her. Gerda craved his forgiveness for whatever sins she must have committed. Tina had heard many snippets and hints but no one had ever told her the full story of Gerda's misdeeds. Surely they couldn't be so very bad. Surely a man with any capacity for love and compassion should be able to forgive his own mother. She stirred herself from the lethargy which was threatening to overwhelm her.

'No, Paul. I'm paid to nurse her. You're tired too and you may not hear her when you're downstairs.'

'You're exhausted. I'll take the listener to my bedroom.'

'You might switch it off instinctively and go back to sleep.'

'All right,' Paul's mouth set stubbornly. He knew what he had to do and he would do it – for Tina's sake. 'Wait here until I come back. I'll not be a minute. He disappeared and Tina heard him going into his room. She leaned her head back and closed her eyes, wondering how long she would manage on her own. Gerda grew so very restless when the drugs began to wear off.

A few minutes later Paul returned. He had discarded his suit for a pair of clean jeans and a thick sweater.

'Come on, Tina, I'll take you upstairs. You can administer the medication then I'll see you to bed – even if I have to undress you and put you there myself.' He looked down at her, meeting her startled gaze. She drew in her breath. She could see by that determined look that he really meant it, and he was quite capable of carrying out his threat, she knew.

'B–but . . .'

'No buts. I'll wait with her for the next four hours. I'll doze in the big chair right beside her bed. I shall be on the spot. So . . .'

'You will?' Tina stared up at him, her brown eyes round with surprise.

'I will, I promise you.'

'Oh, Paul . . .' Tina's voice quivered. She was unaware that love shone in her eyes, in her expression, in the softness of her smile. It was almost more than Paul could bear not to seize her in his arms and kiss her with all the love and passion she had awakened in him. Then his spirits slumped. What point would there be in that? He could barely afford to pay half her salary now, and once he and Ryan completed their separation he would have a mammoth debt to the bank. He was in no position to declare his love to anyone. It would be years before he could afford to take a wife.

He tore himself away.

'Come on then, upstairs we go,' he said brusquely. Tina wondered if he was already regretting his promise to sit with Gerda.

'Are you sure?'

'I'm sure.'

'Will you call me in four hours, then?' she asked. 'The doctor said it was important not to let the interval get any longer to keep the level of pain evenly under control.'

'Will do,' Paul agreed, 'and Tina . . . when I make a promise I carry it out. So relax now and get a sound sleep.'

'All right, and thank you.'

Gerda seemed barely to waken and as soon as Tina had given her the tablets and a drink of water she fell back against the pillows, her eyes closed in sleep. Tina went quietly out as Paul entered the bedroom. She had no wish to witness his first glimpse of his mother but she felt a pang of regret that Gerda might not be aware of his presence at her bedside.

Almost as soon as her head touched the pillow Tina fell into a deep sleep but not before she had set her alarm to waken her in three and three quarter hours. It wasn't that she didn't trust Paul, but she wanted to be awake and dressed again before he came to her room.

Paul's thoughts were in a turmoil as he stood beside the bed looking, without any recognition, at the frail old woman lying there. Her spiky hair was white and sparse, and the skin stretched across her high cheek bones was the colour of old parchment. She looked gaunt and near to death. Suddenly Paul felt deeply thankful that he had at last made a determined effort to see her.

She was nothing like the woman he had visualized. He had seen the photograph of her wedding, standing beside his father, smiling at the camera. In his jaundiced view he had considered it a contrived, unnatural pose. He had also seen a photograph of her at Lucy's wedding in a short brightly coloured dress with matching coloured shoes and her long blonde hair flowing like a pennant. She had not been with his father on that one but she had been laughing up at the man at her side. It was just a picture but he had been so sure she was flirting and he had hated her. Now, looking down at the spectre of the woman she had been he could feel only pity, pity and a deep sadness because so many lives had been affected by her feckless ways – not least his own, and now any future he might have hoped to spend with Tina. He sighed and settled himself in the big armchair beside her bed.

His thoughts turned back to Tina and he wondered how she had come to be outside in the darkness and crouching there behind the wall. In the lights from the truck he had seen the man jump from the tractor and lope away after his long-legged friend. In that instant he had realized it was Nigel Kent, and it had struck him suddenly that Nigel had been one of the four men in front of the chemist's. They had been wearing the same woollen hats pulled down to their eyebrows. But why should they come to Wester Rullion and what could they possibly want with the tractor and trailer? In the dim recesses of his memory he remembered seeing a Range Rover parked in a lay-by about a mile further back along the road. It had had a stencilled picture of a horse on the rear. Had they arranged to meet up with the vehicle?

He frowned, trying to recall the various stories he had heard about Nigel Kent's exploits. None of them had been good and he had believed they were probably wildly exaggerated at the time, now he was not so sure. Nigel was reputed to have worked in his father's engineering company for a time. As the son of one of the partners he had had free access to most of the documents, until it was discovered he had been fraudulently siphoning money into his own bank account. There was also a rumour that he had been in trouble with a fifteen-year-old girl and both had been involved with drugs. Whatever the truth, the scandal had been hushed up according to a fellow student who came from the same area as the Kents.

Certainly Nigel had been at agricultural college as an older student. Paul knew he had been five or six years older than most of his and Ryan's crowd. It was not his age which had made him decidedly unpopular, so much as his bragging and the fact that he was known to cheat both in exams and in anything to do with money. So, Paul reflected, if only half the rumours were true, he would have to be on his guard regarding Lord Nog. He hoped he and his fellow thief had not seen Tina. It seemed unlikely since she would be hidden by the shadow of the wall.

He looked at Gerda and saw that she seemed to be sleeping peacefully. He put his head back against the wing of the chair and stifled a yawn. He must have dozed because the next thing he knew he had wakened with a start.

He felt, rather than saw, Gerda's eyes upon him. He sat up and looked at the bed. She was lying as before but her eyes, the palest eyes he'd ever seen, were open now, scanning his face.

'Paul.' It was not a question.

'Yes. Can I get you anything? A drink?' He knew he sounded stiff and polite. He wondered how long she had been watching him.

'Nothing, thank you.' She closed her eyes briefly. When she opened them again he saw, to his alarm, they were swimming with tears. She blinked them away.

'You're the image of Ewan. You always were.'

'So I'm told.' Paul had believed he could never feel anything but anger if they ever met, instead he found he was ill at ease.

'I know you can never forgive me, but . . . thank you for . . . taking me in.'

'It was Granny's suggestion. And Lucy felt we should.'

'They always lived exemplary lives . . . so hard to keep up . . . when you're a sinner.' It was a simple statement of fact with neither sarcasm nor self-pity in her tone. In fact her voice was low and she was obviously very weak.

'Perhaps you should rest now, conserve your strength,' Paul said awkwardly.

'Too late for that . . . I thought you wouldn't come. So much I wanted to say.' She closed her eyes again. 'Now I don't know where to begin . . .'

'Then please don't try. Just relax.'

'I want you to try . . . try to understand . . . I was spoiled by my father as a child. I grew up selfish, jealous of anyone who had anything better. I didn't believe in God so it was easy to cheat, to tell lies . . . but I never stole anything until . . . until Hubert . . .' She closed her eyes again and she was silent for so long Paul thought she had dozed off to sleep. But she hadn't. She had been assembling her thoughts and gathering her strength. Slowly, often faltering, she began to tell Paul of her marriage to his father, how she had not wanted a child – she kept nothing back. It was like the baring of her soul and Paul could only listen. There were things he had not known and he marvelled that Granny had been so loyal and so careful not to influence him or fuel his bitterness.

'I didn't realize . . . truly I didn't . . . that a farmer's fortune is tied up in his land and stock. I believed Ewan was a wealthy man. I thought he could give me the things I had craved all my life. I was bitter and angry, rebellious – a horrid wife . . . It was only later . . . I realized how dreadfully we had affected your future . . .' Paul was silent, digesting all the things she was recounting. He was amazed that she made no excuses for her conduct. She was growing tired and weak now but still she talked on. He felt a growing pity for her – something he had never expected to feel, something he had believed impossible.

'If only I hadn't been so selfish . . . We could have been happy . . . Ewan and I. He adored you from the moment you were born . . . I know you probably will not believe me – certainly I can't expect you to forgive me – but I regretted what I'd done in a very short time. I knew I had made the biggest mistake of my life, even before Hubert disappeared, leaving only debts behind. I've had a long time to live with my regret. I can never forgive myself, so I can never expect your forgiveness. I sacrificed my child . . . my right to be called a mother . . .' Her voice was growing fainter now and she seemed agitated. Paul glanced at his watch and was surprised to see it was time to administer the medication again to keep the pain at bay.

'Please don't talk any more,' he said gently. 'Is the pain returning?'

'It will not be for long now. Thank you – my son . . . My son.' She closed her eyes tightly. Then she opened them and looked at him with a terrible yearning. 'Will you come closer? Will you let me take your hand?' For a moment Paul stared at her in silence. Something in him snapped. He couldn't go on living a life of bitterness and anger with a woman so frail and utterly spent. He moved to the bed and sank to his knees beside it so that his face was level with hers. She held out her hand and he took it. It was so small, like a little bird, just bones held together by the papery skin. He put his other hand over it, clasping it. She turned her head weakly on the pillow. Their eyes met. Gerda smiled, a sweet, sad smile, filled with regret for the life she could have had. 'My son . . .' she murmured again.

'Oh, Mother . . .' Paul's voice was husky.

Neither of them had heard Tina come into the bedroom, then creep away again, her own eyes filled with tears.

Twenty-Nine

Two days later Gerda slept for the last time, just as Dr Little had warned Tina to expect. It was a blessed relief from pain and from what Tina now knew had been a troubled earthly life.

During her last afternoon of consciousness Gerda had talked for a long time, telling Tina everything about her life from the earliest days she could remember, holding nothing back. Tina had been shocked by some of the revelations, embarrassed by others. Jacquie McTeir at the nursing home in Ireland had warned her that some people recounted their life stories, as though reliving past happiness and sometimes reviewing past sins. She had believed the kindest thing she could do was to listen quietly and offer whatever comfort seemed appropriate, but Tina had felt like an eavesdropper.

Later Tina mentally reviewed Gerda's account of her time at Wester Rullion, the way she had left, and in her own words, taken everything of value. She had even connived in stealing away the best of the dairy herd while the family were at church, and selling them for a fraction of their true value. Now Tina knew Paul had every reason to feel angry and bitter towards her. Yet in the end, when she had needed him, he had been there, and he had forgiven her and granted her the peace she had needed so badly.

Knowing everything that had happened had only deepened Tina's love for Paul. Her heart ached for the small boy he had been, deprived of his father and deserted by his mother. No wonder he had concentrated all his love and trust in his grandmother.

Whatever happened in the future Tina knew she would never forget Paul Maxwell, but now she understood the

259

tremendous obstacle any woman would have to overcome
before she could win his trust, and his love. She knew he
was not immune to her, but passion and desire were one
thing, deep and abiding love was quite another. In her heart
Tina knew she could not settle for less.

The letter from Ireland arrived on the morning of Gerda's
funeral. Tina gave it no more than a cursory glance. Although
it requested an immediate reply she set it aside and prepared
for the day ahead. As ever, the Maxwell family joined together
in a united front and they all attended the funeral in the little
church at Lochandee. Their presence there was not for Gerda
Fritz-Allan, the girl who had brought such unhappiness into
their lives, but for Paul's mother, the woman Ewan Maxwell
had chosen to be his wife.

Afterwards they were all returning to Wester Rullion for
refreshments and Tina and Lucy had been busy cleaning and
baking in readiness.

So it was the following afternoon when Tina took time to
study the full implications of the letter from Mr McNaught.
Apparently the couple who were so eager to buy her great-
aunt's property had overestimated the value of their own,
hence the delay. They still wanted to purchase the cottage
and the land but would Tina be willing to accept five thousand pounds less than their original offer?

Mr McNaught requested an urgent reply. If she accepted
he felt it would be better if she could come over to Ireland
within the next couple of weeks to sign the papers and
wind up her aunt's affairs. Tina smiled wanly. She knew
the papers could all be dealt with by post, although there
was always a chance of delays or packages being lost, but
it was kind of the McNaughts to offer her hospitality once
again. Perhaps she should take the opportunity to tear
herself away from Wester Rullion and Paul, she thought
dully.

Yesterday, when the Maxwells had gathered at Wester
Rullion after the funeral, they had treated her as one of the
family, frequently discussing things which were none of her
business. It was during the chatter that she had realized the

full implications of Ryan's marriage and, more importantly, his withdrawal from the partnership with Paul.

It was all too clear now that Paul could not afford to continue paying her own wages indefinitely. He would be cutting back his stock, and therefore his income, as well as taking out a large bank loan to pay out Ryan's share. Her spirits sank at the prospect of leaving Wester Rullion.

Perhaps a visit to Ireland would help her see things in perspective. She ought to be applying for nursing training if that was to be her chosen career, but she could not work up any enthusiasm for making plans which would take her away from Wester Rullion and Paul. She had promised Ryan she would stay until after his wedding. She had accepted Molly's invitation to be her bridesmaid, especially since Kirsten didn't expect to get home from Australia in time for the wedding. But the rest of her life seemed to stretch in front of her like a lonely path into a desert.

In an effort to shake off her depression Tina decided to walk the one and a half miles to the post box with her letter instead of taking her little car, or waiting for the postman to take it in the morning. She went in to tell Rachel where she was going.

'Oh, Paul has just gone over to the vet's to collect some antibiotics for a cow with mastitis. He could have given you a lift.'

'I feel like a walk. Is there anything you would like before I go?'

'Nothing, thank you dear, except the youth and energy to enjoy the walk with you.' She smiled wryly. 'It's a beautiful evening. I can hear the birds singing their hearts out in the garden.'

'Yes, I shall miss all this dreadfully when I move on,' Tina sighed. 'And your garden beds are looking beautiful now the pansies and violas are blooming.'

'Yes, it was a splendid idea of Peter's to build them up, but I appreciated your help in bringing me the plants and helping me get them all in. I shall miss you dreadfully when you go away to do your training, Tina. Are you really sure it's still what you want to do?'

261

'No, I'm not absolutely sure about anything,' Tina admitted. 'But you've made a marvellous recovery. You don't need nursing any longer, and I'm glad about that. So . . .' she shrugged, 'my life must move on. I'll go and enjoy my walk and see whether I can feel as joyful as the birds by the time I return.' She smiled and closed the door quietly behind her, leaving Rachel to ponder on the blindness of her beloved grandson. It was so unusual for Tina to be in low spirits.

The road was fairly quiet at this time in the evening and Tina strode along briskly, taking care to step on to the grass verge when she heard a car coming. The post box was simply a red box on a pole as they were some distance from the village. She popped her letter in and decided to take a short detour to return. A bit further along the road on the opposite side there was an even narrower road which curved in a loop, taking her almost back to the Wester Rullion entrance.

There were cars coming in both directions and Tina stepped back on to the grass verge, waiting to cross over. She was vaguely aware of the blue five-door hatchback which swept past her on her own side but she paid scant attention to the occupants.

As soon as the road was clear she crossed over and made her way into the narrower road beneath the canopy of leaves which stretched across from both sides. At one time it had probably been a cart track, she thought, but although it was narrow it was tarred and every few hundred yards there were wider points for passing places if two vehicles met. Tina knew there would be very little traffic at this time of day. There were entrances to two farms leading off but otherwise there was no reason for cars to travel this route. On one side there was a long scrubby woodland and on the other a ditch and a fairly steep bank topped by a hawthorn hedge still white with May blossom. In the fields beyond the hedge cows and sheep grazed peacefully in the evening sun.

Tina felt her spirits soothed by the peace of her surroundings. She loved the countryside in every season, but she thought this time – late spring going into summer – was probably her favourite. During the winter she had marvelled many times at the perfect V formation of the wild geese as

262

they headed homeward to the wildfowl reserve beside the Solway Firth.

'I wonder how they know their places so precisely?' she had remarked to Ryan.

'I don't know,' he grinned, 'I suppose it's the same way the cows know which stall they sleep in and which animal leads the herd. I reckon animals and birds have more common sense than we humans sometimes.'

Tina had agreed with him and when she saw two early swallows swooping along she decided they must have some pretty marvellous radar too to navigate all those thousands of miles across the ocean and return to the exact same nest in the little open shed at Wester Rullion.

She had gone perhaps half a mile along the loop road, admiring the shining gold faces of buttercups, a clump of sweet wild violets, lingering patches of bluebells and the glimpses of bright scarlet where the ragged robin bloomed. On the opposite side, beneath the trees there were masses of wood anemones.

She sighed. The countryside would be lovely in Ireland too but her heart ached at the thought of leaving Wester Rullion and its surroundings. She had become familiar with the fields and roads quite quickly in spite of the time she had spent indoors. Both Ryan and Paul had been eager to share their favourite haunts and Peter had his own secret spots, where the best wild mushrooms grew, where he had found a wren nesting, or on top of the hill at Wester Rullion where he went when he needed to clear his head and think. She thought she heard the cuckoo calling and she stopped, hoping it would come again.

She had not heard the car cruising along until it was almost upon her. She jumped to the side, startled, and clambered on to the side of the ditch, balancing there precariously to let it pass. If she had had more warning she would have crossed to the woodland side where the verge was more level. But the car did not pass. It continued to purr beside her and she could move neither backward nor forward.

'There's plenty of room for you to get by,' she told the driver with some asperity, wishing he would hurry up so that she could jump back down to terra firma.

'We're admiring the view, dar-ling . . .' the driver drawled mockingly through the open window. Tina squinted at him more closely, partially blinded by the low rays of the evening sun. Her heart leapt in fear. He was not wearing a woollen hat, and his companion was not the tall lean man, but she was almost certain this was the squat figure of the man called Nige who had been driving the tractor the night someone tried to steal the cattle trailer at Wester Rullion. She looked at the car. Was this the blue hatchback which had passed her as she waited to cross the road after posting her letter . . .?

'There's a lay-be a few yards further along if you want to enjoy the scenery,' she said, trying to keep her voice steady.

'It wouldn't be the same scenery then though, would it, he-en? Why don't you come down off your perch before you fall in the ditch?'

'I shall when you move on.'

Both men gave a loud guffaw at that as though she'd said something hilarious.

'We're not going anywhere.'

In spite of her fear Tina felt her temper begin to rise. She was trapped. There was no room to step on to the road, because she couldn't trust them not to edge the car forward on to her foot if she tried. Without even looking she knew the bank on the other side of the ditch was perpendicular and topped by the thorny hedge with a drop into the field on the other side. Even if she had wanted to attempt jumping across the ditch and scrambling through the hedge she dare not turn her back on the two men.

'Get in the car. We'll give you a lift.' The driver eyed her up and down and she squirmed as his eyes undressed her. She knew exactly what he was thinking. Her heart thumped. Why, oh why, had she chosen such a quiet road to walk on her own? 'I said get in the car,' he repeated and this time the insolent drawl had gone. There was a threat behind the command.

'There's no point,' she said as calmly as she could, 'my husband will be along in a minute to lift me home. He's just been to the vet's.' Swiftly with the lie came the thought of a wedding ring. She straightened her shoulders and put her

264

hands behind her back, apparently defiant and prepared to outface them, but she was struggling to get the signet ring off her middle finger and on to her wedding finger. There was not much water in the ditch but she didn't relish the indignity of falling in while they watched and laughed. Would the possibility of an irate husband be enough to distract them from whatever evil they had intended?

'Husband?' the driver echoed. He frowned. 'But you were at Wester Rullion that night! I saw you!'

'You're one of the thieves.'

His eyes narrowed angrily and his mouth almost snarled, 'So who is your husband?'

'His name is Paul Maxwell.' Please God forgive me for lying, she prayed silently.

'I might have known! That sly conniving son of a bitch. He always said no woman would ever catch him. It was just bloody talk! It attracted the women like pins to a magnet, including mine. Well! We'll see if the arrogant Maxwell still wants you as his wife when we've finished with you.'

Tina stared, terror gripping her throat now. Her ploy had backfired. As Paul's wife he wanted her more than before.

'What do you want with me?'

'Revenge!' He almost spat the word. 'Do your stuff, Tom Tiger.' He moved the car a foot away from the ditch, opening his own door to bar her way as he did so. Tina jumped from the side of the ditch but the other man had run round and he caught her in an iron grip, twisting her arm painfully up her back without a second's hesitation.

'Into the back with her!'

Thirty

Tina screamed in pain and frustration. Both men laughed mockingly. Tina forced herself to go limp for a moment. The man's grip relaxed slightly. In the next second she lashed out with her foot at the man's shins. Her walking shoes were leather and sturdy and the man yelped in pain. She wrenched free, and with another kick at his ankles she ducked beneath his arm and ran across the road into the wood. It was far too thin and scrubby to hide and she headed up the slight incline, praying she could reach the open fields beyond.

In spite of his bruised shins, or maybe driven by fury, the man was fast and he was catching up on her. The slope of the wood was steeper than she had realized and she wished she had chanced running back along the road the way she had come. She glanced behind her. He was definitely gaining. It was then she heard the sound of an engine. There was something coming along the road.

In desperation she doubled back in a triangle. A painful stitch in her side made her gasp for breath, but she was sure she could hear a vehicle approaching slowly. It would have to stop. The blue car was blocking the road. The vehicle must stop. If only she could reach it . . . Then to her horror she saw the driver, Nige, had jumped out of the car and he was running across the woodland to cut her off. Short and square though he was, he could run faster than she could in her present state.

She stopped briefly, raised her arms above her head, and waved. 'Help!' she yelled. 'Help . . .' She ran on, almost parallel to the road this time, putting as much distance as she could between her and the pursuing Nige.

Then she saw the vehicle. It was a farm pick-up. It was

the Wester Rullion truck! She stopped running and shouted as loudly as she could. She tore off her blue fleece jacket and waved frantically. The truck stopped and she sank to the ground. Paul was running towards her. She caught her breath in a sob as both he and the driver of the car reached her simultaneously.

'Tina! Are you all right?'

'Yes, oh yes,' she gasped and saw Paul turn to the other man and catch him by the collar of his polo shirt, shaking him in fury, tightening his grip as he did so.

'How dare you try to harm her?' he growled through gritted teeth.

Nigel Kent looked up into the green eyes, glittering with fury, and spluttered, 'I . . . we were only offering her a lift.'

'No you were not! You were trailing her. I saw a blue car do a U-turn on the main road, in front of me. I saw you turn off on to this road . . . If I'd known it was you . . .' His grip tightened.

'You're throttling me,' Nigel spluttered. Out of the corner of his eye he saw his companion heading back to the car, deserting him.

'I'd like to throttle you!' Paul snapped. 'But you're not worth the bother. What is it with you anyway? You lost your job. Why are you still in this area?'

'I have relations down h—'

'Of course! The charming Bardrops,' Paul mocked.

'And some rather nasty friends so you'd better wat—'

'Oh yes . . .? Like that one . . .?' Paul nodded his head towards the man climbing into the car.

'Your wife's a red-headed vixen!' Paul sensed, rather than saw, Tina stiffen, but he didn't take his eyes off Nigel. 'She lamed him. You're welcome to her. Weren't going to get caught by a woman, were you, Maxwell? Too smart, you thought,' Lord Nog sneered. He glanced malevolently at Tina, now standing just behind Paul. 'He just wanted women to play around with, didn't you?' he said bitterly. 'Including my Iris.' Paul blinked. His grip tightened instinctively. Nigel gasped and spluttered.

'Who?'

'Let him go, Paul,' Tina whispered anxiously. 'He's not worth getting into trouble for whoever she is.'

'I don't know what he's talking about.'

'You bloody well do know!' Nigel swore as Paul slackened his grip a little on his collar. 'Iris Burns was my girl until you came along and took her out. Then she didn't want to know me. She changed after she'd been with you . . .'

'Oh, wee Iris!' Paul exclaimed, then he began to laugh. Nigel grew furious and started to struggle. Paul shook him like a terrier might shake a rat and his face grew grim. 'I had nothing to do with the change in Iris Burns. I took her out once – as a foursome, arranged by Ryan. I didn't even know who we were meeting until Iris turned up. Ryan just informed me she was needing rescued from a persistent admirer. So that was you? Well, well . . .' Paul's eyes narrowed thoughtfully. 'If I remember rightly her parents were very wealthy, weren't they? Are you sure it was Iris you wanted, Nog, or just her money?'

Nigel's face flushed angrily but he made no reply and Paul went on, 'As to the change in her you can give the credit for that to Evelyn Sharp. Underneath the glamour she had quite a kind heart and she helped Iris make a transformation. Blonde streaks and a hair cut, contact lenses and new clothes. She turned Iris into quite a pretty little thing, but she was still shy and no match for the likes of you . . .' Paul gave another shake and then let go so suddenly that Nigel Kent went sprawling on his backside, bruising his thigh on a lump of wood and swearing profusely. Paul stood over him. 'If I see you anywhere near here again I'll report you to the police. Have you got that? Have you?'

'Suppose so,' Nigel grunted sullenly.

'I didn't believe half the rumours I heard about you, now I think you're capable of anything. You've a chip on your shoulder like a mountain and you probably brought it all on yourself. Clear out of the county and do something useful for once. The world doesn't owe you a living, any more than it owes me one.' Paul turned to Tina and put an arm around her shoulders, helping her to the road and into the pick-up while Nigel Kent uttered a stream of foul oaths after them.

Once in the truck Paul turned towards Tina with concern. 'Are you all right, Tina? They didn't harm you?'

'I – I'm fine,' but she couldn't suppress a shudder. 'I – I was so terrified.' She shuddered again. 'He's evil, that man . . .'

'I suspect he may be experimenting with drugs,' Paul frowned. 'He seems to have got into bad company since he lost his job and I think he was bad enough before that.' He put the truck into reverse gear and drove it smoothly backwards until they came to a narrow track, almost hidden from view.

'This is only a cart track but it's dry enough just now. It would take us up over the top of the hill and down on to the other road. It's a bit of a detour but the view is worth it. Do you feel up to it, Tina, or shall I try and turn and go back the quickest route?'

'We'll go over the hill,' Tina decided. She shuddered again. 'It'll give me time to calm down before I face your grandmother and Ryan.'

'Yes, that's what I thought. It was Granny who said you had walked to the post box. I knew I hadn't passed you on the way home so I thought you must have taken the loop road. Then I remembered seeing the blue car and its strange U-turn. I thought I'd just come and check . . .'

'I thank God you did,' Tina said fervently. 'The man called Nige said he wanted revenge. I don't know what he had in mind but I was petrified.' Paul had a good idea what Nigel Kent had in mind and his jaw clenched and his hands tightened on the steering wheel.

'I can understand now why some men commit murder,' he muttered.

'Oh, Paul! I'm so sorry to bring you so much trouble. He's not worth it.'

'You didn't bring the trouble, Tina.' Paul patted her hands briefly where they lay clenched together on her lap. 'Nigel Kent is the kind who makes trouble wherever he is. He pestered the life out of Kirsten for a while, and it was all because she told him I was her boyfriend. She just said it to fob him off but he's too insensitive to see that.'

'Oh . . .' Tina's face flamed with embarrassment. 'I – I

invented a worse lie than Kirsten's,' she confessed miserably, but they had reached the top of the hill and Paul was concentrating on parking the pick-up. She thought he hadn't heard her. He came round and helped her out, holding on to both her hands when she stood before him. His fingers felt the gold band on her wedding finger, turned so that the initialled square of her signet ring was against her palm. He smiled down at her and led her round to lean against the dry stone wall which formed the boundary between two hill farms. He stood, holding her prisoner between his strong arms with her back against the wall.

'So . . .' he said smiling, 'what lie did you invent for dear Nigel, Tina?'

'I – I . . .' Her face flamed anew. 'I thought it m–might scare them off if they th–thought I had a big strong husband who might d–deal w–with them. I told them I was m–married – to y–you, Paul. I'm sorry. Anyway it only made him worse . . .' She hung her head but she couldn't suppress a violent shudder. Paul's arms tightened around her, holding her close against his chest, his chin resting on the crown of her head. He was silent for what seemed an eternity to Tina and she trembled, thinking he was probably angry, or indignant. Then he put a finger under her chin and raised her face to his so that she was forced to meet his eyes.

'I wish with all my heart I could make it true, Tina,' he said quietly, 'but I can't. It's quite impossible.' His green eyes were looking into hers with such intensity that Tina felt she was drowning in them. Then he bent his head to kiss her lightly on the mouth, but her lips parted involuntarily, soft and yielding, and needing him. His kiss became an all consuming world of love and passion and longing such as Tina had never expected to feel in her whole life. She would have given Paul every bit of herself, but he raised his head. He groaned softly.

'I love you, Tina,' he said simply.

'Then . . .?' she stared up into his face, her soft brown eyes filled with yearning.

'But I can't ask you to be my wife, I just can't . . .'

'Oh, Paul . . .' Tina's voice was no more than a whisper.

270

She reached up and cupped his lean face between her hands and he turned his head and kissed her palm. A tremor ran through her. 'I love you too,' she said softly, but clearly. 'I understand now why you mistrust all women and shy away from a commitment as serious as marriage. Your mother told me everything. I know it was wicked of her, I know it must have been so hard for you to understand when she ran away. But she did repent. She bitterly regretted what she'd done. She told me so. Perhaps in time you will learn to put your mistrust aside . . . Even if I have to wait for ever for that to happen, I shall still love you, Paul.'

'Oh God, Tina!' Paul bowed his head and buried it against the softness of her breasts. She stroked his hair gently, soothingly, relishing the weight of him against her. Eventually he raised his head and their eyes met. 'You got under my skin long ago,' he said softly. He grimaced. 'It's true, I did used to say I would never make any woman my wife, and I believed it. After what my mother did to my father I felt I would never allow myself to be caught in the same trap. And then – even before my mother came to Wester Rullion, long before she told me everything, I knew I could trust you with my life . . .'

'Then why . . .?' Tina held her breath, her eyes shining.

'Because the only thing I can offer a wife is a massive great loan at the bank, and no certainty that I'll ever pay it off – unless . . .' He shook his head silently as though rejecting an idea. 'I've considered all sorts of plans. You do know, Tina, that it was Uncle Conan and Aunt Bridie who have been paying your salary for most of the time you've been at Wester Rullion? I can't even afford that, let alone to keep a wife,' he said dully.

'I knew that, Paul,' Tina said softly. 'But you forget I was brought up on a small farm, much smaller than Wester Rullion, and the land didn't even belong to us. There was never much money to spare, but we were happy, Daddy and Mammy and me . . . They loved each other.'

'You have so much ability and the opportunity to make a good career for yourself.'

'I have – if only I could convince myself that's what I want to do with my life.'

'What do you mean . . .?' Paul looked at her sharply. 'I thought you'd set your sights on a career in nursing?'

'It's just something I considered. I enjoy caring for people . . . but now . . .' She looked at him and her eyes were filled with love and yearning.

'One solution I have considered,' Paul said slowly, 'is to sell Wester Rullion and take a job. I wouldn't need a bank loan to stock the farm then and I'd have enough capital to buy you a good house, or I could keep the farmhouse if you preferred . . .'

'You'd consider doing that for me?' Tina's eyes were round and incredulous. 'No! No, Paul, I wouldn't let you do such a thing. It would break your heart – and your grandmother's, after the struggles she's had to keep it for you all these years. No, no. In time you'd hate your job, whatever it was, and you'd grow to resent me for agreeing to such a thing.'

'I'd never resent you, Tina. I've come to realize that even Wester Rullion doesn't have the same appeal when I think of you not being there too. But you're right about Granny, I owe it to her to make a go of it now.' He sighed heavily.

'I have a better solution. Surely it wouldn't be any harder if we worked together than it was when Ryan was off with his broken arm? And we should have only ourselves and Granny to consider then. I have ten thousand pounds from Daddy's sale. You could use it to buy commercial cows to replace the pedigree animals Ryan will be taking with him . . .'

'No! No, Tina,' Paul's jaw set. 'I could never take your money for that. You may need it some day.'

Tina knew then that she must not mention the sum Mr McNaught expected to raise for her when her great-aunt's property was finally sold, and she was 90 per cent certain it would go through this time. The sum was greater than anything she had ever owned or hoped to own, it would certainly cover a good half of Paul's loan from what she'd overheard of the discussions between him and Ryan. If only she could make Paul forget his pride and concentrate on their love for each other, she knew now exactly where she wanted her future to be.

'If I lived and worked with you at Wester Rullion as – as your wife,' she said shyly, 'I wouldn't have to buy a house for myself, no mortgage, no heating, or electricity bills, no telephone, not even any of the new council taxes . . . Surely you could take my money when I'd be having all those things from you, Paul? Surely we could work at Wester Rullion together as your grandparents did? Please don't let your pride stand in the way of our happiness. Life may be too short – like Mammy's was . . .'

'Oh, Tina! Don't . . . I couldn't bear to think of life without you in it now.'

Tina turned to look at the view spread out before them. Paul put his arms around her and she leaned back against him, savouring the warmth of his lean body. They were silent for a long time. Before them the fields were fresh and deeply green in the evening light, sloping down the glen to where the river wound in a wide loop on its way to the Solway Firth. On the horizon the point of Criffel was merging into the purple shadows of evening and the rays of the setting sun painted the horizon with vivid splendour of flame and gold and aquamarine.

'The tide must be in,' Paul said softly, 'I can just see the glint of the water, over there. Look, in that direction,' he lifted an arm to indicate, 'and that's the Cumberland hills and the point of Skiddaw beyond.'

'It's beautiful,' Tina breathed softly. 'Not all the money in the world could buy this moment in time for us.'

Paul was silent. Suddenly he lifted her up and swung her legs over the other side of the stone dyke, setting her down on the flattest top stone he could see. Then he jumped over into the field and stood facing her.

'Why have you put me up here?' she asked in surprise.

'Because . . . you're not a vixen, you are a witch, and you've cast your spell on me. On your own head be it . . .' His lean face split into a grin, but his eyes showed anxiety and concern and the sight of that vulnerable look made Tina ache with tenderness and love. Then to her astonishment he bent down on one knee.

'Miss Augustine Donnelly,' he said solemnly, 'will you do me the honour of consenting to be my wife?'

Tina gasped. Then she leapt down from the wall with a squeal of happiness, straight into his arms. He fell backwards under the impact but he took her with him, holding her close as she spoke against his lips.

'Yes! Yes! Oh yes please . . . Dearest Paul . . .' Each word was punctuated with a kiss and the last one threatened to stretch into eternity.

Through her ecstasy Tina became aware of Paul's arousal as she lay along the length of him, her cheek resting close to his heart. She raised her head and looked down into his face, her eyes wide and bright with happiness and one big question. He groaned softly. 'You are a witch and your spells are torturing me to . . . a wonderful death . . .'

'Shall I do something to cure your torture then?' she asked softly.

'Do you want to . . .?' Paul's voice was husky. In answer Tina rolled to his side and ran her hand down over his stomach. He shuddered in anticipation. Her hand loosened the belt and then the fastening of his jeans. Her fingers moved – delicately, tantalizing. 'A-ah, Tina . . .' She tugged gently and he slipped out of his clothes and turned to her, taking possession of her mouth, pushing aside the loose T-shirt and the lacy cups which hid her swelling breasts. He heard her breath coming in little gusts of pleasure and revelled in the sensations he kindled and felt himself. When he drew away her own jeans he saw a livid patch on her hip, and another on her thigh, where she had collided with a branch in the wood. He kissed them tenderly. He moved on further in a journey of glorious exploration. Then he could bear it no longer. He lifted his head and looked down into her face.

'Tina . . .?'

'Yes . . . oh yes, please . . . now . . . I love you, Paul . . .'

Much later Tina lay cradled in his arms as the darkness spread over the sky. A faint breeze cooled her fevered skin.

'Great, wide, beautiful, wonderful world . . .' she quoted softly, happily.

'With a beautiful woman around me curled,' Paul chuckled. 'I can ask for nothing more.' He sighed. 'But I must help you dress before you catch a cold.'

Eventually they stood side by side, reluctant to leave their own piece of heaven and return to the world. A few yards away some curious sheep watched them, eyes glowing yellow in the darkness. In the distance the lights of the town curved in a semicircle, winking and sparkling like a gold necklace against the purple of the night sky.

'God's in his heaven, All's right with the World.'

Thirty-One

Tina went to Ireland the following week as she had arranged. The sale of Great-Aunt Augustine's property had gone through without a hitch this time, making her richer than she had ever expected to be in her life. She knew it was not enough to pay Paul's loan to the bank but it would go a long way towards it if she ever managed to persuade him to use it, but it was not the money which made her so happy. It was the joy of knowing she loved and was loved in return, for herself, and soon she would become a real member of the family which had taken her into their homes and hearts as one of their own.

She and Paul had decided to keep their plans to themselves until after Ryan and Molly's wedding so that their news did not detract from their celebration, but to those who knew them well their love for each other shone like a beacon for all to see.

Two weeks after Tina's return from Ireland she followed Molly down the aisle to join Ryan and Paul, handsome in their kilts and the fitted black jackets with silver buttons. Her heart lurched with love as Paul half turned to smile at her. Molly looked radiant in her ivory dress of silk chiffon. Ryan's grandmother had helped her choose the empire style and it disguised her thickening waistline perfectly, much to her mother's relief and delight. Tina's own dress was a simple style in buttercup yellow which suited her sparkling brown eyes and auburn hair.

Although Molly and Ryan had insisted it should be a quiet wedding with only close relations, the number of guests was a surprise to Tina. The couple were to have a week in the Lake District because Molly didn't want to travel far.

While Ryan was changing out of his kilt, prior to making a getaway on their honeymoon, he turned to Paul.

'From what I've seen of you and Tina these past few weeks . . .' he grinned, 'it'll be your turn next, old boy!'

'Yes,' Paul nodded, trying to keep his expression solemn, 'five weeks today exactly.'

'What!' Ryan stared open mouthed. 'You've got it all arranged? And so soon? And you've kept it secret! Why, you old son of a gun!'

'Seriously, Ryan, do you think Molly would agree to you both staying at Wester Rullion while we're away? We intend to have a really quiet wedding – just ourselves and a couple to act as witnesses, but I'd like to take Tina away for a holiday before we settle down to the hard work.'

'Oh I'm sure Molly will be delighted. We both owe you anyway.' His smile disappeared and he looked earnestly at Paul. 'Don't think I don't appreciate how generous you've been, Paul. You could have made things very difficult for me, what with the partnership and everything.'

'Och, go on with you!' Paul slapped him on the shoulder. 'Don't you know I'm pleased to be rid of you . . .' he teased. They were grinning as they rejoined the other guests but before Molly and Ryan departed Ryan banged on a table and called for attention.

'You all know how much we appreciate you being with us today . . .' he began.

'You've told us that already!' Norman called jovially.

'And thank you all for being so generous to us,' Ryan went on undeterred, 'but I have a piece of news which I believe you'll all be pleased to hear . . .'

'Is it twins then?' one of Molly's cousins called cheekily.

'No, it's more fun having several goes at that!' Ryan retorted, then quickly, 'The news is that Paul and Tina are going to tie the knot too – wait for it . . . in only five weeks from today!' There were exclamations all round. Only Rachel looked on, smiling serenely, reaching out to pat Tina's arm where she was sitting beside her. She was the only person who knew, apart from Megan and Max, who had agreed to act as witnesses. Ryan waited for the noise to subside. 'What's

277

more they think they're going to get away with only two people there – and themselves of course . . . I don't think that's fair! They haven't invited me!' he grinned. He looked around the gathering. 'But I reckon I can rely on my mum and Aunt Bridie to make them change their minds about that?'

'You bet we will!' Bridie called and hurried over to hug Tina and congratulate Paul.

'It's the best news I've heard for years,' she told them, 'but there's no way we shall let you get away so easily. We Maxwells enjoy a celebration, don't we, Lucy?'

'Indeed we do,' Lucy said, smiling happily at them, adding her congratulations. 'It's wonderful news.'

The following day Tina was surprised when Bridie and Megan, Fiona and Lucy all descended on Wester Rullion to see her.

'We can't let the most important day of your life go by without a wee celebration,' Bridie said persuasively. 'I know you have no close relatives, Tina, but you may have a few friends you'd like to invite, and if you really insist on it being low key we could hire the Lochandee Hall. That's where Nick and I held our reception.' She sighed. 'Sometimes it feels like yesterday, other times it seems a century ago. But the hall has been newly decorated and the council put in a new kitchen recently to comply with all the regulations. We could make it look really nice with flowers and greenery. Fiona, you're really good at that sort of thing . . .'

'It would be a pleasure to do it, if Tina and Paul agree, but Conan has volunteered to pay for a reception in one of the hotels if you prefer, Tina – on condition he can walk you down the aisle . . .' She smiled.

How neatly Fiona gets the difficult bits slipped in without embarrassing Tina, Rachel thought gratefully, watching Tina's expressive face.

'And Kirsten will be home from Australia in three weeks' time,' Lucy said. 'She's desperate to be a bridesmaid if you'll have her as well as Megan? She feels she's really missed out with not being here for Ryan's wedding. What do you think, Tina?'

278

'I – I don't know what to say . . .' Tina stammered, quite overwhelmed.

'Don't know what to say about what?' Paul asked, popping his head round the sitting room door where they had gathered. When they told him his face shadowed anxiously.

'Of course Conan's paying for it all. He feels you've been an absolute gentleman the way you've let Ryan off the hook,' Fiona said. 'I think it would make him feel a bit better if you'll let him give you a sort of send-off to a new life too – and of course, as I was telling Tina, he wants to walk her down the aisle.'

'No wonder you're speechless, Tina!' Paul grinned as he came to her side, slipping an arm round her waist. 'Can you bear it?' he whispered in her ear.

'It's – it's all such a surprise . . . And you're all so generous. But I feel I ought to pay . . .'

'No!'

'Definitely not!'

'Look how wonderful you've been with Mother,' Bridie said. 'We're all in your debt, Tina. If a bit of a celebration will make you happy it will make us even happier.'

'All right then . . .' She looked at Paul. 'Is it . . .?'

'You're the boss, we-ell for now anyway!' he chuckled.

'You'll have to have a proper wedding dress now, Tina,' Megan said. 'I'd lend you mine but you're so much neater than I am.'

'Mine would just about fit you, Tina,' Lucy said eagerly. 'It was a lovely dress and not a style that goes out of fashion either. Fiona's good taste of course . . . But maybe you'd rather choose your own . . .?' she finished uncertainly.

'We hadn't considered anything like that . . .' Tina said, 'but if we're having guests . . .' She looked at Paul. 'You'll have to wear your kilt again. I love you in your kilt. Yes,' she smiled at Lucy, 'if your dress fits me I'd love to borrow it.'

So in the middle of July, with the first of the silage pits filled and the hay made and safely into the lofts, Tina and Paul felt relaxed and happy.

The McNaughts were coming for the wedding and

bringing Jaquie McTeir, and even Great-Aunt Augustine's old friend, Jamie O'Toole, had been persuaded to come with them.

When the reception was over and Tina and Paul had departed amidst showers of confetti and balloons, Bridie turned to her mother.

'I expect you're exhausted after all the excitement?'

'No,' Rachel smiled. 'It's been one of the best days of my life, Bridie. I never dreamed I should live to see Paul so happy, or with such a lovely wife as Tina. It's been simply wonderful having all my family gathered together again in the Lochandee village hall. Ross would have been so proud of you all.'